WHEN

WE

WERE

BRIGHT

AND

BEAUTIFUL

ALSO BY JILLIAN MEDOFF

Good Girls Gone Bad
Hunger Point
I Couldn't Love You More
This Could Hurt

WHEN WE WERE BRIGHT AND BEAUTIFUL

a novel

JILLIAN MEDOFF

HARPER

An Imprint of HarperCollins*Publishers*

WHEN WE WERE BRIGHT AND BEAUTIFUL. Copyright © 2022 by Jillian Medoff. All rights reserved. Printed in the United States of America. No part of this book may be used or reproduced in any manner whatsoever without written permission except in the case of brief quotations embodied in critical articles and reviews. For information, address HarperCollins Publishers, 195 Broadway, New York, NY 10007.

HarperCollins books may be purchased for educational, business, or sales promotional use. For information, please email the Special Markets Department at SPsales@harpercollins.com.

FIRST EDITION

Library of Congress Cataloging-in-Publication Data has been applied for.

ISBN 978-0-06-314202-2

22 23 24 25 26 LSC 10 9 8 7 6 5 4 3 2

In memory of Jeffrey Masarek, my forever friend
(1963-2021)

And above all things have fervent charity among yourselves: for charity shall cover the multitude of sins.

—1 PETER 4:8

WHEN
WE
WERE
BRIGHT
AND
BEAUTIFUL

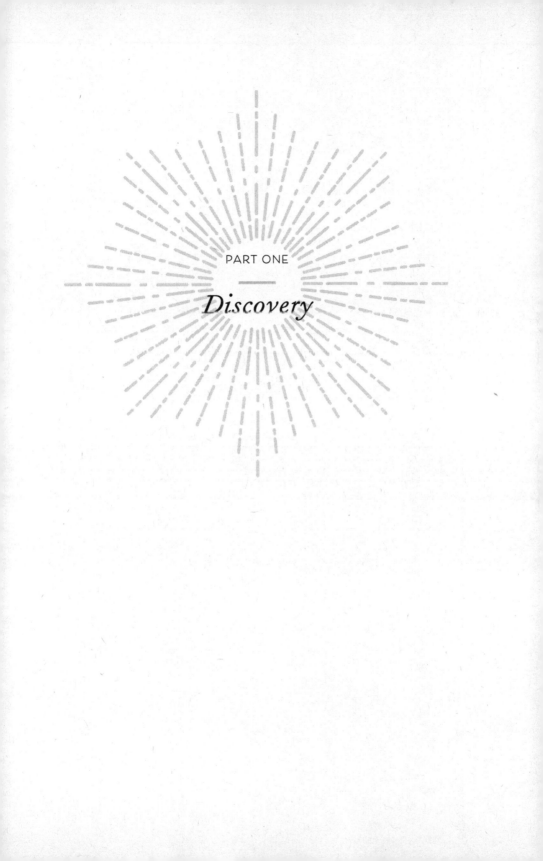

PART ONE

Discovery

1

THIS IS BILLY'S STORY. BUT IF I WERE THE ONE TELLING IT, I would start with Nate's call. For me, that's the pivot point between before and after; the moment I was, for lack of a better expression, jolted awake.

"Cassie? You there?" Nate, my older brother, is shouting into the phone. He's back in New York, and he's frantic. "Where have you been? I've been calling for hours."

"I'm sorry. I was in the library. I shut off my—"

"Cassie, listen, okay? Something awful happened to Billy."

Nate is talking so fast his sentences bleed together. I make out the word *rape*, but that can't be right. Then he says it again.

"Billy was *raped*?" This can't be true. Our younger brother isn't just strong; he's also scrappy as hell. "Is this a joke? If so, it's not funny."

"Come on, Cassandra. Billy wasn't *raped*, he was arrested *for* rape." His voice is tinged with antipathy. "I wish I were joking. The girl is out for blood. She . . ." Trailing off, he leaves me to twist.

At twenty-five, Nate is a typical big brother, as bossy as he is protective. I'm twenty-three, and Billy is twenty-two. Billy and I are Irish twins; we've been inseparable our whole lives.

"Who's the girl, Nate?" I ask, though I fear I already know.

"Diana Holly."

Oh, shit. My body stiffens like I'm girding for battle. If Diana Holly is involved, something is very wrong.

"Yes," Nate agrees, though I've said nothing. "You're right."

Our family is partial to silence, but like many siblings, my brothers and I communicate telepathically. At the moment, for instance, Nate and I are tallying up all the ways Diana has hurt Billy before, and the signs that she'd one day go too far.

Billy is a junior at Princeton, as is Diana. They met last June and dated on and off until he broke up with her in December, three months ago. "Not enough hours in the day" was his explanation, which makes sense. Billy is premed and a serious athlete, so he's buried under a heavy class load and brutal training regimen. He also tutors kids with special needs, children who, like him, have trouble expressing themselves.

"Have you spoken to Billy?" I ask.

"No, just to Dad, and only for a few minutes."

"How is he?"

"Billy? Scared, mostly. Baffled. Losing his mind. But physically okay, I guess."

"I didn't realize he and Diana were . . ."

"Her name still comes up. She knows his weak spots, and you know Billy."

Billy's weak spots are also his core strengths and vice versa. He's defenseless against people in need. After college, he plans to go to med school, become a pediatrician, and subspecialize in something brainy, like clinical genetics, so he can cure childhood aphasia. Sure, it sounds noble. But you know how super-smart people are sometimes big idiots? That's my kid brother. While Billy's tunnel vision makes him an excellent student and an inspired competitor (he's a power sprinter, with a laser focus that can bend steel), it also insulates him. He doesn't see danger until it's too late.

"She's a compulsive liar," Nate reminds me.

"So her accusation is bullshit, then." Despite all I know about Billy, I feel a sweeping relief, like being waved through a DUI checkpoint when I'm stone-cold sober. There's no way I could have gotten a ticket, but I'm still grateful it's over.

"Wait. You thought it could be true?" Nate is incredulous. "*Of course* it's bullshit."

"I wasn't thinking anything, Nate. Lighten up."

"Lighten up? Billy is being *interrogated*, Cassie."

"I'm sure he asked for a lawyer. Everyone with a TV knows if you ask for an attorney, the cops have to back off."

"Never gonna happen. Billy won't ask for a fucking thing. He'll choke out what they want to hear and then clam up until they let him go."

Billy has a speech impediment, a stutter that's triggered under stress. Most days, it's barely detectable, but once he starts, he can't stop. Then he gets embarrassed and won't talk at all, which makes him seem sullen when really he's ashamed. In this way, my brother is more sensitive than most college juniors. He'd never hurt anyone, much less Diana Holly—a girl he loved and still has feelings for.

"Dad wants you to come home," Nate says abruptly, a non sequitur that sounds like a command. "I've been here all day." He has his own place in SoHo, a loft he bought last fall when Billy and I moved out. But from what I can tell, he's usually at our parents' place uptown, taking advantage of their fully stocked refrigerator, private gym, and dry cleaning service.

"Why didn't he call me himself?" Until I left, I was our dad's go-to child. In my absence, Nate has claimed my spot.

"Oh, I don't know, Cassie. Maybe because he's busy with his son being *in jail* and all. Why does it matter?"

I try for a conciliatory tone. "It doesn't matter. I was asking rhetorically. Where's Billy now?"

"In custody somewhere near Princeton. Cops don't dick around with a rape accusation, Cass. He's been arrested, fingerprinted, and tossed in a cell. They're holding him while they investigate."

"But he and Diana *know* each other. He's not some guy in a dark alley. They have a long, sordid history."

"Which will work in our favor, eventually. But last night, he and Diana left a party together. At some point after, the cops responded to a 911 call, and carted Billy off. Dad's down in New Jersey, trying to get him out, but it's the weekend so no one's around."

"Who called 911? Diana?"

"I don't know. I told you, Dad and I only spoke for a second. He said Billy will be home tonight and wants us both there."

I hate when Lawrence makes Nate his messenger, but of course I jump. "I just need to figure out my schedule. I have midterms next week."

I'm up at Yale, taking a refresher class in Statistics and Introduction to Arabic, before I start a six-year PhD program for political science in the fall. No one in my life is happy about this. Last May, when I graduated from Columbia, I was supposed to work at the Stockton-Quinn Foundation, our family's charitable nonprofit. Instead, I moved to New Haven and applied to grad school. I've been living here for six months. I love my coursework. I'm thrilled to be on my own. And yet my family is still waiting for me to give it all up and come home.

"Blow off the exams, Cassie. We're in crisis. And Thursday is Dad's birthday."

"I know it's his birthday, Nate. But I can't disappear."

"For fuck's sake." He snorts. "No one is asking you to *disappear*. Why do you always have to be so dramatic?"

"I don't know, Nate. Why do you always have to jump all over me?"

My brother gets irritated when I talk about Yale. He's on the equities desk at Bessemer Trust and has hated his job from day one. The plan was for me to graduate, for him to quit, and for the two of us to join the foundation together. Instead, I took off. But rather than leave Bessemer—which he can do, at any time—he chose to stay. He's still miserable, but now he blames this on me. Obviously, there's more to the story than impulsivity (mine) and inertia (his), but rather than discuss it explicitly like adults, we taunt each other with insults that are steeped in resentment (his) and guilt (mine).

"So, what happens next?" I ask.

"Dad's at the jail with the Bowtie, trying to get answers."

"He called *Burt*?"

"I know. The guy can't handle a bank deposit. How's he gonna deal with a felony? But it was three o'clock in the morning, and no one else was around. So, for the moment, the Bowtie is our holy savior, shepherd, and redeemer."

Nate and I laugh, pals again, united in our animosity toward the Bowtie. Burt Archer is a longtime friend of our mother. During parties, he stands in the corner like an antique spindly lamp, feigning a friendly affect while pointing out who got fat and who went broke. My parents' circle is lousy with Burt Archers, but my brothers and I loathe the Bowtie the most.

"Is he helping?" I ask.

"Fuck no," Nate replies. "He told Dad he knows a few judges in New Jersey, so he's calling in favors to get Billy released. But he's, like, five hundred years old, so most of his cronies are retired or dead. One thing he can do, though, is stave off the press. The Bowtie is a gossip whore with enough dirt to make a few media dons back off, at least for the moment. If this gets out, Billy will get hammered."

"Maybe not. Billy hasn't had it easy, Nate. He's had his share of problems—"

My brother cuts me off. "He's had rich-people problems, Cassie. Park Avenue problems. The kind of problems that evoke disgust, not sympathy. Billy is the whole trifecta: rich, white, Ivy League athlete. Put those together, and you've got a story everyone knows. The one where the loudmouthed jock gets tanked, loses control, and attacks the nearest female."

"Loudmouth? Billy *stutters*, Nate. He doesn't drink. He rarely goes out. He was in therapy for years—"

"Speech therapy."

"Therapy is therapy, Nate. It counts."

"Look, Cass. You know I agree with you. But these days, it's hashtag-believe women. The world is gunning for white guys, and the rich rapist is a fan favorite. Especially the ending, where he's convicted and dragged away in handcuffs, leaving his family disgraced and penniless."

The chances of our family ending up penniless are nil, even if we're saddled with exorbitant legal fees. But the image of Billy in handcuffs pierces my heart.

"Thankfully, Billy's situation is different," Nate continues. "Diana is unreliable, and her behavior is erratic. Dad said the cops will drop the charges once they get a clearer picture of her and Billy's relationship. In a perverse way, it's better that she was the one who accused him rather than some random girl he met at the party. But in the meantime, we have to keep his name out of the papers and off the internet. Otherwise, his Google hits will follow him the rest of his life."

"You're not worried? Even a little?" My own stomach is in knots that keep tightening.

"No, I'm not worried. He'll be fine. Just get in your car and come home. But do everyone a favor, Cassidy Cakes. Try not to drive like a maniac." Nate's voice is softer and more loving. *Trust me. Trust Dad.* "Cass, we're talking about Diana Holly. It's Billy's word against hers. Who do you think people will believe?"

2

THE DRIVE FROM NEW HAVEN TO MANHATTAN TAKES AN hour and change, longer with traffic. But the last time I made this trip, I went door-to-door in fifty-six minutes. Afterward, when I sat down to Christmas dinner, I was full of myself. I *flew* here, I announced as I slid into my chair. I was *unstoppable*. But no one was impressed, Billy least of all. "What are you trying to prove, Cassie?" he asked sharply, puncturing my good mood. "You're gonna kill yourself one day." I started to protest, but the conversation had turned, and my voice got lost in the chatter.

It's dark outside; rather, it would be if not for the spotlights shining through my windows at discreet intervals. Although it's almost midnight, traffic is brutal. After Nate's call, I decided to wait, figuring the roads would be clear, but, stupidly, didn't factor in construction. So now I'm stuck in a long line of cars, unable to move, with nothing to do except agonize over Billy.

Diana Holly has been angry before, but this time she sounds unhinged. I feel a little unhinged myself, frankly. For me, going home is fraught. When I'm there, I not only have to deal with my family's disappointment, I also have to ward off drama with my ex-boyfriend, Marcus, who can sense when I'm vulnerable. Managing both at the same time is exhausting.

So my nerves were jangled even before I pulled out of the parking lot, but this stop-and-go traffic is sending me over the edge. My foot hovers on the gas, and I'm aching to gun the engine and take off.

Let me stress one thing about Billy. My brother is a fighter. He's overcome more challenges than anyone I know. When he was born, he was so small and sickly, no one thought he'd survive. He was slow to roll over, late to walk, and unable, or unwilling, to talk. When he finally did, he stammered so severely, he was unintelligible. By kindergarten, Billy had undergone a series of surgeries to repair his heart. Between his lousy health and stutter, elementary school was torture, and he kept falling behind. But with help from speech therapists and tutors, he caught up to his peers and eventually surpassed them. Children who stutter, particularly boys, often excel later in life. King George VI and James Earl Jones are great examples of this. So is my brother. At twenty-two, his repetitions (disfluencies, they're called) are infrequent, and he's mastered strategies for heading them off. Still, his impediment is a wily beast, ready to pounce at the slightest provocation. Certain words trip him up; and in moments of high stress, he'll struggle to say simple sentences. It's why his arrest, however bogus, is so terrifying. Like Nate said, if Billy is scared, he can't defend himself.

Nate calls again. Seeing his name, I feel a weight press down on my neck and shoulders. We've already spoken several times, most recently an hour ago. He caught me just as I zipped up my bag. His timing is impeccable, as if he's tracking my every move. There's a fine line, I've come to realize, between loving someone and suffocating her.

A few minutes later, feeling restless and twitchy, I call him back. "I'm on the other line," he says brusquely, like I'm the one stalking him. "It's about Billy."

"You told me not to tell anyone."

"These are people I trust."

I'm skeptical of Nate's sources the same way I'm skeptical of Nate. My brother has a wealthy boy's overconfidence, so he often misses the nuances in a conversation. The next time he calls, for instance, he tells me Billy won't actually be home tonight. "The Bowtie does know a few judges in New Jersey, but they can't release Billy."

"They can't or they won't? Shit, this is bad."

"It's just a question of timing," Nate assures me. "The Bowtie's request came in too late today, so it'll happen tomorrow. Definitely tomorrow."

"Tomorrow is Sunday," I remind him. "No one works on Sunday."

"Prisons are like hospitals; they're open every day."

But there's more, and it's worse. Turns out Diana wasn't the one who called 911. Two boys stumbled across her and Billy having sex in a playground. According to them, Diana was plastered, and Billy was being "forceful" or "aggressive," so they called for help. When the cops showed up, Diana was hysterical and Billy was struggling. They put him in restraints and shoved him into a squad car.

As soon as Nate says "hysterical," I'm reminded of another scene, a different dynamic: Billy's Audi, a sexy two-seater, destroyed. Hood bashed in; headlights shattered. Glass awash on the pavement like water glinting in the sun. And there was Diana standing on the side-walk, still swinging the bat, the textbook definition of *hysterical*. "You can't leave me, Billy!"

What haunts me most about Diana Holly, even more than the vio-lence, is her deceptiveness. When Billy first told me about her, I was thrilled. "She reminds me of you," he said, to which I cracked, "That's gross, Elmo," and we both laughed. But he meant the way she looked after him. Between classes and labs, tutoring, twice-daily workouts and competing, every minute of Billy's life is accounted for. Diana forced him to slow down, eat a decent dinner, relax in front of a movie. She was attentive and caring, which kept him balanced and sane. What a relief, I remember thinking, which of course I now regret; just as Billy probably regrets thinking she and I were anything alike.

Diana Holly, despite her mother hen act, is a manipulative and vin-dictive young woman. She's one of those girls who plays down her attractiveness, like hiding her killer body under long wooly cardigans, as if there's virtue in looking dowdy. She's studying biology, and she's very smart, with a lost-in-the-library quality I used to consider her best asset. It made her seem less vapid, more authentic than the preen-ing show ponies we grew up with.

Women love my brothers, both of whom inherited their father's good looks. Nate is tall and broad-shouldered, with a brilliant smile and carefree insouciance. He's funny and sarcastic, so he gets a lot of play. But Billy is the one girls go truly bonkers over. He's boyishly handsome, with silky black hair that falls in his face, dreamy blue eyes and a wounded affect that fuels their fantasies. While Nate and I always found it amusing to see how far girls would go to get, and then keep, our idiot brother's attention, Diana Holly's cunning and persistence genuinely alarmed us.

I know nothing about the criminal justice system. But I do know Diana, and it seems patently wrong that the cops can lock Billy up without knowing the facts. This is a woman who threatened him when he broke up with her, who stalked him across campus. A few times, she even snuck into his dorm room while he was in class, and was curled up in his bed, pretending to be asleep, when he returned. Billy was so disturbed, he called security. Meanwhile, he's the one in jail; the one who gave up his fingerprints, DNA, blood—the works.

If Billy's been hauled in for questioning, I can tell you exactly how that scene played out: four husky cops working over one lean boy, rapid-fire questions, blinding lights, scary threats. "I am inn . . ." Billy will stumble. "Inn . . ." He'll chew his words, close his eyes. Finally, he'll give up. "Ok-k-kay. Ok-k-k-kay." Billy will agree to anything. He'll even confess to a crime he didn't commit if it means he can stop talking.

When I imagine Billy behind bars, I picture places like Angola or Folsom, where he rots in the hole or gets shanked from behind. If it was me or Nate, I'd worry, of course, but wouldn't spin worst-case scenarios. First of all, I'm female. I have breasts. My survival instincts are stiletto sharp. Similarly, Nate, with his wolfish smile and kingpin's charisma, would have his new inmate buddies tunneling him out by lunch. But Billy is softer than we are, more easily breakable.

Look, Billy and Nate are my brothers, and I love them beyond the beyond, but I'm able to see us objectively, dispassionately. To say our lives aren't charmed is a lie. Doors swing open simply because we're white, wealthy, and blessed with good genes. It's easy to judge us, I know, because I judge myself all the time. Even so, tragedy doesn't discriminate. Like many families, rich and poor, we've faced catastrophic loss, and, equally crippling, lack of purpose. Each of us has suffered; Billy most of all. To say otherwise is also a lie. My point is, you can have everything and still not have enough.

"Billy's in trouble," I say to Nate, who's still on the phone. I think about our parents, scrambling for answers. I've called them both, several times, but they've been radio silent, which is unusual—and frightening. "This won't end well for any of us."

"Have faith, Princess." (When I was little, my nickname was Forever Girl or Sweet Girl, which Nate turned into Sour Girl, Sour Patch, Sour Pickle, Princess Pickle, or just plain Princess.) "We're the Quinns. Nothing can break us. All for one and one for all, remember?"

3

CARS START TO ROLL, AND I ROLL ALONG WITH THEM. A MINute later, there's real movement, so I jam on the gas. Cutting across open lanes, I weave in and out, gaining momentum. Exhilarated, I blow past eighty, eighty-five. The car's vibrations surge through my veins. Bodies in motion stay in motion. Amped up this high, my urges override my good sense. Slow down, I warn myself. Instead, I hit ninety, ninety-two, ninety-five.

My Porsche is a hand-me-down from Nate, who rode it hard and with no respect. The left side is dented, a taillight is busted, and the shocks are a disaster. Still, it's a top-of-the-line speedster worth two hundred grand. It's also an asshole's car and a police magnet, so I get stopped constantly. Plus, I drive recklessly and over the speed limit. "It's like you *want* to get caught," Billy says.

I hear the cop before I see him. His siren blares, then his megaphone. "Pull over at the next shoulder."

Offering him a good-natured wave in my rearview mirror, I slow down. But my heart is thumping. Despite my bravado, police terrify me. It may seem paradoxical to fear the very men our lives depend on, but terror is the point. Like soldiers, most cops are young, male, and bred for violence. When it comes to power dynamics, they can be as lethal as the most hardened criminals. Look how they're treating Billy.

For me, a girl alone on a long stretch of highway, the best defense is a good offense. So, by the time I reach a full stop, I've slipped off my jacket to reveal a barely there camisole. It's a vintage cast-off that I found combing through thrift store racks in New Haven. In my rearview mirror, I tousle my hair while watching the cop step out of his sedan and approach me. It's late March and raw—chilly, rainy, and starting to sleet. So, I straighten my back, sit high in my seat, and pretend I'm not rattled.

Using his thick ring, the cop raps on my window. "You mind?" He's young, about my age. Stocky and cocky with a bleached flattop; military all the way, or at least aspirational. It's dark out, and in the white glare of passing headlights, his spiky hair glows like a crown of thorns.

I widen my eyes and ask, "Something wrong, Officer?" Even I'm embarrassed by my breathy voice, as if we're filming a porn video. It's my weak attempt at humor, but this guy barely glances my way. Instead, he shines a flashlight into the backseat and then up front, across the dash and over to me. "License, registration, and proof of insurance, ma'am."

I gather all three and hand them over. "I was driving too fast." I say this contritely, in my own voice. "I apologize."

"Sit here." Marching off, he's coiled tight, with the pigeon-toed walk of a ballplayer.

Still, I'm hopeful. I have youth on my side. In a few years, by, say, twenty-eight, thirty, the whole enterprise will start to sag. For the moment, though, my face is unlined, my ass round and firm. I'm extremely tall, almost six feet, and lanky, with long legs, slim waist, and large breasts. I have a wild mass of auburn curls and freckles that trail into my cleavage. I'm not a conventional beauty. But because of my height and thick, glossy hair, I'm striking. Besides, money hides a multitude of sins, and I have unlimited resources.

The cop returns, looking peeved. "Speed limit's sixty-five. You were going—"

"A lot faster." I nod. "I know."

"This is—"

"My last chance. I know that too. One more ticket and I'll lose my license."

"Your left taillight—"

"Is broken. I'm on it."

Finally, he smiles—and pulls out a ticket pad. But just as I admit defeat, he steps back and shines his light along the Porsche's curvy exterior. So, I stay quiet, watch him, and wait.

There are two states of male arousal: feral and submissive, each with its own unique tell. Feral men get jacked up in two seconds; they fuck anything in their path. Submissive men are sneakier; they beg for intimacy while pawing their way to climax. On the hunt, both are equally dangerous. Feral guys are fast and ferocious, their aggression is laced with violence; one wrong move and you're done. Submissive men make no explicit demands, but they lack a core, so you serve as filler. They destroy you from the inside out, inflicting deeper wounds that won't heal.

This cop is feral, for sure. He's ogling my car with glazed eyes. "Nice ride," he notes as he chews the inside of his cheek.

I don't let myself breathe.

"You drive too fast," he says. But he's not looking at me. He's looking at my car, at the rich leather seats and high-tech dashboard. The Porsche is a gorgeous piece of machinery, clean lines, smooth surfaces, curves in all the right places.

"Want a ride?" I ask softly.

Around us, traffic shrieks, sirens howl, the wind is deafening, but he's moved beyond sound, beyond language. Where he's gone, nothing matters but want. I understand, Officer, I want to say. I too have unbearable urges, needs I can't satisfy. Without thinking, I take my keys out of the ignition and extend my hand.

He won't look at me, or the keys. "I'll let you go with a warning," he says sharply. His stance, his tone, the way he presses my license into my palm—it's all deliberate. He's reminding me, and maybe himself, who's in charge. "But you better slow down."

"Thank you, Officer." I start the car. Rocketing forward, I go from zero to sixty in a single shot. I glance back every few minutes, but when there's no sign of him, it's both a relief and a letdown. A half hour later, I cross the bridge into Manhattan, still checking to see if he's behind me.

4

Gothic spires. In a city that thrives on exclusivity, the Valmont is one of the earliest and most private luxury residences—and has been since the streets of New York were first paved in gold. Finished in 1880, the building was designed to look like a European castle with turreted towers, medieval-style doors, endlessly high ceilings, and stained-glass windows. Since then, it's housed Mayflower descendants, captains of industry, and political scions. Here, in the kingdom of old money, the Valmont is the most desired castle, and my family holds the keys.

When I pull up tonight, I see the grounds crew working on the exterior. They've positioned Klieg lights along the semicircular driveway, and smoke billows off the glass, bathing the limestone façade in a soft, dreamy mist. Despite its pedigree, the building is only twenty floors high, and one city block wide. It's basically ten mansions stacked on top of each other, with long hallways, hidden alcoves, and doors that lead to doors that lead to secret rooms. *The Valmont* is Manhattan shorthand for an exclusive way of life, and while our neighbors might appear in the society papers or financial news, we aren't celebrities. Indeed, my parents pay PR firms a sinful amount to keep us out of the press (and have forbidden my brothers and me from social media). Even so, our wealth makes us a sideshow act, even among our own gilded circle, so I can't say we're anonymous either.

As I pull into the driveway, Anton Rivera, head of resident relations, strolls out to greet me. Like the carved statues of Venus that line the walkways, Anton is a permanent fixture.

Opening my door, he bends at the waist, as if I'm a visiting diplomat. "Good evening, Miss Cassandra." Anton has the regal bearing of an aristocrat, and it's only when his shift is over and his tie is loose that you hear the Bronx in his speech. Raised somewhere near the Grand Concourse, Anton is a "barrio boy made good" (his words, not mine).

"Anton!" I greet him as I climb out of the car. "You're working late."

"Miss Valmont is getting a facelift. I'm just here to ensure there's no scarring."

Dapper even at this hour in a European suit, silk tie, and pocket square, Anton grabs my bag and accompanies me inside. He communicates with his doormen, porters, valets, and security using earpieces. They look like well-dressed Secret Service agents, and are barely distinguishable from the residents, which is by design. Behind us, a valet is already moving the Porsche to a secure, climate-controlled parking lot underneath the building. Below our feet, a security team watches live footage of the grounds on a wall of monitors. Two guard stations sit at either end of the driveway. The Valmont is a fortress, which means my family is safe and protected, but we're also prisoners.

Locked in step, Anton and I cross the marble lobby. Inside the elevator, I pull out a pack of Marlboros I'd stopped to buy at a bodega. "Smoke?" I ask Anton.

"Ah." He shakes his head. "I'd love one, my dear, but I'm on the clock."

"Fine. But here, take the pack. I bought extra."

Once upon a time when I was twelve, Anton caught me smoking. He never told anyone, but over the years, we've developed a ritual: I offer him a cigarette, he politely declines, and I give him the pack. Residents and staff may coexist, but we don't fraternize, so it's our small moment of connection; and for me, a small act of rebellion. It would drive my parents nuts if they knew that I share a secret, however inconsequential, with a Valmont employee.

As Anton rides with me up to the fifth floor, I scrutinize his face, trying to figure out if he's heard about Billy. His expression is blank, and his eyes, inky black pools, reveal nothing.

Anton is fifty-seven; he's been with the Valmont forty-two years. His son Joey is twenty-four. During high school, he sorted packages for his father. Briefly, Nate and Joey were friends, and occasionally,

Joey would stop by to play video games. When Anton found out, he went ballistic. High-end doorman positions are impossible to come by. They're preserved in families for decades, handed down from father to son, uncle to nephew. Joey's behavior was foolish. He not only jeopardized his own job, he also put his father's career on the line.

"School okay?" Anton asks. "How's Arabic coming?"

"*Ana murie.*"

"Which means what?"

"That I suck, basically. Dumbest move I ever made, taking this class." I speak fluent French and enough Spanish to find the ladies' room. When I finish my PhD, I plan to work overseas—assuming my family doesn't rope me into their foundation. Either way, I want to be prepared. In the next fifty years, Arabic is projected to be one of the most commonly spoken global languages. "It's harder than I thought, so I'm stupid *and* arrogant."

He laughs. "You'll get better. Stay focused and don't look back. It goes quickly. Before you know it, you'll be my age."

"Oh please, Anton. You're like a giant oak. If anyone's gonna live forever, it's you."

Despite a mutual affection, Anton and I never depart from our assigned roles or scripted lines. Our conversation, while pleasant, is all surface and deflection. But don't let this fool you. As a long-serving, high-ranking Valmont employee, Anton occupies a seat of power. Doormen may be invisible, but they're all-seeing and all-knowing. They're here and not here, like a conscience.

The elevator stops, and Anton makes a sweeping motion. "Welcome home, Cassie. We've missed you." His tone is light, but he touches my shoulder and offers a fatherly squeeze. "Take care of yourself, dear girl."

"Thank you, Anton." Flashing a smile, I radiate well-bred confidence and nonchalance. "But I'm a survivor." It's Billy we need to worry about, I almost add. Except Nate told me to keep my mouth shut, so I step out of the elevator and into our foyer. I feel Anton observing my every move. Still, I say nothing. If he doesn't know about Billy, I won't be the one to tell him.

5

THE NEXT MORNING, I WAKE UP TO AN OMINOUSLY QUIET house. It was just as quiet—and eerie—last night. By the time I got home, it was one-thirty. Nate had gone to his place, but Lawrence, my dad, always waits up for me. So when I stopped by the celebration room, expecting to find him, the empty space felt like a rebuke. Hours later, I heard padding footsteps outside my door. When they slowed, I thought it might be him, making sure I got in. But it was more likely Maeve, our housekeeper, who has family in Ireland she calls at odd times. Our house has four quadrants; and I have my own separate wing, with Maeve, on one side of the house. My brothers and parents are on the other side. Being far away used to frighten me, but as I got older, I relished the distance and solitude. To be fair, I'm sure my parents did too.

Being back here makes me ache for Billy. When we were little, the two of us were always together, playing on the terrace or cuddled up on the couch. We're so close in age we liked the same TV shows and movies: *Wonder Pets!,* Elmo, SpongeBob, Disney. The only time we diverged was when I went through a pink princess phase, and Billy stayed loyal to Elmo. He dragged that scrubby red Muppet everywhere.

I'm a terrible sleeper, but must've dropped off at some point last night, because I dreamed that Billy and I were on the beach in Southampton. We were playing hide-and-seek in Hawkins Cove, but there was tension between us, and the mood was grim. Billy started to back away, so I tried to grab him, only his T-shirt was made of silk, and I couldn't get purchase. To my horror, he slipped through my fingers and plunged over the side of a cliff, a ledge, something with a steep drop below. I woke up in a panic; and now, half-awake in my childhood bed, I'm flooded with feelings of loss and dislocation. Nothing seems real, as if time has rewound and I never left.

My phone dings; it's Nate, texting:

u up?
Yes still in bed. You?
In an Uber, don't let Dad leave
Leave?
To meet new lawyer and get Billy
Lawyer?

Typical Nate, leaving me with more questions than answers. I'm about to text him again when I hear a familiar voice in my doorway. "Hey, Sweet Girl. You up?"

Families are complicated. The name on my birth certificate is Cassandra Forrester. On my driver's license, it's Cassandra Forrester-Quinn. I live with Lawrence and Eleanor Quinn, and their sons, Nathaniel and William. I call Lawrence and Eleanor my parents, and Nate and Billy my brothers, except we aren't related, not by blood. My biological parents are dead. Andrew Christian Worthington Forrester (forever known as CW) died when I was three; Rachel Richardson Forrester, when I was five.

"Cassie, honey?" Lawrence's voice is like the ocean. It's gravelly and relaxed, with a hypnotic quality that draws me in and calms me down. "I'm heading out."

I don't call Lawrence "Dad," but he's my father in every meaningful way. While I'm sure lots of daughters believe their fathers are heroes, mine is exceptional. (I bet we all believe this too.) Long before I was born, CW Forrester was Lawrence's mentor, protector, and surrogate parent. So, when he and Rachel died, the Quinns offered to raise me. The idea was Lawrence's, and he says it was a reflexive decision, that he didn't think twice.

"I'm sleeping, Lawrence," I say. "I raced home the second Nate called me. I got in very late—which you'd know if you'd stayed up. Or answered any of my calls."

"Sorry, kiddo," he says. "I conked out. But you keep sleeping. I have to run." He turns away.

"Wait!"

"Cassie, what?" Impatient, Lawrence taps, taps, taps the door. "I'm in a rush."

Still, he hesitates. We're both relieved I'm home. Although I've only been gone six months, and I was here for Christmas, our connection is already fading. I mean, Lawrence is my dad. He'll always be my dad. But our day-to-day routine is over. Now, I'm a visitor, a young woman whose other life, her real life, doesn't include him. So, we breathe for a minute, father and daughter, thinking about Billy; and, also, about us.

"Let's start again." Lawrence steps into the room. A beat later, I feel the mattress dip as he sits down, and then his hand touching my back. "I'm glad to see you, Cassie. I'm losing my mind. Yesterday was like a nightmare I can't wake up from."

I turn over. Seeing Lawrence on the edge of my bed, I feel a hitch in my chest. A valve opens, pressure releases, and tears burn my throat. "I'm worried about Billy," I say.

"We all are." Holding out his arms, Lawrence beckons to me like I'm still a little kid. I shrug off the covers and lean forward. My guard falls away. I bury my face in his shoulder.

"Thanks for rushing home," he says as he hugs me. "It hasn't been the same here without you."

I wait for him to say more, to make a crack about how clean the house is now that I live elsewhere. He doesn't, but I know what he's thinking. Whereas Eleanor is supportive of my move to New Haven, Lawrence has mixed feelings about it. Yale is prestigious, the distance is fine, but *six more years* of school? And a *PhD*? "What about the foundation?" he asked last May when I announced my plans. "Why the sudden change of heart?" I couldn't talk about Marcus, so I told him the partial truth, which was that I felt suffocated, and needed to be on my own. This, he could understand, if not accept. The five of us are always together. Our life is grand and glorious, but also a trap. Money is a noose that yokes children and parents together in ways you can't anticipate. It binds you for life and then some. Even if my brothers and I go through the motions of adulthood—college, job, apartment, marriage—we must never forget where our true allegiance lies. What about the family? Lawrence kept asking. What about us? "Please, Lawrence," I told him. "You can't pull me back. I'm already gone."

A second later, my eyes flood. Soon, I'm crying so hard I soak his shirt.

"Hey, hey, hey, Sweetheart," Lawrence says, patting my hair. "Your brother will be fine. This is all a big mistake. The right lawyer will correct it." When I wipe my nose on my arm, he stands up and whips out a handkerchief like a magician. "Use this. Or just drip snot everywhere. Your choice."

As I take the handkerchief, I notice that Lawrence has lost weight. He's naturally slim, but his button-down is baggy, and his slacks hang loosely on his hips. Otherwise, he looks the same: piercing blue eyes, a shock of black hair, movie-star teeth. In a few days, he's turning fifty-four. He's graying at the temples, and he used to jog so his knees are shot, but otherwise he's still as loose and energetic as a man in his thirties.

"How's Billy?" I ask. "For real."

"Like I said, Cassie, I'm optimistic." He offers a smile. Lawrence has a killer smile. His whole face lights up and fills with warmth; when he looks at you, you shine. But today his upbeat tone is undermined by his bloodshot eyes and hollow cheeks. "Dealing with the cops yesterday was bleak. But now that I've spoken to several lawyers, I'm confident we'll resolve this mess today. As long as we act quickly. The longer he's in the system, the harder it is to get him out."

"Did you get my messages? I tried you, like, ten times. Why didn't you call me back?"

"I was on the phone all day, looking for a criminal attorney. I like one guy—Peter DeFiore. Supposedly, he's the best. Plus, he knows New Jersey courts. Eleanor can't stand him, naturally. And he is a little rough around the edges. But . . ." He pauses. "Regardless, sorry I didn't call, kiddo, but I knew Nate was reaching out."

I scoff. "Nate was selective with the details. Which means I need the whole story from you."

"I wish I had time, honey. But this guy, DeFiore, agreed to meet me at the place where they're holding Billy. He'll be there at"—Lawrence checks his watch—"eleven. I can't be late. He said he might be able to get me inside."

"Inside the jail?"

"Not a jail," he corrects me, sharply. "It's just a detention center."

"I'll come." Standing up, I reach for my canvas tote bag, which is on the floor, open. Leggings, T-shirts, underwear, and bras spill out. Rummaging through the pile, I quickly grab a clean pair of jeans, a sweater, and suede boots, but Lawrence just stands there, watching me.

"Cass, wait. Cassie, stop. It's better if I sort this out alone. Eleanor will be able to tell you more once she gets back. But you won't be able to see Billy. I probably can't either. Regardless, it's best if I meet the lawyer by myself. Eleanor agrees," he adds, as if she's the final authority.

Regardless, regardless, regardless. The way he repeats himself drives me up the wall. It's always like this: I miss Lawrence terribly and feel guilty when I'm away, but after five minutes with him, I feel trapped, anxious to flee. My phone dings. It's Nate, texting: there in fifteen.

A thought occurs to me. "Where is Eleanor anyway?"

"Mobilizing a private militia, of course. Right now, she's having breakfast with Burt and his partners. She's talking to lawyers, judges, anyone who can get Billy home. By noon, she'll have the US Attorney holding a press conference."

"You still haven't convinced me why I can't go with you."

"I'm concerned about Billy." His voice breaks. "He'll be fine. Of course, he will. But the girl is refusing to back down. As is the DA. He wants to make an example of Billy for reasons that aren't entirely clear. So I have to stop this today—before your brother gets further embroiled. And before the press hears about it." He's interrupted by his phone; a ring so loud we both jump. "It's Eleanor." He clears his throat then calls out an upbeat "Hey, hey, honey!"

The change in him is instantaneous, like he stepped through a screen and emerged triumphant. "Everything's moving along great. Yes, Eleanor. Of course, you're upset. I'm upset too. But I promise, it will be fine . . . Yeah. I am. Leaving in a minute." Glancing at me, he points to the phone, mouths *sorry*.

"I'm going with you." My own voice is forbidding; I dare him to say no.

"Of course!" He waves, still talking to Eleanor. "Sounds good!" Then he heads out of my bedroom and into the hall, walking and talking, filling the air with glad tidings and cheer.

6

WHEN I STEP OUTSIDE A FEW MINUTES LATER, THE SUN IS shining, but it's windy. Lawrence's Mercedes idles in the driveway, and I expect to see him behind the wheel, but he's standing under the heated porte cochère, his back turned to me, presumably still on the phone with Eleanor.

"Did you sleep here?" I ask Anton as he escorts me to the waiting car. "Aren't there rules about working too many hours?"

"Yes, there are many rules." He pats my shoulder. "But I appreciate your concern for my welfare."

We both watch Lawrence approach, finally phone-free. He's wearing a ski jacket and thick wool cap. I'm shivering in my light tweed blazer. For a second, I consider going back upstairs for a heavier coat, but don't move. "We're driving to New Jersey," I tell Anton.

"So I hear." He starts to open the driver's side door, but Lawrence is already there. "Got it, thanks," he calls out, waving dismissively as he slides into the front seat. "Let's go, Cassie."

"How did you hear?" I ask Anton quietly.

"Hearing is my job. I take my job seriously. This way I know everything."

Anton is kidding, but I panic all the same. I feel a sudden chill spread along my arms and down to my fingers, which start to tingle. Saliva soaks my mouth. A metal taste permeates my tongue and teeth. "I doubt you know *everything*."

"Knowledge is power, Miss Cassandra," he says, but his voice comes from a remove. He chuckles in slow motion, like a tape played at half-speed.

I hear myself panting and force out words to muffle the sound. "Depends on what you do with that information, Anton." Even as my pulse click, click, clicks. Even as heat spreads across my scalp, I feel myself disappear.

A few years ago, in high school, I went through a difficult period. My best friend, Avery Walker, and I had a fight, a big one. In the aftermath, I was lonely, self-destructive, and hungry for affection. I did what lots of girls do: smoked too much weed, blew off my classes, and started seeing Marcus Silver, a guy who was wrong for me in all the worst ways. Our love story, simultaneously epic and ordinary, started as a slow burn then escalated at warp speed. Marcus was intoxicating. He taught me about insatiable cravings, and how it feels to want more—more fun, more sex, more everything. Soon, I was desperately in love, and after that, just desperate. No one knew he existed. Only Anton, who caught us once in a compromising position. At least I think he did. But he never mentioned it, nor did he tell a soul. In my world, this makes him more trustworthy than family. Still, his words, however innocently he means them, raise all kinds of fears.

"Get in the car, Cassie!" Lawrence shouts. "I don't want to miss this guy."

"Why are you yelling? Nate isn't even here yet—"

As I say this, my brother grabs me from behind. "*Princess Pickle,*" he says, lifting me off my feet in an iron grip. "So kind of you to honor us with your presence."

Nate is a brawny bear with Lawrence's wavy black hair and his own perpetual five o'clock shadow. He's our family's Lost Boy, funny and cynical, but in no hurry to grow up. At the same time, he's surprisingly self-aware for a twenty-five-year-old man whose only true ambition is to surf the world's biggest wave.

"Any news about Billy?" he asks me. "I hope he survived the night. Pretty boys don't fare well in prison."

"Don't say *prison*. Or *jail*. According to Lawrence, it's a *detention center*. Soon, he'll have us calling it a *spa*."

"Tomato, tomahto. Ass rape is ass rape. Just thinking about it makes me jittery; I had to take a Xanax this morning to take the edge off.

Tell you what, Princess. You ride shotgun, and I'll sit in the back like someone's grandma."

"What's the catch?"

"No catch." He knocks my shoulder with his own. "I'm relieved you're here. Dad's been off his nut. I can't handle him by myself."

"Let's go!" Lawrence's tone is clipped. "You two can talk in the car."

I climb into the passenger seat, but Nate is greeting Anton with a bro-man handshake routine. Although my brother's closeness with the staff drives Eleanor up the wall, her disapproval only encourages him to keep it up.

Finished, he opens the back door and slides into the car. "Favorite and firstborn reporting for duty, sir."

Anton leans into my open window. "Have a safe trip," he says to Lawrence, who offers a terse "thank you" before pulling away. Lawrence's snappishness is shockingly off-brand. He's the quintessential clap-your-back, introduce-you-around, buy-you-a-drink kind of guy. But I know Lawrence intimately; and he is far more worried about Billy than he wants to admit.

* * *

We travel in silence. Everyone is preoccupied, and Lawrence's lousy mood clouds the air. Eventually, when we emerge from the Lincoln Tunnel in New Jersey, he turns toward me. "What were you and Anton talking about?"

"Nothing. 'Have a good day; you too.' That was our entire conversation."

"Did he say anything about Billy?"

"Of course not." I stare at Lawrence, but his eyes are hidden behind mirrored sunglasses. "Why would you ask that?"

"The man is always around. I'm just curious what he's heard, what people in the building might know."

"He'd never talk to me about Billy. Even if he knew—which I assure you he doesn't. Give the guy a break; he's just doing his job."

"Why are you so protective of Anton Rivera?"

"Why are you so suspicious of him?"

Learning forward, Nate sticks his head between us. "Oh boy, have I missed the sweet sound of your bickering." He snatches my purse off my lap. "Got any food? I'm starving."

"Hey, that's mine!"

Before I can grab it back, Nate pulls out a tampon, which he unwraps and jams into his nostril. "Excellent for nosebleeds." He bobs forward and I take a swipe at his face, but he's too quick.

"Hey, hey, hey," Lawrence says, but he cracks his first real smile of the day. "Hands on your own bodies." His eyes flash my way. "I'm sorry, Cass. I don't mean to snap. At you or Anton. I'm just worried about Billy and pissed off at the world."

"I understand. You're forgiven. Now tell me what happened."

"I already told you everything," Nate says.

"Which is why I want to hear it again, including what this new lawyer said." I look at Lawrence. "What's his name?"

"Peter DeFiore. No frills, big reputation. His claim to fame is defending men accused of rape or assault. But not high-profile cases. The ones you never hear about."

"And? What does he think about Billy's chances?"

"Not great. He said nine times out of ten, cases like ours—where it's one person's word against another—are settled out of court. He's upfront about the fact that he tries to steer clients away from jury trials, even when the evidence is clear. The outcomes are too unpredictable."

Nate sneers. "So he's pussying out even before he meets us?"

"He was talking in generalities, Nate. When I told him about Billy, and his relationship with the girl, he perked up. So that's good," Lawrence says, but he grimaces.

"What's with the face?" I ask.

"DeFiore said that anyone who hears about Billy's case will assume he did it. His exact words to me were 'The second you started talking, the word *guilty* rang in my head.'"

"That's bullshit," Nate says. "No decent lawyer would say that. I hate this guy already."

"Your mother felt similarly. DeFiore is coarse, but I appreciate his bluntness and can overlook his bad manners. More important, we need him more than he needs us."

Lawrence takes us through the past twenty-four hours. According to the Bowtie, although Billy struggled at first, he was respectful and compliant at the police station. He willingly gave a DNA sample and consented to a blood test and full-body search. "Burt said the detention center isn't terrible—it's not Rikers, thank God. But it's concerning nonetheless. Billy is scheduled to appear before the judge tomorrow, but I'm hoping DeFiore can get him out today."

"Why can't he post bail?" I ask.

"No cash bail in New Jersey. It's a vestige of prison reform from years back."

"See, Cassie?" Nate sighs. "I *told* you there's no bail. You never believe anything I say."

Lawrence nods. "Nate's right. Billy's going to be assigned a score based on how likely he is to return for trial. For all we know, the DA will argue that our finances make him a flight risk. Either way, they can hold him for forty-eight hours. I don't want him to spend one more night in that place."

"It's Sunday, Lawrence," I remind him.

"It doesn't matter what day it is; anything can be worked out."

"With the proper encouragement," Nate adds.

"Whatever it takes." He glances at my brother in his rearview mirror. "I would do the same for you." He pauses. "So far, they're charging Billy with aggravated sexual battery and suspicion of felony rape. But the clock hasn't stopped. The cops are interviewing witnesses, looking at video footage, and photographing the scene. The more evidence they find, the more serious crimes they can add to his charges. Regardless, Burt is confident we'll get the case tossed out way before that happens."

"But if we don't," Nate says, "and Billy goes to prison, he'll get ass-raped every night."

"Nathaniel, that is *not* funny."

"Dad, I'm not trying to be funny. If we go to trial, Billy is fucked. Can you imagine him on the stand, getting twisted up in his own words?" He shakes his head. "They'll *crucify* him."

7

AN HOUR LATER, WE'RE DEEP INTO NEW JERSEY. MERCER
County is eighty miles south of the city, and a whole other world. We
pass cow pastures, scarecrows, working farms, and long stretches of
lush greenery before the view shifts to burned-out storefronts, abandoned churches, a derelict daycare center, and three grimy garages,
one after the other. Soon, we're in a shabby neighborhood that reeks
of unpaid bills and impending foreclosures. The only sign of life is a
large white woman wearing a puffy coat and flip-flops. Lounging on
a stoop, she uses her feet to rock a stroller back and forth.

I watch Lawrence scan the streets. "This is it, I think," he says. He
makes a sharp right, and we head up a steep hill. There are Private
Property signs warning us off, but he ignores them. We reach the sum-
mit, where there's a parking lot cordoned off by long, greasy chains.
Four police cars sit with their noses clustered together. The guard
station is empty, and the grounds are as quiet as a graveyard.

Lawrence taps his horn. Nothing moves.

"Let's go," I say, growing uncomfortable. "We don't belong here."

It's only been two minutes, tops, but Lawrence can't wait. Leaning
on his horn, he demands service with a long, loud, obnoxious blast.

"Lawrence, stop!" I grab his arm.

"If DeFiore is inside, I don't want to miss him. Cassie, let go of me.
Please."

From the car, I have a partial view of the campus, which looks more
like a rural community college than short-term housing for violent
criminals. There's a row of broken-down trailers and four low-rise
brick buildings. Two men, one white, the other Black, wearing khaki
jumpsuits push a laundry cart stamped with MCCF. But there's no

security—no men, no guns, no dogs. Just a faded sign that says Mercer County Correctional Facility half-hidden by a battered van with caged windows and muddy tires.

"This place is a dump," Nate says, glancing at his father.

Lawrence doesn't respond, although I can tell from the hard set of his jaw that what he sees is unsettling. He grew up in a place like this, a blue-collar town called Pittsfield in western Massachusetts. His father, a much-loved Irish tavern owner, died of cirrhosis of the liver when Lawrence was three. A year later, his mother sold the bar to pay off her husband's debts then worked two jobs to put food on the table. Lawrence was expected to contribute, but when his silver tongue earned him a full ride to Groton, an elite prep school, she agreed to let him go. His mom had reservations, to be sure. She didn't want her boy living away from home, much less among rich, spoiled snobs. What values might he learn? What bad habits? In retrospect, her concern is poignant, given that every aspect of his charmed life—career, home, wife, sons, me—can be traced back to Groton.

Despite his disadvantaged start, Lawrence flourished. After high school, he went to Columbia, also on scholarship, then spent years as a media consultant, advising political candidates on PR strategies. Lawrence's genius is exploiting the space between fact-based truth and news-based reality, and he created successful campaigns for contenders in local races before advancing to state and national elections. Through Eleanor, he was introduced to the upper echelon of the country's legal, business, and journalism communities, which helped him build a vast referral network.

And yet, for all his success, Lawrence is a humanitarian at heart. Losing a father so young left him with the persistent need to be loved and do good. So, he was lucky to find Eleanor, with whom he shares a social conscience that informs their life choices. About six years ago, Lawrence started to sour on politics. The country's economic divide sickened him, but so did getting paid to write blustery speeches filled with false promises. When Eleanor encouraged him to switch careers, he decided to use his talent, experience, and influence to benefit those less privileged. I was still in high school when he created the first blueprints for the Stockton-Quinn Foundation, a private nonprofit devoted to wealth redistribution. His big idea is to pair corporate dollars with underserved communities and create social welfare programs at the neighborhood level. (I said it was a big idea, not a novel one.) Lawrence genuinely wants to help people; he also wants never to go back to Pittsfield. To see his youngest child locked up in the middle of nowhere must feel like a cruel twist of fate.

A sharp tap on Lawrence's window startles me. I look up to see a Black man peering through the glass. He raps again, this time with the tip of his rifle.

"You're on private property," the man says. His grin is menacing, but it's his teeth, broken and caked with yellow debris, that shake me up. Once again, I've underestimated the danger factor. Like Lawrence, I have blind spots where trouble seeps in. Next thing I know, I'm in over my head.

"Yes, sir." Lowering his window, Lawrence offers a five-hundred-watt smile. "Good morning!"

"State your business."

"We're meeting my son's attorney."

"Now? It's Sunday. No one gets in or out Sunday. Unless you have cause to be in my driveway you need to turn your vehicle around."

"Dad, let's go." My brother is annoyed. "Cassie, tell him."

"Give me a minute, Nate." Lawrence starts to open the car door, but the guard lunges forward. "The fuck you think you're going?"

Flustered, Lawrence holds up his hands in surrender. His voice drops conspiratorially. "Listen, my boy is inside. May I ask one question?" He hesitates, and for a horrifying second, I'm afraid he's about to offer the guard a bribe—cash, his Mercedes, me.

Lawrence isn't a foolish man, but he does act impulsively, and I can't bear to watch. Until this weekend, our only experience with law enforcement has been speeding tickets (mine), and a few driving citations (also mine), including failure to wear a seat belt (true), failing to yield (true), and recklessness (untrue). Sure, there were dust-ups. In high school, Nate got caught "mischief-making" with toilet paper and shaving cream. Billy once threw a baseball glove so hard he bruised a kid's head. But nothing serious and certainly nothing criminal.

"Lawrence, come on."

"Cassie, I just want to ask a question." On his phone, Lawrence pulls up his favorite picture of Billy, a candid shot from the Lewis School where he volunteers. In it, he's helping a little boy read. Billy's sleeves are rolled up, and his tie is loose. He looks patient and caring as he points to a book while the kid sounds out a word. "That's my son," our dad tells the guard proudly. "William Quinn. He's with his lawyer, right at this very minute. I'm hoping to see them while they're together."

"That ain't a question." The guard trains his eyes on Lawrence. "Turn around and go."

"Look, sir." Lawrence's smile is back.

"He said no!" I grab the phone, which dings with a text. "We're sorry, Officer. We're leaving." I scan the screen. "Look." I shove the phone in Lawrence's face. "It's the lawyer. DeFiore. He's not even here! He's down the hill at a diner."

Lawrence nods and thanks the guard. "Appreciate your time, my brother. We all do what we can."

The second he closes his window, I blow up. "My *brother*?" I'm so angry I'm shaking. "What the *fuck*? It's so disrespectful."

Nothing ignites my fury like Lawrence's man-of-the-people routine. Case in point: He had a cancer scare a few years ago. The day of his biopsy, I bit his head off for flirting with the female med techs. Maybe I overreacted, but he kept making comments about one's "unusual green eyes" and another's "stunning red hair" like they were sorority girls in a bar instead of hardworking professionals at a hospital. "I'm just a friendly guy, Cassie," he said in his anesthetized haze. "I can't help it."

We head down the hill, the guard watching us go. My phone dings; it's Nate texting from the backseat.

> you're too hard on him Cass
> he's impossible
> he's scared, dipshit

Chastened, my face grows hot. We're at a light, and Lawrence takes off his sunglasses to clean the lenses. Sunlight filters through the windshield, illuminating the fine lines around his eyes and lips. He looks fragile, like an old man, and I have to turn away. Otherwise, I'll think about his corny puns and small kindnesses, which he offers even when I'm a brat. And then I'll remember his heartbreak about Yale, but how he still acted the proud dad. And then I'll remember how he played hooky from work, drove me to New Haven, and took me out to a celebratory lunch. And then I'll be flooded with love from my knees to my neck; and I'll wonder if a PhD is worth six years of my life, or if it's a selfish indulgence when he needs my help with the foundation, and now, with Billy.

"I'm sorry, Lawrence." I watch the trees as we pick up speed. "I know you're worried; I didn't mean to yell at you."

He squeezes my hand three times. "We're fine, kiddo. Fine, fine, fine." But he won't look at me either.

8

THE PARKING LOT NEXT TO THE DINER IS PACKED, AND WE'RE lucky to find a spot. Inside, I spy a middle-aged man leafing through a file while forking eggs into his mouth. He's heavyset and disheveled, wearing a suit jacket sized for a much smaller body over a green sweat-shirt with JETS embroidered in white letters.

"That's DeFiore," I tell Lawrence and Nate. "In the back."

Looking dazed, they follow my finger. Our encounter with the security guard shook us all up. We're still getting our bearings.

"No." Lawrence shakes his head. "I saw his website. That's not him."

"It is, I'm telling you." Leaving them, I weave my way through the crowded tables.

"Cassandra Quinn," I say when I reach him. "You must be Mr. De-Fiore."

"Peter." He puts down his papers to shake my hand. "You must be Billy's sister."

"His favorite sister? Yes, I am."

"His only sister, I hear."

"He could have a thousand sisters, and I'd still be his favorite."

Smiling, we size each other up. DeFiore looks like a fast-talking, low-level hitman. His oily hair, frayed jacket, and battered shoes suggest strip-mall storefronts and envelopes full of cash. But his eyes are ultra-cool as he studies my face.

I wave to Lawrence and Nate. "Over here!"

"Cassie was right," Lawrence says as he approaches. "I wasn't sure it was you." He shakes DeFiore's hand. "Lawrence Quinn. This is Nate, my older son. Thank you for seeing us on such short notice."

"You were probably hoping I was someone else." DeFiore gives Lawrence a once-over. "Maybe someone in a bowtie and wingtips."

"You met Burt, I gather," Lawrence says. "He's a bit stuffy."

DeFiore nods. "This morning, on video. I met your wife, too, but only to say hello. I had to rush off." He gestures to his plate. "Apologies for digging in, but my kid will kill me if I miss one more soccer game. Please." He motions to empty chairs. "Sit."

We settle in and make small talk. While we try to flag down a waitress, DeFiore finishes his eggs, a blueberry muffin, and a buttered bagel. He eats ravenously, as if filling a bottomless pit. I marvel at the way he relishes his food. No one I know, not even my brothers, eats with that kind of abandon. As for me, every bite I take demands penance.

"So, what can you tell us about Billy?" Lawrence asks just as a ponytailed waitress appears with a notepad. "You guys ready?" She gravitates immediately to Nate and offers a sweet smile. "What can I get you?"

Nate smiles back. He gives her dazzling teeth, dimples—the full-court press, and the girl's face reddens. "Pancakes, please," he says. His eyes flicker to her breasts where a nametag is clipped. "Amanda. Bacon and coffee." Like our father, Nate considers every encounter with a female an opportunity to showcase his charm.

"I'll have coffee too, Amanda," Lawrence says. "Two eggs scrambled dry. Orange juice. Oh—no toast, please. Cutting out carbs." He gestures my way. "She'll have egg whites. Dry toast. Tomatoes, no potatoes. Black coffee."

"Seriously?" I snap after she leaves. "I can order for myself, thanks."

He chuckles self-consciously. "Sorry, Cass. Old habits."

DeFiore is watching us. "Hard to see them grow up, isn't it, Lar?"

I've never heard anyone call Lawrence "Lar" in my life, and the absurdity of it cracks me up. DeFiore gives me a cocky grin. I like him, I decide. He knows what's what.

"You have a daughter?" I hear Lawrence ask.

"Three, actually." DeFiore sips his coffee. "Six, four, and two. The six-year-old runs the show."

"They're little," Lawrence says. "You still have a few good years left."

I turn to DeFiore. "At ten, we're lovely. Around thirteen, we get moody. By sixteen, we're monstrous. Defiant, uncontrollable, and mean as hell."

"You?" He shakes his head. "Sorry, can't see it. You're too pretty."

I shake mine back. "Guilty as charged, Counselor. I was gruesome."

"Can we please focus on Billy?" Nate snaps. "He's the reason we're here, right?"

My brother is famished, which is clear from the way he rips open the plastic Saltine packets on the table with his teeth and devours the crackers, one by one.

I text him under the table: Sit up. Be nice. Act human. No joke.

His eyes shift from his phone to DeFiore. His face softens, tone shifts. "So, Peter," he says amiably. "Tell us about Billy. Is he okay? We're very concerned."

*　*　*

Nate's life's ambition is to surf the Banzai Pipeline in Hawaii, where the waves run a hundred feet high. He loves the beach. He used to love sports, but then he went to boarding school. Now, he drinks a lot. He snorts cocaine, takes ecstasy, and smokes a ton of weed. He tries to cut back, though not very hard. If *please, allow me* is Lawrence's personal brand, *not trying hard* is Nate's. At Columbia, he had a negative GPA for two semesters. He transferred to Reed, then SUNY Binghamton, but gave up in the end. He has a similar job history. Nate's longest stretch of employment was six months, including the time he tried, and failed, to intern for Lawrence. Our plan to join the foundation was predicated on me doing all the work, so when I took off, he didn't see the point. One of the husbands in Eleanor's set got Nate the position at Bessemer, and when he eventually quits, someone else's husband will find him some other job at some other company. Or Lawrence will re-hire him. Or he'll go back to rehab. Or something. Nate doesn't need a job because he needs the money; he needs a job because he needs a life.

But he's unwilling to feign interest in a phony career simply to fill up his days. So, he's left with no purpose and nowhere to go. Other than surfing, Billy's case is the first thing I've seen him get emotional about since he discovered Hawkins Cove, our childhood hangout in Southampton, when he was eight years old.

I can't tell from DeFiore's expression how much he knows about my brother, though I'm sure the Bowtie offered a preview. The Bowtie's not a fan of Nate's either. But he's keen on Billy because Billy is Eleanor's favorite.

"Incarceration is a shock," DeFiore is saying. "But Billy's holding his own. He isn't bothering anyone. More important, no one's bothering him. Which is good since he's not getting out until he sees a judge. Apparently, he thought he'd be released today. That is not happening."

"But Billy is innocent," Lawrence says, looking stricken. "What's the problem?"

"The problem?" Cocking his head, the lawyer gazes at Lawrence. "That's not how things work, Lar. There's a justice system. We have to act within its confines. Innocent boys go to prison every day—even white ones."

"I realize that, Peter. Of course, I do. But I'm hoping we could, I don't know, circumvent the . . . move things a bit faster. My wife is—"

He's interrupted by the waitress, who sets down our food and asks if we need anything else. No, we tell her; all good. "Let me know!" Her eyes linger on Nate for a moment before she rushes off.

"We can't circumvent anything," DeFiore tells Lawrence. "The process is the same for everyone—slow and painful. In the morning, Billy will be transferred to the courthouse. He'll appear before the judge. The DA will do his thing. We'll do ours. Ten, fifteen minutes, tops." He sits back. "So, as we discussed, I still have a lot to review but it's unlikely I'll recommend a trial—"

"This just happened, Peter," Nate says. "How can you know what you'll recommend?"

"Regrettably, Nate, your brother got himself in a shitty spot. In he-said/she-said situations, everyone's a little bit innocent and little bit guilty. Lawyers hate these cases, especially in New Jersey, because plaintiffs have an advantage here. Plus, Mercer County is a political minefield."

"What do you mean?" my brother asks, a challenge in his tone. Like Lawrence, he wants DeFiore to cut to the chase and set Billy free.

"Several years ago, the previous DA, a guy named Jameson Halliday, was charged with assaulting three female paralegals. This was right after Harvey Weinstein exploded, so his case got a lot of ink. On one side you had Halliday, an older man who wielded enormous power. On the other, you had a large contingent of vocal women with very real grievances."

"Whose side were you on?" I ask.

"Great question, Cassie. I'll plead the Fifth. Halliday was a manipulative asshole with a long, dirty history. But it was a hard case to prosecute. The evidence was weak. Two of the women made lousy witnesses. They ended up settling. It was the right call, but Halliday got off easy. Though he resigned and paid a hefty fine, he didn't have to admit guilt or give up his pension. Everyone left the table unsatisfied."

I snort. "But why would this one case—"

"The next DA comes in and cleans up. Doubles down on victim's rights, reinstates rape shield protections, implements new sensitivity programs, et cetera. Now plaintiffs have an advantage here unlike any other county in the Tri-State area, maybe the whole East Coast."

"And? What does this have to do with Billy?" Nate asks.

"The new DA, the one who will be prosecuting your brother, is Brad Anderson. He has a personal stake in this case." DeFiore pauses. "His wife's sister was Halliday's accuser number one. Halliday retired to Boca Raton and plays golf every day. Meanwhile, Anderson's sister-in-law suffers from crippling anxiety, and hasn't worked in more than ten years. Anderson is rabid."

The waitress offers coffee refills. DeFiore checks his watch, then nods. "One more cup, then I gotta hit the road."

"Does this mean we won't get the case thrown out?" Lawrence asks.

"Thrown out?" DeFiore squints at him and shakes his head. "No way. Not with Anderson. Not in this climate. Don't get me wrong—I understand why Burt might have thought so. Given your son's prior relationship with the accuser, this case looks like a non-starter, especially if Princeton can confirm the girl's stalking and we can produce her texts. But we run into trouble with the eyewitness statements. They . . ." Trailing off, he looks down for a moment, and as I feel my impatience grow, it's easy to picture DeFiore in a courtroom, pausing mid-sentence to heighten the drama. "Two young men saw them at the scene. Both in their twenties. Both college students and unknown to your son and the accuser. So they're credible. And they both said the same thing: your son was assaulting a girl who appeared to be unconscious."

"Objection!" I say. "No way." *Unconscious?* According to Nate, Diana was *hysterical*. What else was lost in translation?

DeFiore turns my way. "Excuse me?"

"Diana Holly is a liar. The accuser—Diana Holly—she lies compulsively."

"She used to sneak into Billy's room when he was in class," Nate adds. "He'd come back, and she'd pretend to be sleeping. Once he was so freaked out, he called 911. The police must have records."

"Maybe they do." DeFiore shrugs. "So what? Those events have no bearing on her state of mind two nights ago. The EMT and sheriff's reports will determine that. Once I get them—and CCTV footage from the streets and playground—I'll know more. Of course, we'd argue it was dark, the witnesses were a distance away, what have you. But assaulting a woman who blacked out is a much higher level of charge. An unconscious person can't give consent, no matter how many times she may have lied in the past."

"Look, Mr. DeFiore," I say.

"Peter, please."

"Peter. Diana Holly is disturbed. If you can establish a pattern of abusive behavior—"

"Knock it off, Cassie," Nate says. "Let the guy do his job."

DeFiore looks amused. "I'll take that under advisement . . . uh . . . Counselor? I thought you were studying"—he checks his notes—"political science?"

"I watch a lot of *Law and Order*."

"Great, so you can be my co-counsel." Wiping his mouth, he turns to Lawrence. "*If* you decide to hire me. I don't mean to presume." He stands up. "Sorry, I have to run."

DeFiore's reticence throws me. I imagined him having an assassin's temperament, the kind of guy who'd rip into Diana Holly like an animal.

"You're hired." Lawrence also stands up. "We'll see you at the courthouse in the morning. Should we bring anything? Do anything? Say anything?"

"Say nothing to no one." On this point, DeFiore is unequivocal. "*No one*. If you feel compelled to speak up, to clear Billy's good name, to call for justice—do not. The only time you should talk is with an attorney present. Me or one of my team." He glances at us. "Got it?"

Nodding, we each shake his hand.

"And Mrs. Quinn?" DeFiore asks.

"No problem," Lawrence assures him. "I'll talk to Eleanor tonight."

We watch DeFiore lumber out. "All due respect, Lar," I say. "Don't be so quick to speak for your wife."

9

THE WORLD OF THE WEALTHY IS SMALL AND CLANNISH. THE Forresters, my biological family, were old-money bankers. CW's father attended Groton, as had his father, and his father, all the way back to 1884. They donated generously to the school, endowing millions of dollars in scholarships for disadvantaged youths. One such recipient was Lawrence Quinn.

When they met, Lawrence was thirteen, and CW was forty-two. Back then, hazing was rampant at Groton, and Second Formers (eighth graders) were the targets. Lawrence was subjected to ice-cold showers, petty theft, and humiliating pranks that could turn violent. Luckily, the Forresters' scholarship program included a mentoring component, and CW spent two Fridays a month teaching Lawrence essential life lessons, like how to beat back a bully or tie a perfect Windsor knot. In turn, Lawrence helped CW, a twice-divorced Wall Street wizard, relive his youth. Ultimately, the program worked as intended: Lawrence had a father figure to admire, and CW had an impressionable young man to mold in his own image.

Lawrence and CW's ad hoc but sincere fraternal connection inspired everything that came next. When Lawrence was in his last year at Columbia, CW introduced him to Eleanor Stockton, who was a senior at Wellesley with his niece, my first cousin Clarey. Sparks ignited, and by graduation, Lawrence had asked Eleanor to marry him with a ring financed by CW. After their wedding, the couple moved into the Stocktons' historic Valmont home (Eleanor's parents had retired to Palm Beach), and a few years later, CW married Rachel Richardson and moved into his family home two floors below. Initially, Eleanor and Rachel kept their distance, but soon their lives were enmeshed.

Eleanor introduced Rachel to the charity circuit. Rachel helped Eleanor find a speech pathologist. My nanny and the boys' nanny were second cousins.

As chairman of Forrester Holdings, CW traveled for a living and preferred that his much-younger wife accompanied him. Rachel, who'd quit her job at CW's bank and relied on his support, was in no position to object. I stayed behind, though not with a nanny or housekeeper. Instead, my parents left me with the Quinns for days at a stretch. Which is why, when CW had a stroke—alone for once, in a Brussels hotel—I was already living upstairs. CW's death sent Rachel spiraling, but Lawrence stepped in. "We'll take her," he offered. "Let me do this for you, Rachel. Let me be a father to Cassie, the kind of father CW would've wanted her to have."

Everyone was pleased. CW could rest in peace. Rachel was unburdened. Eleanor finally had a girl after years of trying. Lawrence could repay his mentor. But two years later, tragedy struck again. Rachel died in a car accident—alone, in Florida, at the wheel—leaving me with no close blood family except CW's older sister and her awful daughter Clarey. When I turn twenty-five, I'll inherit CW's fortune. And yet, despite all the stories of wealthy orphans with calculating relatives, no one offered to raise me. No one except Lawrence and Eleanor Quinn.

People are skeptical of the rich. We are selfish and self-absorbed. We are oblivious to poverty, to the needs of others. We are greedy. We are corrupt. We eat our own. But this isn't all we are. The Quinns are obscenely wealthy. They have everything money can buy. But when presented with a problem that wasn't theirs to solve, they didn't turn their backs, nor did they take the easy way out and write a check. Instead, they opened the door and invited me in—not to visit, but to stay. So, maybe Eleanor can seem cold, and Lawrence tries too hard. Maybe they're not always kind, or good, to each other; maybe they're not good at all. But Lawrence and Eleanor were good to me. For this, and for everything else they've given me, I was, I am, beyond grateful. To a sad, lonely orphan girl, the Quinns were, the Quinns are, are a gift from God.

*   *   *

At midnight, I'm studying at my desk when Eleanor enters my room. She's so quiet, I don't realize she's behind me until I see her shadow in the mirror.

Startled, I let out a yelp. "Oh my God, Eleanor."

"I'm sorry. I didn't mean to scare you." She shakes her head. "I can't sleep, so I'm wandering around, trying to find a place to put myself."

"That's the problem with mansions," I say. "Too many damn rooms."

So it was Eleanor, not Maeve, in the hall last night. Poor Eleanor. In our family, Lawrence is the good cop. Eleanor is all the other cops. She isn't given to overt emotion. To turn to me for comfort—to show up at my door—means she's going insane.

Years ago, Eleanor went beyond the beyond to make me feel welcome here. One special gift was my bedroom. When I was old enough, she let me pick out the colors, mint green and white, and filled the shelves with my favorite books, stuffed animals, and toys. The animals and toys are gone, but the décor in this room has barely changed.

Turning on a lamp, I motion for Eleanor to sit. My floor is still a disaster site. Clothing, boots, belts, and books are strewn everywhere. I move to fold a sweater when Eleanor says "Leave it, dear. It's not important," which is another sign of her distress. Growing up, our bedrooms and bathrooms had to be immaculate, not that she ever set foot in them. I can't actually remember the last time she was in my room, much less on my bed. Under normal circumstances, this breach of privacy would be unthinkable.

At fifty-four, Eleanor still shimmers with youthful glamour. Her golden hair is cut in a chic bob, and she moves with a dancer's poise. Always impeccably styled, she's wearing a teal Valentino robe that could double as a ball gown. Eleanor is a true Hitchcock femme fatale, though her regal bearing lends her a chilliness she doesn't deserve. Perched on my white comforter, she looks lost and afraid.

Earlier today, in the car coming home, Lawrence mentioned, offhandedly, that it's better if Nate and I don't repeat everything DeFiore said. "Better Eleanor hears the 'unconscious' detail from me." Eleanor isn't fragile, just protective of Billy. I'd say "overprotective," but how much protection is too much? That's like trying to quantify love.

"I'm not entirely comfortable with our new attorney," Eleanor says. The warm light illuminates her porcelain skin.

"Lawrence told you?"

"That he went behind my back? That he hired a lawyer for my son without my consent? That he, once again, acted impulsively, with no regard for my opinion?"

I hold up my hand. "I'm sorry, Eleanor, we should've said something."

"Yes. You should have. It's harder for Nate—I understand this. But I depend on you to keep Lawrence in check. Or, at the very least, to keep me apprised of his behavior."

"I wish I could keep Lawrence in check, Eleanor. Believe me. And I'm not making excuses, I swear, but Billy is seeing the judge tomorrow morning. We needed someone fast. Plus, DeFiore is smart, his credentials are decent, and he's handled lots of cases like ours."

"Cassandra, please. His credentials are mediocre at best."

"Rutgers isn't Harvard, but Peter DeFiore is an expert on the local courts, which will be a defining factor in Billy's case. Still, you can watch him in action. If you're still uncomfortable, hire someone else."

"I'm sure he's a fine lawyer, but we need the best—"

"—of the best. I know, Eleanor."

"Yes, someone at the top of his field. But, equally important, we need someone who understands families like ours. Money is not a concern," she adds, as if I needed the reminder.

For Eleanor, money isn't emotional nor is it pleasurable. Money isn't even interesting. Money just is. Her family staked their claim in gunpowder during the French revolution, and then expanded to dynamite, plastic, oils, and chemical manufacturing—the raw materials of daily life. Their fortune has been compounding for generations. Eleanor Anne Stockton Quinn is a socialite. My peers consider this label unflattering; these days, we're socialite-entrepreneurs and socialite-artists, with handbag lines, poetry collections, and podcasts. But Eleanor is first and foremost a lady who lunches. I don't mean to suggest her lunches are vacuous, only to point out that her preoccupations are different from yours and mine.

"Eleanor, listen. His reputation is outstanding. Burt, in fact, recommended him. Would you feel better if you were the one who hired him?"

"If I hadn't been told after the fact? Maybe. Even so, his coarseness doesn't sit right."

"You mean his girth."

"Excuse me?"

"Peter DeFiore is fat."

"Cassie, I didn't see his body. Earlier, I saw him on video, but only from the waist up."

"I'm sure you got the gist of him. DeFiore is ungainly and sloppy, and you're wondering how a man who can't manage his person will effectively represent your son. Here's the thing, Eleanor." My voice is as solemn as a priest's. "Not only are fat people competent, but fat-shaming is *très déclassé* these days."

"Do you really think I'm that shallow, Cassie?" Eleanor smiles.

"Not shallow, per se." I smile back. "*Discriminating*."

"Let's get one thing straight. The only person's appearance I care about is yours. And it pains me to say this, but God Almighty, Sweet Girl; you are a fright."

Eleanor isn't physically demonstrative, so when she reaches out to smooth my hair, I light up from within. But it's not enough. It's never enough. Which is what I mean by insatiable urges. The poor woman has already given me the keys to the kingdom and the family jewels. Still, I want more.

"Seriously, Cassandra. When was your last trim? Tomorrow is devoted to Billy. I want to bring him home and get him settled. But Tuesday, we'll take care of you: tip-to-toe, hair and nails. I'll make the appointments." She glances up, like she thinks I'll disagree, though we both know I won't.

Eleanor has high expectations for her children. I'm female, so my appearance is non-negotiable. Her primary target is my body, which she's been policing since I could walk. "Boys will be boys, Cassandra, even good boys. You're a pretty girl. Why borrow trouble?" As far as she's concerned, it's my responsibility to ensure that I'm never viewed sexually by men—any man, including my brothers. Eleanor was raised in a subculture that enforces firm codes of conduct for both genders, but particularly girls. So, she raised me the way she was raised, the way her mother was raised, the way her mother's mother was raised, and so on, all the way back to that naked slut Eve, whose downfall could've been prevented had she made better choices.

"We have an early start," Eleanor reminds me. "I should lie down. But I heard what you said about Mr. DeFiore and will keep an open mind. And I appreciate you dropping everything to come home. It means a lot to me, and I know it means the world to your brother. Both brothers."

"I'd do anything for Billy, and for all of you. I miss you guys every day."

"I know, Cassandra, but you're where you're supposed to be. Now get some sleep." She brushes my cheek with her fingers. Her touch lingers long after she leaves.

Though Eleanor is a pain in the ass, her dedication to my welfare is more than I deserve. With Lawrence, she raised me like a real daughter—that is, no differently from their sons. Together, they began the adoption process, only it was never finalized because of reasons too complicated to understand, unless you're well-versed in revocable living trusts. I'm sure the decision had to do with money, but whose and how much I have no idea. Nor do I care. Eleanor is the closest I'll ever come to having a living, breathing mother. She took me in when no one else wanted me. She fed, clothed, and protected me. You could say that she and Lawrence saved my life, and you wouldn't be wrong. To this end, I spend an unholy amount of time conforming to her views of how I should look, how I should act, and who I should be. Both of us, I believe, consider me a work in progress.

10

THE NEXT MORNING, THE SKY IS PURE CERULEAN BLUE, AND the sun is bright yellow. It's picture-perfect outside, as if the universe is casting a hopeful glow on today's court visit. Choosing my outfit, I shoot for demure elegance with a come-hither edge, a mix of high and low fashion: chocolate-brown skirt (the Row), silk blouse (Burberry), thrift shop camisole, Louboutin heels, and beige tights (Gap). I wrangle my hair into a messy chignon, clip on my Mikimoto pearl necklace, and set off.

Our apartment spans two floors, and we spend most of our family time in a smaller living area that we call the celebration room. Here, we open birthday presents, trim Christmas trees, and announce good news (hence the corny name). But if I had to pick a favorite spot, it would be the dining room. When we were kids, before my brothers left for Groton, I loved our family dinners. Platters were passed back and forth while we reviewed our days. Cassie, please hand me the salt. Cassie, sit up, dear. Cassie, tell us three good things. Nate, Cassie, Billy. Billy, Cassie, Nate. Three Musketeers. Like most kids, I believed my family was the center of the universe, and I felt proud to be included.

I've only lived in a few places. However, I am well-traveled, and have come to recognize that a house's personality reflects the best and worst traits of its owners. I barely remember my birth parents' home. The Tarrants, an elderly couple, live there now. They have a daughter and son, both older than me. When I was younger and saw the family in passing, I'd imagine that the girl and I were the same person. She was the former me, forced to grow up in a cold, sad mausoleum; and I was the new me, spirited away to a bright, beautiful dreamland. I knew it was childish, but I couldn't help feeling superior to her. I was the anointed one; I had been chosen. I never did go back to my old apartment; trying to picture it conjures a sweep of loneliness, even all these years later. The foyer had a marble floor, so you stepped off the elevator into a hard, sterile space. There was an art gallery, library, and billiards den, plus six bedrooms and a private guest wing. The rooms, long as tennis courts, were overstuffed with antiques, and yet felt cramped and devoid of life. For all its opulence, the house evoked despair, like a spinster who stocks up on Hummel figurines to hide the absence of love in her life.

The Quinns' house, by contrast, is an oasis of warmth and light. They have the same mix of formal and informal rooms, but the couches are plush and inviting. Music plays quietly, even in empty rooms. The air smells of cinnamon and freshly baked cookies. They host parties with friends, business associates, and household staff. As a child, I loved being among the crowd, even if I just curled up on a chair and read. Maeve and the nannies hovered nearby, chiding me to eat in hushed voices. I felt blanketed by affection, welcomed by all. The sight, scent, and sound of the Quinns imprinted upon me so completely I was like a baby duckling, drawn back and back and back.

Heading down the hall, I hear Eleanor and Lawrence arguing in the kitchen and my optimism about the day fades. They're on the far side of the massive kitchen, near the terrace, so they don't see me, but their voices carry across the wide open space.

Side by side, my parents make a stunning couple. Today, Eleanor has on a dove gray Kiton skirt, navy blouse, and understated gold jewelry. I'm sure she's been showered and dressed since dawn, as opposed to her husband, who hasn't shaved in days, and slouches against the counter in baggy shorts, a faded Wellesley T-shirt, and battered loafers.

Lawrence and Eleanor fell in love at first sight, or so the story goes. The way he tells it, Eleanor's society ways, proper diction, and icy elegance knocked him sideways. I can see it too: Lawrence doing soft-shoe, jazz hands, anything, to win her over while she stood back, amused, watching him spin. But Eleanor was equally intrigued. Despite CW's endorsement, Lawrence Quinn was the type of uncultured, unrestrained boy her parents derided. A boy who talked too much and drank too much. Who had the gall to mock her uptight bearing, yet knew enough to court her properly, with handwritten notes on heavy card stock. With Lawrence, Eleanor felt girlish. With Eleanor, Lawrence felt like an insider. Together, they were a perfect couple. So perfect, Eleanor wouldn't sign a prenup. Her parents balked, but she stood firm. In the end, the parties compromised, and Lawrence was welcomed into the fold with a lavish wedding, while Eleanor's fortune remained under her control, the majority sealed in a trust. Lawrence can access their assets, but he needs Eleanor's authorization to spend above a certain threshold. And so the perfect couple lived happily ever after.

This morning, though, I see no happiness, only rancor. Eleanor's lips are pursed, and Lawrence is raking his hands through his hair. I assume they're arguing about Peter DeFiore, but just as I'm about to call out a cheery *hello*, Eleanor says, "She's going with you today. That's why she raced home—to support her brother." And I realize they're fighting about me.

"It's better if I go alone," Lawrence says. "If the press is there, they'll pounce. Until this whole thing goes away, the less we appear in public the better."

"That's why we pay a PR firm. So far, they've done their job."

"It hasn't even been three days, Eleanor. I'm telling you Cassie should not show up in court. Why won't you listen to me?"

"I'm sorry you feel this way," she replies, without sympathy. "But Burt wants the whole family there. A united front, he said."

"First of all, Peter DeFiore is Billy's attorney, not Burt. Peter didn't mention anything about a 'united front.' He said this appearance will last ten minutes, tops. So there's no reason for all of us to drive two hours there and two hours back for a ten-minute show. Second, Burt's specialty is wills and trusts. If we were debating the value of our wine collection, I'd ask his advice. But—"

"Stop it, Lawrence. Just stop. Why are you focused on Cassie? Or Burt, for that matter? My son has been falsely accused of a horrific crime. Every iota of your attention should be trained on him. In the meantime, it's late, so please shower and wake Cassie up. Remind her to wear the Row wool skirt. Oh—stockings, too. She can't walk into a courtroom with bare legs."

"Billy is on trial for rape. Cassie's legs are the least of our problems." In response, Eleanor turns and stalks off. "Where are you going? We're in the middle of a conversation." Lawrence sighs. "Why are you so angry at me, El? I just spent two days in some New Jersey backwater, trying to bring *our* son home. I resent you saying I'm not focused on him."

"I am not angry at *you*. I'm angry at the *situation*. However, you do have a habit of making terrible situations worse. Your stupid stunt could jeopardize Billy's entire defense. And then where will we be?"

"Hey guys." I step into the kitchen and over to the counter, where Maeve is laying out pastries, sliced cantaloupe, and coffee. "I'm here."

"Cassie!" Whirling around, Lawrence looks startled, almost guilty. "You're awake."

"Morning, dear," Eleanor says with strained brightness. "Sleep well?"

Bustling around us, Maeve hands me an empty mug embossed with the letter C. "Yours," she says, and I thank her. Over the years, the C, once crimson, has faded to a dull pink. "Poor Billy," she murmurs. Maeve is sixty-four with translucent gray eyes and pale, paper-thin skin. Like Anton, she's been in my life since day one. Gathering me in her arms, she kisses my forehead. "You're too skinny," she says, her brogue thick even after thirty-odd years in this country.

I hug her tightly. "Promise? Say it again; say, 'You're super-skinny, Cassie. I've never seen you this skinny. Are you sick? Do you feel okay?'"

She laughs. "You're terrible."

Standing at the counter, I fill my mug with coffee, aware that Eleanor and Lawrence are watching me. "So." I spear a piece of melon. "What's the latest? Good news? Bad news? Possible windfalls? Last-minute reversals?"

"We're set," Lawrence says. "DeFiore texted from the courthouse. Billy is being transported over. Now we're debating who should drive to Trenton."

"Why is it a debate? Aren't we all going?"

"We are," Eleanor says. "So is Burt. He'll meet us there." When Lawrence starts to protest, she cuts him off. "For moral support. Burt has known Billy all his life."

"Billy can't stand Burt. He doesn't need or want his support."

"Moral support *for me*, Lawrence. Burt is showing up *for me*."

I try to de-escalate the tension. "What about Diana Holly? Have we heard anything about her?"

For some reason this makes Eleanor laugh.

"What's so funny?" I ask.

She looks at Lawrence. "How similarly your minds work, as if you're both on a single track."

I turn to look at him too. "What's she talking about?"

"It's nothing."

"It's not nothing," Eleanor corrects him.

Lawrence rolls his eyes. "I made one phone call last night. Just one call, to the girl's father, but he didn't pick up and I didn't leave a message. Nothing came of it, but Eleanor is convinced that because of my grievous error, they'll ship Billy to Leavenworth and throw away the key."

"For God's sake, Lawrence," Eleanor says. "Why would you contact the father of a girl who accused our son of sexual battery and felony rape?"

Lawrence throws up his hands. "He didn't *rape* her."

"That's not the point." She stares at him, unblinking, and for a long moment, they don't move.

"Okay," Lawrence concedes. "It was stupid." Exhaling, he blows out a mouthful of air. "I just thought if we could talk, dad to dad, I could make him see that a trial would be just as tough on his daughter. He doesn't want to watch her life get ripped apart, and her reputation trashed, any more than we want that for Billy. No one wins. That's all I wanted to say, Eleanor—"

"This isn't some *deal* you can finesse through back-door channels. The girl and her father are our adversaries." Eleanor's voice breaks. "Lawrence, why is this happening? Billy did nothing to deserve this."

"Come here." He beckons to her, but she doesn't move. "Honey, I promise. Billy will be fine. We'll clear this up, bring him home, and resume our lives. And you're right. It was a mistake. But I honestly thought he and I could figure this out."

"Stay off the phone, Lawrence." She glances at me. "Cassie, dear . . ." She points to my legs. "Find darker stockings. Please, for my sake. Those make your legs look naked." Reflexively, I bend down, but before I can reply, she pulls open the French doors and steps out onto the balcony.

Nothing knocks Lawrence off-balance like his wife's disapproval. "I'll be right back," he says and follows behind her.

* * *

Eleanor uses the terrace as a means of escape, even in the dead of winter. It's more like a heated solarium, with a wet bar, full bathroom, and Zen rock garden. I watch through the beveled glass as Lawrence tries to return to her good graces. Brushing Eleanor's hair off her forehead, he looks into her eyes. As he talks, her body relaxes. Soon, she nods, and this time, when he opens his arms, she lets him embrace her. For one long, tender minute, they sway together, as if dancing to silent music.

Suddenly, Lawrence jerks up his head, as if reminded of something. Looking at me over Eleanor's shoulder, he raises a finger. Nodding, I thumb through the *Wall Street Journal*, but ten minutes later, he still hasn't emerged. Just as I'm about to leave, Lawrence rushes into the kitchen. "Cassie, hold on."

"I need to change my tights," I say tersely.

"They're fine." He tries to catch my eye. "You're mad. At me? What did I do?"

"I'm not mad, I'm upset . . ."

"Cassie, spit it out."

"Why don't you want me to go to court? You did the same thing yesterday with the DeFiore meeting. What's the deal?"

"Cassie, listen, today's appearance doesn't matter. It will be over before it starts. I don't think Eleanor or Nate should go either. This family needs to be as far away from that courthouse as possible."

"What about the Bowtie's idea for a united front?"

"Burt made one passing remark that Eleanor has hooked on to." Lawrence seizes my shoulders. "Billy is innocent. We all know that. But this girl has set a machine in motion, and given the timing and politics, his innocence may not matter. If this case goes to trial, it will blow up into a media circus. I'm trying to protect us, that's all."

I consider this. "You're sure it's not about me?"

He sighs. "What about you, Cassandra?"

I don't expect Lawrence to focus on my problems, but I can't escape them, especially when I'm home. It's more accurate, for instance, to call my difficult period in high school a complete unraveling. At the time, I told my parents I was fighting with Avery, my best friend since preschool. And while we did have an argument, a bitter one, my breakdown was the result of other events, with Marcus at the white-hot center. The truth is, Marcus was married, and despite his promises, would never leave his wife. It was a confusing experience, to love someone who lets you down, over and over. I was ashamed and obsessive, joyful and reckless. It was like a tornado, and I pitched into the vortex with abandon, only to find myself stripped of confidence and dignity—and alone.

Marcus Silver's gravitational pull was so strong I lost myself around him. When times were good, they were fantastic. But there was no bottom, and the only way to survive was to escape. So, I left him. (Then went back. Left again. Went back again.) Then I left town. I've since recovered, although his draw is still intense. Even now, the thought of him unmoors me, so I'm careful not to leave myself open.

You know the worst part? I have only myself to blame. I came on strong; I gave him no room to fend me off. He did say no, by the way. But I kept pushing until he gave in. You can't choose who you love, but you can choose how you behave. I behaved atrociously. Which is why it's too mortifying to talk about.

"What about you, Cassandra?" Lawrence repeats.

I'm exhausting, I know. Still, I can't help myself. "Maybe you're

worried the press will find out about Avery and the . . . you know . . ."
Embarrassed, I trail off. "Maybe you're worried that people will judge
me, judge us. And if they judge us, Billy will lose."

"*Of course*, I'm worried." Lawrence looks incredulous. "But not just
because of Billy. Cassie, I'm worried about how this may affect *you*. I
don't want any part of your private life exposed."

"I have to be there for Billy. He's my brother, and my best friend.
I'm not afraid."

"Well, I am." Lawrence's eyes are clouded with concern. It's like
he's seeing me across a great divide: already ravaged and beyond his
grasp. "And you should be too."

11

MERCER COUNTY CRIMINAL COURTHOUSE SITS ON THE corner of a busy intersection in downtown Trenton. It's a nondescript four-story building that looks like a suburban medical center, and we pass by it twice until Nate calls out, "Over here! Guys, turn around." Inside, armed guards are at the ready, and we have to step through a metal detector, but the lobby is as non-threatening as a dentist's office.

Despite Lawrence's continued rants about the predatory media, I don't spot a single reporter, either on the street or in the building. Still, he scans the four corners, as if expecting a newscaster to leap out, wielding a microphone. He speed-walks ahead of us to the elevators; and then, as if realizing his mistake, doubles back to take Eleanor's arm. Looking unhurried and serene, she swans across the lobby like it's her own living room. There's a stillness and grace to Eleanor I can never replicate, no matter how hard I try.

Seeing Lawrence so keyed up makes my own fear spike, but at the same time, I feel distant, as if all of this is happening to someone else entirely. Nate must see my bewilderment, because he takes my hand and propels me forward.

Upstairs, on the fourth floor, the scenery changes. The light is so bright I'm forced to squint. We walk down a long, noisy corridor, passing courtrooms on either side, each a private theater, with LCD screens advertising the presiding judge. Police stroll beside us, guns holstered but visible. Families sit on benches in groups of twos and threes; a disproportionate number are Black and Brown. Men wear oversized hoodies and heavy work boots; women are dressed for church in colorful blouses, flowing skirts, and gold chains. Huddled together, they look like small football squads listening to the quarterback—their lawyer, most often a white person in a business suit—call off the plays.

Heading to Courtroom 4L, we pass white lawyers shouting into phones, white lawyers holding shabby briefcases, white lawyers with thinning hair and poor diction. "They haven't given us fuckin' discovery, I don't know what to tell you. It's not my fuckin' problem. It's your fuckin' problem, asshole," I hear one say as I move down the hall.

I feel absurdly white and absurdly wealthy, so white and wealthy I float above the bustle. But no one, not one of the Black men, the Brown women, or the white lawyers glance our way.

DeFiore and the Bowtie wait outside the courtroom, a study in opposites. DeFiore is a colossal, oily mess, wearing the same threadbare suit jacket as yesterday. He's swapped a dingy button-down for the Jets sweatshirt and put on a tie, a long, red tongue that unfurls over his belly. Beside him, the Bowtie looks like a slender dandy who has time-traveled here from the Gilded Age. With his white handlebar mustache and infamous paisley neckwear, he's Mr. Monopoly come to life.

"I have good news and not-so-good news," DeFiore says quietly when we're gathered into our own football huddle. "I saw Billy. He's okay. He's scared and angry but resolved to get through this."

"How does he look?" Though I'm addressing DeFiore, the Bowtie answers.

"What are you expecting, Cassandra? Two black eyes and a bloody nose?" He chuckles, a sound that repulses me. "You watch too much TV, my dear."

Given his age and ties to Eleanor, the Bowtie should be a kindly grandfather figure to me. Instead, he acts like I'm up to no good, sparking my deepest fear: I'm an interloper in my own family. Ever since he handled the estates of Eleanor's parents, the Bowtie has slithered as close as he can, while forgetting the first rule of friendship among the monied class: hold your lane. Out of respect for Eleanor, I normally swallow my distaste. Not today.

"Excuse me, Burt, but my brother just spent two fucking days in prison. So I'm not asking for commentary on my television habits. I want to know how the hell he is holding up."

"Cassandra!" Eleanor is mortified.

DeFiore steps in. "Folks, folks. Let's focus. We don't have much time. Cassie, your brother looks fine. Exhausted, petrified, but no dings."

"So, what's the not-so-good news?" Eleanor wants to know.

"The DA is going to argue against release."

"What?" She turns to Lawrence. "What is he saying? They're won't let Billy out?"

"They won't win," Lawrence reassures her. "Peter and I discussed this yesterday."

"No, of course not," DeFiore agrees. "But their argument is meaningful. I don't know what your husband has told you, Mrs. Quinn, but the DA has witnesses, two Princeton students who came upon Billy with the accuser. They're alleging that she was unconscious, er, unresponsive, rather."

"*Unconscious?*" Eleanor grabs Lawrence's arm. "Did you know this?"

Nate and I stiffen; we keep our eyes locked on the floor. *Oh Lawrence*, I think.

"It's a point of contention," he says. "There's no evidence—"

"No *confirmed* evidence," DeFiore clarifies. "We're still waiting. This is Billy's first arrest. He is a model student. They have no legitimate reason to detain him. But Anderson will argue that he exhibited what they call 'willful and depraved disregard for the girl's welfare.' He's sending a message."

"What kind of message?"

"Given the climate, the facts of the case so far, the press—"

"The press? There's been nothing in the press," Eleanor says, her pitch rising.

"After today, there will be, Mrs. Quinn. They're going to use Billy. Make an example—"

"But what about the girl? What about Diana?"

A shadow crosses DeFiore's face. Clearly, he wants Eleanor to let him finish a goddamn sentence, but for all the guy's smarts, he doesn't grasp that she's paying him to let her speak. In fact, she'd much rather shell out three times his rate to a Park Avenue attorney who knew enough to shut his mouth when she's talking, wipe his forehead, and buy a decent suit that fits. "What about Diana?" he asks wearily.

"Diana and Billy's relationship? How does that fit in?"

"Right now, it doesn't." DeFiore starts to add something else then decides against it. Promising we'll all talk soon, he disappears behind a concealed door.

Eleanor looks shell-shocked, and Lawrence tries to take her arm, but she shrugs him off.

"Billy will be fine," the Bowtie murmurs as a sheriff opens the courtroom doors. Laying a protective hand on Eleanor's shoulder, he maneuvers her inside. "As will you."

Stepping forward, Eleanor maintains a safe distance from the rest of us, as if she'd just met us for the first time and wasn't impressed.

* * *

Twenty minutes later, we're seated in the gallery. Everyone is in place—judge, defense team, court reporter—except for the prosecution, whose table is empty. I take in the Honorable Charles McKay, our judge. He's gray-haired, with deep-set eyes, unruly eyebrows, and a formidable frown. So far, he's the most impressive man in the room, though this is probably because he's on the throne, wearing robes.

There are ten rows for spectators. Half the rows are empty, the other half hold women with young children and a few scattered families like ours. Everyone, except us, is Black. At the defense table, DeFiore sits with a younger man, presumably his co-counsel. Heads bent together, the two men crack up. Their levity seems disrespectful, and I wonder if maybe Eleanor was right about DeFiore.

Billy is scheduled to appear first. But fifteen minutes later, we're still waiting. From my bag, I pull out a pen and paper. Nate and I play Hangman. I solve the first puzzle (*N A T E T H E G R E A T I S K I N G*). Nate solves the next one (*B I L L Y Q U I N N W A S F R A M E D*).

Eventually, a slender woman with a low ponytail rushes in. Wheeling a legal briefcase and carrying a stack of folders, she heads to the prosecution table. She's wearing tiny glasses with cat's-eye frames and an olive-green polyester suit. Her hem hangs down and skims her calves. In her dusty flats and pilled cardigan, she looks like she leads Bible study on Wednesday evenings. A bald giant follows behind her, also wheeling a briefcase. A burly bruiser with a thick neck and fleshy jowls, he's talking quietly on his phone. According to the Bowtie, this is Bradley Anderson, the district attorney; the dowdy girl is Maggie Fleming, his deputy.

"We apologize for being late, Your Honor," Fleming says, her voice just above a whisper. "We had a last-minute—"

"Fine, you're here." Judge McKay waves them to their table. "Sit down; let's go."

The prosecution and defense teams acknowledge each other with a perfunctory nod, and then turn to McKay, who opens the show. "What's the case number?" he asks the bailiff, but before she can answer, he asks the DA if they're set.

"Sure," Anderson replies. "We're ready whenever you are." His casual tone surprises me.

McKay beckons Fleming up to the bench and says something inaudible. She nods. Meanwhile, DeFiore and Junior are conferring, as if they have nothing to do with the proceedings unfolding around them.

The side door opens, and a marshal steps into the courtroom, accompanied by a teenager wearing a brown prison jumpsuit, his head bent. His hands and legs are cuffed, forcing him to shuffle forward. When I hear Eleanor gasp, I look again and realize—*my god*—it's Billy.

Billy scans the gallery. I want to shout, *Elmo, Elmo, Elmo; it's me; it's Cassie!* Beside me, Nate is restless. His calf bounces, and I nudge him to sit still.

Under the bright lights, my little brother seems younger and smaller than the last time I saw him. His hair has grown so long since Christmas that the edges curl against his collar. A sweep of bangs hides his eyes, giving him a fawnlike quality. "Let me see that page again," McKay says to the DA. He seems oblivious to my brother, who waits politely for instructions. In the jumpsuit, with his unwashed, shaggy hair, Billy looks like a misunderstood bad boy in a teen movie, the rebel with a heart of gold.

"Okay, let's move on," McKay says, opening a folder. "William Quinn."

The presentation from the DA's office, though short, is harrowing. Fleming does all the talking, and despite her quiet voice, she is curt, brisk, and all business: William Matthew Stockton Quinn was seen forcibly having sexual intercourse with an unconscious woman. William Matthew Stockton Quinn is the son of extremely wealthy parents and has the means to flee. This is reflected in William Matthew Stockton Quinn's detention scores. The way she keeps repeating William Matthew Stockton Quinn terrifies me.

Billy, meanwhile, is gripping the table, his knuckles white.

"Defense?" the judge says. "Can we hear from you?"

Standing up, DeFiore buttons his jacket over his ridiculous tie. His voice booms with the resonance of a Shakespearean actor. "My client is a Princeton scholar-athlete with a 3.8 GPA. He plans to be a pediatrician. He is a well-liked young man with a lifelong commitment to public service and a loving family who will vouch for him. This is my client's only brush with the law. He has a prior relationship with his accuser that will bear on, if not mitigate, the DA's charges. Moreover, it's highly irregular for the State to request remand for a first-time offender." DeFiore steps toward the bench. "Your Honor, we respectfully ask that my client be released on his own recognizance."

When DeFiore finishes, the judge asks Mr. Quinn if he'd like to add anything. Stupidly, I turn to Lawrence, but McKay means Billy, who shakes his head.

"The court needs to hear a verbal answer, Mr. Quinn."

Nate grabs my hand. We hold our breath. "Not guilty" has hard and soft consonants. For Billy, hard consonants—B, D, V, G, K, C—are the most challenging. He'll repeat a G several times until he can hitch it to a neighboring vowel and make a full stop: *g-g-g-g-guilty*. With soft consonants—L, N, S, W—he'll prolong the sound, pressing down with his tongue until he can release: *lllllllove you, C-C-C-Casssssie.*

I love you, Elmo. Just say it. Come on, Billy. Not guilty.

"Mr. Quinn?" the judge prompts.

Billy swallows. "Nnnnot, g-guilllltty."

I exhale, and Nate drops my hand.

McKay reads back the transcript. He denies the State's motion for detention. Prohibits Billy from excessive use of drugs, alcohol, social media, and pornography. Sets a curfew. Reiterates the terms of the restraining order. "You are not allowed to contact the accused or any witnesses."

DeFiore asks, "Your Honor, can Billy return to Princeton to finish his classes and take his exams? The semester is over in six weeks."

"Given the nature and severity of the accusation, I have to say no. He can work out an arrangement with the university to finish his classes or take a leave." The judge looks at Billy. "Also, Mr. Quinn, you will be required to wear a monitoring device. If you go out of your designated area, or anywhere near the accuser, you will be taken back to jail until your trial. Do you understand the limits of your release and are you able to comply with all of them?"

DeFiore leans over, and whispers to Billy, who looks up and nods.

"Again, the court needs to hear your answer, Mr. Quinn," McKay says.

"Y-y-y-yes. I c-c-c-can, Your Honor."

"Fine, then. Pursuant to the laws of New Jersey, the next step is for the prosecution to determine if they want to take this case further. If so, it will be presented to a grand jury—"

"We do, your Honor." Fleming jumps to her feet, raises her voice. "We have determined that this case has merit and sufficient evidence to pursue a conviction."

"Then the case will proceed to the grand jury." Judge McKay bangs his gavel, and just like that, my brother's immediate future is sealed.

12

Billy's speech impediment was psychosomatic. Despite hours of physical exams and pages of clinical assessments, she still lacked a definitive answer for why he stuttered. Why not Nate? What about Cassie? She took him to a psychiatrist who impressed upon her one fact: there is no reason. Billy stammers because he stammers. Nor was there a single reason for his childhood ailments. By his fifth birthday, Billy had been treated for illnesses ranging from ear infections to aortic stenosis. He didn't speak until age three (*Cass*) or say sentences (*Me and Cass read*) or express complex thoughts (*too tired to read me and Cass book*) until nearly four. He spent an extra year in nursery school and didn't start kindergarten until he was six.

I like to believe I helped Billy thrive, because I wouldn't have survived childhood without him. When I was five and my biological mother died, I became preoccupied with death. My fears escalated at bedtime. Falling asleep seemed like dying, and I was afraid to close my eyes. What happened during the nothingness? What if I didn't wake up? Night after night, I lay awake on red alert. When I did sleep, my dreams were terrifying. I fell off mountains, burned in fires, starved in caves. Lawrence and Eleanor tried everything. They read to me, sang to me, left me alone, slept beside me.

Nothing worked until Lawrence came up with a ritual. Each night, he carried Billy to my room, laid him in my bed, and told us stories about our lives. "Epic stories," he called them. Sometimes he went backwards in time, telling us about CW and Rachel, how Lawrence fell in love with Eleanor, how Lawrence and Eleanor fell in love with Cassie, their "forever girl." Other nights he made up tales from the future about Cassie, Billy, and Nate, his Three Musketeers on the beach. Through these stories, Lawrence showed me all the ways I belonged, that I was safe and wanted. His voice was the thread that tethered me to our family, who loved me beyond the beyond. But it was the ritual that connected me to Billy, to the warmth of his body, his silky hair and sturdy presence. Eleanor didn't like Billy (or Nate) to sleep in my bed. She insisted that he return to his own room as soon as our epic stories were over. But sometimes Billy dropped off while Lawrence was still talking. On those nights, his dad let him stay, which filled me with unspeakable joy. Had Eleanor allowed it, I would've slept curled up next to Billy until we were grown. I still would.

* * *

Midafternoon on Tuesday, I'm perched on a chair beside a sleeping Billy when Eleanor steps into his room. She's annoyed. "Let him be," she whispers. But I don't move. "What about your hair? Your appointment is today."

I beg her to cancel it. "He's been asleep since he got home. I've barely talked to him."

Billy's room hasn't been touched in years. Clothes are stacked neatly in drawers, jackets hang in the closet, and running shoes are lined up on racks. Bits and pieces of his childhood are scattered all over—plastic dinosaurs, skateboards, his library of science fiction—and his shelves overflow with trophies, medals, and ribbons. But other than a Princeton pennant and the framed picture of him teaching a kid to read, there's no sign whatsoever of my brother's current life.

As a child, I spent as much time here as I could. After our epic stories, when Billy went back to his own bed, the house became a cemetery. The silence was unbearable. I felt so lonely. So, I waited until the clock said 9:30. Then I tiptoed through the long, scary halls, all the way to Billy's room, and crawled under his blankets. The bed was soft, Billy's body warm. I wrapped myself around him: my arm over his ribs, my nose in his neck, our feet entwined. Close like this, I could finally sleep.

"How long have you been watching me?" I hear.

Billy is propped up against the pillow, naked except for a pair of boxers. His torso is absurdly lean; his chest and shoulders are hairless and pale, and a faint scar, like a faded zipper, runs along his sternum. The paleness cuts off at his biceps, which are tan and rounded with muscle. His forearms, also tan, are roped with cords of tendons that look like telephone wires under his skin.

I offer a sheepish grin. "If I said since yesterday, would you think I'm creepy?"

"Too late; I know you're creepy." Billy stretches. "But please tell me you're kidding."

"Of course I'm kidding. You're not *that* important."

My brother's longer hair makes his face look girlish, but he's bulked up since Christmas and his body is as hard as granite. Sparse hairs trail down to his groin and vanish inside his waistband. Eyeing his phone, he yelps. "Holy shit, it's almost two! Why didn't you wake me up?"

"You said you hadn't slept for days."

"I couldn't. That place was loud, and I was too scared."

Yesterday, on the ride home from Trenton, Billy was quiet. He needed a shower, badly. His hair was greasy and matted; his face, drawn and washed out. He looked defeated. As we pulled out of the courthouse parking lot, he started to cry, which made me cry. Eleanor pulled out tissues, and gave Nate the wad to split between us, like we were little kids. Billy rested his forehead against the window and tried to relax, but every few minutes, some sound—car horn, pothole—startled him awake.

Nate couldn't bear the silence. "So, what happened?"

"Nate," Lawrence warned. "Let him sleep. He's exhausted."

"I am exhausted." Billy's eyes were closed. "That place was, like, major sensory overload. The smell was unbearable. It was a combination of sweat, piss, puke, and Lysol. I tasted it every time I swallowed."

"With *Diana*." Nate was insistent. "What happened with Diana?"

Billy ignored him. "It was grim as fuck. Guys jammed together, no privacy. You're always on guard. I mean, it wasn't Attica. People weren't bashing each other's heads in. But you never knew what was coming. So the threat hung there like, I don't know, like foul air."

After a long silence, Nate said, "Sounds like you miss it, buddy."

Billy grimaced. "With my whole heart." Minutes later, he nodded off. He slept until we got home. Then he took a long, hot shower, ate two bowls of Honey Nut Cheerios, and crawled into bed.

Thankfully, he seems better today. His eyes are brighter, his cheeks have color, and his thick hair is clean. "It's so great to be here," he says. He throws off his blanket with a ferocious yawn and gets out of bed. When he pulls on sweats, I catch a glimpse of the black bracelet around his ankle.

Billy sees me looking. "Coveting my jewelry? It's the latest in men's biometric gadgetry."

"We should ask Nate if he wants one," I say, relieved he can joke about it. "Lawrence too; you guys can be a chain gang."

He grins. "I'm glad you're here, Cass. Good to see your face. Christ, it's been rough."

"Me too, Elmo." My throat wobbles and burns. "I can't imagine. Being arrested—"

"No, I mean the last seven months, with Diana. I feel like I've been living through a long, endless war. This weekend was the last battle, the bridge that blows up in the finale."

"I'm sorry I've been out of touch. I've been a bad sister."

"Forgiveness truce." Billy holds out his hand and pulls me into a hug. Inhaling his soapy smell, I press my hands against his mighty back. Under my fingers, his bare skin feels smooth. "I've missed you," he says. "A lot."

"Me too, Elmo." Then, unable to stop myself, I blurt out, "Why is she doing this? What does she want from you?"

"That's the million-dollar question, Cassidy Cakes. Maybe if I knew, I wouldn't have gotten myself in this position."

"*You* didn't do anything. *She* did."

Booting up his computer, Billy scans the screen. "We both did a lot of things."

It's been forever since he and I have had a real conversation. We text and call each other but rarely say anything. We used to be so close I had X-ray vision into his brain; we shared similar thoughts, finished each other's sentences. Then he met Diana Holly and grew distant. Or maybe I pulled away first. It's easy to blame her, but both my brothers took a backseat when I hooked up with Marcus. My desire for Marcus was intense, urgent, and all-consuming. I had never felt anything like it before. Nothing mattered but him.

"Why the fuck am I so exhausted?" Billy asks, plopping back on the bed.

"Because you were in jail?"

Nate appears at the door. "Wasn't jail, Princess. It was detention." He grabs Billy and squeezes him around the middle. "Finally, you're up."

They wrestle on the mattress until Billy cries uncle. "I'm empty, Nate. Seriously, I'm done."

"Nate wins! The crowd goes wild!" His arms shoot up. "Nate the Great is king!" Dancing on his toes, he thrusts a hand-microphone at Billy. "Mr. Loser, tell our viewers how it feels to give up the title of Strongest Man Ever? Are you disappointed? Will we see a rematch?"

Mr. Quinn, how do you plead? Mr. Quinn, speak up. Mr. Quinn, the court needs to hear a verbal answer.

"How do I feel?" Billy leans forward into the mike. "Honestly? Relieved it's over."

"But your legacy lives on." After one final twirl, Nate heads out. "Late lunch. Dad's making pancakes. Although for you, Mr. Loser, I guess it's breakfast."

Once we're alone, I tell Billy I'm here if he wants to talk. "Anytime. And I'm finished with classes in May. I'll come home for the summer if it will help."

"Thanks, Cassie. But don't rearrange your life for me."

"I *want* to rearrange my life; I *want* to be here. Nate too. We love you."

Billy looks out the window. "You know what's strange? I'm not angry. I should be, but I'm not. This is how Diana operates. When I get busy with classes or whatever, she gets anxious. She calls and texts all day, but that makes *me* anxious and I retreat. So, she'll whip me into a frenzy to get my attention and then we'll be back right where we started."

His resigned tone alarms me. "Billy, Diana is trying to ruin your life. What she's doing is destructive—and criminal. You have to see that."

"Cassie, you don't know Diana. We've been through a lot together. I just want her to drop the charges, so we can go back to normal."

"You can't go back. Even if she tries to drop them, the machine is in motion and the DA can still prosecute. No matter what happens, Billy, this accusation will always hang between you."

"I think we can." Turning to me, he juts out his chin. "I love her. She loves me."

He means this, I realize. "Billy, this isn't love. What you're describing, what Diana is doing, is something else entirely. But there's no way it's love."

* * *

Hours later, I slip out of the apartment, and into the car the Valmont staff has called up for me. It's cold out but the milky sky is full of stars, so I retract the convertible top. As I head east to the FDR Drive, I feel a rush of adrenaline. I step on the gas. The circumference of Manhattan is twenty-seven miles. The fastest recorded time for circling the city is twenty-four minutes, which averages to sixty-six miles an hour. Tonight, I will crush that. Twenty-four minutes includes red lights, which I will bypass. There's always traffic in New York City, but I know the highways like I know my own body. I gather speed, hit forty, forty-five, fifty. Dodging and weaving, I race to the bend of the horizon. Soon, the car falls away. It's just me, flying through space, weightless and untethered. I can't hear. I can't see. I don't feel. Out here, it's as peaceful, as soundless, as sleep. Out here, it's a dream.

13

ON WEDNESDAY, BILLY WAKES UP EARLY. HE TELLS MAEVE to take the day off and makes challah French toast for the whole family. "I need hobbies," he says. "It's gonna be a long spring." He's not as disconnected as yesterday, but his eyes are unfocused, and he's filled with manic energy as he gathers plates and forks. He's panicking, I can tell.

"Cassie," he asks, wearing a white apron patterned with daisies as he dishes up the French toast. "Would you rather I make you egg whites?"

"Thanks," I tell him. "But I'm fine with French toast."

"How about Styrofoam?" Nate asks. "No calories in Styrofoam."

"No fiber either, Smart Guy," I say.

In response, Nate takes a huge bite of French toast. He chews with his mouth open, making sure I can see.

"Seriously, Nate?" Lawrence asks. "How old are you again?"

DeFiore calls while we're eating, and Lawrence puts him on speakerphone. He wants to meet with us tomorrow. Lawrence says sure, absolutely, wouldn't miss it for the world, like it's a movie he's dying to see. His falseness puts me on edge, and it's this edginess that compels me to announce I'm heading back to school after we see DeFiore. "I'm sorry, Lawrence, but I have a midterm, classes, and lots to take care of."

"I'd prefer you stay, Cassie. It would mean a lot to Billy."

"Oh, no way, Dad," Billy says. "Don't put me in the middle. Let her live her life."

"It's not just you," Lawrence tells him. "Eleanor and I need her here too."

This aggravates me. "Keep pressuring me, and I'll leave right this minute. I don't want to fight."

Of course, I want to fight. Otherwise, I would've kept my mouth shut. But being home is taking a toll. I'm not sleeping well, my head is buzzing, and I'm reverting to old habits. Yesterday, while Billy slept, Nate and I got stoned and watched Netflix when I was supposed to be reviewing my notes for my exams. When I'm here, time is elastic, its edges collapse, and I lose track of myself. I'm an adult, but also a child. If I don't set boundaries, I'll give in, and stay forever.

The other issue is Marcus, who's started reaching out again. He, too, has uncanny radar. I let his calls go to voicemail, but the pull to answer makes my fingers dance, my body twitch. I imagine him waiting for his wife to fall asleep then sneaking down the hall to use the burner phone he bought specially to contact me. We haven't spoken in six months, although I admit I save his messages to replay during weak moments. *I need you, Cassie. I miss you. I just want to say hi.* But no matter how much I wish I could talk to him, no matter how much I want to hear his voice, I can't risk getting dragged back in.

Nate texts me:

apologize, princess. be the bigger person. This week is rough for everyone

I know; I'm not an idiot

You're not? His bday is tomorrow. You just said you'd rather sit in class than be with him

Oh shit. Looking up, I realize everyone is waiting for me and Lawrence to finish arguing. "I'm sorry," I say. "I wasn't thinking. Of course, I'll stay for your birthday."

"Thanks, Cassie. That means a lot to me. I'm thrilled you'll be here to celebrate."

He gives me a loving smile, and we focus on our plates, both of us sheepish. Lawrence takes an enormous bite of French toast. "Delicious, Billy," he declares, chewing with gusto. But I'm distracted by memories of Marcus, and pick at my breakfast, unable to taste my food, much less swallow it.

* * *

The day warms up, and in the afternoon, Billy announces he's going for a run. Nate and I say we'll go, too, and change into sweats and sneakers. Honestly, it's the last thing we want to do, but it's the best way to get him alone so we can ask about Diana.

In the park, we head to the Reservoir. Billy keeps what for him is a slow pace, but after ten minutes, Nate and I are gasping.

Billy pats my arm. "Catch you on the flip side." Then takes off.

Nate and I watch him until he disappears. "Think he'll come back?" Slowing down, he wipes his forehead with this T-shirt.

"Would you?"

"Fuck yeah. No way I'd let Diana Holly get away with this."

We sit on the curb. "Do you think she will? Get away with this?"

Nate shakes his head. "No, but even if he wins, he loses. We may not go to trial, but Billy won't walk away unscathed. That's how these things work."

"A few days ago, you said the exact opposite."

"A few days ago, I hadn't talked to Peter or been to court. Now I have. So, yeah, I'm worried. Plus, Billy is acting like this is no big deal. Like this girl isn't fucking up his whole life."

"I think he's in shock, Nate. He doesn't know how he feels."

"So let's set him straight. Let's drive to Hawkins Cove, build a fire, have a come-to-Jesus."

"Southampton is out of range. His monitoring bracelet?"

"Fuck." Nate's face crumples. "He really is a prisoner, isn't he?"

Twenty minutes later, Billy appears in the distance, a blur of joyful fury. Running takes him to a place where he's free and at peace. His head is thrown back. His arms move like pistons. Bathed in the golden glow of the sun, he looks like a Greek god.

"Can you believe that kid is our brother?" Nate asks, marveling.

"He's not a kid anymore."

My brother's body is both a work of art and a machine. He didn't come to running until high school, but it changed everything in his life. He was miserable at Groton and begged to come home. But when a teacher suggested he join the cross-country team, around the same time he went through a growth spurt, a star was born. By fifteen, Billy had an ideal sprinter's body. He gains and loses weight easily and has a higher percentage of what's called "fast-twitch" muscle, so he excels at explosive sports that demand force and speed.

Billy is intense and obsessive when he finds something he likes. Running was no exception. He trained four days a week, eleven months a year. He competed around the state then across the country, breaking records, winning medals, and impressing recruiters. For our family, seeing him run was thrilling, but so was seeing him gain confidence. Now he'd introduce himself without being prompted. He had friends, went to parties. It was a revelation, like watching time-lapse photography of a flower in bloom. But despite his physical transformation, Billy was still inexperienced with girls, and his shyness persisted in college. He was like an innocent kid, naïve and trusting—the ideal target for Diana Holly, a manipulative woman seeking a boy to mold however she pleased.

*   *   *

As the sun sets, Nate, Billy, and I head out of the park. Our shadows stretch along the pavement, so it looks like we've multiplied and are walking with a crowd. The air has grown chilly, and under my tank top my sports bra is damp.

Seeing me shiver, Nate hands me his sweatshirt. "Put this on." I do as I'm told. Meanwhile, he's looking at Billy. "Can I ask you a question?"

Billy's face is flushed and dripping sweat. "If it's about Diana, then no."

"So, you're never gonna tell us what happened?"

"I told you. We dated, we broke up, she got upset. We dated again, we broke up again, she got upset again. Then she got really upset. And now here we are."

"With all due respect, Elmo," I say. "She's a little more than 'up-set.'"

"She's fucking unhinged." Nate flings his arms across our shoulders. "If you can't tell us, who can you tell? We're the Three Musketeers, remember? All for one, one for all."

Nate came up with the Three Musketeers, but Lawrence had planted the seed, calling us the three stooges; the three little pigs; Huey, Dewey, and Louie; Charlie's Angels. Like Nate, my happiest memories are from our summers at the beach. My brothers have July birthdays, and mine is in August. So our weekends were filled with parties, balloons, presents, and cake. Two years in a row, Lawrence hired a plane to spell out *Happy Bday 3 M's* across the sky.

We're almost home when Billy says, "I know you don't understand my feelings for Diana. But we were happy. We had problems, but doesn't every couple?"

"What kind of problems?" Nate asks.

"I don't know, regular. She was a perfectionist. I'm . . . well, you know how I am. But we were crazy about each other. Have you ever heard me say that before?"

Their relationship, Billy reiterates, was fast and furious. He and Diana met in June at Sloan-Kettering, where they were summer interns. Diana's family lives somewhere near Pittsburgh, but she was subletting a studio in the city, so they saw each other every day. It was a fantastic three months. Then when September came, and Billy felt crunched, Diana was surprised. "I told her we needed to slow down. She didn't take it well, which I already told you. She called a lot. She cried nonstop. Then she started following me around."

"Did it bother you?" I ask, thinking of Marcus. At times, I carried on like this, calling and texting him nonstop.

Billy shrugs. "I love her."

"Not an answer, Billy boy," Nate says gently.

"Yeah, okay. It did bother me. But we got back together, and it was fine. Then December rolled around. I told her I had to focus. She said she understood. But when I couldn't see her, she got angry."

"You mean she went nuts," I say. "Again."

Billy nods. Still, he held firm. He didn't see her for a while and felt more in control of his life. Then, last week Diana invited him to a party. Billy doesn't drink. He'll have a beer to loosen his tongue, but alcohol blunts his speed on the track. Plus, he had to study. He told Diana no, but she kept texting him: Don't blow me off, it'll be fun, come say hi, cajoling him until he finally relented.

"And you have all these texts?" I ask.

"Cops took my phone, but yeah."

Billy figured they could talk, rationally, like adults. But by the time he got there, Diana was wasted. He downed two beers and a shot of whiskey to catch up. Unaccustomed to the alcohol, he got very drunk, very fast. They went to a back bedroom and ended up fooling around. A little while later, they left the party together. They stopped in a play-ground, where they kissed on a tire swing then moved to a grassy area. After that, Billy says, it's hazy and distorted. He felt Diana unzip his pants, pull down his boxers and reach for his—

Billy is shaking, his eyes glazed. "I t-told her n-n-n-no. I sssaid n-no."

She started to stroke his penis. He was too far gone to stop. Her dress got hiked up. Billy recalls being inside her but not for how long because he was hit with a wave of nausea. He stood up and pulled down Diana's dress—he distinctly remembers that she wasn't wearing un-derwear. He turned and vomited, when he was suddenly tackled by what felt like a gang of men. He kept trying to get up, but they had him pinned. He threw up again, which made him dizzy, so he closed his eyes. Next thing he knew, the police were there.

"Did you talk to Diana during any of this?" Nate asks.

"No idea."

"Did you think she blacked out?"

"Hell no." On this point, Billy is adamant.

Nate and I put our arms around him. "We believe you, Billy," we tell him. "She won't get away with this."

14

OUR HOUSE IN SOUTHAMPTON SITS ON A HUNDRED AND fifty acres. Along with a blueberry patch, heated pool, tennis courts, and boat dock, we have a private beach that's surrounded by deep and dense woods. Large parts of the area are rough and isolated, so our parents forbid us from exploring. But with Nate in charge, we roamed far and wide. He was a genius at finding things. Under his direction, Billy and I dug for strangers' castoffs, which we treated like buried treasure: loose playing cards told our fortunes, Scrabble tiles spelled out hidden messages, a set of keys opened imaginary doors.

Nate's greatest discovery was a secret hideaway. Twenty yards past the dunes, close to the marshy shore, groups of trees cluster together to create hidey-holes perfectly sized for small children. When Nate stumbled on one of these shady spaces, he dubbed it Hawkins Cove in honor of Jim Hawkins from *Treasure Island,* a book he loved.

My brothers and I spent entire days at Hawkins Cove, which we called HQ. To reach the trees, we had to pass through thick reeds that grew as tall as our shoulders. Nate dreamed up complex missions where we snuck supplies (blankets, Doritos, a Magic 8 Ball) from enemy territory (house) past the DMZ (dunes) down to HQ. But our favorite game was my idea, one I'd stolen from Lawrence. We'd lie down and close our eyes. "Tell me a story, Cassie," Nate would say. "Make it epic." But where Lawrence offered family lore, I spun wild stories that starred three brave siblings who banded together to save the world.

Hawkins Cove was our secret. So was Epic Story. We played for years, probably longer than was age appropriate. Having secrets connected and comforted us, especially after Nate and Billy went to boarding school. (Had I not already lost one family, I would've gone too.)

Even when we're at odds, under the surface, we're as entangled as any natural root system. Which is why, hours after we return from the park, I feel an urgent need to be with Nate. I wait until the house is quiet and then steal into his room.

My brother's chest is massive, and as I burrow against him, I'm reminded that it's been a long time since I've had a man's arms around me. The room is pitch-black, except for a sliver of light that washes over his face. I adjust my breathing so that we inhale in unison, our chests rising and falling as if we share one set of lungs, a single beating heart.

"Tell me a story, Cassandra," he whispers. "Make it epic."

I pause for a moment. "This is Billy's story," I say quietly. "William Quinn is the smartest, most handsome boy ever. He meets Diana Holly, a dangerous witch disguised as a beautiful girl. Unaware of how cunning she is, he asks her out on a date—"

"Flash-forward. How does it end?"

"The jury is about to read the verdict when Nate and Cassie shout, 'Billy Quinn is innocent!' The case is dropped. Diana Holly gets punished. The Three Musketeers prevail." I pause. "Plausible?"

"Christ, I hope so." Nate touches my hair.

"How does the story really end?" My eyes are closed. "You tell me."

"They go to the beach." His voice is dreamy. "They run down to the edge and jump in the waves. Then they float out to sea, never to be heard from again."

I picture myself at seven, eight, nine, a skinny kid in shorts. Scratched, scabby legs. Wind-tangled hair. Wonder Woman Band-Aids. As I start to doze off, I remember one afternoon before Nate left for Groton. We're sitting, cross-legged, in the cove. Above us, the trees form a canopy to block out the hot sun. The air is cool and smells of salt. Nate is fourteen, I'm eleven, Billy is ten. Still young enough to believe in Hawkins Cove, to trust in its transformative properties. In two weeks, Nate will be gone. We'll never see him except for breaks, holidays, and the occasional weekend.

"I d-d-don't want to g-g-go," Billy says, though he's years away from boarding school himself.

"You'll be okay," Nate assures him. "I'll be there."

"Besides, Elmo," I say, echoing Eleanor. "Groton is the best of the best, especially if you want to be a doctor. FDR went there. So did Teddy Roosevelt's son."

"They're not d-d-d-doctors," Billy points out.

"Will Elmo Quinn be a doctor?" Nate holds up our Magic 8 Ball. "All signs point to yes."

I grab it from him. "Will Cassie fly planes like Amelia Earhart?" I'm enthralled by tragic, mysterious women. "Ask again later. Will Nate surf the Banzai Pipeline?"

"Without a doubt," Nate says just as I read, "Without a doubt." We crack up. "Jinx!"

I feel thoroughly, unconditionally happy. I loved Billy and Nate more than I ever loved anyone, even Rachel, my biological mother. At one time, I thought about her constantly, but by that point, she'd been dead for years, and existed only as a few faded pictures and a couple of songs she hummed under her breath. One was a Christian hymn that her own mother, a religious woman, sang to her. *All things bright and beautiful / All creatures great and small / All things wise and wonderful / The Lord God made them all.*

"I'll tell you what happens," I say to Nate now, lying next to him. "Billy will go to med school. I'll fly supersonic jets. You'll surf the Banzai Pipeline. We'll live happily ever after." I pause. "Nate? You up?" Beside me, my brother's breathing is slow and even. "Just wait, Nathaniel," I whisper. "It will be so beautiful."

15

THURSDAY AFTERNOON WE'RE IN DOWNTOWN PRINCETON. The leafy trees, storefronts, and wide sidewalks remind me of New Haven, which feels like a place I visited once, years ago. It makes no sense—I haven't even been gone a week. But I'm so caught up in Billy, my other life has receded; soon, I will barely remember it.

The offices of DeFiore & Associates, LLC are in a renovated Victorian. As we climb the front steps, the door swings open. "You made it!" DeFiore stands on the landing, wearing his same rumpled suit. "Welcome, welcome."

He ushers us into the foyer, a sleek reception space with hardwood floors and Tiffany lamps. Behind that, there's a plush library with built-in shelves, oversized couches, colorful pillows, and leafy plants. Floor-to-ceiling windows wash the room in natural light.

"I call this room my lounge-brary," DeFiore says. "Nice, right?"

"Wow." Lawrence can't hide his shock. "This looks like a luxury hotel."

"You got the eye, Lar. The building used to be a bed and breakfast. But we gutted it from the basement to the roof. We stripped this baby down to the studs."

"Really cool offices," Nate says, following DeFiore into the biggest glass-enclosed conference room on the main floor.

"You've surprised me, Mr. DeFiore." Smiling, Eleanor sinks into a leather chair. "I'm not easily surprised."

"I'll take that as a compliment, Mrs. Quinn. The build-out cost me a fucking fortune. One-point-five mil for the architect alone. But who cares? It's just money."

DeFiore's associate, Mitchell Manzano, shakes our hands. Up close, he looks less like DeFiore's son than he did in court. He's in his late thirties, older than I thought. Today he has on sexy black labor-union glasses, which add an air of maturity. "You should wear those all the time," I tell him. "Women love men in glasses."

He smiles. "I'll take that under advisement."

Beside me, Nate is heads down with Abby Friedman, the trial consultant, who's around Eleanor's age. He says something I can't hear, and when she cracks up, I catch the sparkle in his eyes. Not that I blame him. Abby is a knockout, a voluptuous brunette with great legs. She's wearing an Armani coatdress that emphasizes her curves, but in a tasteful way, and her sky-high Louboutin heels are expertly polished. Striking yet formidable, she projects trust and authority.

DeFiore turns to Billy, who's in pressed khakis and a sport coat. His hair's been trimmed, but his bangs still brush his eyes. "You clean up nice, kiddo. Those jumpsuits make everyone look guilty, unfortunately."

Billy lifts his pant leg to show off his bracelet. "This makes me look guilty too."

"We'll get that off before you know it. Speaking of, let's start. Mitch, the door?"

For the next hour, DeFiore walks us through where we are and what's ahead. He's been working the phones since Monday, trying to sort out the facts. Myriad issues come into play during a trial, but from his perspective, there are three primary questions at stake in this case: when, specifically, Diana went from being conscious to being unconscious; if Diana was unconscious, did Billy know; and if Billy did know, when exactly did this realization occur?

DeFiore's immediate concerns are the EMT and hospital reports, neither of which he's seen yet. However, he read the sheriff's report, which describes Diana as "breathing but unresponsive." This could pose a problem if the emergency techs and intake nurses offer corroborating impressions: an unresponsive woman cannot give consent.

"Still," he says, "the State has to prove that Billy knew she was unconscious but had sex with her anyway. Which isn't easy to do, not by a long shot. And from what I hear, the EMT report is a mess, and their eyewitnesses are recanting. Plus, the responding officers didn't secure the scene, so their physical evidence is probably useless. But I'll know more in another day or two."

"Knock, knock," Felicia Drake, DeFiore's co-counsel, says as she slides open the glass door. "Sorry to be late. I couldn't get off a call."

DeFiore waves her in. "I was telling the Quinns about the sheriff's report."

"A shit show, right?" Felicia is a Jersey girl with thick ankles and a nasal voice. Her pouffed hair is dyed jet-black, and her eyeliner is applied with a heavy hand. "That report does us no favors. Hopefully, the others will say different. But don't worry too much about it; we're still sorting everything out."

Eleanor looks at DeFiore, expecting him to contradict Felicia, or at least apologize for her bluntness. Instead, he nods in agreement.

"I wasn't worried about it until you walked in, Felicia," Eleanor says.

"I'd like to read the report," Lawrence says. "Assuming it's handy."

"Trust me, Lar. You don't. These reports are excruciating for family—on both sides," he adds, as if we've forgotten that Diana has parents too. "The DA is presenting preliminaries to the grand jury next Wednesday. They'll review the evidence to date and determine if it's enough to indict. But our assumption is the case will be greenlit."

"We should be at the grand jury," Nate says.

"You can't," Lawrence says. "None of us can." He looks at DeFiore. "Tell him."

Felicia answers. "Sessions are closed. It's just the prosecution and their witnesses."

"But who'll speak for Billy?" my brother asks.

DeFiore starts to reply, but again, Felicia answers. "No one. And the greenlight is a sure thing, not an assumption. Anderson wouldn't call a grand jury unless he's confident he can get a majority of votes in favor of indictment."

Felicia is a female version of DeFiore, except the same qualities that I find oddly charming in him—large, pushy, bombastic—I find unforgivable in her.

"That's not fair!" Nate blurts out. "What about Billy's rights?"

"At this point, Nate," Felicia says, "Billy has no rights. Rather, his rights don't matter to the DA. Or to the public. No one is rushing to defend rich white jocks, not for rape. And certainly not if a victim is deemed 'unresponsive.'"

Felicia is correct on this point. Billy's profile has obviated any chance of an impartial or fair trial. To be clear: I'm defending my brother here, not defending rapists. I know that sexual violence is dehumanizing. It's life-shattering. It causes victims to feel unsafe in their bodies, often for the rest of their lives. Still, this doesn't make Diana Holly any less a liar. Or my brother any more culpable.

"What's *really* unfair," DeFiore adds, "is that the DA will gloss over the couple's prior relationship. If Anderson is smart—and trust me, he is—he'll zero in on choice details. Like, say, white, wealthy, Princeton, binge-drinking, violence, eyewitnesses, resisting arrest. He'll use them to tell a familiar story. Then he'll pound this story into the jurors' minds, over and over, until they can recite it forwards, backwards, and sideways. Not that repetition is necessary. We all know the story anyway. And a prior relationship, especially one that's loving and consensual, only confuses the narrative."

"That's where we come in," Manzano says. "Our job—and by 'our,' I mean all of us—is to come up with a more compelling story, one where the relationship is central."

Lawrence turns to Billy. "You're quiet."

"Of course, he's quiet," I say. "We've been talking about him like he's not here."

"Get used to that," DeFiore tells Billy. "Soon, you'll just be 'the defendant.'"

"Then 'the rapist,'" Nate adds. "Then the 'inmate.'"

"Nate!" Lawrence and Eleanor snap. But Billy starts to laugh. Nate and I join in, and once we get going, we can't stop. My laughter, loose and alive, unravels inside my chest like a long paper dragon.

"You're an idiot, Nate," I say, wiping my eyes.

"Nate the Great scores," he mutters. "A triumph!" he adds, which sets us off again. Soon, we're doubled over, but my bleating sounds border on sobs, and I have to reel myself back from the brink.

When we finally compose ourselves. Lawrence asks Billy if he wants to add anything.

Billy is nervous. "Ssssssince Friday—when I really was 'the inmate'—it's been hard not to think of myself in the third person. I k-k-k-keep hearing about a guy named Billy and his girlfriend Diana. I don't know those people. What k-k-k-kind of man attacks a woman he loves? And if he didn't attack her, why would she say he did?"

DeFiore waves him on. "Let's play it out. Why did Diana accuse Billy? Felicia, Mitch, and I have lots of theories, but we don't know her. You do."

"Well, anger for sure. When Diana gets angry, she acts out. In this case, she didn't realize what she was doing. Her accusation was, like, a knee-jerk reaction."

DeFiore shakes his head. "I don't buy it. A rape accusation isn't just 'acting out.' It's hard to make a jury believe a girl this smart didn't know what might happen."

Billy's face goes white. "B-b-b-b-b . . ." He tries again. "D-d-d-d-iana . . . ssshe's n-n-n-not like that. Sshe . . ."

"Hey, it's okay." DeFiore pats Billy's knee. "Just playing devil's advocate. Fact is, there are lots of reasons why Diana accused you. Maybe she drank too much, blacked out, and woke up confused, and pissed-off, with the whole story already in motion. All she had to do was agree. I'm not saying that's our defense. But when the time comes, I promise you we'll have one." He glances at Felicia. "Want to do the honors?"

"Why am I always the bad guy?"

DeFiore grins. "Ten to one they already don't like you." He winks at Eleanor. "Am I right?"

Felicia laughs. "Okay, here goes. If we move to trial, our advice is to settle. We will make the best deal we can—"

"Oh no," Eleanor says. "There will be no settlement."

Nate balks too. "No way. My brother is innocent."

"Doesn't matter," DeFiore says. "A trial is about what a DA can prove. How the story sounds to a jury. What evidence is admissible. A whole host of factors, most beyond our control. This will be a high-profile case. You need to consider what's best for Billy—and for the family. If he goes on trial, the press will pry into every detail of your lives and twist their findings to fit their narrative. Even if Billy gets off, you all pay a price. Some families never recover."

"I keep saying this." Lawrence glances my way. "But they don't believe me."

"People never think it can happen to them until it happens to them." Lawrence opens his mouth as if to add something.

"What? Now's the time to talk. Tell me everything. Secret meth addictions. Spousal abuse. I don't care. Once the indictment comes in, you're all fair game. So think about it, folks. Meantime, I need access to your finances. Income, investments, real estate—the works."

"Absolutely," Lawrence tells him just as Eleanor says, "That won't be possible, Mr. DeFiore."

He laughs. "I can see how this is gonna go. Mrs. Quinn, we can speak privately. Also, we have a freelance investigator, so you'll need to authorize the funds to pay him."

"Whatever you need," Lawrence assures him.

"One thing you should do," I cut in, "is load up your team with female lawyers."

"You're very smart," DeFiore says. "Anyone ever tell you that?"

"Everyone tells me that."

"Ask her about Yale," Nate says. "No one is more impressed with Cassie's brains than Cassie."

As we stand up to leave, Billy says, "W-w-wait. I have to tell you sss-something. I quit running. I mean, competing. Last December."

Lawrence looks at Eleanor. "Did you know?" She shakes her head.

"Why?" I ask. "You love running."

"It was too much—Diana, school, tutoring. I told you this."

"I thought you gave up Diana, not track."

DeFiore lays a hand on Billy's shoulder. "I'm glad you shared this. It's just another detail we'll add to the story." He turns to the rest of us. "One last thing. This is the most important thing of every important thing I've told you. In the coming weeks, people will try to contact you—cops, investigators, reporters. Do not speak to anyone unless

I'm there. No one. I cannot stress this enough: keep your mouths shut."

*   *   *

That night, we celebrate Lawrence's birthday. In the cab on the way to Reginald's, our favorite restaurant on Madison, we make a pact to relax. For one night, no talk of lawyers, trials, or doomsday fears. We reminisce about our childhood birthdays: the time Nate lit a cherry bomb and blew up the cake, Billy peeing on my foot after a jellyfish stung me, sleeping outside in tents, our sacred days in Hawkins Cove. Later, at home, in the celebration room, Lawrence opens his presents (ties, books, more ties). Maeve brings out a black forest cake that says *Happy Bday, love Eleanor + your 3 M's*. We sing off-key, lick frosting off our fingers, drink too much wine and for one brief shining moment, the world is ours again.

16

TURNS OUT LAWRENCE WAS RIGHT ABOUT THE MEDIA. A week later, when the grand jury votes for indictment, the press gets wind of the case. The hits start slowly—small mentions on a local blog, a brief mention in *AM New York*—then snowball. Six hours later, by the time the *New York Times* and Associated Press have gotten ahold of the story, my brother is everywhere.

Guilty, guilty, guilty, I can read between the reporters' lines. Almost all the articles home in on his privilege, showcase his All-Ivy record (9.8 seconds in the 100-meter dash), and allude to unspecified "emotional problems." Diana Holly, by contrast, barely registers. "Biology major," the papers call her, adhering to the laws about not naming a rape accuser. "Women's shelter volunteer. Exceptional student." Worst of all, there's no references to their prior relationship.

Enraged, I call DeFiore. "How can they do this? *She* was the one who harassed *him*. *She* invited *him* to the party. *She* forced herself on *him*."

He's unruffled. "Be patient," he assures me. "Everything will come out at trial."

Will it? I wonder. Everything?

DeFiore was right too. As we get closer to Billy's arraignment on April 17, the hits multiply and metastasize, and we are deluged by reporters, bloggers, op-ed writers, columnists, and TV journalists. They phone, text, and email us. They contact family friends, relatives in far-flung locations, and acquaintances we barely know.

"Do not read the news," he reminds us. "Do not talk to a soul."

I can't help myself. Scrolling through headlines, I spot one in *Vanity Fair*—"Ivy Runner Can't Outrace Rape Charge"—and lose hours in a Google black hole. That I can't set the record straight kills me. My desire to talk becomes a need, then an urge. I'm twitchy all the time from biting my tongue.

For the next three weeks, the five of us hunker down at home. Outside, reporters and paparazzi converge on the street, angling for pictures, sound bites, any bits of news. We hire a security detail, including a bodyguard for Billy. Soon, I'm climbing the walls. Anton sneaks me down to the parking lot in the super-secret staff elevator, and I escape to New Haven for a few days. My apartment is small: two bedrooms, one bathroom, and no furniture to speak of. But it's private, quiet, and entirely my own. While I'm there, I make up missed exams, turn in late assignments, and try to pretend everything is fine, fine, fine. Before I leave, I drop off keys for the doorman, who's promised to pick up my mail. "I'll be back," I assure him and reassure myself. "I still live here."

As I'm catching up at school, Eleanor, Lawrence, and Nate are questioned by the police, individually then together. DeFiore and Felicia accompany them to deflect questions and guide their responses. When I ask Lawrence over FaceTime if I should reach out to the police, too, he looks at me like I'm demented. "Why would you do that?" he asks. "*Never* offer unsolicited information."

While I'm away, Nate calls with updates. DeFiore is working hard to make a deal, but so far, no dice. The DA won't agree to any terms unless they include a state prison stint and sex offender registration. We won't agree to any terms but "not guilty." On this subject, at least, we're all united as a family, certain of Billy's innocence and ready to fight as long as it takes. Privately, Lawrence continues to protest a trial, but publicly he's a man on a mission. He's in charge, and Nate—who's taken a leave from Bessemer—is his deputy. They speak with DeFiore's team several times a day, follow up on research, and play out scenarios. Eleanor is doing her part to shore up support. "I'm so grateful you reached out," she says on the phone. "Yes, it's shocking. Yes, the girl is terribly damaged. Yes, we should get together. Yes, this horrible experience will end very soon."

* * *

Suddenly I see cops everywhere. Driving back from New Haven, I stop at a bodega near Columbia. A gauntlet of police is blocking the door. Unable to find a spot, I double-park by a hydrant. I expect one of them to bark *move your car!* But they're engrossed in each other, drinking coffee and laughing, and I move through the huddle like a ghost.

In the back, I spot a familiar figure. He's turned away, scanning the glass cases. But I recognize Powell Porter's hulking shoulders and meaty neck. He's one of Nate's oldest friends.

"How about Heineken?" Powell is asking his date, whose face I can't see. From behind, swaddled in a puffy coat, she looks tiny. Her shoulder-length blond hair is magnificent, the perfect blend of honey highlights and gold lowlights. "I'll get you whatever you want," he adds, "as long as it's Heineken," then laughs at his own joke.

The girl is talking on the phone. Hearing her voice, I realize it's Avery, Avery Walker. My former best friend.

Powell and Avery are infinitely unimportant to me. Yet running into them, unexpectedly and ill-prepared, throws me back to high school as if no time has elapsed. I try to slip out of the store, but it's too late. "Cassie? Hey, Cassandra Quinn—wait up!" I swivel around. "Powell?" I sound surprised and delighted to see him. "Oh my God!" Thankfully, Avery is still in the back, on her phone.

Powell, like all of Nate's friends, is a well-groomed social animal with excellent posture. He has ice-blue eyes, tight blond curls, and a chiseled jaw. His features, which were adorable on a small boy, give him a hard edge as a man. "This is crazy!" he says. "I just spoke to Nate. He's been keeping me up to date on Billy. I still can't fucking believe it."

The Porters and the Quinns have been intertwined for as long as I can remember. Powell's father, McClain, is part of the city's political machinery. Briefly, he and Lawrence worked together; and McClain still checks in from time to time. After making a bundle in real estate, McClain ran for comptroller and served two successful terms. Now, there's talk he'll be the next mayor. New Yorkers adore dashing men-about-town, though McClain settled down a while ago with a woman who helped raise his sons. Powell's brother Deacon is Billy's age, and they're friends, but not nearly as close as Powell and Nate. The older boys met in Little League, and then Powell angled his way into Groton, where they both played football. Unlike Nate, Powell was a genuine star with a massive frame built for destruction. In high school, he tried to fuck me, but I didn't take it personally. Powell is one of those guys who tries to fuck everyone.

"Nate keeps you posted on Billy?"

"*Of course* he does. He tells me everything, Cassidy Cakes. He's like a fucking girl that way."

Of course, he tells me, tells me, tells me starts to echo. A whoosh of blood fills my ears, blocking out sound. My throat closes up. My heart races. The small, cramped store gets smaller and more cramped until it's a box. Trapped in here, I can't breathe.

"The girl?" Powell's voice comes from far away. "Diana? She's lying. Billy's a gentle soul. I don't say that about anyone. We had horny fuckers in our crew. Dash Lovell, Brody Leighton. Christ, I once saw Aiden Ambrose on top of—You know what? Doesn't matter. But Billy? No way. I told Nate to call my dad. He'll help however he can."

Powell Porter is the worst kind of guy: feral masked as submissive. He pretends to give a shit when, really, you're just a means to an end. In grade school, Powell made fun of Billy's stutter ("B-b-b-b-illy"). When Nate found out, he clocked Powell so hard, he shattered his nose. Powell apologized, and he and Nate stayed friends. Nate said he wanted to keep the peace, or for the greater good; I can't remember how he spun it. But like civilized men, they shook hands and moved on.

"Nothing this girl says will stick." Powell's eyes are glassy, and I realize he's stoned. "They dated for *six months*; she was his *girlfriend*! Elmo will be fine, Cass."

"Don't call him that." Using my nickname is crossing a line; it's like calling Billy a retard—which Powell also did, by the way.

At the register, Powell is behind me, so close he steps on my heels. I point to Marlboros and pull out a fifty. "Two packs, actually," I tell the guy.

Powell's face twists. "You're *smoking*? That's so gross." This from a guy who I've seen caked in mud, gulping grain alcohol out of a cleat. "Hey, Ave! Where are you? Look who it is!"

As I watch Avery approach, the store takes on a movie-set quality, realistic but artificial. My head is spinning; and I view the next scene through a scrim. I'm rooted in place, but my mind detaches while the self that remains is anesthetized. At the same time, my other senses sharpen; sounds are richer, smells more pungent. I have the sensation of falling off my own feet.

"Cassandra," she says, sounding like she's speaking through a long, hollow tube. She looks very stoned too. "I'm a blonde now."

"You are very blond," I agree.

Our eyes lock. Years of memories flash between us. I feel my chest ache.

I haven't seen Avery in a long time. We grew up together. As little kids, we rode horses and had sleepovers; as tweens, we got manicures; as teenagers, we learned how to drive. In high school, Nate threw parties when our parents were out of town. Avery and I drank, smoked, and flirted with older boys. It was fun and decadent—though for me, short-lived. Eventually, Marcus got in the way, and Avery and I stopped being best friends, or friends at all. Both of us acted badly, but I acted worse.

Outside, the night air is cool. I return to myself. I'm ready to talk, but Avery murmurs a quick goodbye, and walks away.

"Avery! Wait up!" Powell calls out. "Great seeing you, Cass." He leans in to dust my cheek with his lips. "Elmo will be fine," he whispers. "Trust me."

Trust him? I roll my eyes. When I step toward my car, I see a ticket on my windshield, a gift from the cops. Bent fuckers, all of them.

17

APRIL 17 TAKES FOREVER TO COME, BUT WHEN IT DOES, IT'S too soon.

We drive to Billy's arraignment in thunderous silence. We're all furious—at Diana Holly, at the press, at the New Jersey courts, at each other. In the back, wedged between Nate and me, Billy is wearing enormous white headphones. With his eyes closed and head bobbing, he looks like an astronaut receiving orders from Mission Control. His doctor prescribed Effexor to help lift his mood, and Ativan to help him sleep. It's hard to know if they're working since Billy hasn't uttered a full sentence in days. Mostly, they make his movements slow and slug-gish. Before we left, I dry-swallowed an Ativan, just to dull the edges. Nate swallowed two, so the Three Musketeers are three blind mice, three zombies, three junkies.

Lawrence speeds out of the tunnel so fast he almost loses control of the car. *Do it*, I think. *Hit a wall, plow into traffic, immolate us all.* But he's not telepathic, and we reach the courthouse in record time. When he turns off the ignition, instead of offering optimistic platitudes, he tightens his scarf and barks, "Let's go."

As we exit the parking lot, I put my hand on Lawrence's back, try-ing to comfort him. "Billy will be okay."

"Cassie, for God's sake," he scoffs. "Do you see what's going on here?"

Throngs of reporters are gathered on the street, surrounded by news vans and camera crews. As we approach the courthouse, we're besieged by questions that sound like accusations. *Mr. Quinn, will your son plead guilty? Mr. Quinn, is it true the DA has new evidence? Billy, look over here. Billy, this way. Billy, do you watch porn? Mr. Quinn, is your son a rapist?*

"No comment," Lawrence snaps, herding us up the steps and into the lobby.

"Porn?" Nate says, just as I ask, "What kind of new evidence?"

"Ignore them," he tells us. "Keep walking. Do not turn around."

A half-hour later the courtroom is filled to capacity. We arrived early, so we're in the first row of spectators. The rest of the gallery is over-crowded, so people line up along the walls. From the corner of my eye, I spot a family that could be Diana Holly's. I've never met them, but I'd guess it's her mother, father, younger sister, and grandparents. Diana isn't among them, which isn't a surprise. DeFiore told us she can watch the proceedings on closed-circuit TV in another part of the building. If she is, I wonder if seeing her family so stricken makes her feel as though she's viewing her own funeral. That's what it's like for us, like this is the end of everything, and we're gathered here to mourn my brother.

Ahead of us, Billy sits next to DeFiore at the defense table. Today, my brother is wearing a navy suit instead of prison coveralls, so he looks less guilty than he did the last time we were here. But he seems stoned, and I wonder if, somewhere between the car and the court-house, he took more Ativan. His eyes are lifeless, and his head lolls forward, as if too heavy for his neck.

"What's wrong with him?" Nate's jaw tightens. "Why is he drool-ing like a mental patient?"

"Keep your voice down," Lawrence whispers. He keeps shifting in his seat until Eleanor grabs him. "Lawrence, please. Sit still."

A side door opens. The same judge, Charles McKay, enters the courtroom. We rise. Sit. Wait. Wait. Wait some more. Soon, the movie begins, and there's action, dialogue, and atmospheric texture, but I'm too anxious to listen, too strung out to hear. I've already seen this show; it ends with our hero falling off a cliff.

When McKay lists Billy's purported crimes, I snap to attention.

"Mr. Quinn, you are indicted on five charges, including two counts of rape, one count of attempted rape; and two counts of felony sexual assault, one count where the victim was intoxicated, and one where the victim was unconscious of the nature of the act. To these five counts, how do you plead?"

My stomach clenches as I wait for him to speak.

Suddenly, Lawrence grabs my hand and squeezes it. "I'm sorry," he whispers, out of the blue. "Live the life you want, Cassie. I won't hold you back. I love you, kiddo."

My chest catches. My lungs expand. "Me too. I love you too."

Together, we hold our breath.

Billy stands up tall, thrusts out his chin, and says, "Not"—he swallows hard—"guilty"—swallows again—"ssss . . ." There's a delay, but it's brief. ". . . *sir,*" he says, with extra emphasis.

As I exhale, I feel Lawrence do the same. Drenched in sweat; I'm spent. "Thank God that's over," I say with relief.

"Over?" He starts to laugh, loudly. He sounds like a maniac. "This has just begun."

18

TIME PASSES. DAYS BLEND TOGETHER. SOON, A MONTH goes by. My prep classes are over, and while I'm no more proficient in Arabic than when I started, at least I'm done. My next hurdle is deciding where to live until school starts in September. My choices are New York with my family, New Haven alone, or Southampton, occasionally with Nate but mostly alone.

Billy has no such choices. After he was formally indicted, Princeton asked him to withdraw, and then banned him from campus until his case is settled. Although he can reapply, prevailing wisdom says he won't be readmitted. No college wants an accused sex offender among their community—even if he's exonerated. So how and if Billy can finish his degree remains to be seen. Moreover, medical school is likely out of the question. Again, he can apply. But the internet is all-knowing and everlasting. A quick search for "Billy Quinn" already yields too many hits for an admissions board to ignore. So, it's not just Billy's education that's been derailed; it's his whole future, along with his health and emotional well-being.

The trial is set for October 30, and until then, Billy is required to wear his monitoring bracelet, report to a probation officer, and, somehow, get through each day. Eleanor has plans to take him to a host of therapists and wellness workers, along with the psychiatrist he's already seeing, but I know my brother, and he'll refuse anyone he has to talk to for more than five minutes.

For the next five months, we'll work with DeFiore's team on Billy's defense. DeFiore will continue to press us to plead out. We'll continue to say no, absolutely not; and then as the trial gets closer, we'll say maybe. Like Billy, we have to stay optimistic and resolute, which becomes increasingly difficult with each passing day. Reporters continue to reach out in surprising ways and at unexpected times. "No interviews," DeFiore reminds us. But it's so hard to stay quiet when the story they're telling is based on lies.

Billy's indictment has turned our lives upside down. The five of us are stuck in the house every day, from dawn till dusk, holed up together like snakes in a nest. The constant closeness is wearing, and as tension brews, arguments break out. Teeth cleanings, checkups, eye exams, mammograms—all on hold until after the trial. The funding for Lawrence's foundation is in flux. Nate extended his Bessemer leave then quit. Eleanor's set is gossiping, lifelong friends won't return calls. The Bowtie comes around, which makes everything worse. The press is still camped on the sidewalk with microphones and telephoto lenses. Once in a while, I sit with Lawrence and Nate as they field updates from DeFiore. The guy is never not working. He calls and texts compulsively with news of evidentiary hearings and toxicology reports. Their conversations, which are tense and combative, go on for hours; and more often than not, result in nothing.

Yesterday, Billy made a troubling announcement. "I wish I could go to prison already and get a jump on my sentence." That he'll be found guilty is, in his mind, inevitable. So I guess it's good that DeFiore works so hard. I mean, how do you effectively represent an innocent kid who's not only guilty in the court of public opinion, but who's also given up on himself?

*   *   *

According to DeFiore, the central argument for our defense doesn't hinge on whether or not Billy Quinn had consent to penetrate Diana Holly. Or whether or not Diana Holly was conscious at the time of penetration. Or whether or not Billy Quinn knew Diana Holly's state of mind during the act of penetration. In many ways, what happened on March 24 is beside the point—to us, anyway. That's the prosecution's riddle to solve. To defend my brother successfully, to get an acquittal and keep him out of prison, DeFiore has to answer one simple question: *Who is William Matthew Stockton Quinn?*

"Here's what I'm thinking," DeFiore says. "We'll put the affluence front and center. We can't hide the money or privilege. But we shouldn't play up his childhood illnesses. Strategically, this can backfire. A jury hears *developmental problems*, they'll think *anger* then *tantrums* then *rape*."

"You're wrong," I say. "They'll only make that leap if you push them that way."

It's the end of May, six weeks post-arraignment. I've come down from school to New Jersey. Nate, Lawrence, and I are meeting with DeFiore, Felicia, and Paul Martinez, the private investigator, in their office. Eleanor is in New York with Billy, who should be here but bowed out. "I can't," was his reason.

"No, Cassie," Felicia says, which annoys me. "*You're* wrong. Juries make snap judgments all the time." She likes to pretend we're buddies. Behind DeFiore's back, she jokes about his "Men's Warehouse castoffs." But if he's in the room, she goes out of her way to shut me down and make me look foolish.

I ignore her. "Billy is complicated, but *complicated* doesn't mean *violent. Complicated* means *sensitive. Complicated* means *overcoming adversity*. Show the jury he loved Diana, he was vulnerable, and how in the end, *he* was the victim. The point is *his* empathy and *her* anger."

Lawrence glances at Nate. My brother shakes his head.

"What?" I ask.

Being up in New Haven for the last few weeks has been great. I love having my own space, outside the drama. When I'm there, it feels easier to ignore Marcus, who's still calling me, now constantly. I'm stronger away from home and don't answer. I do have guilt, however, about neglecting the trial. I can tell Lawrence and Nate resent me for flitting in and out of town while they work around the clock.

"You're right, Cassie," Lawrence says. "But proving Diana harassed Billy won't be easy. And we run the risk of alienating the jury."

"My two cents?" We turn to the investigator. Paul Martinez is an unsmiling middle-aged man of average build whose only memorable feature is a gray goatee. This is the second, maybe third time we've met, but I couldn't pick him out of a lineup. "Probably best to steer clear of the relationship."

"Since when?" I'm shocked. "Billy and Diana's relationship is the root of the whole case!"

"Unfortunately, it's not as cut-and-dried as we thought," Lawrence says.

"Which means what, Lawrence? Specifically?"

Everyone's on edge, including DeFiore, who's barely speaking to me. Granted, he's not speaking to anyone, but when I'm around, he loves to flirt; he tells me that I'm brilliant, I'm a knockout, if only he were ten years younger. It's unnecessary and infuriating. But I smile and stay quiet—sometimes I even flirt back—because I can't risk insulting him.

"Princeton has no record of Diana stalking Billy," Lawrence says sourly. He gestures toward Martinez. "You did the legwork. You tell her."

"Your brother claimed the girl snuck into his dorm, showed up in his classes, made a nuisance of herself. But none of this was ever reported."

"So what, Paul? That's one small piece of a larger story."

"For Christ's sake, Cassie," Nate interjects. "That piece is called proof. And we don't have it."

"But Peter said we didn't have to *prove* anything; we only have to *defend*. Right?" I turn to DeFiore for support. "We need to show the jury what kind of person Diana is. I told you about when she was in our house last November? I caught her holding a vase, checking the bottom to see where it was from. She's *obsessed* with money."

DeFiore doesn't respond. The room is silent.

"Peter, I told you about that; how bizarre she acted." I don't want to badger him, but this is important. "Remember?"

Suddenly, DeFiore shouts at me. "Cassie, *enough*! Knock it off." His eyes are blazing. "You don't know shit." He is pissed, beyond pissed, and fed up. Peter DeFiore, Esquire, is a stone-cold killer, I see it now, a feral savage who will fuck you, hard, if you get in his way. "So please shut up for one fucking minute."

My face burns. "I was just making an observation," I say quietly. DeFiore's angry outburst humiliates me, a feeling that's compounded by Lawrence's approving nods. He can't rein me in either, so he appreciates DeFiore taking control. When Lawrence looks at me, he has an air of triumph that unsettles me. My pulse speeds up. My thoughts skip. I start to fracture and soon the room feels unsafe, like the web holding the world together is coming loose. Just leave, I tell myself. Go back to school and stay there.

"Despite your fascination with *CSI* reruns," DeFiore is saying . . .

Law and Order, I think.

". . . *you're* not a fucking lawyer. *I'm* a fucking lawyer. You didn't hire me to show the jurors who Billy Quinn is. You hired me to show them the man they want Billy Quinn to be."

But who is Billy Quinn? I mean, who is anyone, really?

19

MARRYING INTO GREAT WEALTH DOESN'T ENSURE HAPPI-
ness or stability. For some people, living among the one percent does
the exact opposite: it reveals the depth of their wanting. One infamous
woman, born into humble circumstances, married a billionaire. Over
the years, she spent obscene amounts of money on plastic surgery. Her
rumored goal was to look like a cat, which she more or less achieved,
with high cheekbones, feline-slanted eyes, and peaked eyebrows. As
her face changed, she became the subject of tabloid covers and society gossip. It's easy to judge the woman's conspicuous consumption
and frivolous spending, her vanity and bold denials. But to me, she's a
tragic figure. Imagine feeling so unfulfilled and so lacking—for love,
for attention, we'll never know—that you pay millions of dollars to
carve up your face.

My biological mother, Rachel Forrester, has a similarly tragic story.
She was raised in rural Wisconsin. Her parents, a postman and a
teacher's aide, worked hard, lived modestly, and passed away in their
early sixties. She loved them but had higher aspirations; her dream was
to move to New York and work on Wall Street. After graduating from
a small Chicago college, Rachel got an MBA at NYU. Her first job was
with Forrester Holdings, where the chairman, CW, happened to notice
the tall, slender redhead with freckles and light eyes, thirty-four years
his junior. While their relationship seemed unlikely, what began as a
passing attraction evolved into a genuine love affair. But after their
wedding, instead of enjoying her newfound riches, Rachel drank herself into oblivion, and ended up dead at thirty-two.

My memories of CW are hazy—a gruff man with grasshopper
legs, the earthy smell of cigar smoke, a mitt-sized hand cupping my

head, the soft brush of a camel hair coat. Rachel, I remember more clearly. Like me, she loved word searches, card games, and puns. We played Hangman and Scrabble. We watched *Wheel of Fortune*. Though I rarely think about CW, I do wonder about Rachel. Admittedly, my feelings are complex, but I miss her in ways I can't quite articulate. Even when she was alive, I wanted more of her than she could give. It seemed like she was always on the move, always far away, always someplace I wasn't.

Now, I'm almost the age she was when she met CW, and I can better appreciate her situation. Rachel hitched her wagon to a man three decades older who thrust her, with no preparation or support, into his high-society life. I'm sure it felt alien and lonely. She was an outsider, watching a party through the window. My birth likely triggered postpartum depression that caused her to crumble, and then CW's death sent her over the edge. But Rachel's unraveling, unlike the cat woman's, was shorter, swifter, and less visible to the naked eye.

Earlier, I said that Rachel accompanied CW when he traveled. But that isn't the full story. CW insisted she come along with him, partly for his pleasure, but mostly to monitor her drinking. From his point of view, his wife was a danger to herself and only he could save her. But then she got pregnant, and CW realized she could save herself—with my help. "Rachel, my dear, this baby is your saving grace," he told her. "She will give your life purpose." And thus, at seven weeks old and still in the womb, I became the solution to my mother's relentless addiction.

Unfortunately, for all CW's genius, I was a lousy bet. One great lie of modern life is that parenthood is vital and transformative. For Rachel, it was a disaster. Upon my arrival, her drinking ramped up. Overwhelmed, overwrought, and overly indulged, she outsourced my care to day-nurses, night-nurses, live-in nannies, live-out babysitters, and finally, when she ran out of options, her upstairs acquaintance, Eleanor Quinn.

I believe Rachel tried. I have scrawled notes indicating as much.

You're mine forver
Sorry, sorry, sorry, I love you, love you, love you

You're my sweet princess and my heart
Cassie, you and me together 4-ever

The notes are maudlin and little-girlish, rife with misspellings, and likely written while drunk. Still, I cherish each one. They're evidence that she existed, that she loved me. In photographs, we're two happy kids, showing off matching red nails, licking ice cream, napping side by side on the beach. Not much, but not nothing.

I recently asked Lawrence about the car crash that killed her, whether it might not have been an accident. He equivocated, saying we'll never know for sure. Not that knowing would've changed anything. When it happened, I was barely five, and already ensconced with the Quinns, my forever family.

Lawrence's offer to raise me was magnanimous. Selfless. Kind. However, knowing him as well as I do, I'm sure he was equally relieved to be in a position to give back to CW, a man he revered like a god and loved like a brother. So, you see, the world of the wealthy isn't just small and incestuous; we also have our own economy with our own currency. Lawrence, a rosy-eyed dreamer, saw value in me where others saw junk. She's ours now, he said. She's mine and Eleanor's, to raise as we please. In this way, then, Lawrence's unspoken debt to CW was repaid in full, the circle was closed, and my fate set in motion.

* * *

It's June, nine weeks after Billy's arraignment. The weather has shifted again. Summer is here, and humidity has descended like wet fog in New Haven, where I'm living full-time. Here, far from the chaos, I spend entire days not speaking to a soul. I'm free of parents, of brothers. Of men. I'm not oblivious to men, just uninterested. Most important, I'm anonymous. No one knows I'm the "adopted sister" of "accused rapist" or "rapist runner" Billy Quinn. The truth may eventually come out, but for now, I carry my brother the way I carry my other secrets: one self facing the world, the other shrouded in darkness.

I will tell you one sacred secret: I look like an ordinary woman. But inside I have a well of shame that's as deep as I am tall. I'm an orphan. My father is dead. My mother, also dead, was a drunk. But my shame isn't that Rachel drank. It was that she gave me away, quickly, easily, no looking back.

Why? I ask Lawrence. Why did she do it?

Rachel was ill, he tells me. Rachel was weak.

But to me, only one answer makes sense. I'm damaged goods. Too damaged to want, too damaged to keep. The truth, of course, is nuanced, but to a small child, distinctions are meaningless. One day she was my mom, the next day she was gone.

The half-life of a daughter's grief is equal to the length of time she spent with her mother multiplied by the rest of her life. I always feel Rachel's absence. Which is why I try to be a good girl, a good daughter for the Quinns; a better girl than my brothers are boys, a better daughter than they are sons. Nate and Billy are Quinns by birth. They can never be rejected. But my place is tenuous. So I'll do whatever I can to make sure Eleanor and Lawrence love me, if not the most, then at least as much. I do anything they ask, anything my brothers ask. Just, please, please, please I beg you: don't leave me behind.

That sounds so mawkish, doesn't it? Pathetic, too. Like I'm someone who wallows in self-pity.

I lean forward. Let me stipulate, for the record, that I don't feel sorry for myself. My family has been nothing but good—to me and for me. They would never leave me.

"They would never leave me," I repeat, but this time I stammer. "They'd never . . . no one is leaving anyone . . . we love each other . . ."

Christ, it's hot in my apartment. I feel like I'm suffocating. My skin sticks to my chair and makes a sucking sound when I move. I need liquids, moisturizer, a towel, something.

The cop, Haggerty, turns off the tape recorder, looks into my eyes. "Do you need to take a break, Ms. Quinn? We've been talking for"—he glances at his watch—"two hours already."

"Call me Cassie. And no break. We had a deal: one interview."

Scrambling, I gulp water. "I'm just a little flustered; talking to you seems to get me all hot and bothered."

My joke falls flat. Haggerty's eyes are blank.

"We should stop for a few minutes," he says. "Don't underestimate what we're doing. Telling a stranger about your most intimate relationships is——"

"What do you mean by intimate?"

"It's just a word. Doesn't mean anything. Look, I can see you're tired. Let's pick this up another time."

"Don't tell me I'm tired," I say wearily. "It's patronizing."

"Not intentional, Ms. Quinn. I'm just asking if you prefer I come back."

"I didn't want you here in the first fucking place, Officer."

"*Detective.*"

"*Detective.* Can I call you Greg?"

"Detective works, thanks."

Detective Gregory Haggerty is skinny and angular with an over-sized Adam's apple and hawkish nose; a long, lean Ichabod Crane wearing filmy glasses and yesterday's suit. His rumpled shirt and muddy shoes make him look inept. But his eyes give him away. Hard, black, and set deep in his skull, they drill into me, make me sweat and squirm in my chair.

"You win." Exhaling, Haggerty feigns relief. "It's me. I'm the one who needs a break."

"That's just as patronizing," I tell him.

"Again, not intentional, Ms. Quinn."

I feel a spike of rage that blooms into revulsion. I hate Gregory Haggerty, I think. I want him out of my apartment. Asserting these simple, declarative statements boosts my confidence, returns me to solid ground. "Again, call me Cassie." I smile big. "We're friends now, right?"

He's not charmed in the slightest. Men with no sense of humor are exhausting; this guy is soul-killing.

"Can I get you more water?" he asks, as if our roles have reversed, and we're in his apartment, not mine.

I lift my glass, which is empty. I'm so thirsty I can hear my lips pull apart when I speak. "All set," I say. To accept anything from him is to show weakness.

"Why don't you relax while I step out and make a few calls?" Haggerty tilts forward, speaks into his phone. "It's ten a.m. on Wednesday, June fourteenth. This concludes Part One of my interview with Cassandra Elisabeth Forrester-Quinn."

He clicks a button, closes a folder, and stands up, all in one motion. He seems pleased with himself. This is a bad sign. Haggerty's confidence can mean only one thing: at some point during my epic story, I gave myself away.

PART TWO

Investigation

20

I'M SERIOUS. THE HEAT IS DEADLY. OUTSIDE, IT'S, LIKE, A HUN-
dred and ten degrees, and the sun has baked the brick building since
dawn. With the windows closed, my living room feels like the core of
a furnace. When Haggerty showed up, face flushed, hair damp, I considered turning on the air-conditioning. But then decided no, let's not.
This guy wants to talk so badly, let him shrivel up in this hotbox. Let
him walk out of here a desiccated husk.

In the past two hours, I've done most of the talking. I started with
Nate's call in March and recounted all the high points, including
meeting DeFiore, Billy's first appearance, his arraignment, and what
happened next. After that, I told him, I lost the thread. Haggerty kept
pace, asking questions, follow-up questions, and more follow-up questions. And yet, he never mentioned the heat, not once. Even when his
grimy sweat dribbled down his face and stained his collar, he didn't
flinch. So, points to him for grit and endurance. Not that I plan to give
up. Haggerty may have won the battle, but our war rages on.

While he's in the hall, I steal into my bathroom and suck two hits off
a joint. Not enough to lose my wits, but enough to feel faraway and chit-
chatty; enough to retrace my steps, fix any loose ends, and close up shop.

Haggerty's primary questions were about Billy, obviously. "Tell me
a story," he said, just like my brothers at Hawkins Cove. "I'm open to
anything."

I hadn't forgotten DeFiore's instructions to keep quiet: *Do not talk
to anyone without a lawyer present.* But I agreed to talk for two reasons.
The first is personal. I wanted Haggerty to see my family's complexity, our humanity, the day-to-day reality of our lives. The world has
appalling misconceptions about the rich. But we're no different from

people with less money, or no money, not in the ways that matter. We fear our mothers' disapproval. Our fathers mortify us. We forget their birthdays. Our impulsive decisions disappoint them. We form alliances, hold grudges. We behave childishly, indefensibly. But just as we reach the point of no return, there is kindness, forgiveness, flashes of grace. We are normal, everyday people; wealthy, sure; but otherwise just like anyone else, just like him.

If you want to know us so *intimately*, Detective, I told him, pull up a chair.

The other reason I spoke up is tactical. Team Billy is at an impasse. Lawrence has decided, unequivocally, that the risk of losing is too great; he and DeFiore are pushing Billy to take a plea. Eleanor and Nate refuse; they want to go to trial. Billy is too depressed to offer a meaningful opinion. And while I agree with Eleanor and Nate, no one cares what I think, not since I left town, essentially abandoning my family in their time of need. With Eleanor and Lawrence at odds, and questioning DeFiore's every move, we don't have a coherent defense. Time is ticking. If Billy takes the plea, he'll end up in prison. If Billy goes to trial and loses, he'll end up in prison. What could I do? What would anyone do?

DeFiore will be livid, but once I explain, he'll get over it. He may even thank me. Someone had to advocate for Billy. So I gave Haggerty what he asked for, and set the record straight. Knowing he'd check and double-check, I stuck to the truth, even when it made us look bad. I'm not a lawyer, but I am a sister. I know my brother better than he knows himself. Who else but me can create a portrait of Billy that will convince a jury of his innocence? The story is so simple it's stupid: Billy suffered. Billy stuttered. Billy triumphed. Billy has a heart of gold. Billy was an easy mark. Billy fell in love. Billy gave and gave. Billy got burned. Billy got railroaded. Not guilty, Your Honor.

I hear the front door open. "One more minute, Ms. Quinn," Haggerty calls out.

"It's Cassie," I call back. "And no rush." Like I said, fuck you, Haggerty.

It feels good to assert my independence, to tell the truth. I was smart to leave New York. New Haven brings out my clear, steady self. The fighter. The girl that won't quit. The self that disappears when I'm home, with my family.

I brush my teeth, so I won't reek. Unlike Billy and Nate, I'm old school when it comes to weed. I prefer the harsh burn of smoke, like my lungs are on fire.

My phone dings with a text. It's Marcus, killing my mood: Can't stop thinking about you. Remember that first kiss in the park? On the bench? The ducks? Christ, I wish you were here. xx

Oh yeah, fuck you, too, Marcus.

* * *

The first time Haggerty contacted me was back in late April, a few weeks after Billy's arraignment. He said he was a cop, but DeFiore never mentioned his name, so I didn't call back. Soon he was texting me like a possessive boyfriend, so I did some digging. Turned out Haggerty is from Manhattan, a detective in the 16th Precinct, Special Victims Unit. (It's real? Who knew?) Knowing he was bad news, I told myself to stay away. And I did, for months—until today, when the doorman announced that a cop was here. Again, points to Haggerty for tenacity and strategic maneuvering.

Admittedly, I was curious. So I invited Haggerty up, welcomed him in, and before you could solve *BILLY QUINN WAS FRAMED*, he and I were sitting at my farm table, sweating our balls off.

"Start from the beginning," Haggerty instructed. "Don't think, just talk." Bossy, bossy, boom, boom.

I offered my most winning smile, but he stared back with those dead eyes. He's a different animal than most men, neither feral nor submissive. Haggerty is negative space.

"Which beginning?" I asked. "It's an epic story, goes back generations."

"Any beginning, doesn't matter." He was watching me. Normally, I relish this, but the way he latched on was unnerving. "Pick a spot, any spot."

I started with Nate's phone call. Seemed as good a place as any. But soon Haggerty was steering the conversation away from Billy and peppering me with questions about CW and Rachel, Spence, Columbia, Yale—my whole life, basically.

"What do I have to do with Billy's case?" I asked after a while.

"Maybe everything. Maybe nothing. Trying to decide which." He sat back. "So, tell me again why you ran away from home."

"I didn't run away. I'm forging a path. Striking out on my own. Chasing a dream. All the clichés."

"What about the family foundation?"

"I'll work there eventually. It's why I'm going to graduate school. I didn't just pull political science out of the air, Detective. I'm interested in language and rhetoric. I plan to study how it's used as a corrupting influence, particularly in rich countries that hijack and subvert messages. This way, when I do join the foundation, I can make a tangible difference. I don't want to be another vacant, pampered rich girl 'working for my dad'"—I make air quotes—"while I wait for a husband."

"Noted." He nodded. "And the man?"

"Is that a question?"

"You said you also left a relationship, one that was bad for you. Dangerous, even."

"Who hasn't, Detective? We're all trying to outrun a cunning bad boy, aren't we?"

"Tell me about him, about Marcus Silver."

"He's no one. No one important."

"All due respect, Ms. Quinn, but 'no one' doesn't derail your life."

"He didn't 'derail' anything. I used the word to describe what happened to Billy's life, not mine."

Haggerty took out a pad and jotted a few notes. "If you say so."

"My relationship with Marcus is over. It shouldn't matter."

"Of course it matters, Ms. Quinn. It wasn't supposed to happen, and it did."

That's when the dynamic turned. Red flooded the edges of my vision. White noise filled my head. Haggerty was so sure of himself, I got rattled. I added superfluous details. I went off on tangents and had to retrace my steps. I felt skittish, as though he could see all the ways I was compensating. Little in life frightens me, but this man was terrifying.

And now he's back. "Ms. Quinn? Okay to come in?"

"It's Cassie. And yes." When he slides onto the farm bench and pushes Record, I don't waste any time. "So, Detective Haggerty, where were we?"

"You were telling me about your friend, Marcus Silver."

"I have nothing to say about Marcus."

"Oh, I disagree. You seem to have a lot to say on the subject."

His smugness infuriates me. "You need to leave," I say suddenly, getting up so quickly my bench turns over and hits the floor. "We need to be done with this now."

"You say we're done so we're done." He pauses. "One last question: What's your problem with the police?"

"Do you not read the news? Cops are a menace."

"You feel 'menaced'?" Haggerty makes his own air quotes. "How? Did Billy's security detail use the good towels in the powder room without asking?" He smirks. "Fact is, Ms. Quinn, cops are what stand between you and chaos."

"It's Cassie, Detective." I study Haggerty's face, but it's like looking into a mirror and seeing nothing reflected back.

He hands me his card. "Call me anytime you want to talk."

"We're done."

"Oh, I think we'll be seeing each other soon."

"Don't be so sure." I slam the door. But as soon as he's gone it occurs to me that I have it wrong. If I'm the one looking into the mirror, then I'm the one who isn't there. Haggerty's eyes may be empty, but I'm the one with no soul.

21

HAGGERTY IS RIGHT: I DO WANT TO TALK ABOUT MARCUS. I *always* want to talk about Marcus. I'm *bursting* to talk. Especially now that it's over. But I've never uttered a word to anyone. Keeping a secret is difficult, which is why so few people succeed. It demands commitment and vigilance, pain and sacrifice. The willingness, the strength, to take it to your grave.

Worry sets in. I spoke to Haggerty to be helpful; Team Billy might see it differently. Thankfully, DeFiore doesn't call me. But neither does Lawrence or Nate. My worry morphs into paranoia. Maybe they're punishing me for talking to a cop. Or they're furious I abandoned them. Or they're busy. Or the Valmont lost cell service. Could the whole city have gone dark?

By Sunday I'm so panicky I can't sit still. I go to my favorite Neighborhood Café on State Street for breakfast but leave before my food arrives. I lounge by the pool, but it's too hot. My apartment is too cold. I head to the parking lot, where I slide into the front seat of my Porsche, put my keys in the ignition, and debate my next move. I end up going nowhere. I don't even start the car.

On Monday night, I finally break and call Lawrence. "I'm thinking of coming home," I offer casually, feeling him out. "I want to catch up on the case. I miss you guys."

It's after ten; I hear the TV in the background. A panel of experts debating politics. I also hear Nate. "Is that Cassie?" he wants to know.

"Yes," Lawrence replies. "She's asking about the case." He sounds sleepy. No mention of Haggerty, which confirms he has no idea. If he did, he wouldn't let it slide.

"Are you there? Lawrence? I'm *talking* to you." By this point, my purse is in my hand, and I'm racing to my car. When I can't get his attention, my anxiety surges. "Lawrence!"

"Sorry, Cass. I can't keep my eyes open. It's been a long day."

Minutes later, my key is in the ignition. I back out of the lot. I don't even look, just hit reverse and hope for the best. "What do you think?" I ask.

"About what?"

"Me coming home."

"Sounds good." Noncommittal, Lawrence doesn't care. "Hey, Cassie. DeFiore is on the other line. It's late and could be important. Sorry, kiddo. Speak soon."

When he hangs up, fear explodes in my chest. I can feel my pulse in my teeth. I accelerate, fast then faster. Ninety minutes later, when I walk into the celebration room, Lawrence is still staring at the TV, nursing a drink. Nate is gone, but his enormous sneakers are wedged under the coffee table like white bricks.

"What a surprise!" Liquored up and woozy, Lawrence kisses my cheek. "A wonderful surprise." But he's selling too hard. His voice has no connection to his words. "How long you here for?"

I end up staying three days, one more unbearable than the next. Everyone is busy, busy, busy. The celebration room has been transformed into a war room where Nate and Lawrence strategize like the Joint Chiefs of Staff. They're on the phone with DeFiore's team every day. Eleanor is in her office or huddled with the Bowtie. Billy barricades himself in his bedroom, sleeping for twelve hours at a clip. Occasionally, I catch sight of him from behind, hunched over his computer. No one has time for me; and if they do, it's a cursory hello while they tackle more important business. Feeling left out one evening, I accuse Lawrence of avoiding me.

He sighs. "No one is avoiding you." I exasperate him. I exasperate everyone with my neediness, my solipsism, my unwillingness to see that our family is under siege and my brother's future hangs in the balance. I'm a selfish and spoiled girl; I need to back off. "We're focused on the trial, Cassie. You said you wanted your own life. You can't have it both ways, Princess." The way he says Princess sounds snarky.

"Would love to, Cassidy Cakes," Nate says when I ask if he wants to see a movie, smoke a joint, play Scrabble. "But Dad and I are lawyering it up." Together, this implies. Without you.

Here's something I didn't tell Haggerty. Until he was six, maybe seven, Nate and Lawrence were best buddies. They spent weekends together, skiing, mountain biking, and tooling around town. But then I moved in, orphaned and traumatized, and seized Lawrence for myself. It never occurred to me that Nate might be resentful, or if the thought did occur, I ignored it. But when I left, and they reconnected, I realized that Nate must've felt an awful lot of hurt and anger as a child. The same hurt and anger I feel now. Which is the funny thing about families, no matter how much cake you have, someone will always feel starved.

* * *

After that, I stay put in New Haven, even though I'm not taking any summer classes. By mid-July, I feel less rattled. It's blisteringly hot, but I cool off in the pool. When people pass by, I wave and say hi. Music plays in the streets. It's like a soundtrack to the movie of my life, a movie I'm watching and living at the same time. Everything here is easy, or easier, at least. For one thing, I'm able to sleep.

When I first moved in, I had big plans to strip down my life and rebuild. I wanted to transform myself into a whole new person, a wholesome person. Someone with a sense of adventure, a can-do spirit. The kind of girl who could gut renovate a historic townhouse by herself. I'd wear tall green wellies, cover my hair with a red bandanna, and plant cucumbers in the soil. I'd get a rescue puppy named Bo and tie a matching bandanna around his neck. Neighbors would stop by for vodka tonics and salted nuts on the deck. We'd grill steaks and watch the sun set while the kids lit sparklers. Later, after the house emptied out, and the children were home safe in their beds, I'd walk Bo around the block, taking in the quiet neighborhood.

Reality set in. Needing a place fast, I settled for the familiar, a luxury rental in East Rock with a pool, gym, and yoga studio. A few grad students live here, but I haven't met any of them. I'm rusty at small talk and faking good cheer. This is when I most miss Marcus, a man who could capture a room simply by stepping in it. He was funny, sarcastic, and terrifically entertaining, always coming up with new activities to do on the sly. We'd pretend to bump into each other at MoMA and study the art, sneaking sweet kisses around corners when no one was looking. In movie theaters, we luxuriated in each other under cover of darkness. Once we went to a hotel in Greenwich, where he kicked my ass in Scrabble. We swam in the overly chlorinated pool and drank red wine in bed. It was the first time I'd ever woken up next to a man besides my brothers, and despite a bit of awkwardness (bathroom smells, body fluids), it was glorious. When I was with Marcus, my world grew bigger, the sky was infinite.

My life in New Haven, by contrast, is empty of people and things. I've gotten used to it; I even enjoy it at moments, despite my family's skepticism. "You'll be back in two weeks," Lawrence had said when he helped move me in last year. He wasn't being mean, merely shocked I had left, and so quickly. "You're our Forever Girl."

"This is my life now. I'm not coming back."

"If and when you do, you'll always have a place with us, Cass." Again, this wasn't discouragement; it was concern. What I told Haggerty is true: Lawrence is an overprotective father, like many parents of his generation. Of course, how much care is too much care remains up for debate.

My apartment's two bedrooms are similarly sized. One is mine, and I've designated the other as a guestroom by tossing a mattress on the floor. A sliding glass door leads to a tiny terrace. To fill the rest of the space, I bought furniture from Pottery Barn: a platform bed, a wooden farm table that seats eight, two picnic-style benches and several lamps. The bed is king-sized so it's where I eat, sleep, study, and watch TV. That I choose this existence may have surprised my parents, but minimalism suits the new me. I've never lived outside New York or away from my family. I've never held down a job or had to fend for myself. (Of course, I'm neither holding down a job nor paying for this place, but one step at a time.) And yet, once I got over the initial terror, I felt lighter, like I was unshackled from chains I had no idea I was wearing. The downside of my newfound agency is loneliness, but it won't kill me.

You know what would kill me? Going back to New York and returning to Marcus. One way or another, I would cease to exist.

*   *   *

A text appears; it's from Haggerty.

> You want to talk
> No, I don't
> Yes, you do
> I'd never talk to you
> If not me who?

22

I LOVE BREAKFAST, WHICH I EAT EVERY DAY AT THE NEIGH-
borhood Café. For the past two weeks, I've been ordering the same
thing: black coffee and the Little Italy burrito. The Little Italy comes
with two eggs, sausage, peppers, onions, and provolone cheese. Inside,
there's a hash brown patty. Sometimes I add hot cherry peppers. After
I order, I find a table inside. When my food is ready, Eddie will bring it
to me, and we'll talk for a few minutes. He's very friendly. While our
roles are circumscribed—he's a server, I'm a customer—we share a
connection, like me and Anton.

"Little Italy and coffee," Eddie says today. "Right?" He's twenty-
seven and from the Midwest. He's got cowlicks in his hair, expressive
brown eyes, and a lisp I find endearing. "I'll bring it right out."

I met Eddie last fall when I was working on my grad school ap-
plication. I was very serious about the process, which I treated like a
job. Along with studying for the GREs, I wrote letters to my former
professors requesting recommendations, drafted and redrafted my
personal statement, and then hired a doctoral student to proofread it.
I showed up at the café every morning, after the rush, like it was my
office. Soon, I was a familiar face and talking to Eddie became part of
my routine.

Today, I read *Middlemarch* while I sit. After September, it will be
academic journals, so I'm gorging on dense novels, ones I've loved
since high school.

But mostly, I'm enjoying dining out in public, something I can't
do in New York anymore. The press became relentless, so my family
stopped leaving the building. Meals, stylists, and masseuses come to us.
One night, we risked dinner in a restaurant tucked on a side street. All

five of us went, even Billy. It was fine until Nate drank too much and Lawrence berated him for acting sloppy.

"There is *a lot* riding on this, Nathaniel."

Lawrence was so furious I could feel heat rise off his skin. People were staring, and his mouth was twisted into a rictus smile.

But it was Billy who pushed back, not Nate. "Fuck you, Dad," he said before stomping off. "Fuck you, too, Cassie."

"What was that about?" Lawrence asked.

"Brother-sister shit." I stared into my plate. "I ask too many questions about Diana Holly, I have no boundaries, and I should mind my own business. Or something like that."

I was shaken by Billy's vicious tone; he never would've lashed out when we were younger. Now he's easily angered, and quick to turn on me. I understand how scared he is—I'm scared too—but I thought this horrible experience would bring us closer again. Instead, it's pulling us further apart. Why can't it be the same as it was when we were kids?

"More coffee, Cassie?" Eddie asks, holding a pot.

"Oh my gosh." I giggle like a silly girl. "I'm already buzzing! Just water, thank you."

"Your food will be ready in a minute. I'm sure you're starving."

Oh, Eddie, I think. You have no idea.

My conversations with Eddie are pleasant, non-threatening. I don't worry about subtext or hidden meanings. Lawrence has warned me about men. "Not every boy has honorable intentions," he told me, in the awkward, stilted way that fathers have when discussing sex with their daughters. "You need to be smarter. Stay two steps ahead." As I got older, our talks got easier, mostly because they were science-based and cerebral. My takeaway was that men, boys, are always on the hunt; whether conscious of it (feral) or not (submissive). Their brains are more developed than other warm-blooded vertebrates, but they're mammals fueled by testosterone, which primes instincts like dominance and self-affirmation. Sexual satisfaction is hardwired, and they'll achieve it by aggression, deception, or both. Women who don't see the world through the lens of men's needs are naïve or willfully blind.

Eddie is getting a master's in comparative literature. The first time he brought out my food, I was reading *The Shining*. The next time, *Song of Solomon*. The next time, *The Secret History*. It became a joke between us: What is Cassie reading this morning?

"I should introduce you to my wife." He glances at the cover of *Middlemarch*.

I feel a shiver, like the wind has shifted. "Your wife?"

"Sure," Eddie says, affably. "She's a big reader, too; I bet you'd get along great."

"Where did you meet?"

"A study group, believe it or not."

Far off, I hear humming. Maybe I'll meet my husband in a study group too. He'll smile at me across the table. He'll walk me home. We'll go on a date and eat Thai food. He'll kiss me at the door. I'll have the charming, wholesome relationship I've always longed for.

When my Little Italy is ready, Eddie sets it down in front of me. "I will have more coffee," I tell him. "Cream, please."

Talking to Eddie makes me feel sneaky. Like I'm getting away with something by presenting myself as a wholesome girl capable of wholesome love when I'm a dirty degenerate, a con artist who used to fuck a married man—a man with children, no less. That I'll end up with a Midwestern Eddie and become a book-loving wife is a laughable idea. And yet, in New Haven, never say never. Maybe here I can start over as an entirely new person, relive my life, remap my choices.

I pick up my fork and dig in. In New Haven, I eat with gusto. Here, I eat tortillas. I eat eggs. I eat sausage. I eat provolone cheese, hash browns, and hot cherry peppers. I can feel my scrawny body filling out, growing healthy and strong. I feel alive. I eat, I eat, I eat.

*   *   *

Hours later, reading by the pool, I have a chance to practice my social skills. When I look up, a dark-skinned guy is pointing to the lounge chair two inches from mine. This is only significant because there are thirty other chairs around the pool, all empty.

"Taken?" His hair, also dark, is curly. His eyes are black as tar. He's my age, maybe a few years older.

I consider flirting. *Did you mean the chair, or me?* Instead, I wave cheerfully. "All yours."

He tosses down his pool bag, and I study his body. Awesome shoulders. Impeccable arms. Flat stomach. But what I like most is his towel. It's a Mighty Morphin Power Rangers beach towel, circa 1993.

Settling in, he sighs. Above our heads, the sun is a fireball, beating down mercilessly. "Where is everyone?" he asks. "It's a perfect pool day."

"Too humid," I reply. "But I like it this way, white-hot and wet." As soon as the words are out, I cringe. *White-hot and wet?* Gross.

We sit side by side under the scorching sun. Soon, we're both drenched in sweat. I'm desperate to jump into the pool but feel exposed in my skimpy bathing suit. Since when? I ask myself. I'm tongue-tied, not sure what to say, the right way to engage. All I know is how to invite him upstairs, slide off my bikini bottoms, let the afternoon unfold.

"My brother had those sheets," I choke out. "Power Rangers." For a second, I seize up. What if he asks me about Billy?

"The towel was a gift," the guy says. "It's vintage. Ebay, I think."

Thankfully, he doesn't ask about Billy. In fact, he doesn't ask about anything.

For the next thirty minutes, I'm a wreck. How do wholesome people date? Finally, I decide to make a joke. We'll laugh about our awkwardness, the horror of striking up conversation. But when I turn to speak to him, I realize that the whole time I've been spinning, he's been asleep behind his stupid sunglasses.

23

I CHECK THE NEWS EVERY DAY FOR UPDATES ON BILLY'S case. My system is elaborate. I start with a Google search on my phone for any mention of my family. Then I read a hard copy of the *New York Times* I have delivered to my door. Back on my phone, I skim an app that aggregates stories from sources across the web. Finally, I scour every digital New Jersey paper, bulletin, and leaflet from Princeton down to Cape May.

The news is quiet so far. But on the last Friday of July, Lawrence makes a colossal blunder and the hits come so fast and furious the next morning that I have to call Nate.

My brother picks up immediately. We don't bother with preliminaries. "You saw the news," he says.

"I did, unfortunately," I reply. "What happened?"

Nate tells me that Lawrence and Eleanor spent most of yesterday arguing. By late afternoon, Lawrence was fuming. The day had cooled down and the reporters were sparse, so he went for a walk. ("He just *left the house?*" I ask, stunned. Nate snorts. "He loves to bait the gods.")

On the sidewalk, a stranger in a Mets cap sidled up to him. "Lawrence Quinn? I'm Raffi Alexander with PXN News New York—"

"No comment." Lawrence turned back toward home.

"I'm on your side. What they're doing to your boy is unconscionable."

"No comment."

"We all see what's happening, Lawrence. Our sons are in the crosshairs. Every male over age twelve has a target on his back. Billy lost his future over a false accusation! Lawrence, what happened to innocent before proven guilty?"

Hearing this, Lawrence slowed down. "Thank you—what's your name? Raffi?" He extended his hand. "Didn't mean to be rude."

"No apologies. Reporters are ruthless. Your restraint is impressive, Lawrence. If it was my family, I'd be shouting in the streets."

Flattered, Lawrence got excited; finally, someone saw how awful this experience has been, how hard it is to keep quiet. "Not all reporters are ruthless, Raffi. Most just want the story, which I can appreciate. As you may know, I was a media consultant for years, and have great respect for the news. But the reporters who spread lies? Who serve as judge, jury, and executioner? I'd love to give those guys a piece of my mind. Where does this end, Raffi?"

"Great question." Raffi raised his camera. "Quick quote? If you could appeal to the press's better nature, what would you tell them?"

"I really can't. I'm sorry."

"Briefly, please. You're in a position to make a difference, Lawrence. Unlike most men, you're eloquent and persuasive. Lots of fathers and sons are suffering. Can you imagine how just a few words from a man like you will help? Please, Lawrence?"

And just like I had, Lawrence spoke up. "To members of the news media, I respect your profession, but I want you to understand that a boy's future is at stake." Making his plea for restraint, his smile was wistful. "My son is petrified. He's just a kid, only twenty-two. I implore you to reserve judgment until all the facts are out and the truth becomes clear. You'll see that this is a case of anger and revenge. A vindictive, irrational woman is bitter a brief affair has ended, and she's retaliating by destroying my son's future."

So.

The press exploded. As soon as Raffi Alexander uploaded the clip, Lawrence's quote was shared, reposted, and retweeted 1.1 million times. "Dad went viral," Nate says. "The guy's a fucking meme. He may have screwed Billy beyond repair."

After hanging up with Nate, I call Lawrence, who feels awful, of course. He's desperate to make another statement, but DeFiore forbade it.

"*Henceforth,*" Lawrence says, quoting DeFiore, "*all communication from the Lawrence Quinns to the outside world is shut down.* Peter also ordered us to stay out of sight. Well, not you, Cassie, since you're never here anyway."

"I'll come home," I offer, ignoring his dig. "Nate and Billy's birthdays are next week. I want to celebrate with everyone. Triple-cakes. Triple-parties. Three Musketeers."

"It's okay. No one is feeling celebratory these days."

"Tell her she doesn't need to come home," I hear Nate say. "But she should send gifts."

"Speak soon," Lawrence tells me. "Love you, kiddo."

* * *

Marcus's calls have become more frequent. Always in the dead of night. Always when I'm sleeping. "I can't stand this. I can't stand that you left." He's crying, which thrills and disgusts me. To give in and go back is slow suicide. He has a wife, three kids, two houses, a job, all of which he's devoted to. "Please, Cassie, come back."

I hang up. Trailing my fingers along my arm, I imagine they're Marcus's, and relive the first time he touched me. Alone in bed, I feel sad and sorry. I want to cry but refuse.

24

ON SUNDAY MORNING, WHEN THE DOORMAN CALLS TO AN-
nounce a guest, I freak out. It's Marcus. He drove all the way from
New York! Should I let him in? Pretend I'm not home? If I open that
door, there's no telling what might—

"It's okay," I say. My heart is pounding. "Send him up."

"It's a woman." He pauses to get her name. "Eleanor Quinn?"

Eleanor? Eleanor has never visited New Haven, not since I moved.
"You sure?"

There's a pause. "She said, 'Yes, Cassandra, he's sure.'"

"I need another minute." I'm a whirling dervish, grabbing towels
off chairs, scooping clothes from the floor. Although I never told Eleanor about Marcus, I feel sure she's here to talk about him. I don't know
why I think this, but I do. *A married man, Cassandra? A man who offers
nothing but lies? Who betrays his family? I raised you better than this.*

She knocks as I pull on shorts. Opening the door, I give her a smile.
"Eleanor, this is a surprise." Today, she's channeling Jackie Onassis
fleeing the paparazzi. She's wearing oversized black sunglasses, rich
red lipstick, and a scarf wrapped around her head. She looks ludicrous.

"A fun surprise, I hope." She holds up a brown bag. "Double espresso.
Your favorite."

"Fun!" I'm giddy with worry.

She leans forward but not to hug me. Instead, she pats my back three
times. That's as far as she'll go. When I was a child, she zipped up my
coat, smoothed down my hair, and patted me three times—one, two,
three. Firm yet kind, just enough to make me ache for more.

"It's nice to see you," I say.

"And you, my dear. It's been far too long."

"Eleanor, I was home a month ago."

When she takes off her glasses, I note her eyes, red-rimmed and cloudy. Otherwise, she's styled to perfection—perfect hair, perfect nails, perfect makeup, perfect everything.

She gives me a onceover, and I feel the ground shift under my feet. I love Eleanor, so in my descriptions to Haggerty, I softened her. She's never been cruel or intentionally hurtful to me, but she's exacting, brittle. From the day I moved in, Eleanor has curated my appearance with high-minded precision. Hair, skin, nails, clothes, weight, the way I walk, the way I talk, the list goes on. For most of my childhood, I was so skinny, I looked like one of my brothers. But when I was twelve, my body erupted, like a dirty bomb defiling everything within a fifty-mile radius. Eleanor doubled down in response. Modesty was paramount, desire distasteful, and basic human urges—eating, drinking, fucking— suppressed. Cover yourself, Cassie. Keep yourself in check, Cassie. Be pretty, be smart; be good. For Christ's sake, Cassie, be anything but what you are. I rebelled, parading through the house in a skimpy tank top and tiny boxers. *Hey, Eleanor, check me out.*

"Well, don't you look casual?" she says.

I'm wearing ripped denim shorts and a T-shirt. I'm barefaced, barefoot, and my hair is a tangled, knotty mess. Her point, though, is I'm not wearing a bra. "It's summer, Eleanor."

"Mind if I take a tour?" Without waiting for my response, she sweeps through the nearly empty rooms. "You've done wonders with the place, Cassandra. Who knew you had such style?"

"Who knew you had a sense of humor?"

She smiles. "There's my girl. Snappy as ever."

Eleanor won't sit without a proper invitation, so I wave at a bench. "Make yourself comfortable."

"I will do my very best." She slides over as if it's the backseat of a town car: knees together, spine straight, hands folded neatly like white dinner napkins. After a brief pause, she explains her impromptu visit. "We received a report from the lawyer's office."

"About Billy?"

"Of course, Cassandra."

Of course. There's no other reason for her to be here. On the plus side, it has nothing to do with Marcus. I open my espresso and take a sip. It's still hot. "Start with the good news."

"The investigator—Mr. Martinez, the bearded gentleman with atrocious posture, you've met him—is excellent."

"And the bad news?"

"Mr. Martinez's understanding of Billy and the girl's relationship differs from ours. It seems she wasn't really stalking your brother, and he never reported her to campus security."

"Yeah, I know. We already discussed this with DeFiore. Billy said Diana was needy, not that she *stalked* him. I mean, he didn't use that word, specifically. Nor did he say anything to me or Nate about filing reports. We told Lawrence all of this. We also told Martinez before he went digging."

"Well, Lawrence never told me. Neither did Billy. Like you, he's always been less than forthcoming about his romantic life."

I glance at my phone.

"I hope I'm not keeping you?"

"No, I'm good." But she's dragging this out, and I want her to get to the point. When I spoke to Haggerty, I made Diana sound unhinged. I mean, she is unhinged, but I may have overstated some of her actions. So I have to know ASAP if I need to backpedal, and if yes, by how much. "What else did Martinez find out?"

"The DA may be correct. It appears the girl wasn't harassing Billy." She pauses. "It looks more like the other way around."

"Bullshit." She cringes, less at my choice of words than my tone. "Sorry, Eleanor. But Billy has texts proving otherwise. They're on his phone, which I assume the cops still have."

"We were able to retrieve the texts. The girl did send several to Billy. However, it's impossible to parse their meaning."

"So, like most college relationships, theirs was volatile, melo-dramatic, and makes no sense to anyone else. Big fucking deal."

"Mr. DeFiore is still going through discovery. Either way, he thinks it's too risky to paint Billy as a victim."

I sigh. "Again, Eleanor, I know. DeFiore has been saying this for months. You should trust his advice. I've been out of the loop so I can't offer an opinion."

"I disagree. You met the girl. You had dinner with her. You saw them together."

It's true. I met Diana Holly twice—once when she started dating Billy, and again near the end. Billy had described Diana as insecure, which I could see, but it wasn't a deal-breaker. I liked her the first time she met our family, at an Italian restaurant in the West Village. It was June and warm out. She wore a crisp white sundress that could've come from my own closet and casual Tory Burch sandals. Her brown hair was cropped in a pixie cut, and her dangly earrings caught the light when she turned her head. All of us, even Eleanor, found her appealing. Maybe she was a little gushy, but to me, she seemed friendly and forthright. She knew about the foundation, and her questions were thoughtful. "Diana isn't afraid of anything," Billy said. "She reminds me of you."

At the time, I was flattered, but this should've been a warning. If you have no fear, you have nothing to lose; you act recklessly and without restraint. But Billy was in the throes of first love. He and Diana were puppyish and adorable, holding hands and whispering. They seemed happy; and I was happy for them. Also envious, if I'm being honest. I hadn't seen my brother that loose and unfettered in years. They laughed a lot, private jokes. I felt left out—of their relationship, of Billy's life.

Our second meeting in November, was much less successful. Diana came to the Valmont, and everyone was there except Nate. Before we sat down to eat, I stumbled on her in the hall near the celebration room, inspecting our knickknacks and artwork. Seeing her hands all over my family's possessions set me off, and when she held up a vase, I said, "That's from the Ming dynasty. Not Pottery Barn." I must've hurt her feelings because she stammered out an apology and ran off. Next thing I knew, she and Billy were putting on their coats. I felt awful about snapping at her, but she blew it way out of proportion, making him leave without even eating. She kept tugging on his hand, saying "Come on, Babe, let's go," which made her seem manipulative and childish, nothing like the savvy woman I met over the summer. When she and Billy walked out, I made a crack about her clinginess, which infuriated him so much he stopped returning my calls. I should've kept my mouth shut, but her behavior was creepy. She was exactly like he'd described her: needy and demanding, the kind of girl who'd go mental if a boy told her no.

* * *

"I'm sorry, Eleanor. Do you need something from me?"

"I'd like you to come home. Someone has to convince Billy to tell the truth, even if he's afraid it will cast him in a bad light. Mr. DeFiore can't build a solid case otherwise."

"Billy has been interrogated by the police ad nauseam. If they can't get him to tell the truth, what makes you think I can?"

"You were always so close. Remember when you were a little girl, you were afraid of the dark? Every night, you snuck into his bed, before Maeve carried you back to your own room." She looks at me, narrows her eyes. "This went on for many years, longer than what's proper. I should've stopped it, but I was grateful you found comfort." She sighs. "You didn't think I knew. Of course, I did. I'm his mother. I know everything."

My stomach drops as if we're in a plane that's suddenly lost altitude. "Eleanor, we were kids. My relationship with Billy has changed." The air is shallow. I try to breathe. "We're not as close as we used to be."

"You're still his sister."

"That's why you drove all the way up here? To tell me to talk to Billy?"

"To impress upon you the difficulty of our situation. Not just with Billy. With his father as well. Lawrence's stunt with the reporter cost us enormous goodwill. He's insisting Billy take a plea, which is a terrible mistake." She shakes her head. "Lawrence told Mr. DeFiore, without my knowledge, to go ahead and make a deal. Thankfully, the lawyer called me. I am, after all, writing the checks. But he's since threatened to drop the case. Despite my initial reservations, I believe Mr. DeFiore can move us in the right direction, and I'm worried Lawrence will jeopardize our relationship with him."

"Lawrence went behind your back?" I correct myself. "Of course he did. I'm sorry, Eleanor. I'll help any way I can, but I don't know if I can change his mind."

"Cassie, please." She must read the fear in my face because she chuckles, though nothing is funny. "The trial is three months away. Nate, as you might imagine, is of limited use—"

"That's not true, Eleanor. He's working hard to help Billy. Plus, he agrees with you."

"For the moment. But Nate would follow Lawrence into a fire. It's only a matter of time before his father convinces him to change his mind. I'm exhausted trying to fight the man alone. If you're there, he might behave." She stops to shake out a napkin. "I'll be honest with you, Cassandra," she says, switching subjects. "I was worried when you decided to spend the summer here alone. With no classes, I feared you might get bored. But it turns out my concerns were unfounded— you have been keeping busy! You spoke to a detective, I hear. What's his name? Gregory Haggerty?" She's perfectly poised, her breathing is even, but her eyes are glassy, like stones.

Jesus. Haggerty. How does she know?

"I'm a wealthy woman," she says, replying to a question I didn't ask. "That's what my money buys these days. Information. Cassie, your brother has been accused of a crime he did not commit. Do you honestly believe I would sit back and watch his life blow up?" She tilts her head, appraises me. "Sometimes I wonder. For a smart girl, you don't always think."

I sip my espresso; it's the perfect temperature. I love strong, bitter coffee; I wish she'd brought something to go with it, a biscotti, maybe.

After a minute, the room gets too quiet.

"Do you have a question, Eleanor?"

"Did you speak to a detective named Gregory Haggerty?"

"Yes."

"Even though you've been instructed not to speak to anyone without an attorney?"

"I thought I could help."

"Because you worked so hard in law school? Because you know so much about legal strategy?" When Eleanor speaks, her lips don't move, like a ventriloquist manipulating a dummy.

"Eleanor, I'm sorry. After you and Lawrence spoke to the police, Haggerty kept calling me. So, I thought it would be okay. I just wanted to help Billy."

"Cassandra, dear, we have to be a united front. Come home. Talk to Lawrence. Change his mind. That is how you can help your brother." Pressing her knees together, Eleanor swivels around then gets up. "Oh, another thing. It's likely you will be asked to testify in Billy's defense. Lawrence and I differ—"

"He won't allow me or Nate to testify. He wants—"

"I know what he wants, Cassie. But if Mr. DeFiore thinks your testimony will help, you will get on the stand. Our family is our family. We have nothing to hide. Again, the best way to support Billy is to show up and speak up."

"I understand, Eleanor."

"Thank you, Sweetheart. Well, I am off. I would love to spend the day taking in the sights of New Haven. Regrettably, my dance card is full."

When Eleanor leans forward, I recoil. But she is only reaching for the empty coffee bag. "I loved seeing you, Cassie, as always." She opens the door, making an elaborate show of folding the bag into four perfect squares and sliding it into her purse. "Buy yourself a trash can, Cassandra, dear. You are not a child anymore."

25

THE SECOND SHE'S GONE I CALL LAWRENCE.

"Hey, Cass. I'm in the middle—"

"Eleanor was here," I say flatly. "In New Haven—"

"*New Haven?* Why?"

"She's angry at me. You might get angry too. A couple of months ago—well, more like six weeks—I spoke to a detective; a new guy, Haggerty—"

"A new guy? What does that mean?"

"I don't know, Lawrence. He's a cop. His name is Gregory Haggerty; google him."

"What did you tell him?"

"Nothing. I was just trying to help Billy. But he asked . . . the . . ." I should say more but can't get the words out.

"What else?"

"Honestly, nothing else—"

"When someone starts with 'honestly,' I never believe what comes next."

"I swear, Lawrence. He asked a few questions; said he'd be in touch. End of story."

"Well, Peter hasn't mentioned it. So, it probably doesn't mean anything. Still, don't do it again." He pauses. "What did Eleanor want?"

"She insisted I come home. She's back to the 'united front.' She's furious at you for pushing Billy to plead guilty."

"She couldn't say this over the phone?"

"Why are you interrogating me?"

"Cassie, stop. I'm not giving up or interrogating you. Eleanor hasn't spent as much time with Peter as I have. She doesn't understand the intricacies of the law. Billy will have to register as a sex offender, whether he takes a plea or loses at trial. But the plea guarantees him a much shorter sentence. With a guilty verdict, he could get *twenty years*. Do you want Billy rotting in prison until he's forty-two? I certainly don't. Peter is talking to the DA tomorrow. After that, I want all of us to meet with him, including you. I need your support, Cassie. *We can't go to trial.*"

Immediately, I feel trapped between my parents. Nate is on Eleanor's side, but who knows for how long. "My life is here, Lawrence."

"It's a life, sure, but not your real life. Your real life is in New York, with us." He lowers his voice. "We miss you, Cassie. Billy needs you. I need you—not just to fight this case, but to fight Eleanor. Cassie, please. Come home. Don't make me beg."

* * *

I don't know what to do. Lying in bed that night, I'm restless. I want to sleep but can't. I want to call Marcus but shouldn't. We haven't spoken in nine months. I've refused his calls. Deleted his texts. Maintained my silence. But I need someone to talk to, a distraction so I don't lose my mind. The more I consider calling, the smarter it sounds. Is it, though? Or am I trying to justify a short-sighted decision? How much will I hate myself in the end?

Fuck it.

I text, my heart thumps: Call me. Important.

His reply is immediate: Two minutes.

For Marcus, two minutes means anywhere from ten minutes to three days. While I wait, my hand trails down my stomach, my fingers slip between my legs. I check my phone, willing it to ring. It's an old habit, one I thought I outgrew. If I check in five minutes, he'll call. Ten minutes, he'll call. Fifteen minutes, he'll call. An hour later, when Marcus still hasn't called, I feel my skin start to twitch. My eyes fill with tears. Not again. For years I've been on hold for Marcus, waiting for him to finish his call, get out of work, read the last page. He says I'm the center of his world, but his sole focus is himself, his wants, his needs. I left

New York because I couldn't let Marcus Silver be my sole focus too. And now, look. Months and months of restraint blown with one text. You're so stupid, I chastise myself. So goddamn stupid.

The phone rings. "Hey you."

My relief is instantaneous. Once again, I can breathe. "Hey back."

We race through the boring part: How are you? I don't know, how are you? I miss you. I know. Are you dating anyone? None of your business.

Then he slows down. "What's so important?"

"You know." I pause. "Home. Only worse with Billy." I never liked talking to Marcus about my family. For me, he was an escape from their all-consuming, ever-demanding love, from feeling like an insider and outsider at the same time. "Let's talk about you, though. Your most recent text mentioned a first kiss."

"Did I? I don't remember. Was it good?"

"Meh," I say, and we both laugh.

I knew Marcus for a long time before I really saw him. For years, he was another guy, someone's husband, on the periphery. My feelings turned, of all places, in the celebration room, where Eleanor was hosting a black-tie event. The house was filled with men in tuxedos, and I was fifteen and feeling impossibly adult in a strapless dress and spiked heels. My hair was blown out, my lipstick cherry-red and sexy. Standing by the mantel, Marcus was dangling a drink between his fingers, and studying me with an amused expression. He was dark and rugged. Familiar but unthreatening.

"You look handsome." I shivered at my boldness.

"You mean, for an old man?"

"You're not old. Don't say that."

"I'm old enough to be your dad, Cassie." His tone was firm, but playful, too.

It was after midnight, and everyone was drunk. No one noticed the way his eyes lingered on my breasts, his hand brushing mine as he topped off his whiskey. Later, he claimed he didn't touch me on purpose, but when his fingertip trailed along my forearm, the jolt triggered some dormant need, and I was rocked off my feet. From then on, Marcus never stopped touching me. He could be two inches away or a mile across town, and I could feel his fingers trailing down my body, across my breasts, below my stomach and deep into the cavern between my legs.

A week later, Marcus was waiting outside school after classes. He didn't call out to me, just waited until I spotted his face in the crowd. It was exciting to see him. It made me giddy, like he was a celebrity dropping into my boring world. He was wearing jeans and a windbreaker. "It's fun to be in play clothes in the middle of the day," he said. "Are you surprised to see me?"

"Who says 'play clothes' anymore?" I retorted, then cringed. Why couldn't I just be nice?

"Old men," he replied. "You didn't answer my question."

"Well," I said, grateful he wasn't offended. "You look great for an old man. And yes, I'm very surprised. Happily surprised. Very happily surprised." We went for a walk in the park, two people enjoying the sunshine. We're both voracious readers, so we talked about books: *Song of Solomon*, my favorite, and *Catch-22*, his. When he put his arm around my shoulders, I waited for his kiss. Instead, he brushed my hair with his lips. "I can't have a physical relationship with you," he told me.

"I wasn't asking for one," I said, taking umbrage. At the same time, I started aching for him.

"I'm just putting it out there. We can see each other as often as it makes sense, but we can't touch each other." He paused. "We'll wait until you're older. Seventeen."

Seventeen? That was two years away. He had to be kidding, or in denial. As it turned out, we could barely wait six months. I was fifteen and a half when Marcus kissed me the first time.

"You kissed me," he says now.

"Oh my God, I did not. *You* kissed *me*."

Christ, that kiss. On the phone, Marcus walks me through the memory; the way he touched me, the way I touched him. He reels me in slowly, just a few details then a few details more.

Again, we go to the park, only it's Riverside, on the west side across town. It's chilly out, so no one's here. Two ducks waddle by. Marcus and I sit on a bench. Tracing my skin with his finger, he says he'll never understand why men hunt. "Look at those ducks. They're harmless."

I correct him. "Those are drakes," I say. "They're male." I can see my breath as I speak. I'm shivering from the cold and from Marcus.

He asks how I know.

"They're not wearing lipstick."

Marcus cracks up. "You are so clever," he tells me. "Such a clever, clever girl." My body hums with desire.

"Remember the ducks?" His voice, his warmth spreads through me, floods me.

"They were drakes." I am so desperate to feel his skin, taste his mouth, I claw at my sheets. I want to do everything all at once and savor every second.

On the bench, he leans forward. I close my eyes. He presses his mouth against mine. I feel myself falling. A trapdoor swings open.

I stroke myself while he talks. "I love you," he says. He's breathless too. "I love you, Cassie." Losing myself in his voice, I brace my body for the rush, for the heat I can't capture but then I can, then I can. It's ecstasy, all of it. "Cassie, baby."

"I love you, too," I choke out, panting. "I love you forever, Marcus Silver."

26

> your Audi story isn't true. There aren't any records
> Billy never reported it, he didn't want to get her in trouble
> You have an answer for everything
> Apparently I need to

I know what Haggerty wants. I knew the minute I googled him. He's not interested in Billy in any significant way. He wants to know about Marcus. The question isn't why but why now? Why does it matter? Marcus and I broke up more than a year ago. Haggerty doesn't know how old I was when we started having sex. Who cares?

For the record, I told the truth about Billy's Audi; rather, I told Haggerty what I knew. Admittedly, I didn't see it happen nor did I have many details. Lawrence called last December, a week before the holidays to make sure I was coming home. "Billy and Diana had a fight," he said at one point. "Billy's car is destroyed."

"I told you Diana is nuts." I felt vindicated. "Why isn't she paying for it?"

"Eleanor just asked the same thing. I think she's afraid to tell her father. Their financial situation isn't great. That's just speculation, though. Billy was vague about it." He paused. "It was weird—the way your brother was protecting her. I didn't think they were seeing each other anymore."

"You should press charges. At least call the cops."

"Billy doesn't want to."

The story I told Haggerty could've been true. I mean, why would

Billy bust up his own car? I texted him, but he never replied. Nate claimed he had no idea. No one pressed charges. There were no witnesses. So, really, who's to say the whole thing didn't happen exactly the way I described it?

* * *

I dread going back to New York, even if is better for Billy. I hate when Lawrence and Eleanor drag me into the middle of their arguments. One of my worst memories is from when I was nine. It was Christmas morning, and everyone was in the celebration room, waiting for me. When I raced in, giddy and excited, Eleanor jumped up from the couch. "Cassandra!" she admonished me. "Put something on. You can't come in here like that."

I stopped dead in my tracks.

"Get dressed. Go. Now."

What was she talking about? I was wearing a nightgown! Then I looked down. Through the sheer fabric, you could see outlines of my underwear and the tiny buds of my nipples.

"I said go!"

Standing there, I was no longer a girl. I was no longer a person. I was just a body, exposed and alone. I was paralyzed.

Lawrence took my hand. "Let's go, kiddo. I'll help you find your robe." I don't remember what he said, but I know I felt better. Later, I overheard him telling Eleanor she was too harsh.

"She can't walk around like that. It's inappropriate. We have sons."

"She's a child. You frightened her."

"She won't do it again then, will she?"

Two weeks after Eleanor's visit, I'm still in New Haven. I can't stop ruminating about her high-and-mighty tone, or Lawrence's endless questions. The phone rings on Thursday night. It's Nate. "Where are you?" he asks.

"Nice hello. I'm in my apartment. Why? Where are you?"

"Home with Mom and Dad."

"Okay, what's going on?"

My question aggravates him. "Suddenly you care?"

"What's that supposed to mean, Nate?"

"Epic story, Cass. Stop me if you've heard this one. Billy Quinn, star-student, all-Ivy athlete, is arrested for felony sexual assault. His parents are locked in a heated battle. Should he take a plea—ass-rape in prison for seven years—or gamble in court? The trial starts in two months and the defense has no strategy. What *will* they decide? Tune in for today's gripping episode."

"Again, what's your point?"

"You used to haul your ass home in a family emergency. Now our mother has to beg on her knees."

"Eleanor told you she was here?"

"She mentioned it, sure. We have no secrets, Ellie and me."

"Well, Nate, I haven't heard from you in forever. And when I'm home, you're too busy to acknowledge me. So you can lose the fucking attitude." In the silence that follows, we listen to each other breathe. *Knock it off, Nate. We're on the same side. Don't make me the enemy.*

"Okay," he concedes. "Truce. Billy has gone off the deep end. He lays in bed like a corpse, while the rest of us rats scramble for cheese. Except you. I hear you're lounging by the pool, sipping Mai Tais. Ellie said you're very tan."

"Did she. What else did she say?"

"Your shorts are too short, your top is too low, and your apartment is a dump."

"Really?"

"No, not really. But I'm not wrong, am I?"

We both laugh. "Sorry I haven't been home. I needed a break."

"I understand. It's hell. Worse than hell. But I'm serious about Billy. He's, like, catatonic. Doesn't read, doesn't run. Just lies in bed and zombies out on his computer. I realize he's scared, Cass. But he can't step into a courtroom like this. He has to fight."

"So you want me to help get Billy on his feet and persuade Lawrence to back off?"

"You know, Princess, you're a lot smarter than you look."

It's good to hear Nate's voice. I'm not ready to hang up. "Can I ask you a question?"

"Maybe."

"What if we have this backwards? What if Diana Holly is telling the truth? Not about the assault, of course, but what if Billy really did harass her? There's a lot we don't know, Nate. Maybe that's why he's so fucked up. Maybe he feels guilty—"

"Don't be a traitor, Cassie. I'm telling you right now."

"Shouldn't we consider the possibility?"

"Let's say it's true. Let's say Billy texted Diana fifty times a day and stalked her all over campus. Doesn't make him a rapist. Doesn't mean he deserves to rot in prison. Why Dad doesn't realize this makes no fucking sense."

"Maybe he thinks seven years is better than twenty."

"If you support Dad, and betray Billy, I will never forgive you."

"Never," I swear to Nate. "Never. Never. Never. I'd never betray any of you."

* * *

A girl has more confidence at sixteen than she'll ever have in her life. She also has more self-loathing. It's why we're so moody, why our reactions are outsized. Cyclonic drama is how we achieve balance. The world is chaotic and irrational. At sixteen, we lack a way to control it. So we lean into the chaos. We become the chaos. We express what we feel in real time because we believe, mistakenly, that unburdening ourselves will stop the tumult, or at least help us make sense of it.

Marcus's kiss unravels me. At almost-sixteen, I feel powerful, unstoppable. I have thoughts and desires. Cravings I can't yet put into words. My needs, my urges, are all-consuming. Little by little, my life gets reduced. I spend entire days fantasizing about him. No parents or brothers, no classes or activities. Avery is frustrated with me. I won't text her back. I don't invite her over. We barely see each other. "What is going on?" she demands to know. But how do I explain I'm not the same girl I was six months ago? Everything is different. "Nothing's going on, Chickadee," I tell her, using our pet name for each other. "You're overreacting."

I move through my life, my school, my house with purpose. Every action I take, every move I make, is deliberate and calculated. I choose outfits to provoke—short shorts and tank tops, blouses with three buttons undone, uniform skirt hiked up to mid-thigh. Makeup, blow-outs, manicures, pedicures, bikini waxes, stiletto heels, dangly earrings, lacy bras, sexy thongs: once these were part of my costume, playing at being a grown-up. Now they're artillery.

With Marcus, I am cocky, someone I don't recognize but don't necessarily dislike. Look at me. Look at my face, my breasts, my hands. Look at my lips. In a crowd, his eyes track me from corner to corner. This is a whole new excitement, his watching. When I get too close, he sputters, fumbles, loses the thread. What were you saying, Cassie? I got distracted. That I can do this to a grown man is remarkable. At the same time, it's not enough. But I don't know if I can say I want more. Rather, am I allowed? I want more. I need more. The need is unbearable. I tell him this: More, Marcus. More.

Calling him the other night was a stupid, stupid mistake. Now that I've opened the door, Marcus Silver floods in like a tidal wave.

27

AN HOUR AFTER NATE'S CALL, I'M IN MY CAR, ON THE HIGH-
way, swept up in memories. How long will it take to shake Marcus this
time? I press on the gas, only partially conscious of the cause and effect, that the weight of my foot is making the car move faster. I see
the numbers on the speedometer tick up, hit eighty then ninety. I see
myself weave through traffic. But I don't feel my toes or my heel, my
ankle or my leg. I don't feel my body; I don't feel anything.

Soon, I'm heading up Park, guided by the Valmont's spire. Since
April, the building has been on lockdown. The board voted to erect
twelve-foot walls to keep out the press. Security was doubled. Now,
the once-grand castle is bleak and forbidding. The stained-glass windows look like blacked-out eyes. The front door stands open and dark,
the mouth of a monster.

"Hey, Cassie," the valet says when I shut off the car.

Surprised by the breezy greeting, I look up. The man at my door
isn't Anton, but he leans into the backseat in a gesture I've seen Anton
make hundreds of times. He's Anton and not Anton, a second expo-
sure grafted onto a photograph. This Anton is wearing a suit, but he's
younger and seems amused I can't place him.

Then it hits me. "Oh my God, *Joey*. You're working here?"

"Joseph." He lowers his voice three octaves. "I started a few weeks
ago."

"Excuse me, *Joseph*. Or should I say *Mr. Rivera*? Jesus, you sound
just like your dad. You look like him, too."

I haven't seen Joey in at least five years. He has his father's poise and
finesse, but he's taller, skinnier. Holding my tote bag, he escorts me
through the lobby, but stops when we reach the elevator. Only Anton

rides with me all the way upstairs. In fact, I'm likely the only resident for whom he makes the extra effort.

"Congratulations on the job," I tell him.

"Part-time overnight valet. Still have to run packages during the day. My dad is such a hard ass." He looks pleased with himself. "But it's a job."

He doesn't ask about my brothers. Just says "Have a nice evening" and steps back. We both raise a hand as the doors close. Suddenly, I see a camera flash, like a strobe light, in the corner of my eye. My vision blurs. An afterimage burns on my retina. It's me but in memory, years younger, almost sixteen. I'm walking past Nate's bedroom, where he, Billy, and Joey are sitting on the floor, stoned. Nate shuffles a deck of cards. The TV blares. On the screen a naked woman spreads her legs. None of the boys are paying attention. Seeing them together, I get panicky. Joey works for his dad a few days a week. Occasionally, he stops by our house to get high with my brothers. They watch porn; rather, porn plays in the background.

Back in June, when I first spoke to Haggerty, I didn't bring up Billy's extracurricular activities. I wanted to present him as pure of heart, mind, and body. So, I didn't mention that many elite runners (*former* elite runners) are habitual stoners. Athletes who compete at Billy's level truly are machines. The mental and physical pressure is punishing in ways we civilians can't conceive. Marijuana modulates heartrate and stabilizes mood swings. Billy vapes, which his coaches ignored when he was breaking records, but once Diana Holly came along, and he started winning less (never say losing), they told him to buck up or get out. Ultimately, the weed doesn't matter. It's legal, and no worse than alcohol. So why describe him as a pothead whose habit got him booted off the team? As Eleanor says, why borrow trouble?

Same with pornography. For our generation, porn is easily accessible and always available, a utilitarian activity to blow off steam. It's different for Eleanor and Lawrence, who weren't raised on the internet. It would disturb them that Nate was eight the first time he saw a Triple-X video. Billy was likely younger. (I was ten, but it was inadvertent. I clicked the wrong movie on Nate's phone.) For my parents' generation, porn is dirty. The men who watch it, sketchy. Nor would it occur to them that women watch voluntarily. My brothers and their friends, however, make no such judgments.

"Cassie!" In my memory, Nate calls to me, but I keep moving.

"Heading out!" I shout. I have nowhere to go but can't be around Joey.

At this point, Marcus and I have been together for almost a year. By together, I mean he slips away every other week, and we go someplace we won't be recognized. Typically, it's late afternoon, and we ride the subway separately, all the way downtown to the Financial District. Then we meet in the back of a diner. Never the same one, naturally. We sit across from each other, order Diet Cokes and fries, and grind out my homework assignments. This is when I feel most like a couple. Two people in love, solving problems, flirting, showing off. Together, we tackle eye imagery in *King Lear*, algebra of polynomials, militarism of Mesopotamian city-states, the impact force of falling objects. "You know," he says, "it wasn't so long ago that I did all this." But Marcus is older. It was ages ago, a whole different century. "Back then," I tease him, "the world wasn't even in color. It was still black-and-white." Neither of us care about his age. Lots of times, I'm more mature.

And yet, despite our closeness, my dissatisfaction deepens and spreads. Marcus will kiss me and touch my breasts. That's it. Full stop. I'm a virgin, which he knows, but I like to pretend otherwise. I flirt with older men when my parents entertain, especially when Marcus is there and can see me doing it. Older men, I quickly learn, are as hungry for my attention as I am for theirs. "Boys must fall all over you. They must follow you around like puppies." Once, a very drunk man told me that at his age, seventy-two, an erection was a sacred event. "I view each one with awe." I pretended to laugh. The man was *repulsive*. But Marcus is different. He keeps me at arm's length. When he watches me, I feel indestructible, invincible. Then he turns the tables, which used to delight me. Now it frustrates me. He insists we can't sleep together until I'm of age, which is seventeen in New York, even if the sex is consensual.

"What if I get parental approval? What if we go before a judge?"

"Don't be ridiculous, Cassie."

I counter with sixteen and two months.

"Seventeen," he tells me.

Sixteen and a half.

"Seventeen."

I let Marcus say what he wants; we both know it's just a matter of time. Like me, he's a tease. "You picked me, Cassandra," he whispers. "You picked me, groomed me, and broke me down. If we do have sex, it's only because I have no choice."

The tension is unbearable.

"No," I whisper back. "You won't have a choice."

I want to feel his body against mine. Nothing can deter a willful teenage girl who burns with want. Luckily, Marcus is a mass of contradictions. An honorable man, engaged father, and devoted husband, but he also likes to court danger. One night, after weeks of cajoling, I convince him to take me out for drinks. We end up at a tiny bar in the Bronx, a sketchy hole in the wall, where we're anonymous. When we walk in, not one person glances our way.

"See, Marcus?" I say. "Told you."

I'm wearing a full face of makeup, red red lipstick. High heels. Fishnet stockings. A tight leather skirt. I dress slutty for Marcus, the way he likes women. In this way, he's like a man from the nineteen fifties, which I find bewildering and sad. He talks a lot about fucking, he flirts like a dog. He sneaks porn on the sly. He's hired hookers in the past. What about his wife? Does she like sex too? She does not, he says. New subject.

Marcus orders a beer. The bartender looks at me. "Dirty martini," I say boldly, as if this is my usual. My stomach flips over, afraid he'll refuse or demand my ID. "Sure," he says.

I'm not sixteen yet, I want to shout, giddy from the deception.

Marcus thinks it's funny too. "Guess there are no rules anymore."

When my drink comes, I swallow it in one go.

"Hey, hey, kiddo," he says. "Slow it down."

I order another, then a third. Marcus switches to whiskey. Soon, we're drunk. Well, I am. We laugh uproariously at everything, funny or not. He touches my thighs, my face. I lean in too far and almost fall off my stool. When I catch myself, I look up.

I gasp. Anton is sitting across the bar. His son, Joey, is to his right.

Quickly, I grab Marcus. "We have to go." My heart clangs in my chest. I look again. Anton is still there. But is it Anton? I can't tell, it's so dark.

In the cab, speeding downtown, Marcus soothes me. "Don't think twice about it." He's not worried; or if he is, doesn't show it. "You're not sure it was him. Or if he saw us." The other point he didn't make, though I know he thought it: Anton Rivera is a doorman. Joey Rivera is his son. Neither of them is a person worth considering, if a person at all.

28

WOOZY, I STEP OUT OF THE ELEVATOR. THE HOUSE IS DARK except for a dim light in the celebration room. I head down the hall, and find Lawrence slumped in his chair, watching CNN with the sound off.

"Why are you sitting in the dark?" I switch on the lamp.

"Wow, that's bright." He shields his eyes.

Lawrence is holding a wineglass; an empty bottle sits on the floor. Clearly, the stress is crushing him. His hair is matted, his cheeks are sunken. There's a dusting of white stubble on his chin. He looks beaten down.

I shut off the light and sit down on the couch.

"Have a glass of wine," he says.

"Nothing for me, thanks." I don't like to drink with Lawrence, but I'll keep him company. I glance at the TV. "Any news about Billy?"

He shakes his head. "Not yet, but it's coming. Just watch. By mid-September—boom. The whole thing will explode again."

"You still think he should take a plea?" I look at the screen instead of at him.

"Well, Cass, here's what will happen if he doesn't. The press will ramp up their efforts. They will enter this house, take out their knives, and carve up the walls. They will expose every intimate detail they find, meaningful or not, and trump up a story to get readers. Clicks and eyeballs—that's the news model. The public will hang Billy weeks before his trial even starts."

"And Billy will go to prison forever."

"And yes, your brother will go to prison. You know what else? The Stockton-Quinn foundation will lose any hope of funding. No one will offer Nate a job. My clients will dry up. Eleanor will be ostracized. God knows what will happen to you—or where any of us will live once we're forced out of here."

"What are you talking about?"

"Billy will get out of prison eventually. When he does, there's no way these hypocritical Valmont fucks will allow a registered sex offender to live in the building."

Stupidly, I hadn't considered this.

"We can make a deal," Lawrence says. "Yes, Billy will plead guilty, that's awful. But Peter got Anderson down to five years and said they might fold on the registry."

"You're dreaming if you think Anderson will give up the sex registry. I'm sorry, Lawrence, but Eleanor is right. Billy should go to trial. I'm sticking with Eleanor on this one." Eleanor, Eleanor, Eleanor. I repeat her name to piss him off. His willingness to forsake his son disgusts me. Grow a pair, I want to snap. Don't be such a coward.

"If we do, we will forever be known as Lawrence Quinn, father of convicted rapist William Quinn; Eleanor Quinn, mother of convicted rapist; Nathaniel Quinn, brother of convicted rapist; Cassandra—"

"My name is Forrester. I'm not a Quinn, remember? You just let me use that name so I can pretend I'm a part of this family. It's not real."

Lawrence's eyes water as if I smacked him. "You have an answer for everything, don't you?" His tone is nasty.

Haggerty said the same thing. Speaking of Haggerty, I haven't heard from him in weeks. His texts are intrusive and possibly unethical, but I've started to miss them. "I'm tired, Lawrence."

"You know what, Cass? I'm tired too. And no one is helping me, no one is on my side. Not even you. Out of everyone, I thought I could count on you."

"I'm not on your side. I'm not on Eleanor's side either. I'm on Billy's side."

"But I was the one who—"

"Who what? Took me in? Fed me? You're using my being orphaned as a bargaining chip?"

"That's not what I'm saying—" He stops. "Forget it. Doesn't matter. I'm just disappointed. I thought you'd be more loyal. More forgiving."

Forgiving? "Christ, Lawrence. You and Eleanor both—you're relentless."

"No, Cass." Lawrence bows his head. "Billy's our son. We're desperate."

29

PEOPLE WITH MONEY DO CRAZY THINGS. OR MAYBE MONEY makes people go crazy. Once, two brothers, lifelong bachelors, moved into a primitive shack with no indoor plumbing or electricity. They looked like hoboes, lived like hoarders, rarely bathed, and refused to open any mail that could be from the government. This went on until their nineties. After their death, their land sold for almost six million dollars. Turned out they were loaded. So maybe money just makes crazy people even crazier.

* * *

Billy is broody and distant. I understand his unhappiness, and sympathize, but being around him is depressing. It's like when he went off to boarding school. He hated Groton, and called every day, begging to come home. He was shy and self-conscious. He didn't fit in and had a hard time making friends. His stutter returned, only to be made worse by Powell Porter's taunts.

Lawrence encouraged Billy to stay. "You'll get used to it," he promised. "It's brutal, I know. But I survived, and you're ten times stronger and smarter than me. You'll survive too." He believed Groton would teach Billy important life skills. Billy felt like he was being punished for no reason. Eleanor, surprisingly, didn't interfere. "Fathers and sons always struggle," she said. "They'll work it out."

Groton marked a before and after in my brother's life. He left for school a dreamy, gentle adolescent, my twin and soulmate, and returned a confident, if sullen, young man, one I barely recognized. He was still committed to medicine, though his new goal was pediatrics, partly because of his stutter, partly for reasons I'll never comprehend. I am Billy's sister. I know his habits, his favorite foods, and his preferences in music, books, and movies. I can tell you he wants to be a doctor and loves to run, but I can't tell you why. Once Billy graduated from high school, I had no insight into his interior life. My not-knowing implies a lack of curiosity or caring, which isn't true. I am curious. I care deeply. But I don't know how to recapture our old relationship. I realize he's a man, I can see that he's different. And yet, at the same time, I can't believe the small boy I grew up with, the tender kid who loved *Sesame Street,* has been accused of rape.

The next morning, I seek him out. I'm here, I should make an effort. So I put on gym shorts and sneakers, and stand in the door to his room. "Hey, Elmo. Let's go for a run."

He's lying on his side, staring at the wall. "It's too hot."

"Then we'll walk. We can carry parasols."

He doesn't respond, so I move to his bed and lie down. It's a queen-sized bed, so there's more than enough room—or there would be if not for the books, papers, half-eaten sandwiches, and loose bags of chips.

Eleanor must be exhausted. She'd never allow this much clutter otherwise. After Billy's arraignment, Lawrence and Nate cleaned out his dorm room and gym locker, and brought home a carload of suitcases, boxes, and bags. Billy dumped the entire haul on his floor and hasn't touched it since. Clothes are strewn over his desk and chair, dresser drawers hang open, and sneakers are scattered across the carpet like stepping-stones. His plastic dinosaurs, baseball cards, and rock samples are hidden behind stacks of textbooks, water pipes, and a bong.

It kills me to see Billy so unhappy. Except for twice-weekly psychiatrist appointments and meetings with DeFiore, he does nothing except watch TV on his laptop and sleep. He doesn't even look like himself. His once-lean body is doughy. His face is bloated and shadowed with stubble. His eyes are dull and unfocused. He smells foul.

"Come on, Billy. We have a trial to prep for. DeFiore says first impressions are critical. So, you have to clean up and get in shape."

"*We?* Since when do *we* have a trial, Cassie?"

His anger catches me off guard. "What does that mean?"

"You don't live here anymore. I don't need you waltzing in, telling me I'm fat, and acting like you give a shit about what happens to me."

"Of course I give a shit," I tell him. "But you're right. I have been wrapped up in myself. I am sorry for that and will make it up to you. In the meantime, I'm here now, and I'm not going anywhere. Billy, I can see you're scared. We all are. I want to help you, so let me, okay? First, you have to sit up. Please? Look at me."

Groaning theatrically, Billy complies. He won't meet my gaze, but I place my hand on his arm. "Billy." My voice is gentle. "Is there anything about Diana you didn't tell DeFiore?"

"What are you really asking, Cassandra?"

"Will you take me through the night one more time?"

At first, Billy doesn't reply, as if considering where to start. Oh good, I think in relief. We're going to talk. But I misjudged his silence.

A beat later, he explodes, like gunpowder packed into a pipe.

"Who *the fuck* are *you?*" He's so enraged he is spitting. I had no idea he harbored such fury. "Seriously, who *the fuck* do you think you are?" Up on his knees, he shouts in my face. "I told the cops everything! I told the lawyers everything! I have been over that night a hundred times. So, no. I have nothing more to say—not to you." Billy pushes me back. "Get out of here, Cassie. I'm serious."

I don't move. *Hey, Elmo, where are you? What happened to you?* I study him closely, try to catch a glimpse of my brother in this stranger's red face. His eyes fill with tears. Embarrassed, he swipes at them with the back of his hand.

"Hey," I say softly, just as he shoves me, hard, with both hands.

Flying off the bed, I land flat on the floor. My back hits with such force that my breath gets knocked out. Looming above my face, Billy grabs my T-shirt and raises a fist. His eyes are glazed. His jaw is set. He's assessing me with a cold calculation that freezes my blood.

"Do it. I dare you, Billy." He wants to hit me; we both feel it. And I want him to. We feel that too. "Do it, please." My body is jacked up; every nerve, every fiber is tingling. The feeling is as intense, as demanding, as the desire to fuck. "Please, Billy. Just once."

"Stop, Cassie! Jesus." He slumps against the bed. "You're not trying to help me." Billy is crying now, sobs that wrack his whole body. "You're calling me a liar. Which is insane. You're the liar. Your lies ruined my life. Look at me, Cassie. Look what you've done to me. It's time *you* told the truth, not me."

My fear swells and becomes a living thing, slippery and impossible to harness. I force myself to sit still, to stay in this room with my brother and help him find a way out. Meanwhile, I'm cartwheeling, unable to contain the chaos inside me.

"I know you're upset," I say weakly. "But I'm not the one on trial here."

"You should be. If I had the balls, I would tell everyone how fucked up you are."

"My little brother is innocent," I told Haggerty, and I meant it. "He didn't rape Diana Holly."

What I didn't say? He sure as shit has it in him, Detective.

30

SECRETS NEVER DIE. THEY'RE SELF-SUSTAINING ORGANISMS. They exist on a cellular level, so they're part of you, like your hair, your nails, your blood. Secrets grow, divide, and metastasize. You try to bury them. You will yourself to forget. But they fester and swell, roil and spread. Little by little, they rise to the surface. Secrets make your skin itch. Your pulse twitch. They bleed from your pores. Secrets reveal themselves, like shifting tattoos, all over your body.

I'm home three days before it becomes too much. Wearing a baseball cap and sunglasses, I head out for a manicure. It's risky, I know, but it's a Sunday afternoon in August, and most of the press is on vacation. I'd rather face the remaining stragglers than suffocate in my bed.

Summer in the city is not for the weak. The sun beats down from above, streets melt underfoot. The air is heavy, and reeks of urine, unwashed bodies, and rotted garbage.

At the nail place—a cheap one, on Second Avenue—I select the sleaziest, sluttiest red I can find. "Nails and toes, please," I tell the manicurist. Feeling slutty is not the same thing as acting slutty, but it will suffice. I haven't spoken to Marcus since our last call. Nor have I replied to his texts. Already, I feel stronger.

Forty minutes later, I'm at the dryers, staring out at the street, when I see Avery stroll past. *What is she doing here?* She's spotted me too. We lock eyes through the glass. I raise my hand.

Next thing I know, she's sitting in the empty chair beside me. "Presentation of the nails, please" is the first thing she says.

I hold up my fingers, wriggle my toes.

"Nice." Avery nods in approval. "Very nice."

"You like?" I blow on my nails to make them dry faster.

"Love, Chickadee."

In nursery school, we had baby chicks in our classroom. They were so soft and cuddly it was impossible not to squeeze them, especially for Avery, who adored animals. One morning, she was so excited, she couldn't help herself, and squeezed too hard. It was touch and go for a minute, but the chick survived. Still, our teacher forbid Avery from touching them. Avery was inconsolable. So I smuggled one out during recess. "Look!" I opened my coat pocket. "Your chickadee."

Avery's hair is the same glorious gold it was back in April, when I saw her in the bodega. Her creamy skin is clear. She's as skinny as a rail. Normally, I'd be sick with jealousy but I'm so grateful she's talking to me, I'm thrilled for her.

"Why are you stuck in the concrete jungle?" I ask. "No beach this summer?"

"I work in PR. It's a fucking grind. But, hey, it's a living."

"Another day, another dollar."

We both laugh. Neither of us needs to work; we just like to talk that way.

"What about you?" she asks. "No family compound?" Then answers her own question. "Oh, shit. I forgot. How's Billy?"

"Hanging in. We all are."

"That's good. I'm so sorry, Cassie. That girl, Diana Holly, is cuckoo-nutty. Langley knows her from Princeton. Once, she hooked up with Chase Braxton—remember him? His sister Ella was two years behind us? Chase had a girlfriend, which Diana knew, but after, she showed up at his eating club every day for, like, a week. I mean, this was a while ago, but there it is, right?" Avery is somber. "Billy will be okay. I'm sure of it."

I study my fingers. This red is stunning, I decide. "Emma. Chase Braxton's sister. Her name was Emma. I hadn't heard that story. Tell Langley thanks."

Langley is Avery's brother. Seems odd to thank him.

There's a long silence that neither of us knows how to fill. I have to apologize, but "I'm sorry" and "please forgive me" seem insufficient. I hate myself, I want to say. If I could, I'd go back to Miss Meredith's class and meet you all over again. I consider telling her the truth about

Marcus, which is the biggest offering I can think of. Especially if I describe how harshly he rejected me.

After our drunken night in the Bronx, Marcus cools off. Maybe Anton saw us. Maybe he didn't. Doesn't matter. Marcus decides it's too
risky. He doesn't contact me for a week. Then two. I text Avery, suggest a movie. She ices me out for a day then agrees. "I'm sorry I've
been so fucked up," I say when we meet. "I have a crush." Avery wants
to know about him, what he's like, where he goes to school. "He's
older" is all I say. "Doesn't live around here." We used to dissect every
minute of every day. I know my lack of detail is hurtful, and I can feel
her keeping a protective distance. But by then, losing Avery is the least
of my problems. I'm also losing the rest of my life. Before Marcus, I
was a superstar: straight As, Model Congress, Model UN. After Marcus, I hit the earth at full tilt. Unable to stop myself, I text him over and
over and over and over: Please, I need you

Finally, a reply: Tuesday afternoon. Riverside. By the ducks.

My heart seizes. I text back:

They're drakes

He doesn't respond. And then:

Xoxo

I'm overwhelmed with relief. Which is why, in the park, when I
lunge toward him, his refusal is so shattering. "No." His voice is sharp,
angry. "Stop it."

"Stop? Why?"

"We can't see each other anymore."

"But you *told* me to meet you."

"I made a mistake. I'm sorry."

Marcus walks off. I'm left alone on the bench, with the ducks. Alone
and exposed, alone and unloved, alone and unwanted. It's not over, I
decide. He'll come back. I'll just wait.

Months pass. I wait. I wait out his shitty business deals. I wait out his
conference calls. I wait out his sad, sexless marriage. I wait out his cold,
brittle wife. I wait out his porn and his hookers. I wait and I watch. I
measure everything. I am hyperaware of any change, on guard for a
sign. I learn patience, I learn endurance. I learn no one can wait this

long. No one, not even me, the strongest girl in the world. I call him. I beg. "We love each other. Please don't leave me."

"This is over, Cassie. You have to stop."

He's still angry. This is my fault. Why did I come on so strong? Why did I force him to go to a bar? My shame and self-loathing curdle in my stomach. I wield them with gusto. I self-destruct. Drink too much. Smoke too much. Lash out for no reason. I call Avery an idiot, make plans and blow her off. Do it again. Then a third time. We've been best friends for most of my life, but I can't stand one second in her presence.

Finally, she's had enough. "I'm sick of your shit. You're a selfish bitch." I know she's right. I break down in tears. But Avery is a teenage girl too. She, like me, is an ambush predator. She wants me to hurt as much as she does. Next thing I know, the rumors sweep through Spence like wildfire. Every day, a new one circulates: *Cassie Quinn cheated in AP History. Cassie Quinn fucked Powell Porter. Cassie Quinn is hooked on Adderall.*

Forsaken by all my friends, I can't leave my room. I cry in my bed, won't go to school. When my parents ask what's wrong, I tell them, conveniently, that Avery and I had a fight. "She turned everyone against me." They're appropriately horrified. "No one is more dangerous than a teenage girl," Eleanor says. She threatens to call Avery's parents, but I beg her not to, knowing it'll just make things worse. Marcus, meanwhile, still isn't returning my calls. I hate him beyond all rational thought. I hate him so much I can't swallow. I can't breathe. I'm drowning in my own misery. I lose ten pounds, the one upside.

Frightened, Eleanor takes me to a social worker, a psychologist, a psychiatrist. No one can help me. Not because they don't try, but because they don't know I'm waiting. Finally, I see a shrink who suggests inpatient treatment. I'm skeptical but agree to check into a psych ward for three days. Surprisingly, it helps. In the hospital, we talk about feelings. When you feel so much, the doctor says, you get confused. So your feelings may be about other feelings than the feelings you're feeling.

Is she speaking English, I wonder? I don't know this language. Aloud, I apologize. "I'm sorry," I tell her. "I don't understand what you're saying. Your words make no sense."

Feel your feelings, she repeats. Feel your feelings.

From this, I gather one insight: the only way to leave this place is to surrender something sacred. So I tell her about Marcus. He acted like he wanted me, and I think he did, but then one day he didn't, and left me alone with my feelings.

What are your feelings? she asks.

"Sometimes, I feel rage, sorrow, and desperation. Other times, I feel love, affection, and adoration." What I don't tell her is that my feelings are so deep they're deadly, and I feel all of them, all at once, all the time. It's too much to bear so I try to feel nothing.

She thanks me for sharing. Sometimes, she tells me, we mistake kindness for love. Gratitude for devotion. Pity for desire. As I told you, Cassie, it can be confusing.

It sure can, I agree, lacing up my sneakers, grabbing my coat. Thank you; you're very nice, thank you; goodbye. I race out of there feeling nothing.

I text him. Then I wait.

I'm sixteen and one-quarter. No longer a kid. A woman who knows her own mind. A woman who's seen hard times. And just like that, something shifts.

Marcus replies: I miss you. I miss the ducks.

Marcus calls. "You weaken me."

Finally, I think.

The next time we meet, he kisses me, hard. I want you; he tells me. I've wanted you for so long. I can't stop myself. I can't help myself.

No way, I think. I can't tell Avery any of this. I realize my nails are dry. She's watching me. "Let's get a drink," I say instead.

"Let's." She pauses. "Cassie, I—"

"Yes?" I look up. If I were a better person, I'd say, I'm sorry, Avery. I really screwed up. I lost my mind and here's how it happened.

"Billy will be okay," she says.

"Thanks, Avery. Your hair looks amazing. It's perfectly you. I'll text you," I add, which I mean sincerely, but she's already out the door and back on the street.

31

THE NEXT NIGHT, LAWRENCE AND I ARE IN THE KITCHEN, FOR-
aging for food. He's eating Oreos, half a sleeve, one at a time. Seeing
Avery has put me in a foul mood I can't shake. But Lawrence is pissing
me off too. Sometimes all it takes is the sound of him chewing to trigger
my rage.

"Where's Eleanor?" he asks, looking around. I nod at the terrace.
"With Nate. They're both brooding."

"In the dark?" At the French doors, he watches her through the
glass. "She's smoking again," he says absently, as if addressing a studio
audience. "She promised to quit. Now look."

"Everyone makes promises, Lawrence. Give her a break." I take
raspberries, blueberries, and blackberries out of the refrigerator and
cut them into a fruit salad. He plucks a blueberry from my collection
and puts it in his mouth.

I snatch my bowl out of his reach. "These are mine," I say. "Get
your own."

"Oh wow, Princess, you're selfish."

He's teasing but I won't engage. "Maybe I am. What of it?" Behind
me, he puts both his hands on my shoulders, requesting a truce. I shrug
him off.

"Why are you mad at me?" he asks. "What did I do?"

"I'm not mad. I'm not anything. I just think you're wrong about
Billy."

"I got that memo, Cassie. Your opinion has been registered with
the committee. But I'm closer to the case than you are. I speak to
Peter every day. Not for nothing, but you've been out of town all
summer."

Lawrence digs two fingers into my bowl, scoops out more berries, and slides the juicy clump into his mouth. Grinning, he shows off stained lips and teeth.

I don't laugh. He's right: I am angry. I'm infuriated. My anger may be disproportionate to the crime, but it feels righteous. "Lawrence, gross! You're repulsive."

Repulsive. The word distracts me. When I was a child, if a word was multisyllabic and sounded grown-up, I repeated it incessantly. *He's repulsive.* The word reminds me of something, a movie? A picture? An image seeps in, a flicker of light from below a closed door. A man and a woman on a bed. The woman's legs are open. *Repulsive.* The man is standing above her, holding his—*He's so repulsive.* My skin twitches. I blink.

"Jesus." Lawrence's eyes widen, and I can tell I've hurt him. "What's gotten into you?"

"*Stop asking me that!*" Fury, erupting as tears, stings my eyes.

"Cassandra." His voice is strict, paternal. "You're in a bad mood. That's clear. But don't take it out on me. We disagree about the trial. It's not the end of the world. You're not a child anymore, Cassie. That girl is gone. You can't punish me for not giving you what you want. Those days are over."

A surge of white noise fills my head. My heart starts to race. I lose feeling in my fingers and toes. I know this is true, of course this is true, but when I'm here, in this house, time collapses. I'm thrown back to the past in the present tense; there's no before and no after.

"What do you mean, *gone?*"

"You've matured." Lawrence doesn't realize I've left, that I'm split, that I am twenty-three and sixteen, adult and child, woman and girl. "You've grown up. Act like it."

Act like it, act like it echoes in my ears. "What?" I ask, not because I didn't hear, but because I need him to explain.

"You can't treat me like shit," Lawrence says slowly like I'm an idiot.

"I'm not!" I'll treat you however the fuck I want, I think. "I'm just living my life—at least I'm trying to. But every five minutes, I get called back here. So I race home. Every fucking time. It's like I'm not a real person; I'm just a doll you can manipulate any way you want."

My anger centers me. My pulse slows. I'm able to breathe. I return to the now, the real now, as the past now recedes.

Back in the kitchen, my self clicks into place, reassembled. I glance out the French doors. On the terrace, Eleanor and Nate are sitting side by side. He's smoking too. In the near darkness, plumes of smoke rise into the air then disappear. Sprawled in his chair, Nate is gesturing emphatically, as if making a point. The tip of his cigarette glows. Next to him, Eleanor's spine is straight, and her ankles are crossed. Seeing her so self-possessed, I feel a crush of sorrow for Lawrence. He seems lost and alone. Cast out. I can't remember the last time the family turned against him. In fact, I don't think I ever have.

I resolve to be nicer. He's just trying to keep his son safe. "You're right," I say gently. "That was mean. I'm sorry. Here." I push the bowl of berries across the counter. "There's enough for you."

* * *

On Wednesday morning, the valet brings my car around. I've been home less than a week, but I've reached my limit. I'm heading back to New Haven. Classes start after Labor Day, I told my parents, and I need to get ready. They balked, and rightly so. It doesn't take three weeks to prepare. So, I countered with two visits: for my birthday on August 20 and for one meeting of their choosing with DeFiore. Deal, we agreed.

I'm about to slide into the driver's seat when I notice Anton and Joey huddled with a third man under the porte cochère. I wouldn't think twice, except there's something familiar about the man's threadbare jacket and the way he slouches forward, as if to seem shorter. When he turns sideways, I see his profile and almost pass out. It's Greg Haggerty, the fucking detective.

I get into my car, but Haggerty has already spotted me and is speed-walking over. "Ms. Quinn," he says grandly, grabbing my door before I can close it. "We meet again."

"What the fuck? Are you *following me?*"

"What are you gonna do?" He chuckles. "Call the cops?" His face is flushed from the heat, his thin hair pasted to his scalp. Seeing this reminds me of his unannounced appearance in June, our two-hour conversation, his probing questions.

"Seriously," I ask, hoping I don't sound as uneasy as I feel. "Why are you at my parents' house?"

"Don't worry. I'm not here to see you. Just catching up with old friends." He waves toward the door, where Anton and Joey were standing. They're both gone.

"What could you possibly want from them?" I try to swallow, but my throat's dry as dust. I think about that night in the Bronx. The bar, shadowy inside, neither dark nor light. Fizzy laughter. Fishnet stockings. Garish red lipstick on a starched white collar. Idiots, me and Marcus. It's like we were trying to get caught.

Haggerty doesn't answer, instead he studies the Valmont. The building is the crown jewel of New York real estate, but any structure that stands for a century and a half will be leaky, drafty, and plagued by mold. Paying for upgrades is an expensive proposition, and while every resident has the means, none of them wants to open their wallets. This, by the way, is how the wealthy stay wealthy.

"This place has seen better days, Ms. Quinn."

"Call me Cassie. We're old friends. And you've seen better days, too. No offense."

"Right for the heart." He clutches his chest. "You have a tongue like a dagger."

"So I've been told." I pause, change the subject. "Rich people like old things, the older the better." I wave at the Valmont. "It's a funny thing about affluence, Detective. The real rich never talk about money or flash it around. The middle-rich, newly rich, and never-rich are the ones who need to show off."

"Explains why Lawrence is such a peacock."

"He's not a peacock. The man has more money than he'll ever spend."

Haggerty laughs. "Lawrence has no money, Ms. Quinn. We both know that."

"It's Cassie. And what's your problem with Lawrence?" I don't give him a chance to reply, mostly because I'm not sure I can believe anything he says. "Well, I need to head out. Good talk, Detective."

"I think you do want to talk, actually. You've been telling me about Marcus Silver since our very first conversation. I didn't even have to ask. You dropped him on my doorstep like a cat drops a mouse." His keys chirp, and a black SUV lights up. "See you soon, Ms. Quinn."

32

THE FRIDAY BEFORE LABOR DAY, WE GATHER IN DEFIORE'S office. The place is deserted; he's the only one working over the holiday weekend. He called us in because he thinks the DA's latest offer is worth considering. My parents, in turn, summoned me. "You still owe us one visit," Lawrence said. "I'm cashing in my chit." I've already fulfilled my birthday obligation by coming home for steaks on the grill, lots of champagne, and presents in the celebration room. We tried to act joyous, but Nate got trashed, Billy was a bitch, and my parents bickered. Thankfully, I was too stoned to care. Today, I'm not stoned at all, and anxious to get this meeting over with.

"Let's talk the offer through like adults," DeFiore advises as we take our seats at the long conference table.

I cannot believe I'm here. Up at school, I was able to distance myself from the case. I regained my sanity. I saw Eddie at the Neighborhood Café. I chowed down on Little Italy burritos. I swam every day. I bought textbooks, notepads, and brand-new pens. After a lazy, sluggish summer, New Haven is coming alive. Students are returning to campus, and by next week, the restaurants and bars will be packed. Seated in this freezing room with my cranky, fucked-up family, talking about my sullen brother's rape trial, I resent being pulled back into this life, this mess.

"As I said, five years is the best offer we're likely to get." DeFiore's cheeks are rosy with a soccer-field sunburn. He turns to Billy. "I am confident in my recommendation that you take it—and fast."

I roll the word *confident* on my tongue. A *confident* man, a *confidence* man. Like Lawrence, DeFiore is confident people will listen when he speaks. His confidence inspires trust, a willingness to believe what he says despite evidence to the contrary. Also, like Lawrence, DeFiore repeats himself ad nauseum until it's easier to give in than to continue arguing.

Billy's case is taking a toll on my family. I see this every time I leave and come back. My parents and brothers are bedraggled and pasty like they haven't seen daylight for months. Eleanor is fully made up, but the top button of her jacket is loose, and her stockings have a run.

"What are the terms?" Eleanor asks.

"Felony rape and assault of an unconscious person. In return, he's offering five years in a level-two minimum-security facility. Billy will serve three years, less for good behavior."

"What about the registry?"

"Yes, Eleanor; he'll have to register as a sex offender. That's non-neg—"

"No." The word is out of her mouth before he can finish.

Lawrence looks at his wife. "Don't be so quick." He turns to Billy, places a hand on his knee. "What do you want to do, son?"

My brother shrugs. Mumbles a non-answer.

"Billy!" Lawrence is pissed. "We're asking you a question."

Raising his head, my brother glances at DeFiore. I can't tell if he's stoned and thinks he looks normal or if he's intentionally moving in slow motion.

"Billy, listen," DeFiore says patiently, "if we try this case and lose, you're looking at twenty years in a level-five prison. Level-five is a maximum-security penitentiary. That means a whole different kind of life."

"Then don't lose," Nate says. "Last April, you wanted to go after Diana with both barrels. Now it's okay if my brother gets locked up for five years? What happened to speaking out for all the innocent men caught in the system? Whose lives have been ripped apart by hysterical feminists and false accusations?" He turns to Billy. "You didn't do it. Don't let your lawyer fuck you because he turned out to be a pussy."

"Nate," Lawrence says. "Tone it down."

DeFiore is unfazed. "I told you this before, Nate. But I'll keep repeating it until it sinks in. A trial isn't about innocence. It's about what a DA can prove. And their evidence seems solid."

Nate scoffs. "Jesus, Peter. A few months ago, their evidence was shit. It changes every day. Which is it? Solid or shit? Make up your fucking mind."

"I said take it easy," Lawrence snaps. "Or excuse yourself." He apologizes to DeFiore.

"It's fine, Lar. I understand his frustration." DeFiore tries to explain. "The prosecution's evidence *is* weak. But it's solid enough to tell a believable story. They have credible eyewitnesses, CCTV footage, and corroborating reports. They have semen and vaginal tearing. They have interviews with the girl's friends, family, and roommates. They all say the exact same thing." DeFiore ticks off his fingers. "One, the girl broke up with Billy, which made him angry. Two, he stalked and threatened her on several occasions—"

"Peter," Nate interrupts. "For God's sake, *he* broke up with *her*—"

"Three, on the night in question, the girl blacked out and Billy raped her."

"The hospital report was inconclusive—"

"And four, Billy shows no remorse."

"What are you talking about? How is he not showing remorse?"

"I'm looking at him right now. Billy, sorry pal, but you do not look the least bit remorseful. You look like a privileged, pissed-off jock who's never been told 'no' in his life."

Billy's head jerks up. "What the fuck? You don't even know me."

"Hey, hey, hey." Lawrence makes a patting gesture. "Let's stay civil."

"You people don't get it," DeFiore says. "Anderson will decimate Billy. They won't just bring in witnesses from the scene. They'll wrangle every person the girl has ever met to testify against him. They'll say he is damaged, violent, and dangerous. They'll paper the room with pictures of the girl's face and body. They'll go after him like rabid dogs. I've seen every piece of evidence. It's enough to put him away for a very long time."

"You told us that most of it is circumstantial or inconclusive," I say.

"No, the sheriff's and EMT's reports *are not* inconclusive. They both say the girl was unconscious. She scored a thirteen on the Glasgow coma scale. Fully aware is fifteen."

"But they can't prove Billy *knew* it," I say. "And we have evidence too: Diana's texts, pictures of them kissing, the shattered Audi. You must've spoken to the insurance company. So why can't you argue that Billy is a victim of a culture where accusations are no longer questioned? Where women's feelings eclipse men's civil rights? I mean, you'll say it more eloquently, obviously, but isn't that what you originally planned?"

"It's risky, Cassie. Let's say we argue three points. A passionate affair that ended badly. A consensual hook up between former lovers. And a rejected girl hell-bent on revenge. When we explain the blackout with binge drinking, it's a plausible narrative. We chip away at the evidence, raise reasonable doubt, and end up with a hung jury. Then again, if we make the girl the aggressor and Billy the victim, we might alienate everyone. The press, the public, the court, not to mention the jury. He's too rich and too handsome. People are already gunning for him."

The room is quiet for several long minutes.

"Then focus on Billy," Eleanor finally says. "On his prior hardships, his commitment to public service, his plans for medical school. He's a good kid, Mr. DeFiore. Can't you use that to his advantage?"

"If we talk about how good Billy is, Mrs. Quinn, then we also have to talk about where he came from. His values. Each one of you. We open the door for the DA to put the entire family on trial. If that happens, some of you will have to testify, which raises more problems than it solves. To a jury, family members are the least objective and therefore the least credible."

"I thought you wanted us to testify," I say.

"I did. Now I don't."

"Well, Mr. DeFiore, that's what we want."

"Put the family on trial, Mrs. Quinn, and it is open season on everyone." DeFiore looks directly at me. Unafraid, I hold his gaze. He blinks first.

Eleanor doesn't seem to notice. "Mr. DeFiore, stop finding reasons not to do your job. You won't just focus on Billy, of course. You'll also focus on the girl. Show the jury who she is too. She pursued Billy and pressed him for a commitment. She coerced him into attending the party. She took drugs. She drank too much, blacked out, and woke up confused. She blamed her mistakes on him to save herself embarrassment, and to hurt him for rejecting her. My son is a solid citizen. Look at all he overcame. Look at our family, how we took in Cassie, gave her a home and a family. She's willing to testify. Aren't you, Cassie? You'll get on the stand and talk about your brother."

"Of course, Eleanor. I'll do anything for this family."

"There are lots of risks in that approach, Mrs. Quinn."

"We'll take them, Mr. DeFiore."

He appraises us, one by one. "If we do go to trial, it will take a lot to get ready. Not on my side—on yours. A trial is like a staged play in front of an audience. It happens in real time, so there's no room for error. Each of you is part of the cast, even if all you do is sit in the gallery. You'll be scrutinized as closely as the principal actors. You'll need to work hard to prepare. Listen. Take notes. Rehearse. Follow directions down to the letter."

"We're up for it," Nate promises. "Whatever we need to do."

"Let me think about it." Again, DeFiore glances my way, but I study my hands. I can barely sit still. The God-awful twitching is killing me.

* * *

On the way home, Lawrence and Eleanor are snapping at each other. Like a summer squall, the air in the car grows dark and foreboding then the skies split apart.

"I don't appreciate the way you kept interrupting me, Eleanor," Lawrence says sharply. "You may disagree, but at least let me finish my sentence."

Eleanor glances out the window. Her eyes are hidden behind large sunglasses, but there's the hint of a smirk on her lips. "Lawrence, I don't appreciate you jeopardizing my son's future."

"*Our* son. If anyone is jeopardizing Billy's future, it's you. You're jeopardizing all our futures. Why would you let Cassie and Nate testify? They're not DeFiore's clients. Billy is. DeFiore has no reason to protect the rest of us."

"We don't need his protection! None of us is hiding anything— except you, maybe."

"What am I hiding? We've been married for thirty fucking years."

"Let's start with your money issues, your job issues, your crazy foundation—"

"What money issues?" Lawrence's eyes widen. He looks genuinely bewildered.

"It seems to me that a man who is unable to provide for his family, a man who is dependent on his wife to feed himself and his children might have a few money issues." She adjusts her glasses. "Just a thought."

The color drains from Lawrence's face. His breathing grows ragged. For one shocking second, he is wholly unfamiliar, a man who'll rear back and roar. Instead, he glances behind him, at me and my brothers. Then his anger flickers and goes out, like a blown light bulb.

Cracking his window, Lawrence lets in a gust of hot air. For a partnership to endure, he once told me, one person has to be the peacemaker. Someone has to take it on the chin. "Eleanor," he says softly. "I don't want to argue. We're all we have. We'll work this out."

"Of course we will." She stares at the passing scenery. "Of that I have no doubt."

In the backseat, Nate reaches across Billy to nudge me. *We need to fix this.*

33

HOURS LATER, NATE PUSHES ME TO GO FOR A DRINK. "LET'S get out of this house. Put on your shoes, Cassie."

"You barely speak to me. Why should I go anywhere with you?"

Snatching a Columbia ballcap off a hook, he pauses. "Please."

Feeling pathetic but grateful for his attention, I follow him out the door like a dutiful dog.

When we step into the muggy night, he asks a valet to hail a cab. I look around for Anton or Joey, but neither is working. "Isn't it weird that Anton hired Joey?" I ask Nate, wondering what they told Haggerty about me. "Have you spoken to him?"

"To Joey? About what? We have nothing in common. For one thing, he's gainfully employed." Nate's voice is clipped. "And no, it's not weird at all. These jobs get passed down all the time. You've lived in this building your whole life, Cassie. How do you not know that?"

"Nate, what's your problem? Are you mad because I've been away? I come home every time you call. Is it because I blew off the foundation? I'm sorry I left you in the lurch, but it's been over a year, and you have to let it go."

A cab pulls up, and we slide into the back. Nate directs the driver to Mercer Street, and then says, "Cassie, this may come as a shock, but not everything is about you. I don't give a shit that you went to grad school. Your life is your life. Be free and prosper. Nor do I care about the foundation. I'm aware this project is more pie-in-the-sky bullshit from my father. At the moment, Billy is my primary concern. Mom and Dad are headed for mutually assured destruction. We need to figure something out."

The city is quiet. The cabdriver navigates the empty streets, and we make it down to Tribeca in record time. "Thanks, man." Nate hands him a fifty. "Keep it."

He leads me inside a sports bar, where we're hit with a blast of cool air and loud music. The interior is upscale and clubby, with polished wood floors and leather stools. Large-screen TVs hang on the walls, each showing a different sport—baseball, soccer, golf.

"Hey, Tess." Nate introduces me to the bartender. She's a slender brunette with short, spiky hair and muscular arms. "Two Absolut and tonics. Double limes for my sister, please."

"You remembered the limes." This makes me so irrationally happy I almost tear up.

"It's a lime, Cassie, not a kidney. Why are you always such a drama queen?"

"I don't know, Nate." I shake my head. "Why can't you just let me have it?"

Our drinks arrive. We clink glasses then sit. It's not uncomfortable.

"Dad says you start classes next week. Excited?"

"Yeah. Looks like it's really happening."

"I'm glad, Cass. It was a smart idea. I mean, what else were you gonna do? Live with Mom and Dad forever?" He glances at me sideways. "Or maybe you had a different plan?"

"Like what? Killing Eleanor in her sleep and stealing her fortune? I don't have that kind of strength. Nor do I need her money, thank God."

Nate holds up his glass. "Well, here's to your great escape. May it last longer than mine." He finishes his drink in one swallow. "Another Absolut and tonic, Tessie. Actually"—he checks my glass—"two more, please."

The drinks arrive and we clink again. Then Nate says, "DeFiore is giving up."

"Maybe not. Maybe he's trying to do what's best for Billy."

"Shoving a plea down his throat is not what's best. You have to convince DeFiore to stay the course. Promise me you'll talk to him."

"And say what?"

"*Do your fucking job, you sloppy fuck; don't pussy out.*"

"I can't imagine that will go over well, Nate."

"Aw, Cass. Don't be modest. DeFiore is your biggest fan. You know you have the magic touch with middle-aged men."

"Has it occurred to you that DeFiore may be right? We don't know what really happened with Diana. I tried talking to Billy . . ." I trail off because Nate's jaw has tightened.

"Leave him alone." He bites off the words.

"But if we can get him to tell us—"

"Did you not hear me?" Nate's voice is acid. "Billy does not want to talk to you. If you keep trying, you'll be sorry."

Tess sets down our drinks.

"Thanks, Tessie. You're the best." Nate pushes a glass my way. "Two limes for the girl with the big mouth who needs to shut the fuck up."

I try to defuse his anger. *Don't be mad at me. Please, Nate.* "Tess has awesome arms."

"You should see her ass." *It's not just you. I'm mad at everyone.* He gives me a goofy grin. "Shots? Hey Tessie, two shots of Jager, please."

I screw up my nose. "Repulsive." *They're so repulsive.*

"You're repulsive," Nate says. We watch Tess as she pours two green shots and slides them over. Nate holds one up. "L'chaim." He downs the liquor and smacks his glass on the bar. "Awesome."

An hour later, my brother and I are many drinks deep. While Nate is engrossed in a conversation with Tess, I excuse myself and go to the ladies' room. Sitting down to pee, I lose my balance and hold out my hands to steady myself. I'm drunk, but not so drunk that Nate's crack about older men doesn't bother me. I never told him about Marcus, but Joey may have. Although if he did, wouldn't Nate have said something to me? I splash water on my face and return to my seat.

In the short time I've been gone, a girl who's not Tess has donned Nate's baseball cap and is perched on his lap. She's stunning, with straight white-blond hair. Her silk dress is barely a slip, and the skinny straps slide off her shoulders, exposing the curve of her breasts. Nate has one of the straps between his teeth.

"This is Leslie," he says, batting his eyes like a cartoon character. Bent over her phone and texting, texting, texting, Leslie doesn't acknowledge me.

I feel someone come up behind me and place his hands on my shoulders. "Cassie, long time." Powell Porter's voice makes my body recoil. I don't want to turn around, but when I do, my smile is dazzling. "Powell," I say. He's with his brother Deacon, whom I nod hello to. Still smiling. Always smiling.

Spotting his buddies, Nate jostles Leslie off his lap so he can greet Powell. Soon, they're clapping each other's backs and shouting while Leslie wanders off, wearing Nate's cap, fingers still flying over her phone.

Waving a hundred-dollar bill, Powell beckons to Tess. "Heineken, please!" He turns to his brother who asks for an Amstel. "Make that two Heineken, Tessie."

"Powell," Deacon asks. "Why are you such a dick?"

"Sorry, Tess," Powell calls out. "Just one."

He and Nate laugh like this is the funniest thing they've ever heard. Deacon looks at me and rolls his eyes. "Fucking asshole, right?"

"He's your brother, so it would be rude to comment. But yeah, he's a big fucking asshole. When your dad runs for mayor, he'll have to hide Powell in a closet. Otherwise, he can kiss Gracie Mansion goodbye."

Deacon cracks a smile. He's a leaner, thinner version of his brother. They both have the same blond curls, but Powell's hair is cropped close to his skull and Deacon has a long, lion-like mane. His round, wire-rimmed glasses make him look like a bohemian musician, but he's actually a computer genius. Like Billy, Deacon goes to Princeton, although he's in their famed math department. According to Nate, he's already fielding job offers from Google and Facebook.

"Cassie, you look great," Deacon says. "When was the last time I saw you?"

"Two summers at least. You and Billy were headed to the airport for—what? Three weeks in Southeast Asia?"

"Oh yeah! It was a month. Great trip, but your mom was mad as fuck. Billy hadn't told her about the extra seven days, and she was anxious to have him home." His face sobers. "How is he?"

I don't answer Deacon because his brother is touching me again. "Cassidy Cakes," Powell says. "What's the good word? Nate says you're starting grad school. An Eli." His voice is accusatory, as if my brother had told him a lie.

"Come on, Powell. What's the first thing you learned in kindergarten? Hands on your own body."

"Still as uptight as ever. Guess some things never change." Sucking down his beer, Powell smiles. "So, did you and Avery ever reconnect?"

"Actually, I saw her a few weeks ago. Are you guys dating?"

"*Dating?* Avery and I can barely make it through one evening without an argument." His eyes light up, like he's stumbled on a sunken treasure. "If I recall, you and Avery had your own tête-à-tête."

"That was forever ago, Powell."

In high school, during one of Nate's blowout parties, Powell sidled up behind me and pressed his cock against my ass. "I'm gonna split you in half," he growled. A year later, he cornered me in Nate's bedroom and wrestled me to the floor. Powell was heavy, like a tank. His weight flattened me as he thrust a knee between my legs, dug his fingers into my thighs. I was struggling to push him off when my brother walked in. "Whoops," Nate said, misinterpreting. "Didn't mean to interrupt." Powell scrambled to his feet. I ran out of the room, trying not to cry.

He's repulsive, I think now. *Repulsive.* Pressure pulses behind my eyes. "I have to go," I announce, licking my teeth. My mouth is numb. Earlier Nate offered me cocaine; I should've said no. When I try to stand up, my legs give way. I grab the lip of the bar for support. Behind me, I hear Powell talking to Nate about Billy.

"I know *for a fact* he's innocent. *Of course,* he's innocent. He can't plead out."

My lips are tingling. "What the fuck do you know, Powell?"

Nate whirls around. "Lighten up, Cassie. Deacon and Powell are on Billy's side."

"Seriously?" Powell is indignant. "You think I don't know how a guy gets railroaded? Brody Leighton's cousin? At Duke? Met a girl on Tinder. Took her for dinner. Used a condom. Stayed the night. The whole fucking nine. Still, the girl reported him. Next thing the guy knows, he's booted out of Duke and working at Best Buy."

"A condom?" I feign incredulity. "That's consent right there, brah."

"Don't be an asshole, Cassie," Nate says. "Can't you just relax for once in your life?"

"Actually, no, I can't." My jaw aches, my head roars. Nothing makes sense. Why is he discussing Billy in public, much less with Powell? It's our family's private business. "Nate, he doesn't know anything about Billy's case."

"We know everything, Cassie Quinn." Powell slides his hands over my bare legs. "Everything about you, everything there is to know."

Oh, how I wished Nate had rushed to my defense. In my fantasies, when he saw Powell humping me, Nate shoved him aside. He raised a hand. Made a fist. Boom! Again and again, Nate punched Powell's lights out. Get off my sister, get off her, get off her, get off her.

"Get off me!" I smack Powell's chest with open palms. "Get the fuck off me."

"Hey! That hurt." Powell is laughing.

I'm shaking. I need to calm down. I stalk off to the ladies' room again, and when I return, Powell and Deacon are gone. Nate orders two more drinks. I sip mine slowly, trying to straighten up. Soon, the bar is almost empty. It's just me and Nate, and he's wasted.

"Why were you such a bitch, Princess?" Nate's supporting his head, barely, with an elbow on the bar. "Those guys believe in Billy. They're standing by him. That means something." He signals for Tess. "Absolut and tonic, please, Tess-tosterone, Tess-ticle, Tess-la, Tess of the d'Urbervilles."

"You sure you need another drink, Nate?" Tess looks at me.

Shaking my head, I mouth a *no*. I pull on Nate's arm. "Come on. Let's go home."

He won't budge. "Those guys *know* Billy is innocent. Their support matters. We need them."

"I understand, Nate. But we have no idea what really happened that night—or what they'll say about Billy in court. Maybe he should take the deal. I told you, I tried talking to him, but he got angry at me. I just wanted to help. I didn't mean to piss him off."

Nate's eyes flutter open; suddenly, he's wide awake. "Cassie, for someone so smart, you are so stupid. Billy is never gonna talk to you. *Never*. Billy hates you, Cassie. I mean, he doesn't *hate* you—he *loves* you, you're his sister. But he can't stand the sight of you."

"What are you talking about?" I'm panicking. The bar feels too dark and too loud. My scalp prickles.

"You know, Cassie. Don't pretend you don't. Diana and Billy broke up because of you. You're the reason for this whole mess. It's your fault. So don't you dare suggest that he plead guilty just to save yourself." Nate stands up. "I love you, Cassie. You're my sister and a sour pickle, but you are also one dangerous cunt. Right now, I wish we never let you into our family. Actually, I wish we never met you." He staggers out.

"Nate, wait." My eyes fill. "Nate, don't leave me." *Nate, I have no idea what you're talking about.* But I do know, of course I know.

34

ALONE, I TRAVEL UPTOWN. WHEN I FINALLY GET HOME, IT'S two-thirty. I stop by the celebration room and find Lawrence in his recliner, flipping through channels. The TV casts off murky shadows that move across his face, making him look like he's underwater. Though he's still wearing the button-down shirt and khakis he had on earlier today, he took off his shoes. On the floor, near the coffee table, his loafers are neatly aligned. They're expertly polished, but both backs are broken where he slides into them.

"You came home." When he glances up, Lawrence's glasses go dark. For a second, he appears to have no eyes. "I wasn't sure you would."

"Stop saying that." I'm very twitchy, too twitchy to sit with him. My brothers hate me. I don't blame them. "You're my family. Where else would I go?"

"You've been drinking."

"So what?" I'm not as drunk as I was earlier. Between the mean things Nate said and the cab ride from Tribeca, I sobered up fast.

"Cassie, I'm just trying to connect." Lawrence sounds hurt. "I've missed you."

You're repulsive.

He pats the couch. "Come, Forever Girl, have a seat. Tell me what's what." There are no whiskey or wineglasses around, but I can smell the booze. "Where's Nate?"

"At his place. We went to a bar in SoHo." I yawn. "I'm exhausted, Lawrence."

"Just two minutes. Please?" His voice, deep and gravelly, pulls me toward him. "It's lonely without you." I do as he asks. Together, we stare at the soundless TV.

"I'm happy you're home," Lawrence says softly. When he talks, I see two heads, his own and his shadow, on the wall. "Everything is better when you're here." He reaches for my hand, which he cradles, gently, in his own.

My breathing slows down. His nice words take some of the sting out of Nate's. Everything I've missed rushes forward. His deep voice. His steady presence. How he tries so hard to make things right. His earnestness. His faith in me. Lawrence enrages me, but I miss him. He makes me nuts, but I love him. Opposing ideas can be simultaneously true; one reinforces the other even as they're both canceled out.

Without warning, my eyes fill, and I let myself cry. It's such a relief, I feel a shift in my chest and my anger weakens. The hard edges loosen, pieces crumble away. What's left begins to soften and slowly awaken. "I miss you, too, Lawrence," I say finally.

When he grins, I see both apprehension and hope in his face, a father worried his forever girl is gone but equally sure she can never not love him.

He's quiet. After a while, I assume he's fallen asleep, but when I get up, he grabs my arm. "I don't know how we got here, kiddo. Once upon a time, I was a cocky young buck with my whole life ahead of me. I felt like a king. I had a stunning wife, three amazing kids, everything money can buy. But it's gone. My career, my family, my boys, you—all of it, gone."

"It's not gone, Lawrence. We're still here. I'm here."

"My best days are behind me, Cassie."

The true story of Lawrence's career is one of overestimated potential, exaggerated promises, and outsized ambition. He started at McKinsey, primed for the C-suite, but corporate life bored him senseless so he quit. After that, he kicked around for a while, did a bit of consulting, a lot of networking, and ended up in politics, where he found his footing. Ten years in, Lawrence was having a terrific run. He was instrumental in the election of two New York state senators and helped to reposition a few others. Word got around. Soon, he was clearing up DWIs, burying sex scandals, and handing out campaign jobs. Eleanor sniffed at this work, which she called lowbrow and undignified.

But Lawrence was happy. Happy enough to set his sights on the big leagues. With Eleanor's backing, the sky was the limit—a national election to manage, maybe even the presidency. But Lawrence aimed too high and got exhausted or distracted—both, more likely. He was never good with details, preferring the meet-and-greets to the sit-and-work. He made mistakes, minor blunders at first, then unforgivable lapses. Clients went elsewhere; referrals dried up. Soon, he was finished. The architect of his own ruin, he had only himself to blame.

At fifty-four, Lawrence has reached the end of the road. Most men in his position would have retired long ago. Some, the morning after their wedding. But he's still thinking big. And to be fair, his nonprofit is an excellent idea with several sources of funding and great potential— that is, if he were conscientious or diligent. If he could focus. If he had leadership qualities. If he were a different man entirely.

The next time Lawrence speaks, he sounds despondent. "Cassie, someday soon you'll marry a nice guy, have a bunch of children, and enjoy a happy life. I want that for you."

"I don't think I'm the marrying kind, Lawrence. Or stable enough to be someone's mother. Girls like me . . ." I don't finish. Better not to talk about girls like me.

He glances over. "Just don't forget, okay? When you're sitting by the fire, with your new family, don't forget. Don't forget we had a life together, once."

"I could never forget, Lawrence. You saved me."

"You saved me too, kiddo." He switches off the TV; the room goes dark. "Let's just sit for a minute. Let's just enjoy each other."

It is nice to be here, with Lawrence. His voice comforts me, and soon my twitching subsides. We used to spend hours in this room, just talking. No subject was off-limits. Like when I was ten and stumbled on my first Triple-X movie. I went directly to Lawrence and told him about it. I was all twisted up. He was uneasy and stilted. But eventually he found his words. "Grown-ups watch these videos together as a way to feel close to each other," he explained.

"But they're disgusting."

"You may think differently someday."

As the years passed, my questions led to more conversations, ones I might have had with Rachel if she were alive. Or Eleanor if she'd been inclined. Lawrence didn't judge or get mad. He gave me answers, offered opinions, and told me stories. I learned about his brothers, whom he missed a great deal. About the bullying at Groton, which was *relentless* and *devastating* (his words). About money. About how he tried, so hard, to be a supportive husband and conscientious dad. The more I heard, the more I wanted to be just like him: strong and noble, loyal and honest. I loved that I was the one he chose to confide in. Admittedly, with Eleanor's society schedule and my brothers away at school, no one else was around. Still, he gave me the greatest gift a father could give his daughter, even though I wasn't his real daughter, and he wasn't my real father. Lawrence made me feel less alone at home, and later, less alone in the world.

"We were happy, weren't we, Cassie? We were a happy family once?"

"I think so," I say softly. "But I'm not really sure."

35

IT'S THE FIRST WEEK OF SEPTEMBER, MY FIRST DAY OF CLASS. Everything has come together. Today I am a new girl, wholesome, fully realized and present. Yale is gorgeous. The buildings are gorgeous. Being here, I'm gorgeous too. I pass ornate cathedrals, arched entranceways, open green spaces, and towers that rise two hundred feet in the air. I understand this is only one part of the city. Minutes away, ramshackle buildings crumble in neglect. Hungry children live in squalor. The elderly die alone. Like impoverished Manhattan, impoverished New Haven is not my town. But the disparity helps me appreciate what I have while churning up guilt and unease.

My appearance today would make Eleanor proud. Despite the warm weather, I'm dressed like a virginal schoolgirl: white blouse with Peter Pan collar, tweed jacket, pleated skirt, and sensible heels. My hair is twisted into a dignified braid. My makeup is minimal: mascara, eyeliner, and a sheen of lip gloss. I hold my books to my chest and stroll up Prospect Street like I've landed the starring role in the all-female remake of *Dead Poets Society*.

At the corner, my phone rings. It's Lawrence, but I don't answer. "Hello, hello, my Sweet Girl," he'll say in a voice so euphoric it scrapes the ceiling. "Wishing you luck." Then he'll ask, nonchalantly, where I've been, what I'm doing, why I haven't been in touch, when I'm coming home. "No pressure, Cassie. We just miss you here." I'll get snared in our usual push-and-pull. When I hang up, in the space between cutting him off and aching with doubt, I'll brim with youth, vitality, and the possibility of freedom.

The ringing stops. A minute later, it starts again. I shut off my phone, tuck it away.

"Let's introduce ourselves," the instructor says in my first class of the semester. "Anyone want to start?"

Lawrence will call me every day for the next several weeks. Occasionally I'll ignore him; most times I won't. My strength is not enough to sustain me. For now, though, for this one moment, I can say no. "My name is Cassandra Forrester," I say to the room. Today, I am no longer a Quinn. Here, in this class, I am reborn.

*   *   *

A few weeks later, I'm drinking iced coffee at a diner when a shadow passes over my computer. A man stands behind me.

"I get the sense you're avoiding me, Ms. Quinn."

"What makes you say that, Detective?"

"Cop's instinct." Haggerty slides into a chair across the table. "You don't look so good."

"If that's your attempt at flirting, so much for your instincts."

"Your brother's trial is in three weeks. Getting anxious?"

"Not at all. Billy is innocent. Justice will prevail."

"That's optimistic given where he's sitting." Haggerty flags down a waitress and orders an unsweetened iced tea. She turns to me. "More coffee, hon?"

"I'm just leaving, thanks." I dig out a few dollar bills, which Haggerty plucks from my hand.

"She'll have another iced coffee. And a slice of apple pie with whipped cream, please."

"I don't eat pie, Detective. You're, like, the shittiest cop ever."

"The pie is for me, Ms. Quinn." Stumped for a comeback, I say, "Oh. Duh." We both crack a smile. But once the waitress leaves, I cut to the chase. "What do you want?"

"We're looking at other issues related to the Lawrence Quinns." He sits back. "Tell me about Lawrence's business—where the money came from, how it flowed, et cetera."

"I told you everything. I have no other details; rather, nothing of significance to you."

"You'd be surprised, Ms. Quinn, by what I consider significant. Which is why I repeat my questions. The story you've been telling me is very different from the story I'm hearing."

"Are you saying I've been lying to you?"

"Sure. Maybe not lying, but distorting, omitting, overplaying. Not that it matters—to me or to your brother's case. Billy is guilty. We have eyewitness statements, CCTV tapes, and physical evidence. Facts are facts, Ms. Quinn. They're not transmutable. My focus is interpretation. The lies you tell because you're not conscious they're lies. Or, you do know they're lies, but you don't, or can't, admit that they're crimes."

"I don't know what you're talking about, Detective."

"You know exactly, Ms. Quinn." Haggerty sits back.

The waitress returns. "One apple pie with whipped cream." She sets down the plate. "Iced tea and more coffee."

Haggerty thanks her, far too effusively for a piece of pie.

"You can't be serious," I say. "What was that about?"

"I'm an appreciative customer. You'll find that I'm always serious, Ms. Quinn. And I think you are too. I think you've been wanting to talk for years."

"You sound more like a shrink than a cop." I keep my voice steady, my hands still. My jaw is clenched so tightly I'm grinding my teeth into dust.

"I grew up in Massachusetts. Poor family, big brains." He pauses, as if this should mean something to me. "Scholarship kid."

"And?"

"I went to Brown, did a BA in psych, had my heart set on med school. But other subjects caught my interest."

"What kind of subjects?"

"Sex crimes, for one." Haggerty sticks a fork into his pie. Whipped cream oozes through the tines. He takes a bite, chews, and swallows. "So, tell me about the business."

"I already told you."

"Humor me."

"Lawrence used to advise political candidates on media strategies.

Now he's creating a charitable nonprofit to reduce poverty and hunger in the United States."

"Sounds noble. What does he want you to do?"

"I told you this too. He'll be the face of the foundation. I'll be the brain trust. Together, we're the whole package, the head and the heart. We were all set to get started, but I flaked out." I shrug. "Like with you and med school. One day you're a doctor; next, you're having a go at sex crimes."

"I investigate them. I don't commit them."

"Oh, sorry. You weren't clear."

"Now what? Now that your brother's been arrested, how does that change things?"

"Don't know that it does." Leaning across the table, I get so close to Haggerty's face I can smell his aftershave. I swipe whipped cream off his pie and lick it, slowly, off my fingertips. "You're handsome. For a cop."

Haggerty doesn't smile back. "Stop." His voice is as hard as his eyes. I bet under his baggy clothes this guy is a savage. "I am not playing."

"I'm better than this?" My voice is just as hard. I'm a savage too. "Flirting is beneath me? Frankly, Detective, your questions are beneath you. You don't care about Lawrence's business or the foundation. Tell me what you really want, and then we'll have a conversation."

"You know what I want. I want you to tell me about Marcus Silver. He doesn't show up on any Google searches for men aged thirty-five through seventy in the Tri-State area."

"So what? I already told you: it's over."

"But it happened. You were a minor. He was an adult. It's a crime. What if there were other girls? No one wants a predator roaming the streets."

"There was no one else."

"Only you." Haggerty smirks. "You know that for sure?"

"I'd bet my life on it." I pause. "Let's say this is true. I was a minor; he was an adult. But what if it only happened once? *One time* before I turned seventeen. You'd arrest a man for *one time*? No credit for all the other times he held out?"

"That's not how the law works, unfortunately."

"Okay, let's say he leaves his wife, and we get engaged. What could you charge him with? Statutory rape of his fiancée?" I think of Mary Kay Letourneau, a teacher who went to jail for raping her student, a minor, whom she later married. It's possible, I concede.

"I'm sorry, Cassie." His voice is a whisper. I notice he calls me *Cassie*. And says it with kindness. "Marcus Silver will never leave his wife. Not even for you."

"Oh, I know. We broke up, remember?" I try to sound confident, but Haggerty's conviction, the finality of it, is chilling.

He changes the subject. "Here's something I don't get. You call Lawrence Quinn your father, but he isn't your father. And Eleanor Quinn isn't your mother. Your real parents are dead, correct?"

"Lawrence and Eleanor are my real parents. They raised me."

"But they're not your legal parents. Any reason why they didn't adopt you?"

"Money. My trust becomes available next year. By not adopting me, Lawrence said my money is my money, and has nothing to do with my place in his family."

"There are legal ways to protect money. But okay, that's one story. What about Eleanor?"

"Eleanor pushed for adoption, but in the end, she agreed with Lawrence."

"And you believe it? You seem like a skeptical woman. I mean, these reasons seem plausible." He shrugs. "But there are always other interpretations."

This pisses me off. "Like what?"

"First, the Quinns don't need your money, so Lawrence's argument is weak. Unless, of course, he and Eleanor divorce." He pauses. "Second, if Eleanor wanted to adopt you, you would've been adopted. She isn't a woman who defers to anyone. Especially a man who failed to fulfill his duties as husband and provider."

"Lawrence hasn't failed—"

"Cassie, the guy's been sponging off her for thirty years, and seems to have forgotten the money isn't his. I have to assume this makes

Eleanor very angry. So, maybe the Quinns didn't adopt you because they didn't want you in their family. Not really. Not the same way you wanted them."

As Haggerty baits me, panic sets in. My body grows numb, my throat closes. I'm splintering. I can hear and see Haggerty but he's far off and fuzzy.

"That's not true." I choose my words carefully. I must be precise. If I'm not, Haggerty will realize I've checked out. "They took care of me." I feel an aggressive need for a fight, for sex, anything to block the drilling in my ears.

"Cassie, they never claimed you as their own."

A wave of cold sweeps over me. Haggerty has to stop talking. Another wave hits me. The cold is coming up through the ground into my bones.

Haggerty is studying me. "You okay?"

"Fine."

"Billy's story doesn't add up."

"Doesn't make him a rapist." It's October, and this diner is overheated, but I can't stop shivering. "Doesn't make him a criminal."

"Billy Quinn raped Diana Holly. He will be held accountable. Every man should be held accountable for his crimes." He smiles. "Don't you see? I'm on the side of the angels, Cassie. I want to get the monsters."

Standing up, I knock the edge of the table. "I have to go."

"We're just talking, no need to be afraid."

"I'm not afraid. I'm just sick of the sound of your voice." Heading out, I turn around. "Maybe I'm the monster, Greg. Maybe it's been me all along." Admitting this makes the coldness recede. Finally, the truth is out. I brace myself for Haggerty to agree.

Instead, he says no, I'm wrong. "No one believes that but you, Cassandra."

36

I STAY AT SCHOOL. I ATTEND CLASSES, PARTICIPATE IN STUDY sessions, and consider my dissertation. I don't read the paper or watch the news. Billy is in a separate chamber of my brain; a chamber I seal off for all of October. But as the days shorten and the nights get chilly, I know I need to go home. I tell my professors I have a family emergency and will miss a month of classes. I promise to make up the work. You have to go, they insist. Family matters most.

* * *

My second morning back in New York, I wake up to an empty house. Now that I'm here, everyone is gone. No one has left me a note. Billy's trial begins Monday, three days away, and the press has returned en masse. Reporters swarm the Valmont, lobbing questions at anyone who passes by. It's a mess for everyone coming or going. Where the hell could my family be?

I text Lawrence:

Where are you guys

No reply.

The silence in this house is a beating heart, alive and pulsing with darkness. It weighs me down, makes me sluggish even as my mind races.

Why didn't you wake me up? Where's Eleanor?

I'm jangly being in my childhood bed. Paranoid about Haggerty. There's a low-grade buzzing in my head.

I text Nate:

Where are you?

Nate has inherited his father's self-absorption. They both lure me in then cast me out.

What are you doing? Where are you? Please reply!

Nothing, nowhere, silence.

I can't stop thinking about Haggerty. Same question: I know what he wants; I just don't know why. Why is it such a crusade? Why now? I look at the question from every angle, but the answer is encrypted, and I can't crack the code. I have no one to ask except—

"Hey, kid." It's Lawrence, upbeat and self-assured. His voice fills me with relief. He stands at my door, chewing on a straw like a man without a care in the world.

"Where were you?" My mind slows down, my body ramps up.

"Out for coffee." He's still chewing.

"And Eleanor?"

"With Billy and Nate, suit shopping." He leans on the doorframe. Glances behind him. "Cassie, listen. DeFiore is coming over later, and we'll take you through everything. I know I'm a broken record, but you have to prepare."

I stop listening. I'm alone with Marcus. We're in his house. His family is gone for the weekend. He's drinking, and his mouth fills with whiskey. First, I smell it. He pats the couch. "Move closer." Then I taste it. Whiskey burns on the tongue. It's for grown-ups, a smell and taste I'll forever associate with him, with wanting and needing and illicit secrets.

For an hour, Marcus's sole focus is my pleasure. He touches and strokes until I am limp, until I am crying and begging, please, Marcus, please.

"Please what?" he wants to know.

Please, I think. It's too much. "Please don't stop" is what I say.

Marcus kisses me until there is nothing else, just his mouth, his tongue. His voice brings me along, steady and reassuring. His eyes are half-closed like he's drugged. His fingers slide inside me. My own eyes close; I, too, am drugged.

Cassandra. His voice changes. It's deeper, stronger. The voice of a man who isn't amused, a man considering serious business. "Stay with me," he says. I stay, of course I stay. Where else would I go? He is urgent. "I need you; I need you." His palm hovers over my nipple. He brings it down slowly. He barely skims the surface, but the feeling the feeling the feeling. When he looks at me, there are tears in his eyes. There is nothing else; there is only this; only us. The stillest point of the turning world.

My body is between us, young, agile, flexible. I can't live without you, he says. You own me, he says. Your tits, your pussy, your ass. I can't live without these feelings, he says.

Suddenly, the therapist makes sense. Feel your feelings, she advised.

Our feelings dominate us, push us forward, make us dizzy, desperate. Our feelings reduce us to want. Our feelings clarify there is no turning back. We spend one night together. But for me that night is my whole future. That night, my life with Marcus is laid out, glamorous and heady, like a long red carpet unfurled in our honor. Together, we race toward the rest of our lives.

The story of Marcus + Cassie is a story of true love. It's the story of a beautiful man's beautiful voice; a voice that says, come be with me, come, Cassie. A voice I will follow to the ends of the earth then over the side. I wait and wait and wait, and now he is sliding into me, so strong and so hard. We are moving so closely. This is how you build a girl from the ground up, from the inside out; you give her a voice she can follow and then lead her forward. Wherever you go she is there because she is becoming a woman, she is becoming herself. I am coming, Marcus. I am, I am, I am.

PART THREE

Judgment

37

PEOPLE OF THE STATE OF NEW JERSEY V. WILLIAM MATTHEW Stockton Quinn begins this morning at the Mercer County Courthouse in downtown Trenton. We pull into a parking space a few blocks away, all five of us in the Mercedes, with Lawrence behind the wheel. Summoning his courage, he breathes in and squares his shoulders. "We're here." He shuts off the car then walks around to Eleanor's side and opens her door. She offers her hand, his Queen.

Head high, Lawrence canvasses his surroundings. Today, he's dressed for success, wearing a charcoal Brioni suit that accentuates his trim build. DeFiore didn't want him or my brothers to wear sunglasses, so Lawrence's face is bare. A stunning blue tie brings out his stunning blue eyes. His polished shoes tap on the pavement.

A security detail meets us at the corner. As we head up the street, we're consumed by fear and doubt. But DeFiore insists appearances matter, so we raise our chins and stride forward. We move in a single scrum, flanked on both sides by bodyguards. On the next corner, we fall in with DeFiore, his defense team, and four uniformed policemen, who escort us the last few blocks to the courthouse.

It's an overcast and blustery day, one that feels raw and damp, despite an absence of rain. The wind whips through the sky, lifting our hair and ruffling our clothes. My skirt flares up, exposing my thighs. Earlier, Eleanor chastised me for the length of my skirt. "Of all days, Cassandra? Everyone will be looking at you!" She was right, but I wore it anyway.

The wind makes conversation difficult, but soon I hear a low rumble that grows louder as we get closer. The interest in Billy's case that dropped off after his arraignment has returned with a frightening intensity. His alleged crimes have hit a national nerve. Across the country, morning shows are airing segments. Trial reporters live-stream the play-by-play. Radio shows are inviting callers. Everyone has an opinion. Most of the coverage is, unfortunately, negative. Billy is called Pretty Boy Quinn, Rich Runner Rapist, Princeton Rapist. Even the papers of record, the *New York Times* and *Washington Post*, are embracing the rich rapist angle.

The crowd outside the courthouse is immense and deafening. Hold-ing up signs—JUSTICE FOR SURVIVORS and IRRATIONAL, VINDICTIVE YOUNG WOMAN—angry females of all ages chant *rapist, rapist, rapist, prison, prison, prison*. Across the street, groups of burly men wear T-shirts that say THE REAL RAPE VICTIMS ARE THE FALSELY ACCUSED. Several link arms, forming a human chain, and shout *innocent until proven guilty is an American right*.

The press is here in full force too. A convoy of news vans block the curb. Reporters mill around the perimeter, bantering with each other as they check their phones. Several are filming lead-ins. One guy in his fifties wears a suit jacket, a tie, and faded jeans. "Tight as you can," he instructs the cameraman. "Nothing below the waist."

"It's Billy Quinn!" someone calls out. "He's here."

Spotting us, reporters surge forward. They shout questions at Billy, each a variation on *Are you a rapist?*

Facing them, DeFiore holds up a hand. "Billy Quinn is innocent. He has taken and passed a polygraph test. We have no other comments at this time."

The cops bark orders and push back the crowds. "Let 'em by. Move, move!"

We wind through a narrow channel of gawkers. It's chaotic and claustrophobic, and I try to find Haggerty among the bodies. He hasn't appeared since the day he ambushed me. For the past month, his lack of contact meant nothing; now, it's a critical sign. If Haggerty shows up for Billy's trial, it's bad news. If he doesn't, we'll emerge unscathed.

As always, Lawrence leads the charge. He doesn't answer any ques-tions, but neither does he cower. He looks directly at the reporters. Come and get me, he taunts them. Give me your worst.

Trailing behind him, I marvel at his public persona. There's a rise in his arches, a swagger in his hips; nothing to suggest that only a few hours ago, he was slumped on the edge of the bed, un-showered and unshaven, imploring his wife to give in.

Over the weekend, we checked into a swank hotel in nearby Princeton, our home away for the next three weeks. Earlier this morning, I was in my parents' room borrowing toothpaste when Lawrence's phone rang. The three of us froze.

Lawrence picked it up. "Good morning, Peter," he said stiffly.

A giddy DeFiore boomed through the speaker. He had the DA's final offer. "Anderson agreed to four years!" His voice made Eleanor flinch. In his excitement, he apparently forgot he was talking about prison. "Billy will be out in two, less with good behavior."

Four years? Eleanor mouthed and shook her head, but Lawrence didn't react.

She pointed to the phone. Her nails were painted a rose quartz pink to match her lips and cheeks. The custom-blended color, selected by our crisis consultants, is uncharacteristically soft, and makes Eleanor look like an entirely different person. Same with her hair color, which went from socialite gold to relatable honey. Along with newly cut bangs and a mauve cardigan—voilà!—a cold, inaccessible matriarch became a warm, sympathetic mom.

Lawrence leaned in, close to the phone. "We'll take our chances in court, Peter."

DeFiore pressed. "Lar, listen to me. I'm not fucking around. It's a high-profile case, and they'll make Billy pay for all the boys who got off easy. We're looking at twenty years with no allowances. Your son won't get out of prison until he's forty, at the earliest."

"Thank you, Peter." Lawrence closed his eyes. "But no thank you." His eyes were bloodshot. He reeked of last night's gin. DeFiore had already hung up, but Lawrence still held the phone, ready to hit speed-dial and say he was wrong, we'll take whatever pittance Anderson will give.

I started to speak when Lawrence interrupted me. "Sweetheart, look!"

Eleanor and I glanced up at the same time. Lawrence angled his phone, so we could both read the screen: "Rape Trial Kicks Off for Princeton Star Runner."

The headline scared me. "Jesus," I said. "It's really happening, isn't it?"

Eleanor scoffed. "Billy is innocent. He can't plead guilty to something he didn't do."

"His innocence doesn't matter," Lawrence reminded her, "if De-Fiore can't persuade a jury of it. Eleanor, we have to consider the four years."

"The stakes are high," I added.

Eleanor studied us closely—first her husband, then me. "You two are in cahoots again? If you really feel that way, go home. I won't have any negativity in court. Billy will be exonerated, and we will return to our lives." She said this like it was a prophecy, but her sweet pink lips made it difficult to take her seriously.

On the other hand, maybe Eleanor is right. If appearances alone can determine the outcome, our side will win by a landslide. DeFiore's team, along with our publicists and consultants, have coached us on what to wear, how to walk, when to sit, when to stand, when to ignore a question, when to respond, and what to say. Only the attorneys will be speaking today, but each of us is prepped and ready to achieve maximum positive impact.

Billy, for instance, strolls, hesitantly, on the balls of his feet, a sensitive young scholar, upset by all the attention. He is Eleanor's son; and today, like her, he is unrecognizable. The astronaut headphones are gone, replaced by nerdy, black-rimmed glasses with non-prescription lenses. Thanks to a low-carb, high-protein diet, he's twenty pounds lighter. Without the extra weight, his body is lankier and less physically imposing than at his arraignment. Wearing a fitted new suit and shiny leather shoes, my brother holds our mother's arm, as if squiring her along a promenade. Beside him, Eleanor has on a nondescript tweed skirt suit and low-heeled pumps. Gigantic tortoiseshell sunglasses hide her eyes. Her hair is puffed-up from the wind. Earlier, she'd wrapped her head in an Hermès silk scarf to protect her blowout, but DeFiore nixed it the second he saw her with a gruff, "No, no, no. No way."

Next to me, Nate looks like a younger, stiffer version of Lawrence in his own bespoke Brioni and silk purple tie. Among us, he's been the hardest to prepare, mostly because he's so furious—about the trial, the press, Diana Holly. I've missed most of the rehearsals, so I hadn't realized he's also still furious at me. We've barely spoken since the end of the summer, when he stormed out of the bar. When we do, our interactions are largely transactional ("What time are we leaving?" "I don't know, ask Dad."). I think he's pissed off that I bailed on the war room sessions. Or maybe he's pissed off that I failed to convince Lawrence to back off the plea. Or maybe it's just easier to stay angry at me. Either way, I'm giving him a wide berth.

DeFiore and his associate Mitchell Manzano (sexy and trustworthy in glasses) are behind us, along with a shocking number of women. By my quick count, there are seven females on our team: DeFiore's partner Felicia Drake, jury consultant Abby Friedman, two interns, and three women I've never seen before. For all I know, they were hired as extras just for the optics. Everyone is tastefully dressed, tastefully coiffed, and tastefully accessorized with sensible heels, leather totes, and chunky gold jewelry. Lost among the women is the Bowtie, unable to hide his displeasure. Last night, he chauffeured Eleanor to the hotel and expected to escort her up the avenue this morning. DeFiore said no way. "I don't care who's angry at who. The Quinns drive together, walk together, and sit together. Lawrence, I want you on Eleanor's right. Billy, you're on her left. Nate and Cassie, you're closely behind. Burt, I have no idea why the fuck you're here, so find a place in the rear. Listen up, Quinns. You're a happy fucking family. Try and look like one."

As we head up the steps and into the courthouse, it's pandemonium. The cops try to keep order. Reporters surround us, thrusting cameras in our faces. We're being jostled and yelled at. Nate's eyes are wide in alarm. "Jesus," he mutters. "This is bad." I'm shaking with terror.

"Hang in there, kids," Lawrence tells us. Speaking robotically, he fixes his eyes on a point in the distance. But I know every line of his face, every muscle in his jaw. Eleanor's decision to proceed with this trial is killing him. "She's impossible" he says to me at every turn. "But she's my wife." It's how he apologizes.

As we head through the lobby, Lawrence grabs Eleanor's hand. For a second, I think he's going to bring it to his lips. Instead, he squeezes it three times. Eleanor squeezes back three times, and I wonder what it means.

"It's freezing in here," I say, rubbing my skin.

"Want my jacket?" Lawrence asks, holding it out.

I nod; and when he drapes it across my shoulders, he pats my upper arms. We exchange smiles as we stop at the elevator. To the crowd, he's a loving father reassuring his frightened daughter. Don't worry, Honey, we'll be okay. Promise? Promise.

Today's arrival is one of the trial details that DeFiore has choreographed down to the minute. Our entrance is his opening statement. Good morning, ladies and gentlemen. Ignore what you've read; forget what you know. Here, for your consideration, are the Lawrence Quinns. Well dressed. Well mannered. Female friendly. Approachable. Undaunted. We are a united front. We are New York royalty. We are the all-American dream.

38

"ALL RISE!"

The midsized courtroom is filled to capacity. People are lining the walls. Every row in the gallery is occupied. As Judge Charles McKay steps out of his chambers and approaches the bench, everyone jumps to their feet. Conversations cease. The mood turns somber.

I'm standing with my family in the first row of spectators. We're directly behind Billy, Felicia, and DeFiore, who are at the defense table. It's a frustrating setup. Billy's back is to us, so we can't see his face unless he leans back or turns around. The best we can do is gauge how he's feeling from the tension in his neck and shoulders. We're too far away to pat his arm or whisper encouragement—not that we would. DeFiore told us to sit still and shut up, no matter what happens. Our seating assignments were equally specific. The Bowtie is at the end of the row, on the aisle, with Eleanor situated to his right. Lawrence is on Eleanor's right, I'm next to Lawrence, Nate is on my right, and Abby Friedman is next to Nate, at the other end of the row. We'll return to these positions every day until the trial ends.

McKay settles in. Today, his hair looks freshly shorn and his crazy eyebrows have been trimmed. When he turns to the gallery, his face is solemn.

"Be seated." He looks at the attorneys. "Does either side need to address anything before I call the jury?"

"Nothing from us, Your Honor," says Bradley Anderson from the prosecution table. Seated beside him, his deputy Maggie Fleming shakes her head.

"Nor us, Your Honor," DeFiore says.

The judge turns to the sheriff, who says, "All rise for the jury."

I'm not a reverential person, but this collective show of respect humbles me. A jury trial is a meaningful event, one that will decide the rest of a young man's life. Apparently, the officers of the court feel similarly. At Billy's first appearance, the prosecutors walked in late while DeFiore and Mitchell yukked it up. Today, lawyers on both sides sit up straight, ties adjusted, skirts smoothed.

But the real shocker today is DeFiore, who looks like a bona fide attorney. He must've booked a session with the crisis consultants, too, because his gray suit is tailored with knife-sharp creases. His shirt is white, free of stains, and neatly pressed. Gold cuff links add panache. A pair of half-glasses are perched on his nose. Does he wear glasses normally? I don't remember. Either way, he's a man to be reckoned with.

Months ago, DeFiore explained how visuals are as critical as the legal arguments. Which is why Felicia Drake, not Mitchell Manzano, is acting as co-counsel. By positioning Felicia next to Billy, the jury will see him interact positively with a less attractive woman. Beside my naturally elegant brother, Felicia looks ungainly and matronly. Today's walk from the parking lot has loosened her chignon, and her face is moist with perspiration. Her suit jacket is too snug; from behind, her bra lines are visible. With every hand on his shoulder or pat on his back, she's putting on a subtle but effective show for the jury as they file in, one by one.

The jury box is to the left of the bench. Soon, eight men and four women fill the twelve seats. Most bend their heads, but a few crane their necks and gawp, as if dazed by the lights. The majority sport weekend gear: jeans, sneakers, and puffy vests. DeFiore told me that as the defendant's sister, roughly the same age as Diana, I will get scrutinized without pity. The jury will wonder about my relationship with Billy, what kind of influence I had growing up, how my presence in the family shaped his views of women, sex, and relationships. "You are supportive and demure," DeFiore said. "That's what we need to see. Supportive. Demure." He gave me a once-over. "To the extent that you can."

"Meaning what?"

"You ooze sex, Cassie. Don't look surprised, or pretend you're offended. It's a compliment. But button up your sweater and cross your legs at the ankles. Like a lady," he added, glancing at Eleanor. "Like your mom." When he said this, Eleanor caught my eye, and we both made a face.

Sitting up, I run my fingers through my hair. The wind blew out my curls, leaving them long and unruly. Ignoring DeFiore's instructions, I take off my sweater, and unbutton my blouse, exposing a hint of cleavage. Let them look, I think.

Most of the men on the jury appear to be in their forties, whereas the women's ages are harder to gauge. There are twice as many men. According to Abby, who has studied jurors for thirty years, this is what we want. "Older males will see their younger selves in Billy. They're tired of defending their behavior. When they were his age, it wasn't a crime for boys to touch girls, et cetera. Women are less predictable. Some will love Billy and be put off by Diana. Others will identify with Diana and want to crucify Billy. Females are fickle creatures." Today, Abby is wearing a dark blue Celine shirtdress and tailored jacket. She looks gorgeous. Nate shows her something on his phone, and they both cover their mouths, trying not to laugh.

Judge McKay is giving instructions. "I will not allow phone, laptops, or other devices. Any and all will be confiscated then donated to Legal Aid. Anyone caught posting photos of the jury, courtroom, defendant, or lawyers on social media will be held in contempt of court."

As if on cue, a phone rings. McKay glances around, pissed. "Whose phone is that?"

It belongs to Bradley Anderson, the bald giant prosecutor. He's on his feet, fumbling to shut it off. "I apologize, Your Honor."

"DA Anderson, you understand these rules apply to you as well, right?"

"Yes, Your Honor. It won't happen again."

"Ladies and gentlemen, the rules of this courtroom are very important. If everyone adheres to the instructions you were given during voir dire, we will get along fine."

The jury nods. They understand; they will follow the judge's orders.

A few exchange amused glances about Anderson's faux pas. They have to take this trial seriously; shouldn't the lawyers do the same?

Diana Holly's family is here, positioned behind the prosecution, though she's not with them. Just like at the arraignment, she never has to set foot in the courtroom. She can watch, and even testify, on closed-circuit TV. As the victim, she gets compassionate one-on-one assistance. An advocate from the DA's office will accompany her through each stage of the proceedings, explain what is happening and why, and escort her (and her family) to a safe space if she feels overwhelmed. My brother, by contrast, is forced to sit here, in this courtroom, all day, every day, and face a public shaming. As the defendant, he has no one to hold his hand or pat his back. Forget justice. He'll never be innocent, not inside this courtroom or out on the street, not after what Diana has done.

After a series of long interruptions, McKay finally reads the charges against Billy—two counts of rape, one count of attempted rape, and two counts of felony sexual assault, one where the victim was intoxicated, and one where the victim was unconscious of the nature of the act.

Immediately, all eyes shift in Billy's direction. He sits up tall in his seat. He's taking notes, an earnest student. When the judge finishes, Billy raises his head, acknowledging he heard what was said. Then he looks at the jury, as if to show them he's not afraid. He's been wrongly accused, and only wants the truth to come out. Felicia Drake reaches over and pats his arm.

"Your Honor." Standing up, Anderson lumbers toward the bench. His gigantic size makes his movements feel aggressive. "Last night, we filed an amended witness list. We seek the court's indulgence in allowing us to do so at this late hour."

Before DeFiore can object, McKay says, "I will take up this matter at another time. Now, can we please get started?"

Anderson scowls, annoyed, it appears, by the judge's ruling.

After a lunch break, the afternoon passes slowly. Along with additional instructions for the jury, there are many interruptions, including a boring back-and-forth between the attorneys about the State's exhibits. At several points, the discussion gets heated; and when Anderson lashes out, McKay reins him back in. The room is filled with tension, and by the time five o'clock arrives, everyone is eager to go.

As the jury leaves, I notice them scrutinizing the red-faced Anderson with disdain. DeFiore has told us it's foolish to read meaning into anything we see. "Juries are faithless. In the morning, they cheer you on. By the afternoon, you're a pariah." Still, Anderson's demeanor rubs the jurors the wrong way, particularly the men.

This is significant, I can feel it.

39

THE NEXT MORNING, JUDGE MCKAY CALLS ON THE PROSE-
cution to present opening remarks. Before he finishes, Anderson is already up on his feet and ready to go. He tries to close his jacket, but the
material strains against his girth. A button falls off in his hand. The DA
was already as solid as a tank, but in the months since the arraignment,
he's packed on ten, maybe fifteen pounds. While this isn't much for his
frame, like some ex-athletes, he's added the bulk of the new weight in
his gut. Anderson uses this fact to introduce himself.

"Would you believe this suit was too big last April?" He holds up
the button for the jury, as if entering it into evidence. "My wife tells me
to lay off junk food. She's right. Trust me, my wife is *always* right."
Offering a sly grin, he pats his belly. "But I'll get divorced before I give
up burgers and beer."

Last night, my parents, brothers, and I left the courthouse in high
spirits. After the long, tortured wait for the trial to begin, the end of
day one brought relief. *Finally*, we said. The Bowtie booked a private
room in a restaurant two towns over. All the men ordered prime rib,
Eleanor and I shared a whole branzino, and everyone drank wine, so
the evening had an air of triumph. We clinked glasses, toasting Billy
and the absent DeFiore. For the first hour, it was fun to be together.
But as dinner progressed, Lawrence and Nate drank too much, and
Eleanor got annoyed. She'd insisted we not discuss the trial, but Nate,
plastered, couldn't help himself.

"Anderson is fucking up. Did you see his face when the judge kept
overruling him? The jury can't stand him. It's so obvious."

"Neither can McKay," Lawrence added.

Nate lifted his glass. "Here's to the DA going down in flames."

This morning, Anderson assumes a folksy intimacy. To me, his performance feels forced, but the jurors eat it up. His burgers-and-beer comment earns him a hearty laugh. Clearly, his trial strategy is as complex and as nuanced as ours. How many times, I wonder, did he practice the button popping off his jacket before he got it exactly right? Who sewed it on just loosely enough?

"I appreciate you being here," he continues. "Trials are long and tedious. Over the next three weeks, you'll hear intricate testimony from lab techs, police officers, ER doctors, psychiatrists, and other forensic experts. If you're anything like me, you may find it difficult to absorb so many technical details. But I encourage each of you to do your very best. Why? Because we're here to get justice for Diana Holly, a courageous woman who was violated in the most depraved way. This trial will affect every woman you know, and lots of women you don't. We are pursuing justice, which is an ideal this country was founded upon. So, your continued engagement is meaningful to Diana, to Mercer County, to the state of New Jersey, to the United States of America, and to our global community."

The DA is so full of convoluted bullshit that no one is prepared for his sharp pivot.

"This trial is about rape." His gray eyes harden into pieces of flint. "It's not about sex. It's not about relationships. It's not about passion or love. This trial is about rage." He waits a beat. "Privilege." Another beat. "Power." Another beat. "Violence." Then he turns to Billy, takes him in. "Because that's what rape is about: Rage. Privilege. Power. Violence."

The courtroom is silent.

"Rage. Privilege. Power. Violence."

A woman in the jury box coughs.

"The defendant, William Stockton Quinn, is a rich, privileged boy from a rich, privileged family. How rich? How privileged? His family has a net worth north of seven hundred *million* dollars. That's equivalent to the combined wealth of the poorest quarter of the human race. Middle-class people—people like me, maybe people like you—can't conceive of this much money. Or the kind of life this money provides.

But that's the only life the defendant has ever known. From the day he was born, he got everything he needed, anything he asked for. He attended a top boarding school, Groton. The best private college, Princeton. Were he not sitting in this courtroom, he'd be applying to the best medical schools, Harvard and Yale. Wherever Billy Quinn goes, doors fly wide open."

Seven hundred million dollars? Where did he get that number? We're probably at five, maybe six hundred, including CW's money, which isn't mine yet. Anderson's estimate is a king's ransom; a number so enormous it sounds mythical.

Visibly excited, Anderson bounces on his toes. He describes, in exaggerated detail, the symbols of our wealth: multiple homes, exclusive addresses, exotic vacations, luxury vehicles.

I watch Eleanor. Her body is stock-still, her face unruffled, but I know she is recoiling inside. To discuss money in such graphic terms is vile, like describing bodily functions. As for me, I listen carefully, respectfully. But I can't grasp Anderson's point. We are rich. We are gross. So what? Meanwhile, the audience hangs on every word. We may be loathsome capitalists, but indiscriminate spending is the ultimate aphrodisiac. One male juror is checking me out with newfound curiosity. I'd bet one of my many mythical stacks that hearing about my net worth gives him a raging hard-on.

"Me? I'm just a working-class kid from south Jersey," Anderson continues. "Dad was an electrician. Mom was a nurse. We didn't travel in the same circles as the defendant. We barely lived in the same hemisphere. But I was recruited to play football for Harvard, so I met boys like him in college. I considered some of them friends. We studied together, worked out, went to parties. I dated their sisters. All lovely, smart girls who made it clear that while I could certainly buy them dinner, we had no future. I would never visit their homes or meet their families. One girl told her friends I was NQOCD." He looks at me, the defendant's sister. "You know that expression? Not quite our class, dear." As if amused by the memory, Anderson chuckles. "Boys like the defendant are handsome and fun-loving. They're quick to pick up the tab and order another round. But they're dangerous. Having grown up with everything, they want for nothing. They have no boundaries or limits. They're used to everyone, parents, teachers, girls—especially girls—giving them whatever they want. But the penalty for failing to satisfy their whims is incredibly high. What they're not given, they take."

Bradley Anderson couldn't be more transparent. By differentiating himself from Billy, he's trying to make the jurors take sides. *I'm nothing like this guy. In fact, I'm just like you, Juror Number Seven. I'm middle-class. I cheat on my diet. I watch sports on TV. So, if I can judge Billy Quinn, you can too. Go ahead. Judge him. Harshly.* But Brad Anderson is lying. Not small white lies either. He's telling whoppers.

"The defendant suffers from severe emotional problems." (Lie.) "Early on, these problems were manifested in a childhood stutter." (Lie.) "Now, he is plagued by unhealthy addictions, and an inability to have intimate relationships. Particularly those of a sexual nature." (Lie.) "In grade school, the defendant's volatile behavior disrupted the classroom. He was held back, which made him older and bigger than his classmates. He used his size as a weapon, bullying the other students until he was shipped off to boarding school." (All lies.) "Over the years, the defendant became a lonely misfit, always on the outside looking in. He was easily angered and quick to hurt others. For a brief period, organized athletics offered an outlet. But in college, he was kicked off the track team. Why? Because he acted out in fits of rage and unpredictable physical violence. The same way he did when he was five years old."

Lies, lies, lies.

"In the next three weeks, the State will describe how the defendant and Diana Holly met sixteen months ago in a medical lab. The defendant was instantly captivated. He asked her out, several times. Finally, she agreed. The defendant's lawyers will try to convince you that he and Diana had a consensual love affair that went on for many months. This is categorically untrue. Within three months, Diana felt the need to separate. By December, she wanted O-U-T. We will prove that the defendant's kind and well-mannered behavior masked a tormented, unstable interior. He was erratic. Moody. Prone to explosive tantrums. In his presence, Diana started to feel unsafe, then petrified."

Petrified? Of Billy? The kid with the stutter clinging to a Muppet? Nate must be thinking the same thing because he looks at me and rolls his eyes.

"Diana told the defendant she wanted to break up. She told him not to contact her. But the defendant didn't like hearing this. On the contrary, instead of respecting her wishes, he ignored her requests, and waged a campaign to change her mind. He sent emails and texts. He called and called. He snuck into her room when she was in class and pretended to be asleep in her bed when she returned. Diana didn't know what to do. She believed the defendant was vulnerable, possibly mentally ill. She feared that if she reported his behavior, he would be asked to leave Princeton. She knew he'd wanted to practice medicine since childhood. So, instead of protecting herself, she continued to protect him. She said nothing to anyone and lived in constant fear. Meanwhile, the defendant's rage continued to escalate until March 24, when it erupted in a burst of depraved violence."

When Anderson stops, I assume he's finished. But he ambles over to the defense table and positions himself directly in front of Billy. As he speaks, his voice deepens and his chest expands, like he's filling the courtroom with the heft of his body.

"Let's return for a moment to the defendant's emotional issues. What were they, exactly? Why did they have such a claim on his mental health and well-being?"

Anderson rests his hands on the table. Leaning forward, he looks at Billy expectantly, as if waiting for my brother to answer. He stands, unmoving, for an uncomfortable length of time. I start to feel twitchy. I suspect Billy does too because he keeps his head bowed.

Finally, Anderson speaks. "I'm no psychiatrist. However, it's a documented fact that when a child is raised with too much money and too few boundaries, he grows up unwilling to accept 'no.' He throws tantrums. Exhibits antisocial behavior. At the same time, he feels worthless. This, too, is a documented fact. Children who are given too many beautiful things without earning them—money, toys, cars—lack a sense of accomplishment. They are absent a core self. The kind of self that well-adjusted people nurture with loving relationships and trusted friends. They carry shame about their families and about themselves."

Anderson is describing every wealthy kid—every wealthy person—who's ever lived. By his accounting, every single one could be a rapist. But then he says something that stops me cold.

"The State will show that Billy Quinn is hiding a secret. A secret he has harbored since childhood. This secret festered inside him for years. It made him isolated, self-destructive, and, as you will soon hear, extremely dangerous."

I jerk my head up. What secret? I glance at Lawrence, but he's bent over a notepad, scribbling like a madman.

"Because of this secret, the defendant has a fraught relationship with his family. He has no long-term relationships. He graduated from high school having experienced little intimacy with girls, despite his good looks and athletic success. Diana Holly was the first female he ever shared his secret with, except perhaps his sister."

When Anderson pauses, everyone looks at me. He waits. I try to swallow but can't.

"Diana was troubled by the defendant's secret, but he made her swear never to repeat it. *Or else*, he said. Although Diana agreed, she also encouraged him to get help. When the defendant refused, she broke up with him, at which point he became frantic. He feared that if Diana revealed his secret, the fabric of his life would rip open. Would she protect him? Would she expose him? The defendant couldn't risk it. Everything—his education, his future, his parents, his brother, his sister—depended on her silence. Soon, his fear turned into rage. He hunted her down, day after day. Begged her to stay with him. No, she replied. No. Leave me alone."

I can't believe the jury is buying this. But from the way they lean forward and their eyes track Anderson's movements, it's obvious they are, every single one.

The DA continues to talk, establishing the ways that Billy terrorized Diana, and which evidence the State will present to prove them all. A half-hour later, Anderson still hasn't identified Billy's secret.

"And then one fateful night," he continues, "March 24, the defendant's shame and fear overwhelmed him. On this night, Diana Holly invited the defendant to a party for a single reason. To tell him to stop harassing her and insist he get help, for his own sake. She believed it was a safe meeting place because people were around to protect her, including her best friend. Unfortunately, her plan was thwarted. When Diana talked to the defendant, he got angry. She pleaded with him, but to no avail. Thirty minutes later, she left. But the defendant followed her. And in a depraved act of rage, privilege, power, and violence, the defendant brutalized Diana Holly. He brutalized her while she was unconscious. When she couldn't say no or defend herself. On this night, the defendant destroyed Diana Holly's life. And for what?"

A long pause.

"For what?" Anderson asks again then answers himself. "For a secret."

The jury is riveted; clearly, they want to hear Billy's secret. Admittedly, a part of me does too. Instead, Anderson says, "Look at the accused. On the surface, he's a handsome, ambitious young man. But inside, he's deeply angry and deeply troubled. This man raped a young woman while she was unconscious, and, for all we know, has raped other girls and will continue to rape—"

"Objection!" Felicia Drake is furious. "Speculative and inflammatory!"

Anderson doesn't miss a beat. "I'm discussing the evidence I'll introduce during trial."

Judge McKay brushes Felicia back. "This is an opening statement. I'll allow it." But he glares at Anderson. "Watch yourself. It's only the first week." Looking at his watch, he makes a decision. "We've been going for a couple of hours. Let's break for lunch. We'll resume at one." He strikes his gavel.

Anderson relaxes. The timing pleases him. He knows that every single person in this courtroom is dying to learn Billy's secret. But we all have to wait.

40

DEFIORE HAS RESERVED A MEETING ROOM FOR OUR FAMILY'S use during the trial. It's in the building, on the same floor as the courtroom, and we congregate there during the break. The room is spare, with bare walls, a long conference table, and two credenzas. The table seats sixteen, so the five of us spread out on opposite sides. Menus are consulted, lunch is ordered. Soon, phones, laptops, iPads, charging cords, water bottles, tote bags, and notebooks are scattered everywhere.

I am so anxious I worry I'm having a stroke. Perspiration soaks through my blouse. What the hell is the secret? Booze? Billy's never been a drinker. Weed? He doesn't get high as often as I do; does that make me an addict too? Drugs? Money? Did Billy start gambling and not tell us?

I want to discuss Anderson's statement, but don't want to be the one to bring it up. I wonder if the DA knows about Marcus. Does it matter if he does? That's my secret, not Billy's.

Nate is sprawled across a chair, jacket off, tie unknotted, absorbed in his phone. His face has already started to shadow, and I bet DeFiore will tell him to shave again before the day is over. Next to him, Billy has donned his astronaut headphones and stares into space. His blue eyes are glassy and vacant, as if he's been drugged.

I try to find a comfortable position. The leather chairs are plush, but nothing feels right. Why am I the only one freaking out?

"You kids okay?" Lawrence asks from across the room. He's at the head of the table, the chairman of the board, with Eleanor, his trusted consigliere, by his side.

Do they know the secret? They've seen all the evidence. They must know what Anderson is referring to. I'm kicking myself for missing the last few months of war room sessions.

Lawrence's shirtsleeves are rolled up. A sliver of light peeks through the blinds and highlights the dark hair on his forearms. I focus on them to help steady myself.

"We're fine," I choke out, just to fill the air with sound. "Curious about Anderson's strategy. Some of his statements were very . . . I don't know . . . provocative."

"He's making the whole thing up," Eleanor says flatly. She's gazing into a mirror, reapplying her sweet pink lipstick.

I can't get used to her bangs; I startle every time I glance her way. A younger, gentler woman has replaced the Eleanor who raised me.

"Can he do that?" she asks. "Just pull facts out of the air?"

I assume she's referring to the story about her depraved son raping his unconscious girlfriend until she adds, "*Seven hundred million?* Where did he come up with that? We're nowhere near the vicinity."

"We knew this would happen," Lawrence announces. "They'll say anything to malign us." He makes it seem like he's responding to Eleanor, but in fact, he's sending me a message. *We'll be fine, kid. Trust me.*

"So he's allowed to lie?" Nate asks. "Are there, like, no rules at all? Why can't Peter stop him? Or get the judge to stop him?"

"That's not how trials work, son. But Peter will present our case, and when he does, he'll make it right." Again, he's saying this to comfort me. But he still doesn't mention the secret.

The food arrives, but no one moves. A platter of sandwiches sits on a rolling cart, along with a bowl of fruit, bags of chips, and a plate of brownies. Wrapped in plastic, everything looks revolting.

"Billy," I say casually. Then I lean over, nudge him with my finger. He takes off his headphones.

"What do you think Anderson is talking about? What secret?"

Across the room, Lawrence is studying his phone, but I can tell he's frozen in place, awaiting the answer.

"No idea. Could be anything." Billy puts his headphones back on and stares at his phone. "Weed, probably." He shrugs.

"I'm not worried about Anderson," Lawrence says. "But we should get ahead of this. Where's Peter?" He looks around for DeFiore, who's out in the hall, shouting into his phone.

"I bet it's weed," Nate says, shifting his eyes toward Billy.

Nate knows about Marcus, I think. Though the thought has occurred to me before, countless times, at the moment it seems absolutely true.

"Who gives a shit," we hear DeFiore say. "Fuck that guy. Tell him I said no way."

As Lawrence gets up, Eleanor grabs his arm. "Let it go. Let's just have a quiet lunch."

"I don't want to have a quiet lunch, Eleanor. I want to talk to Peter."

She won't release his arm, which surprises me. Why isn't she up on her feet, berating DeFiore for letting this happen? Clearly, I've been out of the loop for too long.

Lawrence shakes her off. At the door, he motions to DeFiore. "We have questions."

Standing up, Nate surveys the food. "There's one turkey sandwich," he tells Billy. "It's yours." Nate positions the sandwich, fruit, and pretzels on a plate with care, as if Billy has broken both arms and can't feed himself. He spreads yellow mustard, not the spicy brown kind, on both sides of the bread. He opens the pretzels and shakes them out onto the plate. He sops up the juice from the fruit then sets the plate on the table, unfolds a napkin and fills a cup with Diet Coke. "Here you go, buddy." He squeezes Billy's shoulder. "You should eat."

Billy nods. "Thank you."

"I don't like Anderson," I announce, needing to speak. If I don't, I'll explode. "He's a pompous jerk."

My brothers exchange glances that say I am beyond stupid. "Well, okay, Cassie." Nate sneers. "Thanks for the legal insight."

DeFiore steps into the room. "Try not to worry about what you heard today. They're going to say terrible things about Billy and about all of you. But our case is airtight."

Since when? This morning, he was pushing us to quit. But now that the trial is underway, maybe there's no room for doubt. DeFiore seems unfazed by Anderson's statement, and I realize that having seen the discovery, he knew it was coming. This means all of them—Lawrence, Eleanor, Billy, and Nate—have already discussed it. The only one who doesn't know is me.

"We're going to be fine," he adds.

This doesn't pacify Nate. "Anderson lied. Is he allowed to do that?"

DeFiore bites into one side of a sandwich. Pastrami, tomatoes, and mustard leak out the other. He grabs a napkin, wipes his chin. "In the legal profession, truth is a malleable commodity. It can be molded, like clay, to mean what you want."

"But then nothing means anything," Eleanor says.

"He's telling a story, Mrs. Quinn. We are too. The jury gets to decide which one is more plausible—and, in this case, more palatable. Anderson is a good lawyer. He knows which truths can be stretched. Witnesses, however, are under oath. Committing perjury is a crime. Don't get me wrong, witnesses lie all the time, but we take everything at face value—unless it works to our advantage not to."

"You still plan to put Billy on the stand, right?" Nate asks.

"I would like to, Nate, but only if I feel confident that he's prepared. If not, Anderson will gut him. It only takes one stumble." He and Nate glance at Billy, who is hunched over his food, headphones on, orbiting through space.

"We'll get him ready," Eleanor says, also looking. "Whatever it takes."

"I knew this would happen," Lawrence mutters. "I knew we'd end up here."

"Lar," DeFiore says evenly. "We haven't 'ended up' anywhere. We're still at opening arguments. You need to pace yourself, my friend. This is a marathon, not a sprint."

Nate is preoccupied. "The jury needs to hear from Billy, especially if Diana's testimony confirms all the bullshit Anderson is telling them."

"This is what I meant, Nate, about witnesses being under oath." DeFiore tries to explain. "Diana can't just say whatever she wants. Anderson will coach her, sure. But she can't make claims that are blatantly false—like she and Billy had no prior relationship, or that she was sober at the party. Right now, she's protected by rape shield laws. We can't talk about her drinking habits or prior boyfriends, anything like that. But if she makes a false statement, the shield laws change, and she opens the door to these discussions. That's why, if you listen carefully to Anderson, you'll hear very few facts. It's all conjecture and pseudo-psychology. He doesn't want his witnesses to say something we can prove false. Instead, he's relying on made-up theories and big ideas, most of which are bluster. Happens all the time. The less evidence, the bigger the performance."

Nate and Eleanor look skeptical.

"Sit tight. Our turn will come." He addresses the room. "Anything else?"

"It's such a cliché," I blurt out.

"What's a cliché?" DeFiore asks.

"The bullshit the DA is selling. Young man has problems. Problems lead to rejection, rejection leads to anger, anger leads to assault. This can't be Anderson's whole argument."

DeFiore nods. "Sure it can. And if I were in his shoes, I'd do the same. Without much proof, he has to rely on a familiar narrative. He's adding drama to ratchet up the stakes. But strip away the color commentary and it's a story we know by heart."

"But it's so simple."

"Yet so effective." DeFiore pockets another sandwich. Looks at Billy. "And often true."

* * *

Back in the courtroom, Anderson can't wait to get started. As soon as McKay says go, the DA is up on his feet and talking, as if no time has passed. "What is the defendant's secret? What had him so anxious? What made him so angry?" He pauses to let us get our bearings.

The judge cuts him off. "I'm sorry, Counselors." He nods at De-Fiore. "We have to adjourn. An issue has come up this afternoon that demands my full attention."

Are you kidding? I want to shout.

Anderson is annoyed; McKay has ruined his big reveal. "Your Honor, can we just fin—"

"Court will resume in the morning." The judge strikes his gavel.

Dazed, I walk out, so nervous I'm numb. As Lawrence hightails the car to the hotel, I sit in the backseat like a robot. "So, it's weed?" I ask Billy. "The secret?" I poke him. "Weed?"

His eyes are closed. He nods.

"But weed doesn't make people violent; how can that be the secret?"

"The DA will say anything," Lawrence calls out. "Don't worry, Cassie. It's nothing. If it were, Peter would've told us."

He's right; of course, he's right.

At dinner, I go through the motions. I pick up my fork, chew, swallow, and try to ignore the screams in my head. Afterward, alone in my room, I get stoned and drown in loud music blasting through my AirPods. How will I survive three weeks of this?

In court the next morning, Anderson is champing to begin. He hustles, back and forth, near the jury box, a linebacker eager to annihilate the home team.

"What is the defendant's secret?" he asks, quoting himself from yesterday. "What had him so anxious? What made him so angry?" A long pause. "The defendant, a twenty-three-year-old student, a world-class athlete in the prime of his life, has"—another pause—"erectile dysfunction, a condition more common in a seventy-year-old man. He has watched pornography since he was a child. Now, he is so addicted he cannot sustain an erection without it."

Nate nudges me, smirks. For the first time in months, we connect. *Porn? That's it? The whole world watches porn.* I am so relieved I almost laugh out loud.

I told you not to worry, Lawrence texts. You really can trust me.

Seated beside me, Lawrence reads my screen then squeezes my arm. "I swear," he whispers.

For the next two hours, Anderson lays out the State's evidence. But rather than drive home the most damning details from the sheriff's and EMT's reports, he focuses instead on the science behind porn addiction: why videos are so dangerous, how technology feeds on the brain, how watching porn predisposes young men to dehumanize women.

"You will learn that the defendant sees his first pornographic video at age seven. You will hear evidence that he continues to watch, compulsively, for the next sixteen years. Witnesses will testify that by the time he meets Diana Holly, he is watching pornographic videos for hours at a stretch. This behavior disrupts his schoolwork, social life, and extracurricular activities. He stops tutoring. He is kicked off the track team. He is deeply depressed. He watches more than eighteen hours a week. He is caught in a cycle of binge-watching, shame, attempts to quit, and relapse. You will hear from the State's expert how pornographic videos came to rule the defendant's life."

I glance at Eleanor. She appears unimpressed by this. So does the jury. Earlier, they were hanging on Anderson's every word; now they shift in their seats. One guy is dozing; another is scrolling through a phone hidden inside his notebook.

My confidence surges. The DA's presentation is lackluster and one-note. He uses too many words to say what he means and repeats the phrase "pornographic videos" to the point of distraction. Even as he bashes Billy into a pulp, even as he graphs Billy and Diana's relationship from flirtation to violence, even as he walks the jury, moment by moment, through the alleged rape, Anderson can't hold the room.

Finally, McKay cracks his gavel. "We'll adjourn for lunch."

41

IN THE AFTERNOON, IT'S OUR TURN FOR OPENING STATE-
ments. DeFiore has implored us to take every day as it comes, but the
second he stands up and buttons his jacket, I know we will win. Once
again, he's pulled himself together. He's no lumpy, dumpy mobster;
he's Peter DeFiore, Esquire, polished in his courtroom blues: a well-
fitted navy suit, a navy tie of appropriate length, and heirloom cuff
links. While Anderson relied on hysteria and theatrics, DeFiore zeroes
in on evidence. He is measured, thoughtful, and persuasive.

Watching DeFiore address the jury, I wish Haggerty were here,
if only to relish the shock on his know-it-all, Ichabod Crane, lemon-
sucking face when Billy is acquitted.

"Despite the district attorney's assertions," DeFiore begins, "this
case isn't about money, power, or privilege. Nor is it about violence.
So, what is it about? Well, let's start with the evidence we know to be
true. The facts both sides agree on, and witness testimony supports.
Fact one: Billy Quinn and Diana Holly had an intimate relationship.
Fact two: this relationship started in June, the summer before their
junior year at Princeton University. Fact three: the couple ended this
relationship in December, six months later. Fact four: the couple kept
in touch, sporadically, between December and March. Fact five: Diana
invited Billy to a party on the evening of March 24. Fact six: the couple
engaged in sexual intercourse on the evening of March 24.

"This, unfortunately, is where our agreement ends, and disagree-
ments begin. The State wants you to believe Billy Quinn and Diana
Holly dated only briefly. However, we will introduce Deacon Porter,
Billy's best friend, who will testify that he joined the couple on dates
from June through December. Similarly, both sides disagree on what

happened during their relationship and who eventually broke it off. We disagree on what happened in the aftermath of that breakup. We disagree on the reason Diana invited Billy to the party. We disagree on what happened at that party. We disagree on whether or not the sex was consensual."

Hearing this, I sit more comfortably. Nate and my parents do too. DeFiore is competent, holding his own. Thank fucking God.

"While each of these points makes for compelling discussion, this case is *not* about what we agree on and what we don't. So, I'll ask again: What is this case about? Why are you here? What are you being asked to decide?"

Looking at the jury, DeFiore makes eye contact with each member, one by one.

"This case lies in the answer to three questions. One, did Billy Quinn believe that Diana Holly wanted to have sex on March 24? Two, did Diana lose consciousness on March 24; and, if so, was this before she and Billy engaged in sex? Three, if Diana was unresponsive before they engaged in sex, did Billy know it? That's it—three questions.

"During this trial, you will hear witness testimony about the charges against my client. Each charge relates to these questions. To be perfectly frank, as Mr. Anderson and I present our cases, much of the issues we discuss will have nothing to do with the charges against my client, or the three questions you must answer. Regardless, you'll be expected to listen, remain objective, consider the evidence you have seen and heard, and reach a verdict. Most important, you must reach your verdict with the absence of doubt. This means the State must prove that the answer to these three questions is yes. An unequivocal yes."

"He's good, right?" I whisper to Nate.

"Yeah, he's great. So shut up."

"Unfortunately, the State has a problem. They must offer tangible evidence for every statement they make. This is the law. The law isn't based in supposition. The law has integrity. It is rooted in proof. But as you may have already figured out, the State's evidence is weak. So, instead, they're offering a fictitious story about a boy named Billy

Quinn. A story based on conjecture, and fake psychology. But they want you to believe this made-up story and send my client to jail."

The jury is listening. I find this encouraging.

"Successful stories are like successful lies. They diverge from the truth by a matter of degree. DA Anderson is a good storyteller. But that's what he's telling you—a story. A story that sounds like the truth and yet is not the truth. A story with many details, none relevant to the charges against my client. A story rooted in sham science and made-up psychology that sounds technical but proves nothing."

DeFiore strolls over to the defense table and lays a hand on Billy's shoulder.

"One example is the DA's claim that my client watches porn. Watching porn is not a fetish. It is not deviant behavior. Porn did not influence Billy's feelings toward women. Many men watch porn. Many women do too. However, we are not here to render judgment on people who watch porn, including Billy, because his private life is not on trial. As I said and will keep saying, the law is unprejudiced. The law doesn't care about someone's sexual preferences or proclivities. It doesn't judge someone's choices. And yet, it's clear to me, and it should be clear to you, that the State plans to do just that. The DA will try to pathologize his habits, will contend these habits led to violence. This story, rife with misleading claims, prejudicial suppositions, and phony evidence, is designed to lead you to false conclusions. I may not be as good a storyteller as the DA. But I am a good truth-teller. My job is to deconstruct this fake story and recast it as truth. I will ensure that you learn the truth of what happened on March 24. I will ensure you hear facts that are supported by scientific evidence."

I want to cheer.

"And so, on behalf of my client, we ask that you keep these three questions in mind as both sides present our cases. We ask that you listen to the witnesses and assess the scientific evidence. We ask that you understand the facts. Finally, we ask that when the State fails to deliver an unequivocal 'yes' to the three questions at the heart of this trial, you tell the truth and deliver a 'not guilty' verdict. Thank you."

Judge McKay looks up. "Let's take a break."

I feel good about DeFiore's statement. Though it was shorter than Anderson's and less dramatic, it was unpretentious and credible. His job is to pull apart Diana's accusations and show an alternative argument. We don't have to prove anything; we only have to provide reasonable doubt.

We spend the rest of the afternoon listening to the State's first witness, a woman who worked in the lab with Diana and Billy. Her wireframe glasses and no-nonsense haircut make it easy to picture her in a white coat. Anderson leads her through a series of science-related questions that have no point, but luckily, McKay calls him out. "I trust you're going somewhere." As it turns out, Anderson goes nowhere, and court is dismissed.

We leave the building in high spirits. Day three is over, and still no sign of Greg Haggerty. Good news, I tell myself, clutching at anything.

42

OVER THE NEXT WEEK, THE STATE CONTINUES TO PRESENT its case. Each morning, we eat breakfast, don our trial personas, and drive to the courthouse. Despite having four cars at the hotel, plus the Bowtie's Bentley, we cram into Lawrence's Mercedes for the first few days. After that, we start traveling in different cars, in various combinations. The most frequent is me with Lawrence, Billy with Nate, and Eleanor with the Bowtie. But we always gather in the parking lot and walk to court as a family, a united front.

The protestors still show up every day, blocking the sidewalks and filling the streets. As the trial continues, both sides grow louder. An anti-porn splinter group has arrived, too, mostly middle-aged women in pink pussy hats. They yell *pervert, pervert, pervert* and wave signs saying PORN DEGRADES US ALL. Given the severity of the charges against Billy, these women seem to be missing the point.

According to Nate, I'm the one missing the point. "Porn is easy," he explains on the fourth day of the trial. Entering the lobby, we try to ignore the hordes on the courthouse steps. "It's shorthand for male dominance. Or female powerlessness. Or whatever dynamic puts Diana in a one-down position. For them, porn is a symbol of Billy's debauched mind and our culture's indifference to violence against women."

"Listen to you." I'm amused. "Did you just pull that out of your ass?"

"I read an op-ed. But it sounds good, right? I mean, it could be true. Then again, what do I know? You're the scholar. I flunked out of three colleges."

"Don't sell yourself short. Besides, I'm so far behind in my classes, I'll never catch up."

"You'll be fine. Haven't you heard? We're worth seven hundred mil." He puts his arm around my shoulders. "Rich people get all the breaks."

Nate's decided to be nice to me again. I appreciate having him there to help me make sense of the trial. Not that I ever doubted Nate's intelligence, but Billy's arrest has brought out a studious, diligent side I didn't realize he had. He follows every testimony, scours the news reports, and offers DeFiore suggestions. He also, apparently, reads editorials.

From inside the lobby, I watch the women on the street. Their shouting is muted, but their mouths are open holes, their eyes vengeful slits. Their fury is unnerving. Where does that kind of rage come from? Do they hold it in the rest of the time so that they can unleash it here? What happens if they never let it out?

"Cassie, let's go." Lawrence is prodding me. "You're dawdling."

You're repulsive. A memory stirs, unbidden. Tangled pubic hair. The flash of a penis. A woman reclining on a bed. *Pervert, pervert, pervert.*

"Don't let them get to you," Nate says. I must look upset because he's insistent. "Seriously, Cassie. The protests mean nothing. Billy isn't addicted to porn any more than he's addicted to weed. The DA's theory has nothing to do with the charges. It's all theater."

"But what if he is?" A sheet corner coming loose. The bounce of a flimsy mattress. *Repulsive* starts to echo.

"Doesn't make him a rapist."

The women's accusations nag at me. You're a pervert. *You're repulsive.* I feel like I've made a mistake that needs correcting, but can't remember what, exactly, I've done.

* * *

In the courtroom, the mood is convivial. People who were strangers a week ago have become like old friends. Family members, reporters, attorneys, and building personnel greet one another warmly. Behind me, I hear murmurs of "good luck" and "hang in there" to Diana's parents. As the defendant's family, we're not entitled to well wishes; instead, we garner icy stares and sneers of disgust.

On days four and five, the State details Diana and Billy's relationship, from the lab to the playground. This time Maggie Fleming does the honors. Since the arraignment, she's traded her cheap skirt and flats for a big-girl suit and midsized heels. Her long Bible hair is swirled into a complicated updo. She questions Diana's friends, relatives, roommates, and family members, all of whom testify that yes, Diana and Billy went on a few dates. Yes, she liked him—at first. Yes, he watched a lot of porn. ("Objection! Hearsay.") Yes, he changed. Yes, he became agitated, withdrawn, and ill-tempered. Yes, yes, yes, his mood plummeted, his grades dropped, and he got kicked off the track team.

Collectively, the witnesses are earnest, consistent, and credible. It's clear that they care about Diana and aim to do right by her. They describe her as a serious and studious, if naïve, young woman who suffered from low self-esteem. Shocked that such a handsome, wealthy guy was interested in her, she was flustered and unsure how to respond. "She doesn't realize her own beauty," her mother laments. "Everyone sees it except her." Diana was flattered by Billy's attention, but her father, who met him during Parents' Weekend last fall, was wary. "He's too perfect. The minute I met him, I knew he was hiding something behind his pretty face and fancy manners."

Still, Diana continued to date Billy, the witnesses say, even as his porn addiction ramped up and his volatility intensified. When school was back in session, she suggested they separate. Billy reacted poorly. Anderson presents a photo to the jury that is admitted into evidence. Exhibit A-19 is a close-up of a wall in what appears to be a dorm room, punctured with fist-sized holes. Yes, her former roommate says solemnly. The defendant lost his temper and punched out the wall.

It's impossible not to sympathize with the Diana being portrayed here. Even so, her absence from the courtroom does the State no favors. Since we can't see her facial expressions or bodily reactions, she is less a person and more an ideal. Meanwhile, the flesh-and-blood Billy comes to life. Hour after hour, the jury sees dismay register in his eyes. He shakes his head and furrows his brow, which makes the female jurors' faces soften. Watching him, we all feel his suffering. He's not the damaged sociopath we hear about. He's a living, breathing human male whose life has been blown apart.

It helps that DeFiore is at the top of his game. During cross-examinations, he's deliberate and methodical. He finds holes in witnesses' statements, dates that don't sync, narratives that diverge. It's no easy task; there's not one big lie he can reveal. Instead, he has to chip away at the State's story, little by little, one detail at a time, and slowly cast a shadow of doubt.

On day five, the State interviews Liza Franklin-Wallace, Diana's best friend. Clad in a plaid dress, black blazer, and sky-high leather boots, Liza appears sharp and fearless, an ideal sidekick for the mousy, insecure Diana.

"How would you characterize the accused's behavior when Diana broke up with him?" Fleming asks.

"Billy—excuse me, the accused—was hurt. At first, he left her voicemails and love notes, begging her to reconsider. But his weepiness morphed into aggression. He hounded her. Once, he showed up in her bed while she was in class. Imagine walking into your room, turning on the light, and finding a six-foot man waiting for you under the covers. She was petrified!"

"But Diana didn't want to call the police?"

Liza shakes her head. "She was afraid he'd lose his shot at medical school."

I don't buy it. If Diana was that scared, she would've gone to the cops. But Fleming has anticipated my skepticism.

"So, instead of reporting the defendant to the authorities, she invited him to a party?" the attorney asks. "That seems like a strange thing to do if she was so frightened of him."

"Diana wanted to confront him. I suggested she do this in a public setting with friends nearby. I told her to tell Billy if he didn't back off, she'd call the police."

"The party was your idea, not hers?"

"Yes. I regret it greatly. I feel sick to my stomach every time I think about it."

"Does Diana always do what you tell her?"

"No, not always. But I tend to be the boss in our relationship." Liza smiles, but only with her mouth, not her eyes. She's got a haughty quality shared by many Ivy League–educated women, one that suggests she knows more than everyone else.

"But you did encourage her to invite the defendant to a party on March 24?"

Yes, Liza says, I encouraged her. Yes, it was foolish. Yes, she had a vodka tonic. No, I'm not sure how many. Yes, the defendant drank too. Yes, I saw them go into a bedroom together. No, I don't know what happened when they were alone. Yes, when they came out, Billy was enraged. ("Objection! Calls for speculation.") Yes, I was worried when Diana left with him. No, they didn't leave together. I meant I was worried when Billy followed her. Yes, I tried to stop her. Yes, I tried to stop him. Yes, I should've gone. No, I didn't. Yes, I regret my decision.

Liza's voice cracks. "Yes, of course I regret it."

When the State is finished, DeFiore steps up. Fleming was persuasive but no match for DeFiore, who is a rabid pit bull. Moreover, Liza doesn't see him coming, which, for a haughty Ivy Leaguer like me, is delicious to watch.

"Good afternoon," DeFiore says, and then proceeds to drop a sheath of papers. Stumbling, he bends to retrieve them. Liza watches with a grin that smacks of arrogance.

"Ms. Franklin-Wallace, you stated in direct testimony that when Billy and Diana broke up, Billy was hurt. That he—quote—hounded her—unquote. What exactly did he do?"

"He called and texted her incessantly."

"Did you ever hear these calls or see these texts?"

"No, but Diana—"

"You also said Billy showed up, uninvited, to her room. Again, did you see this?"

"No, but—"

"So, everything you know about their breakup came from Diana, correct?"

Liza doesn't appreciate the way DeFiore keeps cutting her off. She appeals to the judge. "Can I finish a sentence, please?"

"A yes or no answer is sufficient," McKay replies.

"To repeat," DeFiore says, "everything you know about their breakup came from Diana, correct? So, you have no idea if Billy broke up with her. Or if it was the other way around, correct?"

"Yes, but—"

"But what?"

Liza appears stricken. "Yes, that is correct."

"Let's move on. Ms. Franklin-Wallace, when asked about the party on March 24, you stated that you and Diana had a vodka tonic before Billy showed up. How many drinks, exactly, did you and Diana have?"

Liza leans forward. But she's lost her confidence, and her voice is inaudible. Twice, the judge asks her to speak up. "Four," she says.

"Four drinks total?"

Liza falters. "No."

"No what, Ms. Franklin-Wallace?"

"Four drinks each." She pauses. Her eyes dart from DeFiore to Fleming and back to DeFiore. "And two shots of whiskey."

"Two shots total?"

"No."

"No what, Ms. Franklin-Wallace?"

"Two shots each."

"So, to restate: by the time my client arrived, Diana had consumed four vodka tonics and two shots of whiskey. In your opinion, how did the alcohol affect her?"

"She was relaxed." Liza's face relaxes too. "We were dancing. We laughed a lot. She was happy. Upbeat."

"Anything else? Loopy? Forgetful? Excited to talk? What's the word? I can't remember. It means *free*, but that's not it. *Unconfined?*" DeFiore fumbles but smarty-pants Liza is all too eager to help.

"*Uninhibited?*" Liza's hand flies to her mouth.

DeFiore nods. "Yes, thank you. *Uninhibited*. Diana was *uninhibited*. So, to restate: by the time my client arrived, Diana had consumed four vodka tonics and two shots of whiskey. She danced. She laughed. She was happy, upbeat, and *uninhibited*." He looks at the gallery then the judge. "No further questions, Your Honor."

"No, that's not what I meant. I was—"

McKay says, "You may step down, Ms. Franklin-Wallace."

A gratifying day's end. DeFiore has accomplished his goal: cast doubt on Diana's version of events. Haggerty hasn't shown up, another positive sign. Adjourned until Monday, we pile into our cars and return to New York.

*   *   *

"Busy, Princess?" Standing at my bedroom door, Nate holds an ancient Scrabble box. "Want to hang out?"

I take out my earbuds. "I haven't played in forever."

"We can play Scrabble. Or . . ." He flips open the lid; inside are two joints.

Fifteen minutes later, we're lying on my carpet, studying the ceiling.

"I still can't get over the size of this room." Nate exhales a plume of smoke. We watch it dissolve into nothing. "You were so spoiled."

He is correct. A room fit for a princess. Bedroom, office nook, walk-in closet, and a bathroom suite that could house a family of four. It was lonely though. Still is, sometimes.

"Nate, it's been twenty years. Let it go."

Moments pass. How many is anyone's guess.

"So, what do you think?" he asks eventually.

"About what?"

"How this epic story will end. Will Billy Quinn get acquitted? Finish school? Be a doctor?"

"Absolutely." I don't hesitate. "No question."

"And you? What will you do?"

"Quit Yale. Be Amelia Earhart. Fly jets. You?"

"Big waves, baby. Ride the surf a hundred feet in the air."

A knock on the door startles us.

"Oh, sorry." It's Lawrence, looking confused. "I thought you were alone."

"Lawrence!" I shout. "Go away. This is Hawkins Cove. No parents allowed." I crack myself up. Beside me on the floor, Nate eggs me on.

"Sacred space, dude," he tells his father. "You need to G-O, go. Kids only."

"Sure," Lawrence repeats, faking a smile. "I'll leave you children alone."

Seeing him relegated to the sidelines fills me with superhuman strength. Already giddy, Nate and I can't stop laughing. Holding my stomach, I try to sit up. I should be nice, let Lawrence in on the joke. But by the time I can speak, he is gone.

43

DURING WEEK TWO, BOREDOM SETS IN. TIME STANDS STILL as Anderson and Fleming tag-team street cops, detectives, EMTs, pharmacists, and a slew of forensic experts who take us through sets of tedious and confusing scientific data. What does become clear, however, is that DeFiore underplayed the State's evidence. They have more than enough, much of it troubling. Even so, most of the witnesses are older men who seem ill at ease out of uniform. Their bodies are unnaturally stiff, their answers overly rehearsed. They're armed with props, all designed to situate us at the playground and break down the action in easy-to-follow steps. But Anderson moves through them too quickly. We're shown maps, diagrams, blueprints, and timelines, one right after the other, in an avalanche of details. So, rather than being able to digest the most vital facts, we're buried under minutia.

Watching a trial unfold in real time is nothing like seeing one on TV. There's no wrap-up commentary at the end of the hour. Instead, we suffer through stretches of testimony where the same point is made repeatedly. We hear two police officers describe, in painstaking detail, the patch of lawn where the alleged assault took place, including its square footage, soil density, grass height, and footprint patterns. Photographs of the tire swing are passed around, and entered into evidence, as are Diana's dress, sweater, bra, ankle boots, and socks. Some of these photos have been enlarged to poster size. Anderson holds them up for the judge and jury—and the reporters in the gallery—then stacks them on easels where they sit until the witness is dismissed. But even if the pictures were interesting—which they're not—how many shots of a lacy bra do we really need to see? Similarly, Diana's underwear was missing from the scene, but what could've been a compelling set of questions flattens into a mind-numbing dissertation on chain of evidence. Briefly, a frisson of excitement is ignited when DeFiore suggests that Diana may have foregone underwear altogether ("What's the expression? *Commando?*"). But the objection to his query is sustained, and the comment is stricken from the record.

A skinny, white-haired pharmacist catalogues every substance the couple consumed: beer, vodka, whiskey, Jell-O shots, and marijuana (strain: Sativa, Acapulco Gold). Then he recites how each one alters brain chemistry and bodily function. His testimony is jargon-heavy and impossible to follow. Nor can I figure out why McKay allows so many interruptions. DeFiore is constantly on his feet, objecting and requesting sidebars, which means every few minutes the action moves offstage while we're left to figure out what's happening.

"We're doing great!" I told DeFiore at lunch after the pharmacist's testimony. "You're killing it."

"Don't get too excited," he said. "Advantage is a pendulum. It swings both ways."

Unfortunately, he's right. Slowly but surely the State gains traction. To my horror, Anderson starts pulling Billy apart, one detail at a time. Surprisingly, the pivot point for his success turns out to be porn.

For the next two days, we hear a series of witnesses offer damning testimony, starting with a gangly IT expert who examined Billy's electronics. Basically, he intimates, the defendant is a perverted porn addict. Eleven hours a week is considered compulsive for college-aged males. So my brother, who watches an average of eighteen hours a week, with a high of twenty-four, is a dirty, drooling lunatic who can't keep his hands out of his pants.

"This is bullshit," I murmur.

Nate nods. "But titillating." Looking around, I see this is true. The jury is spellbound.

Lawrence overhears us. "Porn," he whispers, disgusted. "Pseudo-psychology conjured out of thin air. This whole argument is repulsive."

You're repulsive.

I glance up. When our eyes meet, my face registers for him. For the past seven months, Lawrence has been distracted; or maybe it started earlier, when I jetted off to school the year before. Though he looked at me, it was clear he wasn't seeing me. Before that, he was always aware of my presence. There was a pulse in the air, a live wire joining his body to mine.

Now I feel like we're reconnecting again, which makes me unreservedly blissful. At the same time, I hear the type of porn Billy was watching before the party on March 24. "The defendant focused on subjects like Gangbang, Hardcore, and Dominance," the IT guy says. He gets nervous, starts spelling out words he's unable to say. "Videos called *U-g-l-y B-i-t-c-h Gets F-u-c-k-e-d* and *Drunk Girl Gets a Mouthful.*"

Fear blooms in my chest. My heart starts to race. *You're repulsive.* A man's hand reaches down; I see a flash of naked skin. Blue sheet with tiny pink flowers. A patch of wiry hair.

"You okay?" Lawrence's whisper is thick with emotion. "Sweetheart?" His hand reaches down, he touches my own naked skin. Every nerve feels electrified. "Cass?"

My chest flutters. A cyclone whips up inside me. Dizzy, I shake with its force.

"Fine," I say.

I've split. One me is here. The other has taken off. Calm down, I coach myself. Slow and steady. Just breathe. My head is buzzing. Light flashes in my eye.

"Fine, fine, fine," I assure Lawrence. "I swear."

Next up is Dr. Helmsley Fordyce, renowned psychiatrist, porn expert, Cambridge scholar, and Harvard professor whose bona fides make even Eleanor sit tall and take notice. Dr. Fordyce is a silver fox, a charismatic man in his sixties with a plume of gray hair and a British accent that makes him sound simultaneously wise and ironic.

After offering a lengthy intro and résumé, Anderson digs in. "Dr. Fordyce, what can you tell us about men like the defendant who start watching porn at a very early age?"

Dr. Fordyce nods. "Approximately seventy-three percent of males who start watching porn before age ten are more prone to erectile dys-function than males who start watching when they're older. Similarly, of these men, sixty-eight percent admit to having negative feelings toward women. And ninety percent admit to harassing, abusing, and committing acts of violence, specifically against women."

"*Ninety percent*," the DA says. "*Ninety percent* of young men who watch porn admit to committing acts of violence against women."

"Objection!" DeFiore shouts.

I know these numbers are bogus. Statistics can be skewed up, down, and sideways. They cast no light on Billy's guilt. And yet, the audience is buying it. Fordyce's voice is melodious, his affect persuasive. His material is provocative, and he's meting it out in bite-sized bits that leave us craving more. "Porn contains disturbing messages, overt and subliminal. Kids—I'll say 'boys' because, statistically, the population skews male—are repeatedly shown, for instance, that no doesn't mean no. Instead, by pushing, trickery, or physical violence, women can be persuaded, or forced, to perform desired sex acts."

Here, Anderson makes a brilliant move. He invites Fordyce to step down, and then returns to the rape so he can illustrate, in cold hard facts, the connection between porn and violence. He recalls, at a rapid-fire clip, the eyewitnesses, detectives, EMTs, and hospital personnel who saw Billy at the crime scene or examined Diana right after. One by one, the witnesses testify that the defendant was out of control, that Diana was unconscious, and that Billy knew this but penetrated her anyway. The Glasgow coma score—13 out of 15—is raised no less than seven times. Pictures from the physical exam—bruises, lacera-tions, swelling—are admitted into evidence and published to the jury. One of the boys who helped tackle Billy asserts that my brother, who was looking into Diana's eyes while he was on top of her, seemed aware of her condition. During his cross, DeFiore forces the kid to admit that the playground was dark, and he has no idea what he saw, but it's not enough to mitigate the damage.

Anderson turns to the judge. "Permission to show one final photo-graph, Your Honor."

When DeFiore sees what it is, he strenuously objects. But he's overruled, the picture is entered into evidence, and then passed around the jury.

"My God," a woman says.

Anderson holds up a poster-sized replica and sets it on an easel.

"Jesus," Nate murmurs.

"Shush!" Lawrence hisses, though he, too, stiffens.

In the photo, Diana is asleep in the grass. Her clothes are torn off. Her hair is matted with leaves, pebbles, and pieces of dirt. There are bruises on her legs, and scratches on her face. Her skin is pale white against a tangle of dark hair. She is fragile and alone. A young girl, someone's child, beaten to shit.

44

WE TAKE AN HOUR-LONG BREAK. IN THE CONFERENCE ROOM, the five of us are subdued. No one mentions the photograph. Instead, we study our phones. Back in court, the DA recalls Dr. Helmsley Fordyce to the stand. As the doctor sits down, the room is quiet. A new understanding has passed among the gallery. The stakes have been recalibrated. These are critical issues. Matters of life and death.

When the DA speaks, his tone is respectful. "Doctor, you said earlier that watching pornography can have a disastrous effect on a developing brain. Can you elaborate?"

Fordyce nods. "Current science is only beginning to reveal the neurological repercussions of porn consumption in children, but we've known for years that the impact on the mental health and sex lives of young boys—and girls—who watch porn is catastrophic. Briefly, I'll explain a concept called neuroplasticity." He smiles at Anderson. "Stop me if I'm nattering on."

"No, no, Doctor." Anderson makes a rolling motion with his hands. "Continue, please."

"Neuroplasticity is the ability of neural networks in the brain to change through growth and reorganization. Basically, it explains how the brain can adapt, master new skills, and store memories. The process peaks during childhood and adolescence then decreases as we get older, which means two things. One, a child's brain is, literally, shaped by his experiences. And two, these experiences determine a large part of his character for the rest of his life." He looks at Anderson, who, again, gestures at him to keep going.

"The properties of video pornography make it a powerful trigger for plasticity. The brain is wired to respond to sexual stimulation.

Put simply, when the body requires sex, the brain remembers which sources to tap to reexperience pleasure. But over time, the brain gets bored, and needs more exciting stimuli. With porn, there's a leap from conventional sex to group sex, for example. Or forbidden imagery like pedophilia. Many times, it's violence. While my work isn't focused on selection, we do know that children who view porn at a young age develop a hypersexualized view of the world, which is itself another danger. Porn leads these kids down hallways they might never have traveled if the door wasn't opened that first time."

I'm listening intently, too intently. When Fordyce says "a hypersexualized view of the world," it triggers a memory. Suddenly, my body is plunged into water. I have the strange sensation of drowning, as if gravity doesn't exist anymore. My throat closes up. I can't swallow. Lawrence and I are watching a movie. I'm young, thirteen, I think. Was I thirteen? I can't say for sure. I remember saying yes, of course, I want to watch; I'm not a baby.

In the movie, a man is standing over a bed. A woman lies on her back. Her legs are spread. This confuses me. Why isn't she wearing pants? She looks very unhappy even though she's smiling. "Keep your mouth shut," the man commands. I feel like he's talking to me. "Don't move." He grabs his penis, angrily, as if wielding a weapon. There is a flash of naked legs. A rustle of sheets. They're light blue with tiny pink flowers. The flowers are in rows, like a perfect garden. Those flowers are pretty, I think, wishing my sheets had flowers. "This guy is in a lot of these movies," Lawrence is saying, like he's the director, recapping the scene for a graduate seminar. "His name is Marcus Silver. The men tend to be anonymous, so it's weird I'd remember him. In porn, it's women who are the brand-name stars." I have no idea why Lawrence is telling me this, but I wish he'd shut up. This is *repulsive*, I think, a word I'm proud to know. But I can't bring myself to say shut up to him, which means I'm younger than thirteen. More likely eleven or ten, and this was one of his educational moments. Maybe it was when I told him about the naked people I saw on Nate's phone? Keep your mouth shut, the man said. I'm talking to you.

My body trembles. I can't stop blinking. Hypersexualized. Forbidden. *You're repulsive*. Who's repulsive? Me. Here's the thing, the super-secret, I hated the movie but didn't say stop. I kept watching, and part of me, part of me liked it. I am repulsive. A slutty slut at ten years old.

I turn to Lawrence. What have you done? I was just a kid. Right? Wasn't I?

I'm trapped here, in this courtroom, on this bench. Trapped, always, with Lawrence, my gift and my curse. Cassie + Lawrence forever and ever.

"Cassandra," he whispers sharply, his hand on my thigh. "What is going on?"

Lawrence's hands, hairy and masculine, scrolling his phone, pecking a keyboard, sliding along my skin. His hands, under tables, behind doors, reaching for me.

"Nothing, Lawrence," I promise. "I'm fine. I told you that."

His voice flows through my veins like blood. He seeps into every crevice, clogs every pore. This is how I keep him close, how he possesses me. I will never escape Lawrence. I will never escape Marcus. They are one and the same. The secret, special men who loved all of me.

And yet, how can this be a secret? How can anyone not know? To me, Lawrence + Cassie is as obvious as the sky. *How can you not see him all over my face?*

I look at Billy. Time stops for a minute. And then something terrible happens. As I watch my brother, composed and contained in his suit, it occurs to me that maybe I've been wrong all along. Maybe Billy is a criminal. Maybe he did rape Diana Holly. Look where we are. A judge wields a gavel. Prosecutors rifle through briefcases. Defense attorneys take notes. Why would they be here if my brother wasn't guilty?

Fear fills my senses. My mouth dries up. I bend over, trying to calm myself.

Lawrence puts his hand on my back. "You okay?" he whispers.

I shrug him off. "Why do you keep asking me that?" I hate to be babied; I'm no one's baby. "I said I'm fine."

But I'm gasping for air. You can't sit in a courtroom with a boy, any boy, even your own brother, and not question his innocence. Too many women in the world have come forward. They have too many stories. What shocks me, and keeps shocking me, is that their stories are about men we know—loving men, caring men; men trusted by wives, revered by daughters. Men like Lawrence. Wives like Eleanor. Daughters like me. So, yes, I do have to wonder about Billy because I know, better than most, that anyone is capable of anything. Tap deeply enough, and you'll find we're all monsters below the surface.

45

THE DAY ENDS ON A SOMBER NOTE. WE LOWER OUR EYES
and quietly file out of the courtroom. One by one, people look away
from Billy, who's become tainted, radioactive. The tide has turned
against us; I can feel it.

I'm deluged by memories. I'm a senior in high school. Lawrence
and I are a couple, sweethearts. We are together, in the same house,
eating the same meals, but we're also separate. He's still married to
Eleanor, though he will soon leave her. "After college," he promises.
"It will be easier." Plus, after college, I'll be closer to my king's ransom, and we won't need Eleanor's money. "Just wait a little longer."
He pauses. "Please."

Most women wouldn't believe Lawrence, but I know I can. I've
known him my whole life, and we've been Lawrence + Cassie since I
was twelve. Not sexually, not in the beginning. Intimately. Privately.
Look at all we survived: missed connections, jealousy, suffocation, his
refusals, my meltdown. Waiting. More waiting. But along the way we
had the park, the ducks. And each other. Besides, what choice do I
have? To say no isn't an option; the idea never even occurs to me.

"Okay," I agree. "I'll wait."

I graduate from Spence and enroll in Columbia, across town and
up a couple dozen blocks. I move into my own apartment on Riverside Drive, ten minutes from the Valmont by cab. Right by the park,
our special bench. Lawrence visits frequently. I'm seventeen then eighteen, finally an adult. I've never known such freedom. Out of Eleanor's
house, away from her disapproving eye, I spend entire mornings
without clothes. I stand in my small galley kitchen, in broad daylight,
my windows wide open. My body will never be this firm again. I flash

the Upper West Side. No one tells me what to wear, when to eat, who to fuck. Our sex is consuming, satisfying; unobserved and finally, truly alone. Lawrence can't keep his hands off me. "I can't stop," he tells me. Neither of us can.

These afternoons aren't enough. We both want more. Someday, Lawrence promises, we'll have a kitchen, his-and-her cars, our own celebration room. "Call me 'Sweetheart,'" he begs when he's wrapped in my arms. "Say I'm your sweetheart."

But someday is too far away. "Now," I say.

"When you graduate," he reminds me. He'll tell Eleanor it's over; he doesn't love her anymore. He loves me. "You're the Forever Girl. My one and only."

Two years pass. I study stupid shit.

Two more years pass. I study more stupid shit. Sometimes I care, mostly I'm waiting.

Finally, I graduate. For me, there are champagne toasts. Two strands of Mikimoto pure white South Sea pearls. Diamond stud earrings. Fifteen thousand shares of Class A stock. A round-trip ticket to Morocco. For Lawrence + Cassie, there are bickering and tears, arguments and ultimatums. Opposites coexist. It's the best time of my life and the very, very worst.

Lawrence + Cassie devolves. We are as fraught and miserable as spouses in a thirty-year marriage. Fights are never resolved; resentment can't be assuaged. We are always seething, always tense. I make a pronouncement. "I'm going to grad school; I found a program. It's at Yale. Have you ever seen Yale? It's gorgeous."

"You went to see it?" He can't believe it. "When was this?"

"When you were with your wife."

"What about me? What about us?"

"I knew you'd do this, Lawrence. You're so fucking weak." I'm frantic with rage and scared half to death, but I'm doing it. I'm going.

There is begging, and promises are made. "Wait a little longer," he tells me.

"I'm done waiting, Lawrence." Far off in the distance, Rachel is humming, singing a sad lament about beautiful things. In this moment,

I realize she's speaking to me. I walked away, Cassie, she is saying. But I wasn't leaving you; I needed to do it for me.

I can do it, too, I tell myself. I have to do it.

I leave Lawrence, the Valmont, New York, Eleanor, Nate, Billy—my whole life. And ever since that day, he's been dragging me back. Every conversation—my selfish behavior, his business that's barely a business, the foundation that will never take off, my responsibilities, my obligations, my future—is about Lawrence + Cassie. Billy's trial is about us. Lawrence doesn't want me to meet DeFiore. He doesn't want me to go to court. He doesn't want me to testify. He wants Billy to plead guilty. He's willing to sacrifice his own son. All because of us.

Lawrence + Cassie is my darkest secret and deepest craving, my festering sore. What the mind closes off, the body remembers. Memories fade, emotions die, but the skin erupts, the flesh screams.

"After the trial," Lawrence promises. We're alone in the car, heading to the hotel from the courthouse. "We'll be together. I'm begging you, baby. Don't leave me."

"I don't know," I tell him as he tries again to reel me back in. His hand strokes my bare thigh. "I don't know." Maybe.

* * *

Our culture is obsessed with predators. Ever since I was a child, I've been warned about older men who groom young girls for sex. The details change, but never the message: girls are weak and foolish; men are dangerous and canny. Predators are everywhere.

Are there really that many dumb girls? That many violent men? (I don't know the answer; I'm simply posing the questions.)

A predator is careful about his selection; out of a hundred girls, he'll choose one. But it's not as if the girl waits, passively, to be chosen. In her own way, she chooses him too. The man and the girl are familiar to each other; they share feelings they believe are uniquely theirs—strong urges, insatiable needs. Previously, these feelings were shameful, which is why the man is so relieved to find them in her. The girl is just grateful to be loved, to be seen. These feelings are their special language, their private means of communication.

Their relationship is symbiotic, a mutual experience. The man breaks down barriers, but the girl offers herself up. Each word, every gesture is calculated. So is the response. Can I get you a drink? Call you a cab? Walk you upstairs? Days pass, months. Can I touch you? Kiss you? Take off your bra? Touch your breasts? Pull down your pants? Occasionally, years. But the endgame is clear. Can I love you?

Yes, she says. Please.

I'm not suggesting predators don't exist. But not every man is a predator and not every girl prey. Like any relationship, dynamics shift. Emotions wax and wane. But you can't say every girl has no agency, that we're all weak and foolish, that we don't know our own minds. To deny me choice over my body is to deny me a self. To deny me a me.

My relationship with Lawrence Quinn evolves over years and more years. People have misconceptions about affairs between older men and young women. That they're rooted in power and centered on sex is one. Older men push younger women into behavior they don't want is another. But our relationship is rooted in trust and centered on love. Lawrence didn't touch me until I was ready, despite how often I asked, how forcefully I pushed, all my ultimatums.

He loves to tease me about this: that I'm predator and he's prey. "You picked me, Cassie," he says in jest—in jest because he's naked and splayed underneath me like Christ on the cross. "You picked, groomed, and broke me down. I had no choice. I had to say yes."

"You had . . . you . . ." I'm panting. Bearing down, I fuck him harder. Sweat rolls off my skin. I lick salt from his lips. "You had . . . no choice . . ." He has no choice.

Afterward, flat on our backs and soaking in sunlight, we laugh and laugh at the absurdity.

46

I CAN'T SLEEP IN THIS HOTEL. ALONE IN MY BED, SEPARATED from Lawrence by a single wall, I ache with desire. My dreams, hallucinogenic and vivid, are Technicolor movies that I watch and experience simultaneously. They're so immersive, I can't be sure if they're dreams or alternative lives. I work hard to decode the baroque symbolism and hidden messages, but nothing makes sense. All I know for sure is that we're running out of time.

A few of my dreams feature Hawkins Cove. I'm with my brothers, who are in their twenties, but absorbed in childhood activities, like digging holes. In one, I leap over ragged rocks that are slick with blood. The water is threatening, dark red, viscous, and whirling with rage. Billy is there, too, taunting me by refusing to speak. I try to get his attention, but he backs away and then dives, headfirst, into the bloody water, as if over a cliff. Don't leave me, I want to say, but my words are stuck. I wake up crying with my throat raw.

The night before the State rests, it's me and Billy again in my dream. Only this time, I'm the one backing away; it's me who's about to fall. My mouth is filled with grime, pieces of garbage and dirt that I scrape off my teeth in handfuls. Billy is holding my T-shirt, but not tightly enough, so I lose my footing. I suspect he pushed me. I don't want to believe this even as I know it's true. Meanwhile, I'm screaming *Elmo, stop,* but my mouth is too full for him to hear me. Besides, it's too late. My brother has already turned away, and I'm spiraling in midair.

* * *

On Thursday morning, the prosecution presents its final witness. Anderson announces her name in a game-show baritone. "The State calls Diana Angelina Holly."

Excitement ripples through the gallery. She's here? Heads swivel to Anderson, over to DeFiore, back to Anderson. Where? Where is she? Will we see her on video or in person?

"Your Honor," Anderson says. "I beg the Court's indulgence for another minute." Apparently, his celebrity witness is MIA, because he's gesturing to Fleming, who's bent over her phone, texting like mad. "Excuse me for a second," she says to McKay, pocketing her device as she speed-walks out. "I'll be right back."

While we wait, Anderson plods over to the defense table, where he blocks the jury's view of Billy, as if building suspense. Since day one, DeFiore has reinforced the need for Billy to stay calm, especially when Diana is nearby. "The jury *wants* you to go ballistic. They *want* to see you melt down. If you do, it makes their job easier. I am begging you, Billy. Keep your cool, no matter what anyone says to you or about you."

"Be a Sphinx," Felicia Drake added. "Do not react."

Billy has followed these instructions to the letter. Day after day, he listens intently and takes notes. He looks so engrossed even I forget he's medicated. Every morning as we leave the hotel, he swallows a high-grade sedative. If not for the pill, he'd tap his pencil, squirm in his chair, and shift back and forth. Today, when he leans back, he looks serene, if semi-comatose. He has the faintest grin on his lips. I've seen this smile before, during races, right before he makes one last push and snaps the tape. It's Billy's tell, the way he unconsciously signals he knows he's about to win.

The door swings open. Diana Holly appears. Backlit by the mid-morning sun, she strolls down the aisle like a pageant queen, escorted by Fleming. The courtroom is still. We hear the rustle of gauzy fabric and the squeak of patent leather as Diana approaches the bailiff and raises her right hand.

At the defense table, my brother has come to life. Briefly, he turns to his mother. His eyes are open and crazed with terror. He's jiggling his foot. His face is bleached of color. His victory smile has vanished.

* * *

"Thank you for joining us," Anderson says gently. For the past two weeks, the DA has moved through his interviews with swift efficiency—staccato questions, in-and-out, boom, boom, boom. Now, with Diana, he is slow and obsequious. "You have no obligation to be in this courtroom. That you are is a testament to your bravery and integrity."

Diana nods. In my memory, she was small and pushy, with a pixie bob, a greedy personality and nonstop flattery. But today, I don't see any of this. Diana Holly is a pretty girl. Her brown hair has grown out and falls in waves that frame her face. One side is held back by a tortoiseshell clip. She has round eyes and full lashes. She's softer and more ladylike than I remember. On the other hand, she's wearing a fluffy sweater over a rose-colored dress, so maybe that's why. Or because she's not wearing makeup. Mostly, Diana looks pale, sad, and exhausted. I'm sure she is sad and exhausted, considering what she's been through.

Peeking at Eleanor, I try to get a read on her thoughts. She's watching Diana, but her face, as always, is inscrutable. She, not Billy, is the Sphinx.

"So, tell us a little bit about how you came to know the defendant."

"We . . . I . . ." Diana is trembling, and her voice is too low to be heard. McKay doesn't ask her to speak up, though, so we're forced to lean forward and strain.

She clears her throat. "Billy and I met in a lab at Sloan-Kettering. Cancer research—pancreatic cancer. Cellular studies."

"Can you tell us about these studies?"

"Sure. Pancreatic tumors are encased in a thick protective tissue." Finding her comfort zone, Diana relaxes. She raises her voice to an audible level. "We were looking at ways to collapse this cell barrier and make the tumors more susceptible to therapeutic drugs."

"Is this what you want to do when you get out of school? Cancer research?"

"Not research, no. Oncology. I want to treat kids with cancer. Billy and I had this in common. We both want to work with children."

"Were you surprised when the defendant asked you out?"

"I was. Billy could date anyone he wanted. He was very handsome—
I mean, he still is." Diana blushes, her bare cheeks turn scarlet. "It
feels weird to talk about him when he's sitting in the room." She offers
Anderson a sheepish smile. "I was surprised he was interested in me.
Also intimidated."

"Diana, you're premed at Princeton University. You've won countless academic awards, including the Sloan-Kettering internship. Many
people have testified at length about your achievements. Why would
you, of all people, be intimidated?"

"I look great on paper." Diana pauses. "Not even 'great.' Compared
to my classmates, I'm average. But inside, I never felt smart enough.
Or pretty enough. So I had to work feverishly to catch up. I studied
all the time and got perfect grades. Picture a pudgy girl with glasses
who hides in the library. A country mouse from Pittsburgh—not even
Pittsburgh, a tiny town nearby. So yes, when he asked me out, I was
overwhelmed. He was, he was . . . I don't know . . . everything—"

Again, she blushes deep red. But this time, I am moved by her hon-
esty. Diana Holly has become real to me, and I see the girl I liked when
we first met.

"Billy is handsome and smart. And *way* out of my league. He's also
charming and seductive. Truth be told, I got seduced by his looks, by
his money, by all of it. Then, as I got to know him, and saw he wasn't
perfect, we became incredibly close. I couldn't bear to be apart from
him, even for a day."

"But there were problems?"

"Yes. Billy is troubled, emotionally, I mean. Everyone has issues,
of course, but Billy's problems were deeper and more dangerous than
I first realized. They affected every aspect of his life, including our
relationship."

"What kinds of issues?"

Diana looks at her hands. "Anger issues, drugs—marijuana mostly."

I glance at Billy. Though he appears relaxed, I can tell from the
line of his shoulders that it's taking every ounce of his strength not
to react.

"Pornography," Anderson says. Though it's not a question, no one objects.

When Diana nods, a lock of hair falls in her face, and she tucks it behind one ear. "Yes. But the problem wasn't just drugs or porn. It was quantity and intensity. Billy gets stoned every day. Same with porn. Billy watches *a lot*. It seemed normal at first, at least for a college-aged guy. But by July, I realized he was hiding how often he watched."

"How so?"

"He's on his devices all day. But if I so much as glanced at his screen, he'd scramble to close it. He wasn't always fast enough. I saw people having sex, orgies or whatever. Other times, it was the opposite. He'd stare at his computer with his eyes glazed over, completely unaware of my presence. It was creepy and unsettling."

"So what did you do?"

Diana shakes her head. Her eyes fill with tears. Anderson waits.

"Nothing," she whispers. "I was insecure, and so grateful he liked me. I was afraid if I said anything, he'd break up with me."

"You just let it go?"

"I tried to talk to him about it once, but he told me to mind my own business and I stopped bringing it up. But when school started, I told him he needed counseling and we should spend time apart."

"And what was the defendant's reaction?"

"Billy has a temper. When it's triggered, he lashes out."

Anderson refers to Exhibit A-19, the dorm room wall with fist-sized holes. "Like this?" He places the photo on an easel. "Did the defendant do this? Did he make these holes in reaction to you saying you wanted to break up?"

"Yes, he punched the wall."

"How else did pornography affect your relationship? Was it just the fact that he hid how often he watched? Did you distrust him? Or was there more to it?"

"No . . . I mean, yes, he was untrustworthy. But when I confronted him, and he stopped sneaking around, it got worse. Porn permeated our relationship. Billy also . . ." Diana stumbles. "He can't maintain an erection unless he's watching, so he positioned his computer next to the bed. He watched videos while we . . . uh . . . made love. It was humiliating. I was sure it was my fault. I wasn't pretty or sexy enough. I figured if he needed porn because of a deficiency in me, then I had no right to ask him to stop. I was ashamed. I *am* ashamed. I didn't think I deserved better . . . I just . . ." She starts to cry. "It was unbearable."

Anderson asks if she needs a break.

"No. I want to finish." She gathers herself. "By November, I realized Billy's problem was bigger than me. Or rather, had nothing to do with me. Like any addictive behavior, it was compulsive. He couldn't stop."

"What happened?"

"We were at his parents' home in New York."

"You got along well with his family?"

"I thought so. I only met them a couple of times. They were very gracious. But I was intimidated, the same way I was with Billy in the beginning. His mother and sister are so glamorous. Cassie was extra nice. I could tell she was anxious to be close to him again. That night she drove all the way from New Haven just for dinner."

On this point, Diana is correct. I drove home because I was curious about her and Billy. According to Lawrence, she was clingy and they might be breaking up. So I wanted to see if my brother and I could be friends again. I also planned to have a stern talk with Lawrence about his own clinginess. His constant texts and calls were driving me up the wall.

"Billy was agitated that night," Diana continues. "We were in the den, having a drink before dinner, and he kept jumping up to use the bathroom. At first I thought Cassie was making him uncomfortable. I knew—well, Billy had told me—that everyone gets tense when she's home. Then I realized he was sneaking off to watch porn. It was like a light bulb went on. In that moment, I understood he was an addict, it wasn't my fault, and we'd both be happier if we broke up for good."

Wait, no! That's not true. Billy never got up—not once. And I remember this because, like Diana, I was tracking his every move. I watched him come into the house and take off his coat; I waited for him to hug me. Instead, he brushed by me, and guided Diana down the hall.

"Billy!" I called out. "No hello?" Diana said hi, but he kept walking, tossing off, "Oh, hey, Cassie," over his shoulder. Later, we were in the den: Billy, Diana, Eleanor, and me. Billy was being very cold, and I tried to make conversation, but he barely acknowledged me. So I went to find Lawrence, who was in the celebration room, and let him know Billy and Diana had arrived. When I walked out, I ran into Diana, who'd been peering into random rooms, gawking at their size. She was holding a vase, but upside-down as if checking for a manufacturing label. "I'm sorry," she said, startled. "I didn't know you were here." I didn't care about the vase, but I was stung by Billy's shitty treatment. I made a nasty crack, and I think Diana was embarrassed because she wouldn't look me in the eye. "I'm so sorry," she kept repeating then rushed off. When I got back to the den, she was tugging on Billy's hand. "Babe, I don't feel well. Babe? Do you mind if we head out early? Babe?" The whole thing was fucked-up and rude.

"And then what happened?" Anderson is asking Diana.

"I broke up with him. I mean, it took a few weeks, but eventually I told him it was really over."

"And how did he react to that?"

"Badly. Like Dr. Jekyll and Mr. Hyde." She shakes her head. "I went to his dorm room to tell him, and when I started talking, he picked up his baseball bat. I got scared. Honestly, this was unusual. Billy has never hurt me, not physically. But the bat freaked me out. 'Billy,' I said. 'I wish you'd put that down.'"

"Did he?"

"No. He just kept smacking the thick part against his hand, in this menacing way. I didn't know what to do, so I just kept talking. I told him I cared about him and didn't want to hurt him. But we couldn't see each other anymore. At first, he didn't reply, so I thought he was okay. But then he blew up. I mean, he was a maniac, yelling and swinging the bat. Not at me, at the furniture. Then he ran out to the parking lot behind the dorm and started bashing in his own car."

Nate nudges me and whispers, "Do you believe this? Why would he do that?"

Anderson holds up a photo. "I'd like to introduce Exhibit SE-33 into evidence." He hands the photograph to the jury members, who pass it down the line. It's the windshield of a car, shattered to bits. Glass is everywhere—inside the seat, on the pavement, across the hood. He places a poster of the image on an easel.

"Is this Billy's Audi?"

"Yes," Diana replies quietly. "That's his car. That *was* his car, I mean."

When McKay cracks his gavel, the sound is like a gunshot. "Let's break for lunch," he says.

47

I GRAB DEFIORE'S ARM AS HE WALKS OUT OF THE COURT-
room. "Can I speak to you? Privately? I promise it won't take long."

"Sure, Cassie. Always." But he looks spooked, like he's just witnessed a fatal crash. "I have to make a couple calls, and then I'll come
find you." Patting my arm, he hustles away.

I stop in the ladies' room where I run into Eleanor at the sink. It
creates an optical illusion, as if there are four of us. "It's warm in this
building, no?" she says to my reflection.

"I guess" is all I can manage.

"I need water, Sweetheart," she says, then touches up her lipstick,
and snaps her bag shut. "I'll get you some as well." A marvel of tran-
quil restraint, Eleanor could be anywhere: a department store lounge,
the lobby of a hotel or private club. That she happens to be in a federal
courthouse, where her son happens to be on trial, a trial he happens to
be losing, is neither here nor there. "You should eat something," she
tells me. "Dinner might be late this evening."

Soon after, I'm sitting with Nate and Billy in our usual conference
room. DeFiore has brought in an outside firm to consult on the case—
never a good sign, according to Lawrence—and unfamiliar lawyers
have been in and out all morning. The place is a disaster zone. Breakfast and lunch trays have been plundered. Ramekins of cream cheese
and half-eaten sandwiches are drying out under the recessed lights.
Dirty plates, soiled napkins, and empty chip bags litter the table. Laptops and iPads are plugged into walls, and cords are everywhere.

Wearing his signature headphones, Billy is sprawled in a chair with
his eyes closed. Next to me, Nate holds out a bag of pretzels. Digging
in, I take two and eat them, then go back for more.

"What's bothering you?" He squints at his computer, reading the news. "I haven't seen you eat a carbohydrate since the fourth grade."

"Diana's testimony shook me up."

Glancing at Billy, Nate lowers his voice. "She's a decent witness. I mean, she's probably lying about everything. Still, I believe her."

"She is lying. That story about dinner. I was there. Billy didn't get up, not once. I mean, it's a small detail but it's not true." I pause. "We're losing, Nate."

Out in the hall, Lawrence and Eleanor are arguing. This is a new development; until now, they've never argued publicly. Nate puts in earbuds, but I move closer to the door. "It's a bloodbath," I hear Lawrence say. "Let's take the four years."

Eleanor scoffs. "There is no 'four years.' That deal was off the table when the trial started. You know this, Lawrence. Don't pretend otherwise."

"This is *your* fault, Eleanor. I wanted to take it."

"Folks!" DeFiore is pissed. "Knock it off!"

Lawrence apologizes, but Eleanor is quiet. I hear the tap of her heels as she walks away, and wait for him to chase her. Instead, he steps into the conference room. "Whoa!" he exclaims, looking around. "You kids must be starving. You seeing this, Peter? Even Cassie is eating!"

Ignoring him, I turn to DeFiore. "We're fucked, aren't we?"

He shakes his head. "No one is fucked. We're right where we want to be." He tries to sound reassuring but his eyes dart all over the room. "We still have our whole defense—" Mid-sentence, he pivots. "You had something to tell me, Cassie?"

"She's lying," I say. "About the dinner in November. Billy never left the den." I remind him of that evening, the parts Diana left out: how I bumped into her in the hall, the way she was ogling our house, the vase, my comment, her embarrassment, their rushed departure.

"Yeah, I know." Browsing through emails on his phone, DeFiore is only half-listening. "Eleanor also told me Diana is lying. No need to worry, though. We've got this covered."

"What does that mean? How is this covered?"

DeFiore has moved to the lunch trays, where he picks over the small bits of crusted bread that remain. Chewing thoughtfully, he's somewhere else, far away from the trial, away from the Lawrence Quinns, away from this whole sordid mess.

* * *

Back in court, Diana completes her testimony. For the balance of the afternoon, we marinate in Billy's anger. His explosive anger. Shocking anger. Destructive anger. My brother, William Matthew Stockton Quinn, a young man of many dimensions—athlete, scholar, volunteer, brother, son—is reduced to only one: rapist. A note replayed so many times and so perfectly pitched that by the time Diana finishes, I don't understand how Billy can be allowed to leave this building. We should hang him from the rafters and watch him swing.

Diana remains tearful. "The breakup was bad. But the aftermath was worse."

Next to the jury box, two easels hold posters we've already seen: the fist-sized holes in Diana's dorm room and the shattered windshield. Now, as she describes Billy's escalating aggression, Anderson presents a third poster. Exhibit A-21 is a cell phone screenshot with a series of texts:

We're not finished.
You can't tell anyone.
Do not do this, Diana. I WILL NOT LET YOU.
You'll ruin our lives.
It's not true. Nothing you're saying is true.

Yes, Diana confirms, I did receive those texts from Billy. Yes, he harassed me. Yes, he threatened me. Yes, I was frightened. *You fucking bitch,* he kept saying. *You can't do this.* Yes, I worried for my safety. So, I invited him to a party. Yes, I believed I'd be safe. Yes, I realize now this was foolish.

"Why didn't you tell your parents?" Anderson asks. "Or go to the police?"

"I considered it. Several times. But I was afraid of what might happen."

"To you?"

"Yes. But also to him. Billy behaved badly, but he's not a bad person. If I involved the police, he would've been suspended or expelled. He couldn't apply to medical school or be a doctor. He'd lose his whole future, and it would have been my fault."

"What happened when the defendant showed up at the party?"

"I'm ashamed to say I don't remember much." Diana exhales. "Except for a few images, most of my memories are fragments." Her voice is raspy. "Excuse me." She sips her water.

"Take your time," Anderson coaches. "We're in no rush. We know this is difficult."

Diana's hair has come loose from her clip. She brushes it away with her fingers. "Before Billy showed up, I was nervous. I had a few drinks, but I'm sensitive to alcohol. One glass of wine makes me tipsy. Before I knew it, I was very, very drunk."

"Do you remember texting the defendant before he arrived?"

"No."

"Do you remember kissing the defendant after he arrived?"

"No. We went alone to a bedroom to talk privately. I remember kissing there."

"Did you tell the defendant you wanted to have sex?"

"I don't know. I do remember Billy pulling down his pants, but not being able to get an erection."

"Why do you remember that?"

"Because he went ballistic. He started yelling, called me a 'fucking bitch.' I think he was afraid I would tell people." She steals a glance at Billy. "I never would've told anyone."

"Is that why you left the party?"

"Yes. I told him we were finished. 'I don't love you anymore,' I said."

"Did he follow you?"

"Yes, he did. And we ended up at the playground."

"And you started kissing again?"

"Yes." Diana's eyes well up. "We were kissing again. All of this is hazy, but I remember saying 'No, Billy. I don't want to do this.' After that, it goes black. Next, I'm waking up in the hospital. My body ached and I had a cut on my head. I was wearing a T-shirt and sweatpants I'd never seen before. My socks and bra were missing. The nurse told me I'd been assaulted. She had to do a rape kit. I couldn't believe it, but knew it was true."

"How did you know it was true?"

"I told him 'no.'" Diana clears her throat. "I said 'No, I don't want to do this. Get off me.'" She starts to cry again, but this time makes no noise. "I said no," she whispers.

Lawrence was right, I decide. We should've taken the four years.

The courtroom is silent. In front of me, at the defense table, Billy is shaking his head, but whether it's because he's horrified by his behavior or appalled by Diana's lies is unclear. He just seems flattened.

Lawrence is next to me; Eleanor is on his left. They sit rigidly, actively not touching. With their earlier argument unresolved, anger wafts off their bodies like fumes. Under normal conditions, Lawrence would've been down on his knees, begging for her forgiveness. Instead, his jaw is set and he's grinding his teeth with indignation. He's furious at Eleanor for not taking the deal.

Fuck her, I bet he's thinking. Fuck her forever. Catching my eye, he pats my thigh. Then he squeezes my hand three times: I. Love. You.

I don't respond. My own hand rests on my leg like a dead fish.

Anderson isn't finished. One by one, he places a series of poster-sized collages on the easels. Each is made up of snapshots taken from the crime scene, the hospital, and the rape kit. The posters are graphic and difficult to look at. But the images are clear. Bruises on Diana's arms, hips, and thighs. Bloody lacerations on her face. Cuts on her elbows. Welts on her back. Broken capillaries in her eyes. Again, a young woman, unconscious, on the grass.

These easels, starting with the punched walls and ending with the battered girl, tell the story of Billy Quinn and Diana Holly. The hard evidence is laid out chapter by chapter, image by image. While we study them, the courtroom swells with the truth of Billy's anger: savage, destructive, indelible.

"I have no more questions," Anderson says then turns to DeFiore. "Your witness."

Anderson is gloating. Returning to his table, the DA moves with a brand-new nimbleness, as if a tremendous weight has been lifted, as if inside, he is nothing but feathers.

48

AFTER A BRIEF RECESS, DIANA IS CALLED UP AGAIN, SEATED,
and reminded that she's under oath. She looks wiped out, but I notice
a glint in her eye. A small hint of steel that suggests she will not be
defeated.

Rising from his chair, DeFiore buttons his jacket. "Ms. Holly, for
the record, I represent the Defendant, Billy Quinn." He steps forward.
"May I ask you a few simple questions?"

"Yes," she tells DeFiore quietly. "You may."

"Thank you." His voice, by contrast, is booming, and echoes off the
high ceilings. "For the record, are you aware who my client is?"

When Diana's eyes shift to Billy, DeFiore offers her a sympathetic
smile. He has to tread lightly. Before the trial began, he explained that
cross-examining a victim of sexual assault is a minefield. If he goes too
far—too many intrusive questions, for instance, or too harsh a tone—
the jury will side with Diana. Same if he doesn't go far enough; her
story will stand uncontested. He has to find inconsistencies in Diana's
story without calling her a liar; it means attacking her *claims* without
attacking *her*.

The mood in the courtroom is tense. Stripped bare by Diana's testimony, we're raw and jittery. We sense drama afoot the way a dog's
panting portends a brewing storm. Recognizing this, DeFiore is tentative. His movements are languid. He smooths his hair. Removes his
glasses. Then he begins. "Ms. Holly, earlier, you said that when you
became aware of my client's alleged porn addiction, it bothered you.
Is this true?"

"Yes."

"You also testified that porn permeated your relationship. That it was unbearable when my client's compulsion interfered with his ability to perform. Is this also correct?"

"Yes. It was unbearable to be with a man who needed porn to . . . uh . . . function, basically."

"Ms. Holly, are you against porn in general? Meaning, do you have a general objection to people watching pornography?"

"No, I'm not generally against porn."

"And, in fact, you watched porn with Billy, didn't you?"

"I didn't watch porn before I met Billy, but yes, we did watch it together once in a while."

"And did you enjoy it?"

"Objection!" Anderson calls out. "Relevance?"

"Sorry," DeFiore says. "I'll rephrase. You enjoyed seeing Billy happy, right?"

Diana looks at her hands. "Yes."

"In fact, you and Billy watched porn at your suggestion, correct? For instance, when you realized he enjoyed porn, and, more to the point, porn enabled him to perform, wasn't it your idea, not his, to position the computer next to the bed?"

"I wanted to be a supportive . . . I don't know . . . partner . . ."

"Ms. Holly, please answer with a yes or no, and then you can explain. Again, wasn't it your idea to position the computer on the desk?"

"Yes, it was my idea."

"Would you say that porn enhanced your sex life?"

"Yes, sometimes."

"Let's change the subject. Ms. Holly, you're from Squirrel Hill, an expensive suburb of Pittsburgh, correct? Perhaps the most expensive. Is it fair to say your family has a lot of money?"

Diana grins for the first time. "Well, there's money and then there's money."

The jury laughs. Diana must've picked up Eleanor's catchphrase from Billy. If Eleanor recognizes it, she doesn't show it. She stares ahead, brick faced.

DeFiore isn't amused. "I'm not sure what you mean. Are you implying that your family is wealthy, but your parents—and you, I assume—have higher financial goals? Is that why they named you Diana and call you 'princess'? For the Princess of Wales?"

"No. Lots of parents call their daughters 'princess.' It's a term of endearment."

"Did your family have royal aspirations? To be New York royalty, like, say, the Quinns?"

Diana chuckles nervously. "Of course not."

"But they did encourage you to date my client so that you might benefit financially?"

"No. I mean, yes, they encouraged me to date Billy, but only because they liked that he was smart and headed to medical school. My dad is a heart surgeon." She looks up for a second, searches for her father in the gallery.

"But didn't your father say he was suspicious of Billy? That in fact he *didn't* like him?"

"I don't remember."

"Ms. Holly, did you have designs on my client's money?"

"No."

"But you testified you were seduced by his wealth, that he was irresistible. You also testified that on the night you were with his family, his sister Cassie caught you wandering through their house, gaping at the rooms. Correct?"

"Objection!" the DA shouts.

"No, I never said his sister found me wandering through their house."

"Oh, my mistake. But you did walk through the Quinns' house before dinner, correct?"

"Yes, I did."

"So, you were impressed by the Quinns' home?"

"Of course. Anyone would be. The Valmont is a landmark building. It's a historic apartment."

"But you weren't interested in the Quinns' money?"

"No, not at all. I understood their money had nothing to do with me."

"But it would if you and my client got married, correct?"

"If we got married, I'd have to sign a prenuptial agreement."

"Which you knew because you and my client had discussed the future, correct?"

"Yes. At the start of the relationship, we talked about a lot of things."

"Did you talk about the future on the night you were with his family in November?"

"We may have. I don't remember."

Why is DeFiore so hung up on that night? What am I missing? I remember finding Lawrence in the celebration room. "Be right there," he said. Upon leaving, I bumped into Diana, who was in the hall, holding a porcelain vase upside-down. "That's from the Ming dynasty," I snapped. "I'm sorry," Diana said, caught. She put down the vase gently. "I'm so sorry."

"When did you realize that my client's porn-watching problem was problematic?"

"Late July, early August."

"Ms. Holly, I'm confused. You testified that you and my client discussed the future in November, correct? Yet now you're saying his habits were so problematic for you in July that you broke up with him soon after. Isn't it true, then, that my client's habits don't bother you *at all*? That your objection to him watching porn is merely a story you believe you have to tell for the sake of this trial?"

"Objection!" Anderson jumps to his feet. "Badgering the witness."

DeFiore holds up his hands, surrender-style. "Withdrawn. New question, Ms. Holly. Isn't it true you brought up marriage to my client one week after your first date? And you continued to bring it up, even after my client asked you to stop?"

"I don't remember."

"And wasn't it *Billy*, not you, who tried to break off the relationship in September? And wasn't it *you* who refused?"

"No, it didn't happen that way."

"Well, isn't it true that you texted my client twenty times in a one-hour period?"

"I don't remember."

"And in these texts, you begged him to stay with you, correct?" De-

Fiore marches over to the defense table. He motions to Felicia to hand him a stack of papers with multicolored exhibit stickers hanging off the side. He shows the stack to Anderson, who nods, and then DeFiore requests permission to approach the witness.

"You may approach," the judge says.

"Diana, I'm going to show you what has previously been marked as Defendant's exhibit L-432. Have you ever seen these before?"

Yes, Diana says. I've seen those before. Yes, I'm familiar with the contents of this exhibit. Yes, those are my texts with Billy.

"Ms. Holly," Judge McKay says. "Can you read these messages into the record?"

"*Don't do this, Billy. We love each other. You know you love me. Please, Billy. Call me. Why are you ignoring me?*"

"Ms. Holly, I believe you were dishonest in your testimony today when you described your relationship with my client. Isn't it true that the pornography complaint is irrelevant?"

"I wanted to connect with him any way that I could."

"Were you trying to connect with him or trap him in a relationship with you?"

"I did not want to trap him. You're twisting my words."

"And isn't all your testimony today really due to the Quinns' money? You took a self-guided tour of their landmark home, coveting their priceless artifacts, because you want that life, correct? And when Billy felt smothered, you panicked, didn't you? Isn't it true my client said he wasn't ready to talk about the future? But you wouldn't let it go, correct? You pushed harder. So, he told you about a prenup, hoping to deter you, correct? But it didn't. Instead, you continued to press him on a commitment, correct?"

"Objection! Badgering the victim."

"Your Honor," DeFiore says. "The defense is allowed to explore whether or not the victim's outcry is truthful, as well as any motivation she may have for her claim of rape."

"I'll allow it, but rephrase your questions, and move away from this portion."

"Thank you, Your Honor. Ms. Holly, in the previously identified texts, you remind my client that you love each other, and you beg him to 'not do this,' correct?"

"Objection to characterization of begging," Anderson says.

"Overruled."

"But he didn't respond, which made you even more desperate. So you invited him to a party, where you could seduce him, correct? He didn't want to come, but you kept pushing, correct? And when he finally showed up, you encouraged him to drink and smoke pot. And you drank so much you became uninhibited, correct? So uninhibited, you brought him to the playground and had sex with him. The same way you had all those other times, correct? But my client *still* refused to resume your relationship, correct? This hurt you, didn't it? So you saw an opportunity. A nurse suggested you didn't want to have sex, that you had been assaulted. And you thought, 'I can make him pay for hurting me.' So, you went along with the rape accusation. Yet the fact remains: there was no rape, correct? You drank until you blacked out. And you wanted to have sex because you wanted—"

"Objection!" Up on her feet, Maggie Fleming is railing, "Objection! The victim is clearly upset." Meanwhile, Diana is sobbing. "No, this is not correct. Billy *raped* me. I said no."

DeFiore is cool. "Your Honor, we are allowed to examine her motivations. However, we will stop for now. We have no more questions."

McKay turns to Anderson. "Anything further from the State?"

"Yes, Your Honor." Anderson asks Diana to clarify her testimony about the night of the party. He moves slowly through his questions, but Diana is too shell-shocked to answer. Mumbling incoherently, she confuses the sequence of events, and contradicts herself a few times, muddying her earlier statement. "I don't know," she keeps repeating. "I don't know."

Finally, Anderson gives up. "No more questions, Your Honor."

"You may step down, Ms. Holly," the judge tells her.

Blinking, she appears confused. Step down? That's it? I'm done?

"No more witnesses." Anderson is not happy. "The State rests."

"We'll resume Monday with the defense," McKay says. "Court dismissed."

49

OVER THE WEEKEND, WE FEEL THE NEED TO COME TOGETHER as a family, even if no one says so explicitly. Friday night, we drive back to New York and sleep in our own beds. On Saturday morning, all five of us gather in the celebration room and spend the day there. We try to refrain from talking about the trial but it's the only thing on our minds.

Toward dinnertime, Nate builds a fire. "Peter was a champ yesterday," he says, adding paper. There's a whoosh, and the blaze ignites. "His cross was amazing."

The room fills with warmth. Moving closer to the hearth, I hold out my hands. "He definitely cast reasonable doubt. And raised a ton of questions."

"So what?" Lawrence is adamant. "The girl was convincing." Sipping scotch, he watches the fire crackle. "Those posters were very powerful. Peter couldn't mitigate their impact, no matter what he said."

"You're wrong, Dad. He found every hole in her story." Nate nudges me for support.

"I agree." Personally, I think Lawrence's animosity toward DeFiore has nothing to do with the lawyer's performance. Lawrence can't stand that every time he turns around, DeFiore and Eleanor are huddled together, freezing him out. "He raised a lot of good points."

"Doesn't matter," Lawrence repeats. "The evidence was solid and incriminating. Far worse than Peter let on."

"So, you think Billy's guilty, Dad?" Nate asks. "Is that what you're saying?"

"No, Nathaniel. Of course not. But let's not kid ourselves. Peter has to do a lot of damage control."

"Shut the fuck up, Dad," Billy snaps. "Why are you talking about me like I'm not here? You need to back off. Peter is doing a great job."

Diana's testimony has jarred something loose in Billy. He hasn't said much, but last night, after the reporters dispersed around eleven-thirty, he went for a long run. This morning, he got up at the crack of dawn, lifted weights, showered, shaved, and cleaned his room. Now, he's spoiling for a fight.

"I know you admire him, son. But I don't think you understand what we're up against."

"What don't I understand? The part where we let my lawyer do his job? Or the part where we listen to you, and I go to prison for the rest of my fucking life?"

"I wasn't the one who hung you out to dry," Lawrence says, looking at Eleanor. "We didn't have to go to trial." Of course it's true that Lawrence didn't want to go to trial. But it wasn't about Billy. It was about Lawrence + Cassie.

Seated next to me, Lawrence's body trembles with desire. He knocked on my door last night, late. He must have been desperate, knowing the whole family was home, but taking the risk, anyway. I pretended to be asleep, still angry with him. In a few days, I'll ask about the video he showed me. He'll offer a non-apology. *If I did, I'm sure it was meant to be educational. I don't remember, Cassie. It was so long ago. Regardless, I'm sorry if you misinterpreted my intentions.* I'll let him twist as long as I can. Then I'll give in. Lawrence and I have a long history. We're not together today, but tomorrow is tomorrow. There are thresholds you cross when you love someone. You make allowances. You forgive the unforgivable. You sacrifice yourself for his pleasure. Especially after all he has given you.

Eleanor finally speaks. "Lawrence, please." Her voice is tight. "Shut the fuck up."

The next morning, DeFiore stops by for brunch and a pep talk. Cross-examining Diana has revitalized him, and he's full of enthusiasm in his Jets sweatshirt and grungy khakis. Digging into his French toast, he tells us to buck up. "We're in the catbird seat, Quinn family.

It's the bottom of the ninth, we've got a man on second, a runner on third, and no outs."

"At least you're not overconfident," I say.

DeFiore cracks a smile. "Hey, hey, hey." He points his syrupy fork first at me, then at Lawrence. "Enough with the negativity. You need to shine, shine, shine come Monday. This is our last stand, my friends, our Battle of Little Bighorn, our Alamo—"

"Those were bloodbaths," Nate says.

"It's a metaphor, Smart Guy." DeFiore swallows. "Okay, here's what's next. It took Anderson eight days to drag out his case, but I can wrap up in five. My goal is to finish by Friday, so the jury will appreciate our expediency."

"Five days is impossible," Lawrence says, and Billy rolls his eyes.

"It's possible, Lar. We have half the number of witnesses. More importantly, Thanksgiving is the week after next, and McKay will sequester the jury after we rest. So, if we finish by Friday, they'll take the weekend to deliberate then hand in their decision by Wednesday, latest, before the long holiday weekend."

"How do you know this for sure?" I ask.

"Nothing is 'for sure,'" he replies. "I've just seen patterns over the years. Juries will belabor a guilty verdict, especially if it means prison. But they'll gladly vote 'not guilty' if it means we wrap up by turkey time."

"Well, Peter. You're the expert." Lawrence's contempt is obvious.

"You're right, Lar," DeFiore snaps. "I am the fucking expert. And as the expert, I've decided I want you, Cassie, and Billy to testify."

"Not me?" Nate asks.

"Sorry, pal. Demographically, you and your brother are too similar." He looks at Eleanor. "And you're too biased."

"You really think this will be over by Thanksgiving?" Billy asks.

"I do, Billy boy." DeFiore clutches my brother's shoulder. "All it takes is reasonable doubt. One questionable assertion, one conflicted juror, and boom-chicka-boom, you're home free."

50

ON MONDAY, WE'RE BACK IN COURT AT TEN O'CLOCK SHARP, raring to go. Word has spread that Deacon Porter, son of McClain Porter, may be testifying for the defense; and that McClain himself might appear. The gallery overflows with spectators, along with crowds of Billy's supporters: boys he grew up with, athletes he competed against, classmates from Groton and Princeton. They are quiet and respectful, but excitement ripples through the air.

Across the room, Billy glows. Overcome by so many familiar faces, he can barely sit still. I recognize several and the sight of so many clean-cut, spit-polished males fills me to bursting. I'm so moved that when I spot Avery, I rush through the crowd and fling myself at her. "Thank you for coming," I say, hugging her. "Wouldn't miss it, Chickadee," she says, hugging me back.

Today, the courtroom is filled with reminders of Billy's affluence. But for once it's a good thing. DeFiore has been hammering home Diana's mercenary interests, so our family's wealth is front and center in everyone's mind. Most of Billy's friends came with their mothers, who are equally well turned out in designer slacks, cashmere twinsets, and understated jewelry. Our circle radiates good breeding, civility, and money, money, money, which has the jurors starry-eyed.

Re-pressed and re-primped, DeFiore wastes no time getting started. He shoots his cuffs and turns to the jury. "Defense calls Deacon Abington Porter."

Deacon moves to the witness stand with panther-like grace. As he gets closer, I do a double take. His resemblance to his brother Powell is uncanny now. Deacon's shoulder-length hair has been sheared off, leaving him with a cap of blond curls. He's replaced his glasses with contacts and removed the diamond stud from his ear. Wearing a sharp suit, silk tie, and lace-up wingtips, he looks handsome, well bred, and morally fit.

After Deacon is sworn in, DeFiore establishes that he is Billy's best friend, lifelong confidant, and ersatz brother. "So, you've met Diana Holly?"

"Yes, my girlfriend, Channing, and I had dinner with her and Billy a few times."

"What were your first impressions?"

"She was overly friendly, gushy, to me, but standoffish to my girlfriend. Chan can be intimidating to other women, though, so while I didn't find Diana's behavior unusual, it did surprise me. Billy hasn't had too many girlfriends, so he probably didn't see how rude she was. I would've preferred to see him with someone more mature and self-confident."

"So, you didn't like Diana?"

"I was disappointed Billy chose her. She kept calling him 'Babe' and touching him in an inappropriate way. We were in public, but she put her hands all over his body. I'm an easygoing guy, but this disturbed me. Once, Chan and I were so uncomfortable, we went home right after dinner instead of getting drinks with them at another bar."

"Did these impressions change as you got to know Diana?"

"No, sir." Deacon shakes his head. "If anything, she became more demanding of Billy—of his time, his attention. It was painful to watch."

"Did anything else about her give you pause?"

"My father is a career politician, and my brother and I learned early on how to identify women who don't have our best interests at heart. Diana was indifferent to Billy's class load and training schedule. She was also overly focused on his trust fund. I grew up with a stepmother like this. So I've seen women hunting for a rich husband—"

"Objection!" Anderson jumps up.

Deacon covers his mouth. "Oh, sorry. My mistake."

I don't know Deacon well. I can't say if he's always smooth or if this is a class-A performance. Not that it matters. He comes across as trustworthy and authentic.

"Did she mention wanting a future with my client?" DeFiore asks.

"I had drinks with them fairly often, three times over the summer, and two or three times in the fall. Diana never failed to bring up their future, even intimating marriage."

"Did my client participate in these conversations?"

"At first, sure. But at first, we all want to marry our girlfriends. Check back in six months." Deacon pauses for scattered chuckles. "Seriously, by September, Billy felt differently. He wanted to break up but was afraid of Diana's reaction. Her possessiveness was off the charts. She called and texted nonstop, keeping tabs on Billy's whereabouts. She even called me to check up on him."

"Let's switch topics. You grew up with my client. Did you know that he watched porn as an adolescent? And still watches porn frequently?"

"With all due respect, sir, what male—adolescent, teenage, young adult, old man, decrepit dinosaur—doesn't watch porn? I mean, *come on.*"

This gets a couple of cheers in the audience. Annoyed, McKay calls for order. "Please answer the question, Mr. Porter."

Chastened, Deacon nods. "Yes. I knew Billy watched porn. I can't say if he still watches, but most guys I know don't stop. We slow down, though, for sure."

"As a young man, did my client seem overly preoccupied with pornography?"

"Everyone in our crew was preoccupied. But I don't think any of us, including Billy, were *overly* preoccupied."

"Did my client ever mention that he had trouble maintaining an erection?"

Deacon sighs. "Our generation never knew a time without cell phones, so for us—me, Billy, our friends—porn was always available. It's like a public utility, lights or water. You flick the switch and there it is. I'm sure many of us have had occasional erectile trouble." He pauses. "But to answer your question, no, Billy never mentioned a problem, not to me."

"Did he tell you he and Diana watched porn together?"

"Yes, he did."

"Why would he tell you this? Isn't it private?"

"Billy is my best friend. We went to daycare together. We talk about a lot of things. In this case, he was explaining why he wanted to break up with Diana. She was too possessive. The private details were part of a larger conversation, though he did say watching porn together was Diana's idea and it made him uncomfortable."

It occurs to me that Deacon is lying. Why would Billy tell him about his sex life? He and Deacon barely talk. It's all too neat, too perfectly oppositional.

DeFiore shows the jury a cell phone screenshot. Taking a cue from Anderson, he places a poster-sized copy on an easel. "After Billy and Diana broke up, did you know she sent him harassing texts?"

Deacon nods. "Yes, I saw the texts."

Again, why would Billy show Deacon his texts? I feel like I'm watching a split screen. On one side, a polished young man demands justice for his forever friend. On the other, a long-haired bohemian drifts in and out of Billy's life. Impulsively, I turn around and look at the crowd. Powell sees me and raises a hand in greeting; flustered, I do the same.

I try to pay attention to Deacon. But this double vision is driving me mad, one world layered on top of the other, neither of them reality.

"Did you know he was meeting Diana at the party?"

"Yes. In fact, he asked me to go. He wanted to confront her, which sounded crazy. I told him as much. I couldn't make it, but believe me, I wish to hell I had."

Again, how likely was it that Diana and Billy had the same exact motive for attending the party?

"Did you think Diana was hoping to win back Billy's affections?"

"Yes, sir. I did."

"Why did you think this, Deacon?"

"She dropped off a package in Billy's room."

"I'd like to introduce Exhibit V-232." DeFiore holds up a plastic bag, which he shows to Judge McKay then passes around the jury. It's a pair of women's lacy underwear, along with a note: *I won't need these 2nite.* "Can you explain what this is, Deacon?"

"I assume it's Diana's underwear. The note wasn't signed, but who else would send it?"

"Objection!" Anderson is spitting. "The State has no record of this evidence."

"Counselors!" McKay snaps. "Approach the bench."

The judge and attorneys have a heated, protracted discussion. We're not privy to the content, but it's clear DeFiore has crossed a line. "Understood," he repeats. "It won't happen again." Eventually, the underwear is ruled inadmissible, and the testimony is stricken. Even so, the jury can't un-see what they've seen.

51

TRUE TO HIS WORD, DEFIORE MOVES QUICKLY THROUGH
the rest of his witnesses. Over the next three days, we hear from Billy's
friends, professors, coaches, and classmates. All offer similar details:
Yes, Billy's excitement about Diana was short-lived. Yes, Diana constantly talked about the future. No, Billy didn't reciprocate. Yes, Billy
broke up with her. Yes, she was shattered. Yes, she sent threatening
texts. No, he didn't tell the authorities.

"Why?" DeFiore asks Darnell Lansing, Billy's former teammate.
"If Billy had concerns, wouldn't it make sense to call the police? Or
campus security?"

"Honestly, sir, the idea of calling the police never occurred to me."
Darnell is a serious young Black man in his first year at Johns Hopkins
Medical School. He has a sculpted flat top, a heavy brow, and the ner-
vous tic of rubbing his eyes.

"Did you not take Diana's threats seriously?"

"No, I did, absolutely. But I doubt the police would, not in today's
climate."

"What do you mean by 'today's climate'?"

"You've heard the expression hashtag-believewomen? At Princeton, women are not doubted, no matter the circumstances. If a woman
says she was raped, cops swoop in, guns blazing. It's not the same for
men. If I were to complain that a former girlfriend was threatening me,
the cops would laugh in my face."

"Objection!" Anderson is on his feet. "Speculation."

"Sustained." The judge turns to DeFiore and opens his mouth as if
to speak but merely shakes his head.

For some reason, this rattles DeFiore. "Mr. Brown . . . uh . . .

Darnell . . . Excuse me, please." At the defense table, he rifles through his notes. "Darnell," he says but falters again. ". . . no further questions, Your Honor."

Until now, McKay appeared neutral. But DeFiore's attempt to introduce Diana's underwear has exposed the judge's bias. He repeatedly sustains the State's objections and admonishes our side for petty infractions. Worse, the jury is following his lead. Every time DeFiore talks, they cross their arms and sit rigidly in their chairs.

Collectively, the witnesses for the defense are as earnest and credible as those for the State. They describe a gentle, studious young man who is enamored of Diana until her interest in him feels controlling and materialistic. Every time he pulls away, she gets clingy. When he tells her it's over, she blasts him with calls and texts. Finally, he agrees to meet at a party where he plans to confront her. Once there, Diana tries to seduce him, first in a bedroom, then a playground. When their consensual sex is misinterpreted, Billy is hauled off to jail. Meanwhile, a nurse suggests rape. Diana realizes this is a way to get, if not Billy's attention and money, then at least payback for his hurting her.

On Wednesday, the defense explores the events of March 24. DeFiore re-interviews several of the State's witnesses, and introduces new psychologists, behavioral specialists, and IT experts. Again, we're presented with a moment-by-moment breakdown of the evening, but this time from Billy's perspective. We see enlargements of Diana's texts, inviting him to the party (Come on, Billy. It'll be fun; have 1 drink) then admonishing him for being late (Why aren't u here! Where are u? Don't blow me off, Billy. I'm serious). We're shown a blurry snapshot of Billy and Diana dancing, another where they're kissing.

The head of the Lewis School attests to Billy's generosity and patience. DeFiore holds up a photograph, Exhibit B-3940, the one where my brother is helping a boy read. Beside me, Lawrence enlarges the same shot on his phone and zooms in on Billy's face. I pat his arm and whisper, "Billy will be okay."

"DeFiore sucks," Lawrence whispers, sounding like an inconsolable child. "That stunt with the underwear should've gotten him disbarred."

We hear from a medical technician who explains that yes, Diana tested 13 on the Glasgow coma scale, but there's no way to tell when she blacked out. Or, equally important, if Billy was aware she was unresponsive.

We hear from one of the policemen called to the scene. "The defendant did resist arrest initially. But he was inebriated and disoriented. Once he realized what was happening, he willingly gave a DNA sample. He also consented to a blood test and full body search."

We review photographs of the bruises on Diana's body. "Is it possible," DeFiore asks the intake nurse, "that these bruises were present prior to the alleged assault?" She replies no, not all of them were present, but agrees some could have been. Similarly, the vaginal tearing was minimal, and may or may not indicate assault. "It's impossible to say with one hundred percent certainty," the nurse contends. "I can only confirm 'maybe.'"

"No further questions, Your Honor," DeFiore says.

*   *   *

Day by day, hour by hour, DeFiore chips away at Diana's testimony. By Thursday, he's presented an alternative narrative. Billy, DeFiore tells us, is guilty of many things: poor judgment, insensitivity, selfishness, and terrible communication. The one crime he is not guilty of, however, is rape.

"I believe it," I tell Nate for the third time. "I have reasonable doubt. I'd vote not guilty. But will the jury?"

"Why do you always do this, Cassie? Peter is doing great. Why can't you be optimistic?"

"Why can't I ask a question, Nate? Why do you always shut me down?"

It's lunchtime. We're in the conference room with DeFiore, Felicia, Abby, and Mitchell. Around us, the table is covered with piles of detritus: crumpled coffee cups, charging wires, balled-up napkins, and a week's worth of newspapers and magazines. Everyone is scrolling through their devices. When the trial started, a prominent senator wrote an editorial that ran in the *Washington Post*, decrying young women who accuse men of rape when in fact it's "just bad sex." Since then, there's been a flood of op-eds arguing for and against Billy Quinn. Guilty? Not guilty? Predator? Victim? At this point, it could go either way.

The room is quiet after my exchange with Nate. Our anxiety has spiked, and we're all hunched over the table, scavenging the internet for gossip, commentary, debates—anything to allay our worst fears. In forty minutes, DeFiore questions his last witnesses. Tomorrow, Lawrence, Billy, and I testify. Then both sides give closing statements. We are, in fact, running out of time.

52

FRIDAY BEGINS JUST LIKE ANY OTHER DAY. WE'RE AWAKE, dressed, and outside the hotel with a half-hour to spare. Eleanor rides to court with the Bowtie, but that's not unusual. In our car, Lawrence, my brothers, and I bark at each other, but that's not unusual either.

When we pull into the parking lot, the phone rings. Lawrence hits speaker.

"Just a heads-up, I'm recalling Diana Holly," DeFiore says. "So we probably won't rest tonight."

"Why?" Lawrence looks exasperated. "You said it was crucial to wrap up on Friday because next week is Thanksgiving." Turning to me in the passenger seat, he widens his eyes: *Can you believe this guy?* Angling for peace, I offer a wan smile.

"I said it made sense strategically, Lar. Not that it was crucial."

"You're splitting hairs."

"Let's talk when you get here." DeFiore signs off with a cheery "Chin up! End's in sight," to which Lawrence mutters, "Fuck you."

"Come on." I try to coax a better mood. "Give the guy a break."

"I'll give him a break when you give me one."

Last night, Lawrence called from a bar a mile up the road. He wanted me to sneak out of the hotel and meet him. When I said no, he pelted me with: *You're selfish. You're giving up on us. You, you, you.*

"You owe me an apology," I say. "That was unfair."

"Forgive me." He glances in his rearview mirror. I turn around too. My brothers are both wearing headphones, and Billy's eyes are closed. Lawrence squeezes my knee three times. For. Give. Me.

I squeeze his: I. Will. Try.

Like I said, regular morning: same argument, same non-apology. But when we see DeFiore, I know something is very wrong.

"Good tidings, Quinn family!" he says, ushering us into the conference room. "Big day today! *Big* day!" His too-hearty hello is jarring. So is his territorial energy, the way he paces the perimeter of the table as if establishing dominance.

"Are you okay, Peter?" I glance at Nate. *He's acting strange, right?*

Very, Nate agrees with his eyes. "Why don't you take a seat, Peter?" He pats a chair.

"I'm fine," DeFiore says. "I'm golden."

"Where's Felicia?" I try to block his path, but he does an about-face. It's so obvious it's comical.

He doesn't answer. That's strange. Why is he ignoring me? I'm DeFiore's favorite Quinn. Even when there's tension, he's thrilled to see me. But today there's nothing. No flattery, no leers, no pats on the back. Just a manic lawyer making what feels like a last-ditch Hail Mary.

DeFiore looks around. "Where's Mrs. Quinn? Is she coming?"

"Here!" Eleanor strolls in, escorted by the Bowtie, who is dapper in a cashmere scarf and camel coat. "Apologies for being late. Horrendous traffic." She turns to her husband. "Well, you know."

"Actually, I don't." Lawrence's voice is clipped. "We got here with time to spare."

DeFiore cuts in. "Let's get going, shall we?" He opens his arms. "So, Quinn family. Some news: Diana Holly's testimony was not entirely accurate. We need to set the record straight."

"About that dinner?" I ask. "In November?"

Again, he doesn't reply.

"Peter? You're asking about that night?"

Studying his phone, DeFiore nods. "Among other issues."

I should feel vindicated. I was the one who told him Diana lied. Instead, I'm sweating. My twitchiness morphs from worry into alarm.

"Is this a good idea?" Nate asks. "You don't want to look like a bully."

"Oh, absolutely, Nate. The goal is to cast doubt on her credibility.

We have an unimpeachable example. After, we'll proceed as planned: Lawrence will testify, then Cassie, and we'll finish up with Billy."

Behind me, Eleanor asks, "Are you sure about this, Peter?"

"Yeah, Ellie. I'm sure. I'm positive."

A look passes between them.

"Ellie?" Lawrence says, confused. "Since when are you Ellie?"

*   *   *

In the courtroom, the gallery is filled, but the jury hasn't been called in yet. For the next hour, the defense, prosecution, and judge engage in a complicated and testy exchange. From his seat next to Eleanor, the Bowtie explains what's happening. DeFiore is asking to recall Diana because she misspoke about the texts she got from Billy. This bears on their relationship generally, and the events of March 24 specifically. "In other words," the Bowtie says, "Diana's untruths will illustrate to the jury that Billy isn't guilty of the crimes he's being tried for."

"Why don't you just call them 'lies'?" I whisper.

Eleanor shushes me. "I can't hear."

DeFiore is speaking. "Your Honor, on page 142 in the record, Ms. Holly testified upon direct examination—I'm paraphrasing—that the text communication my client sent to her was motivated by his wanting to continue their relationship. When in fact it was something else."

"Counselor, you had a full and fair opportunity to explore this issue when you cross-examined Ms. Holly the first time."

"Yes, Your Honor. However, the defense believes that Ms. Holly misstated the truth upon direct examination by the State with respect to the State's Exhibit A-21."

"If this is a stunt, Mr. DeFiore, you will personally pay in the form of a censure. But I will allow it."

Anderson is pissed. "The Defense had the chance to cross-examine her. This is merely an attempt to cast the accuser in a bad light." Clearly out of options, he finishes with, "Let the record reflect my objection."

"Objection noted. Does either side want to bring anything else up?"

They do not. The jury is called in and seated. Diana approaches the stand with apprehension. Today, she's wearing a Kelly green dress and a lighter green scarf. Her cheeks and lips have a bit of color, which makes her look less washed out.

DeFiore stands up. "Your Honor, permission to show Exhibit A-21."

Permission granted; he situates one of the State's posters near the witness box. It's a screenshot of the texts Billy sent to Diana after their breakup. DeFiore asks her to read each text aloud.

We're not finished.
You can't tell anyone.
Do not do this, Diana. I WILL NOT LET YOU.
You'll ruin our lives.
It's not true. Nothing you're saying is true.

DeFiore turns to her. "Before I ask about these texts, I want to review statements you made under direct examination. Is that okay with you?"

Diana's voice is shaky. "Yes, that's fine."

"Previously, you stated Billy has a secret. He is addicted to pornography. You also stated that during the party on March 24, he became angry, even enraged, because, quote, he was afraid I would tell people, unquote. Why was he angry?"

"He couldn't maintain an erection."

"So, he was angry at himself, correct? Not angry at you?"

"I have no idea. Both, probably."

DeFiore points to the screenshot. "Does this text refer to Billy's same fear?" Using a Sharpie, he circles you can't tell anyone. "That you will tell people he's addicted to porn and unable to maintain an erection during sexual activity?"

"Yes," Diana says.

"Just to be clear, Cassie. On March 24, my client was enraged about his impotence, correct?" DeFiore's eyes widen. "Excuse me. *Cassie* is Billy's sister. I apologize for the mistake, *Ms. Holly*. Again, to be clear: my client was afraid you would reveal his secret, correct?"

I freeze. This was no mistake. DeFiore intentionally mixed up our names. But why? Suddenly, I'm terrified.

"Yes," Diana says. But her eyes are wide; she's terrified too.

"Okay, new topic, *Ms. Holly*." DeFiore smiles sheepishly. But where someone else might see embarrassment, I see bloodlust. I remember when I pissed him off, how he bared his teeth then ripped into my throat. He's about to rip into Diana, who's aware it's coming and yet leaving herself open.

"Ms. Holly, you testified that Billy's sister, Cassie, made everyone in the Quinn family tense. Can you explain what you meant?"

Hearing my name again, I gasp. The air is too shallow; I can't catch my breath.

"Cassie is moody," Diana says. "She runs hot and cold."

"You also stated that you believe Billy's behavior was your fault. That he got angry because of you. What did you mean by this statement?"

"I meant he got angry because I knew his secret."

"I don't understand. You're saying Billy got angry on March 24 because you knew he was addicted to porn? Or because he was impotent? Or because of something else entirely?"

"I don't know . . ." Diana falters. "I don't know why I said that."

"Okay, no worries," DeFiore tells her casually. "So, to restate: Billy got angry at you because he was impotent, and he was afraid you would tell people. Is this statement correct?"

Anderson objects. "Asked and answered!"

McKay sustains. "Get to the point, Counselor."

"Sure." DeFiore is keen to comply. "My client has a secret. But he is not addicted to *pornographic videos*, is he, Ms. Holly? Nor is he impotent. Nor does he need porn to perform sexually. Does he, Ms. Holly?"

Seeing Diana wince, I have to close my eyes.

"No," I hear her say softly.

"Miss Holly, you deceived the court when you made these claims, didn't you?"

Silence. The judge requests an answer. "Remember you are under oath." His sharpness is jarring. I open my eyes. Diana is crumpled in her seat.

"Billy has several secrets," she says, and it's clear she's starting to break.

"But which secret, specifically, made him angry? And which secret, specifically, was he afraid you might tell people?"

More silence.

"I'll ask again. Billy Quinn does have a secret, correct? But it's not porn, is it?"

Beaten, she looks up. "No, it's not."

"When did you discover Billy's secret?"

"In November. At his family's house. Before dinner."

"And you told Billy what you discovered, correct? That's why he broke up with you?"

"Yes."

"Billy is referring to this secret here, correct?" DeFiore points: You can't tell anyone.

"Yes."

"Then, a few months later, on March 24, you brought up the secret again. This scared Billy, correct? It also made him angry, didn't it? That's why you said his anger was your fault, correct? So, I'll ask you again, Ms. Holly: *What is my client's secret?*"

Diana exhales. She studies her hands. "I knew Billy had issues with his sister. He talked about Nate, but rarely about Cassie, even in passing. He acted like he didn't even have a sister. But the night we were at his parents' house, she showed up unexpectedly—"

"This was in November?"

"Yes. In November. That night . . . I realized . . . I saw . . ." Her eyes fill with tears.

"What happened, Ms. Holly?" DeFiore's voice is gentle. "What did you see?"

"It was before dinner." Diana looks directly at me. "I saw Billy's father with his sister. Lawrence had his hand . . ."

The courtroom is quiet. I feel like I'm standing on a ledge a thousand feet in the sky. Air rushes past my ears. I'm suffocating.

"His hand." She turns to Billy, openly crying. "Lawrence's hand." Billy bows his head. I assume he's crying too.

Lawrence's hand is cupping my breast. We're laughing. He's such an idiot; a horny boy with a perpetual hard-on. He's forever fondling me behind doors, as if my body isn't mine but his to play with as he pleases. *Boob-honk*, we call it. *Got one—honk. Got the other—honk, honk.* I tell him to quit it. We're about to eat. Walking out of the room, I'm still laughing when boom—there's Diana Holly in the hall, holding a vase.

That she saw us never crossed my mind, not once. But now it hits me: the vase was a prop. She was just pretending to check the label.

Diana clears her throat. "Lawrence had his hand on Cassie's breast."

"Diana, stop!" Billy shouts. "Don't, please. I'm begging you."

"Counselor, silence your client."

DeFiore keeps drilling. "What's the secret, Ms. Holly? What made Billy so angry and afraid? What secret destroyed your relationship?"

"Billy's father and sister have a sexual relationship. They were kissing. When I told Billy what I saw, he didn't believe me. But I saw them!"

The courtroom erupts. I hear a shout, "No!" It's Eleanor, the Sphinx. She's up on her feet and shrieking in a voice I've never heard before. "No, No, No."

"Order!" The gavel slams. "We'll take a break."

Eleanor rushes out of the room, the Bowtie close on her heels.

My phone dings with a text: #TimesUp #MeToo

I turn. Haggerty's in the back. Seeing me, he waves.

53

TEN MINUTES LATER, MY BROTHERS AND I ARE IN THE CON-
ference room. We'd shuffled back here, silently, like zombies, neither
looking at nor speaking to one another. Unsure what was next, we sat
down to await further instructions.

Our silence fills the room. I sit on one side of the long table. Billy
and Nate are across from me on the other. The air is so heavy it crushes
my neck and shoulders. I want to say something, I need to say something. But I'm struck dumb. *Guys? Guys? Guys?*

The minutes tick by.

Lawrence appears in the doorway. "You kids see Eleanor? We
should find her." Instead of doing this, he walks into the room. His
movements are jerky and robotic, as if his limbs are controlled by a
puppeteer. He sits down between my brothers. So, now all three men
are aligned on one side of the table, and I'm alone on the other.

"Insane accusation," Lawrence is muttering. "Absolutely insane. I
have no idea what game Peter is playing. But I will find out. Obviously, nothing the girl said is true." His eyes shift from Nate to Billy,
Billy to Nate, begging for a response, a *fuck you, Dad*—anything but
this deafening silence. "You know that, right? Come on, guys. Talk to
me." The only person Lawrence won't look at is me.

My brothers focus on their phones. "Peter texted," Billy tells Nate,
speaking over Lawrence as if he's invisible. "He'll be here in a few
minutes."

My body is on fire, every joint aches. I'm paralyzed. Unable to
move, even to shift in my seat. I'm separated from my brothers, separated from Lawrence, separated from myself. The more I detach, the
easier this will get. Soon, I'll be invisible too.

"Insane." Lawrence's voice is shrill, almost hysterical. "Did you know this, Billy? Did Peter tell you what he had planned? This is an insane legal strategy."

Billy gets up from his chair, and looms over Lawrence like a nightmare come to life. He's breathing hard, as if he just finished a long run, and chewing the meat of his inner cheek. He's so pissed off I hear his jaw click.

"Shut up, Dad," he says evenly. In response Lawrence makes a bleating noise that my brother perceives as laughter. "Something funny? What the fuck is funny here?"

Suddenly, Billy's elbow shoots out. He rams his father's face so hard Lawrence's head snaps back. It happens so quickly it's like a cartoon. Oddly, the casual violence doesn't shock me as much as his words. "If you don't shut your fucking mouth, I will destroy you." Leaning in, Billy is shaking with white-hot fury. "Nothing would give me more pleasure."

My brother is guilty. He raped Diana Holly. The knowledge comes to me fully formed just as Lawrence cries out, "Billy. Son."

I sit with the idea. I turn it over. Bat it away. My brother brutalized an unconscious woman. Oddly, acknowledging this frees me up. If I can accept this one fact, then I can accept others. *No*, I caution myself. *Do not*. But the puzzle has already been solved; I clicked the last piece into place. To pretend otherwise would make me complicit. Part of the conspiracy. Haven't I been doing this all along? Didn't I always know deep down about my brother, even if I didn't want to?

Nate has Billy in a bear hug. Billy shrugs him off. "It's over," he says, adjusting his lapels. "I'm good."

A red bull's-eye has appeared on Lawrence's forehead. The wound makes Billy's guilt public, and allows me to see him as an outsider might. My brother is a young man who assaulted his father and raped his helpless girlfriend. In a selfish way it's comforting. At least I'm not the only appalling member of our family. I may have behaved unforgivably. But so has my brother. I may have driven him to hurt Diana. But he's a monster too.

I remain frozen in my chair, the statue of a girl as she shatters.

Hearing DeFiore lumber down the hall, I sit with Lawrence, Billy, and Nate as if this is perfectly normal. *We're fine*, I scream. *This is all very fine*. And yet how do I incorporate this new knowledge into my life? More important: What should I do about Diana Holly? Do I announce what I know? Send her an email? Contribute to a victims' fund?

My brothers return to their places. Heads down, eyes on phones. As soon as DeFiore walks in, Lawrence stands up, enraged. "What the hell are you doing?"

DeFiore's nostrils flare. "What does it look like? I'm keeping your son out of prison."

"By telling lies? *Disgusting* lies. This is my *family*. I demand that you issue a statement refuting what you said."

After letting Lawrence rant a little longer, DeFiore asks, "What's with your head?"

Lawrence touches his temple as if he has no idea. "I walked into the door."

"Cover that, my friend. Last thing we need is you looking like an abused spouse." Chuckling, he asks if I have any concealer. "Your dad needs a touchup, Cassie."

"Wait a second, Peter," Lawrence says. "You need to explain how—"

"Hey, hey, Lar. I don't need to explain a fucking thing. You're not my client." He turns to Billy. "That must've been brutal, kid. Diana's testimony. I apologize. Not knowing how it would land, I couldn't tip you off. But you did great. Your reaction was perfect." DeFiore speaks dispassionately, as if he's Billy's Little League coach and just changed the batting order. He turns my way. "It's not personal, Cass. No hard feelings, I hope. Jury had to know Diana lied about the texts. If she lied about the texts, she'll lie about anything. Including rape." He studies my body just as dispassionately. His eyes graze my neck, breasts, thighs, and crotch, leisurely, brazenly.

DeFiore knew about me and Lawrence all along, I realize. The dirty slut, the sleazy father, the whole fucked-up family. He was just waiting for the right time to use it.

"But it's *not true*, Peter," Lawrence insists. "What you said about me and my daughter. It's not true."

"Not the point." DeFiore checks his watch. "Court resumes at eleven-thirty. I'll finish with Diana. We'll break for lunch. Then start again at two—"

"We have to go *back*?" Billy's voice catches. "How can the judge let this continue? Diana perjured herself."

"No, not perjury. She *misremembered*. Different legal concept entirely." DeFiore's laugh is sinister. "Of course, we're going back. Anderson doesn't want a mistrial any more than we do. To be frank, this could work in his favor. Familial anger is primal. He'll say Diana tapped into that and you lost your marbles. Killed the messenger, so to speak. We'll have to see."

I realize something else. Even more than winning, DeFiore loves the game—shuffling players, pitting us against each other, tossing off ideas just to watch us react. However shrewd and manipulative I imagined he was, he's likely twice that.

The way DeFiore's eyes shine with excitement disgusts me. At the same time, I want him to use every trick he knows to grind Anderson into pulp. And there's my answer: I won't do anything for Diana. None of us will. We are complicit. We are responsible. We carry her like we carry our other crimes. The show must go on.

"Great, Peter," Lawrence says. "You've not only slandered us, you've also jeopardized the verdict. Really fucking great."

"The girl gave a convincing testimony. The jury bought every word. People were tearing up. We didn't have a guaranteed win. So, I took a calculated risk. You'll thank me later." He pauses. "Okay, moving on. Lar, you're up after lunch. I'll run out the clock till five. Over the weekend, Cassie and Billy will rehearse. Monday, they'll testify. Tuesday, closing arguments. Wednesday, verdict." He points to Billy. "Then you're home free."

"Unless I go to prison."

DeFiore lifts his head. "Stay positive, my boy. Ain't over till it's over." Turning, he heads into the hall, and then he trills like a fat lady, singing.

54

"LAWRENCE? YOU OKAY?" I'VE BARELY SPOKEN TODAY. MY
words are clotted in my throat. I take a sip of water but can't swallow.
The water sits in my mouth until I'm gagging.

He mumbles something I can't hear.

"Lawrence?"

We're alone in the conference room, still seated on opposite sides
of the table. Concerned about Eleanor, Nate and Billy went to find her
before the trial resumes. Walking out, Billy fired off one parting shot.
"This is all your fault." Though he was looking at Lawrence, he was
talking to me. "It's insane" was the most I could muster, shaking my
head. "Absolutely insane." But I knew what he meant. It is my fault.
For the first time in forever, my brother and I were actually in agreement.

The welt right above Lawrence's eye is livid. A knot has risen
under the skin. Ignoring it, he taps on his phone, furiously, like he's
signaling Morse code. He's oblivious to his head, to his surroundings, to me.

"Lawrence?" It comes out as a whisper. "There's another option."

He doesn't look up from his screen. "What kind of option?"

"We could admit we love each other. I mean, we're consenting
adults." Do I even want this? I've wanted it for so long. And I want
Lawrence to want it. I'm just not sure about myself anymore. Still, I
keep going. "What if we just say yes, it's true?"

An extended pause. "We could, kiddo. We certainly could do
that." He rakes his hand through his hair, one of his stalling tactics.
Another rake, then another. A loose strand snags on his wedding band.
"Although . . ." He searches the ceiling. "Don't you think it's better

for Billy if we wait? Until after the trial? Why give the other side more ammunition?"

"I don't want to wait. I don't," I say. To state this is to humiliate myself; still, I crave worse. "It's all gonna come out anyway. Haggerty knows. The cop. That's why he keeps calling. He knows about us. He may have people who will testify. Against you." I don't not want it. But is that the same as wanting it?

Shock registers in Lawrence's eyes. "*You told him?* Cassie, you promised not to talk to him again."

"I didn't tell him anything. He told me." My heart is pounding so hard I'm surprised Lawrence can't hear it. It's knocking in my ears, louder and louder.

"It doesn't matter. You were seventeen. It only happened once. I drank too much. It was a moment of weakness. Recklessness. Irrationality."

"I was sixteen, Lawrence." You weren't reckless or irrational, I want to say. You were happy. We both were. "I was a girl."

"You were of age. That's the story. If that's the story it doesn't matter. Besides, he needs you to build a case, right?" Lawrence studies the wall as he speaks. His fingers play a silent piano on the conference room table. "Without you, he has nothing."

Like I said, I know Lawrence, intimately; I know every line, every muscle, every freckle. I've traced the birthmark on his inner thigh with my tongue. So I know he's calculating not just his next move but his fifth, tenth, fifteenth move down the line. Moves that may or may not bring us to the forever he promised me.

I can't risk it. I'm too scared. "You're right," I say. I pull my concealer out of my bag. "Without me, Haggerty has nothing." I shift my body closer.

Lawrence's head swivels toward the door, as if remembering where we are.

"No one is out there," I assure him, dabbing makeup on his skin. I press my lips to his hair. "You're mine, Lawrence. My sweetheart. No one knows you the way I do. No one knows what you like. I'll do anything you want. A sexy dance, another woman, two men—your call."

I lick his earlobe, suck it until he shivers. "I'll drain your cock dry in one go."

He moves away. "Cassie, come on." But he's suppressing a grin, an all-boy, sneaky, mischievous one. He's hard as a rock.

Remember this, I tell myself. He's a dirty dog you can train.

"We had a plan, Sweet Girl. Just a few more days." Under the table, his hand strokes his crotch. Head back, eyelids fluttering, he's lost. "After that, it's you and me." Then, as if to remind himself, he adds, "I promise."

Remember, remember becomes a mantra, a necessary directive, my key to survival. I'm trying, I'm trying, but the past is elusive and the now is slippery. I'm not sure what's true anymore. What rights do I have here? What is mine to demand?

Years ago, in the hospital, the therapist explained that my feelings for men, for Marcus, were confused and confusing. Somewhere along the way my wires got crossed then shorted out. I didn't understand at sixteen, but now I think I do. All this time, I've been confusing pity with desire, gratitude with devotion, obligation with passion. But even if pity and gratitude are shitty reasons to hang on, they're still reasons. They're my reasons. Besides, why do I need reasons in the first place? Why does it matter? You can't choose who you love. Love chooses you.

"Oh shit." Realizing we're late, Lawrence regains his composure. "I'm sorry, Cassie. We have to wait. Just a little while longer." He stands up, adjusts his trousers. "Billy is my son."

"What am I?"

"Excuse me?"

"He's your son. What am I?"

Instead of replying, he leans over. I relax for a kiss. Instead, he pats my shoulder. "I tried to protect you. Back in March, I begged you to stay away from the trial. You can't deny that. Cass, nothing here is real. It's a play, a performance. We're acting out parts in a prewritten script. Don't forget what you know. What we have. What we are to each other. Christ, kid—that thing with your tongue? I practically came in my chair."

Why does it matter? A man's hand reaches down, a flash of naked skin. Blue sheet with tiny pink flowers. *You're repulsive.* Because, like Haggerty said, it happened. It keeps happening. You're twenty-four years old and a child of ten. You want to say no but don't have a voice. Your only option is yes, please, yes, please, yes, please.

My nerves are frayed. Everything hurts. I can't take much more. "Lawrence. I don't want to wait." I'll be good. I'll stop acting out. Please don't leave me behind. I can't be alone. "I want you to choose me."

Already in motion, Lawrence pretends not to hear. He stands tall, inflates his chest, and transforms into his public self. Striding out, he's a man on a mission. I'm hot on his heels. But instead of following him back to court, I head into the elevator where I call an Uber. I'm on autopilot, unsure where I'll go or for how long, unsure of anything, just that I need to keep moving. On the street, a mass of reporters spot me. "It's Cassie, the sister!" one cries out. But as they start to descend, a black SUV pulls up to the curb.

It's Haggerty. "Get in," he says.

55

WE DRIVE THROUGH DOWNTOWN TRENTON. MY MIND IS racing. I can't shut it down, and I don't know why. I used to be able to block out my thoughts, cauterize my feelings. But now everything rises, torturing me.

There's a McDonald's on the corner. Pulling into the drive-through, Haggerty orders two coffees and two breakfast burritos. "Ever try one?" he asks. "It's my go-to meal."

"I used to eat them all the time," I say indignantly, thinking wistfully of Eddie and the Neighborhood Café.

"McDonald's? They're the best." He smiles.

"McDonald's is disgusting, no offense." I pause. "A place in New Haven."

We continue to drive, sipping our coffee. The burritos sit, untouched, in a bag on the floor. Haggerty glances at me sideways. I ask if he heard all of Diana's testimony.

He nods. "I bet that was awful, Cassie. I'm sorry."

My eyes fill with tears. "So, what happens next?" What I mean is, how do I live in my family? As a daughter? As a sister? How do we move forward? What do I say?

Haggerty is thinking more immediately. "My money's on Anderson. Your brother is a rapist. Maybe he was drunk. Maybe he didn't mean to. But facts are facts. Billy was out of control. He wanted to hurt someone. That night, it was his ex-girlfriend."

I see Billy's elbow clip Lawrence's face. Lawrence's head snap back. My body recoils, a delayed response.

"He's going to prison, Cassie. Diana's perjury might get the case tossed on appeal. But he's guilty. The jury knows it." You do too, he doesn't say.

I look out the window. "So, what do I do now?" Again, I mean, how do I reconcile the idea that Billy Quinn is a rapist with the fact that Billy Quinn is my brother?

Again, Haggerty misinterprets. "Go on the record. Help yourself, help other survivors."

"Victims, you mean. I am nothing like those girls."

"Because they're braver than you?"

This throws me. "Braver? I'm not the one crying to the press and the police. I'm not blaming my problems on everyone else. I'm the one with the real life."

"You call this real life? Pinballing up and down ninety-five?" He laughs, but not unkindly. "You were a child, Cassie. You were abused. Tell your story. Set yourself free."

"My *story*?" Again, I'm indignant. "Lawrence and I are *together*, Detective. I won't testify *against him*." But the more I insist, the less confident I feel. "I mean, what should I say to my brothers? To Eleanor? How do I fix our family?"

Haggerty scoffs. "If you and Lawrence run off to New Haven, do you honestly think Eleanor will invite you over for Christmas dinner? Or did you not consider that?"

If I tell him the truth, that I never thought that far ahead, or with any real specificity, he'd never believe me.

"Cassie, come on. You're smarter than this. I've met too many men like Lawrence over the years. There are no happy endings here—for you or for him."

"Lawrence isn't like other men." Haggerty doesn't understand. "I wasn't a victim. It was my choice." We're talking peacefully, rationally, but I'm spinning so fast I'm dizzy.

"Not every victim is a victim. Some graduate from Columbia and go to grad school at Yale. Some are picture-perfect. Some change the world. Call yourself whatever you want." He unwraps a burrito for himself and passes the other to me. While he wolfs his down, I take a tentative bite. I can't believe how delicious it is.

"I've never considered a life without Lawrence," I say quietly. "I try, but he's always there, even when he's not. I don't know how to live without him. I don't know how to be a person. I can't do what normal people do, go on dates, talk about myself, have a job, plan a wedding, walk down the aisle. Who would want to marry someone like me? And kids? If I can't protect myself, how could I ever protect a child?"

"You grow up. You learn how to live. We all do. No one is normal. In fact, I bet you'll be a better wife, a more empathetic mother. As for your family, when you're ready, you'll forgive them."

"Forgive *them*? I'm the one who ruined us, who . . ." It's too intense to think about, like staring into the glare of white light.

"They didn't protect you."

"They didn't know."

"Cassie, there are no secrets in families. We sense when something is wrong, or off, even if we can't say exactly what it is. To say Eleanor didn't know is bullshit. She should've known. A parent's job is to know. She brought you into her home. She raised you. She promised to protect you. And you know what? She failed."

Pulling into a parking lot, Haggerty shuts off the car and makes his pitch. "You won't testify alone. We have witnesses. Anton and Joseph Rivera, Maeve McAllister—they all spoke on the record. Did you know Lawrence offered Anton Rivera money to keep him quiet?"

"Who told you this?"

"Eight years ago, Rivera came to me with his concerns. He was iffy about testifying, but I could've pressed. Not that it mattered. When I tried to pursue it, I got shut down. Your family was too well known. Too powerful, too connected. But then Billy was arrested, and so I contacted DeFiore and worked with his team. Mostly his investigator. Paul talked to everyone I couldn't reach." Haggerty opens his hands. "Two birds, one stone."

DeFiore. What a piece of shit. "You're not my client" he told Lawrence. Instead, he used him as bait. Me too.

"So, what's the problem?" I ask.

"We need you."

"I can't," I say reflexively. "It's simply not possible." After the trial, Lawrence promised, we'll be together. "This is your fight, Detective; not mine. Speaking of—I have to get back."

"For Lawrence's testimony? Why would you put yourself through that?"

"It's fine. He'll say he knew Diana was trouble. That's it." What else could he say? He told me he wasn't ready to admit the truth. Please wait, he asked. Just a little longer.

"And what about her testimony? What about you?"

"I'm background noise, the puppy the Quinns rescued from the gutter. My role is to make them look decent, open, magnanimous. Lawrence will deny everything Diana said. He'll call it a baseless accusation, and it'll be one more way to undermine her credibility."

"I wish you were right." Haggerty starts the car. "Cassie, Lawrence is desperate. Desperate men do desperate things. Come on, I'll take you to the hotel. You can pick up your car and drive to Connecticut."

Haggerty is the one who's desperate. He'll say anything to get me to vilify Lawrence. But he doesn't know Lawrence, not like I do. "Sorry," I tell him. "I have no choice."

56

IN THE COURTROOM, I SIT ON A BENCH IN THE BACK, AWAY from my family. Around me, strangers are gawking, craning their necks to catch a glimpse of my face. But I don't care. I'm fine, fine, fine. Steeling myself, I focus on Lawrence's testimony.

After swearing him in, DeFiore asked preliminary questions, mostly about Lawrence's occupation and marriage. Now he's homed in on Billy.

"Your youngest son, Billy, had medical issues, correct?"

Yes, Lawrence replies, Billy was born prematurely. Yes, he had heart complications. Yes, he failed to thrive. Yes, he had a stutter. Yes, he was bullied. Yes, his early life was challenging.

"Was this difficult for you?" DeFiore asks.

"It's excruciating for any parent to watch his child struggle. It affects the whole family. We also had other stressors. Billy was nearly two when a dear friend, my surrogate father, passed away. His daughter, Cassandra, moved in with us to help alleviate pressure on his wife, Cassie's mother. Sadly, she died in a car accident two years later. So, in addition to Billy's ongoing medical care, we were dealing with Cassie's grief and helping her acclimate to a new life."

"Is this typical for your social set? Raising someone else's child?"

Lawrence chuckles. "Very atypical. But my wife is an atypical woman—gracious, kind, and generous beyond words." Searching the gallery, he fixes on Eleanor and smiles. I can't see her face from where I'm sitting, though I'm sure she's performing admirably for the jury. "Cassie was a precocious child. Losing her parents had lasting repercussions. We were very concerned about her mental health. But together, we survived this terrible time, and became stronger. I'm proud of all three of my children."

Lawrence touches his eye, as if wiping away tears. Despite the heavy concealer, the red spot where Billy hit him pulses like a siren. "Three Musketeers. That's what we called them." His voice catches. "When they were little, I mean."

"Tell us about your own childhood, Mr. Quinn," DeFiore says.

"Objection," Anderson says. "Irrelevant."

"It speaks to the defendant's upbringing and home life."

"I'll allow it." Judge McKay turns to Lawrence. "Make it brief."

Lawrence nods. "I struggled as a child, but differently than my sons. My father died young, leaving us broke, and my mother worked two jobs. In high school, I was offered a scholarship to an elite prep school. The experience opened many doors, but also left me feeling caught between worlds." He clears his throat. "I've always felt like an imposter. At Groton. At Columbia. Even in my current life. Incidentally, I married an heiress from the Upper East Side. At my own wedding, I wasn't sure if I should walk down the aisle or serve our guests canapés."

Scattered laughs. Lawrence is a master, selling himself without selling at all.

Anderson looks annoyed. "Relevance?"

"We're moving on." DeFiore gestures to Lawrence. "What was it like when Cassie came to live with you? How did her presence affect your family?"

"We welcomed Cassie with the best of intentions. Perhaps, in retrospect, we acted impulsively. But she was bereft, a little girl in a heartbreaking situation. Unfortunately, we didn't realize how fragile she was or how much she needed. Nor did we anticipate the ways she'd disrupt our home. This wasn't her fault, of course. She was a child, and it was a lot of upheaval."

"Can you characterize her relationship with the defendant?" DeFiore asks.

"They were so close in age and so closely tied we called them 'the twins.' Over time, though, Billy's devotion to Cassie made him too dependent on her, which confirmed that our decision to send him to boarding school was correct. Being away enabled him to separate from

Cassie and make other friends. Same with Princeton. For the first two years, Billy thrived. Then he met Diana. Right away, I saw she was needy and unstable, a bit similar to his sister. Billy already had so many pressures that Eleanor and I feared Diana would take advantage of him."

"Mr. Quinn." DeFiore pauses. "Lawrence." His tone is engaging, affable, as if he and Lawrence are terrific friends. Knowing what De-Fiore is capable of, I study my hands, unable to watch. "Diana testified that she saw you kissing Cassie before dinner in November."

"That is not true." Lawrence is adamant. "It did not happen."

"Then why would Diana say it did, Lawrence?"

Lawrence sighs. "What Diana saw was *Cassie* trying to kiss *me*. I was fending her off."

What? The world drains of sound. My ears ring with white noise. And yet, it makes perfect sense. I think, deep down, I always suspected this was coming. Someday, Lawrence would forsake me.

"Can you elaborate?"

"As Cassie moved into the teenage years, her behavior became worrisome. She was bright and willful, but also cunning and headstrong. She was so anxious to feel loved, she acted out. Cassie pushed every limit. It was cute at age five, when she demanded another story or refused to go to bed. But soon it was destructive. She put herself in jeopardy. Smoked marijuana. Drank to excess. By sixteen, I couldn't control her. She was dangerous—to herself and to me."

"In what way?"

"Cassie doesn't recognize boundaries. As a child, she insisted I sleep in her bed. When I said no, she'd sneak into her brothers' rooms. While it seemed innocent at first, over time it became increasingly provocative. Many adolescent girls test limits, but Cassie went too far. She wore skimpy shorts and stringy tank tops, even after Eleanor expressed her dissatisfaction. She brushed up against me. She kissed me on the lips. Touched my private parts. As a parent, as her father, it was troubling—and frightening."

Shame and anger swirl inside me. *Help me, Nate. Help me, Billy.*

"So," DeFiore asks, "would you say her behavior was predatory?"

Lawrence grimaces. "No, no, no." He shakes his head. "I wouldn't use that specific word. But I will say that I was trapped. Cassie gave me ultimatums. She demanded I kiss her and touch her. I was her father, the man who raised her. I was so worried. I felt so helpless. Eventually, she threatened to accuse me of abusing her, sexually. I told Eleanor, and together, we got Cassie help. The best doctors, the best therapists, the best treatment money could buy." He pauses. "We had her committed to an inpatient facility."

"Did the situation improve?"

"Yes, it did. Cassie does well in structured environments. Two years later, she went to Columbia. Graduated magna cum laude. Now she's starting a doctorate at Yale. But in moments of insecurity, she'll revert to old behaviors, like driving recklessly. I don't want to tell you how many speeding tickets she's racked up in the past few years. When Billy brought Diana around, I think Cassie felt threatened, like her brother was casting her aside, so she raced home from school to assert her place in the family. She also acted aggressively toward me. Which is what Diana witnessed: Cassie trying to kiss me, to seduce me. Her misguided attempt to confirm that I love her. Please." Lawrence holds up his hands. "I don't want to demonize my daughter. Cassie has suffered tremendous loss. Normally, she's strong and courageous. But on occasion, her fears get the better of her. As my wife used to say, 'there's no one more dangerous than a teenage girl.'" He pauses, catches himself. "To herself. In the sense that teenage girls are self-destructive."

For a split second, DeFiore's face twists in frustration, but Lawrence, lost in thought, doesn't notice. I remember him in the conference room, squeezing himself, vacant with lust. Dwarfed by the enormous table, he looked diminished. Pitiful. A prisoner of his own cravings.

DeFiore asks firmly, "Lawrence, to reiterate, you were not kissing Cassie? There was no sexual relationship?"

Stirred, Lawrence shakes his head. "Absolutely not," he says adamantly. "The idea is insane—absolutely insane. I'm sorry my family has been subjected to these lies." He looks at Eleanor as he offers this apology, imploring her forgiveness. Please don't be angry, he begs.

I will make this up to you. Which I know because he begs me this same way.

Suddenly, there's a shout. "This is bullshit!" Nate jumps to his feet. Scanning the gallery for me, his face is flushed. "It's you, Dad. You're the predator. Cassie was a kid. She did nothing wrong—"

"Order!" McKay smacks his gavel. He admonishes the gallery, and the trial resumes. Meanwhile, I'm trapped here, on this bench, in my body, so angry I could kill someone.

*   *   *

Hours later, I'm racing up 95 toward New Haven. After Lawrence's testimony, I called an Uber, with instructions to the driver to meet two blocks from the courtroom. Then I hid in the ladies' room until he arrived and ran out of the building. He ferried me to the hotel, where I picked up my Porsche, shot Nate a text (Thank you. I'll call. xx), and headed north.

I'm driving so fast the car is vibrating. The top is down, and the chilly wind pulls my face and whips my hair around like a flag. Traffic is heavy, so I weave across lanes, searching for holes. Every vehicle I pass is a near-calamity.

A mile from campus, there's a turn I like to take at Mach speed; the kind of turn that's hit or miss, as far as survival. Fifty yards out, I rocket forward. Driving this fast feels like flying, like nothing can touch me. As I commit to the turn, my wheels skim the pavement. I give myself over to the car. It's out of my hands; I have no control. Nor do I care. I close my eyes, just for a second, just to feel the darkness—

An air horn jolts me awake. WAKE UP! A giant rig passes by; the driver blasts me again. WAKE UP! WAKE UP!

My car starts to skid. I careen out of control. I try to steady myself, hug the curve, right the wrong. I slam on my brakes, lead with my chest, and hit the steering wheel full force.

A third blast. The driver waves. I raise my hand. I'M UP. I'M UP. I'M UP.

57

THROUGH THE FOG OF MY HEADACHE, I HEAR MY PHONE ring, impossibly loud. When I reach for it, sharp pain riddles my chest. The ringing stops. Then starts again. It's Lawrence. He's already left a series of voicemails. "I had no choice. Cass, call me, please. Let's figure this out." He honestly thinks there's a way back.

I won't lie, the pull to believe Lawrence is real. It would be easy to give in, to put this behind us. But I'm angry too. If it's his word against mine, I know who people will believe. Soon the anger will fade, and I'll get weepy and sentimental, but if the universe could grant me one wish, I would stay rooted in place, strong and defiant. *Please*, I think. *Don't let me weaken.* I'm split between the me who's here, inside my skin, and the me who's outside, watching. For the first time, however, one of us is asking for help.

My apartment is musty. I haven't been here since before the trial started, a lifetime ago. In the kitchen, I crack a window and light a joint. Wake and bake, an old favorite. I still have a life, I remind myself. I still have school, my friend Eddie, Little Italy breakfast burritos. A future. The idea makes me laugh. How did Haggerty put it? *You call this real life?*

Lawrence keeps hounding me. More texts. More voicemails. Texts from Nate. A call from Haggerty but no message. Nothing from Billy. Or Eleanor. Christ, she must hate me.

A bang on my door startles me. It can't be Lawrence, so it has to be Haggerty. Who else could slip past the doorman? I send him a text: go away

His reply is immediate: let's talk

He keeps banging until I give in. But when I open the door, I see Eleanor.

"Oh my God," I say. "What are you doing here?"

"Oh my God is right." She hands me a brightly colored bag. "Double espresso. And biscotti." But she's flustered. "I'm not sure where . . . I should've called . . . I didn't know . . ." She clears her throat. "After Lawrence's testimony, I didn't go home. I couldn't. I stayed at the hotel, in Princeton . . . I was up all night . . . thinking . . ." She exhales. "I just had to see you. But I shouldn't have shown up, unannounced. I apologize."

Immediately, I'm suspicious. She wants something. "Eleanor, you're my mother," I say. "You're allowed to show up whenever you want."

"I haven't been much of a mother, I'm afraid." Eleanor's bangs hang over her eyes, which are bloodshot and filmy. Seeing her this way makes me feel superior, which is ironic since I'm the one with nothing.

Taking her coat, I guide her inside, and gesture to the table. "I'm surprised to see you. I thought you'd never speak to me again."

She sits down, sips her coffee. "Like you said, I'm your mother. Mothers forgive their children in ways they never forgive themselves."

"Seems premature to talk about forgiveness when we haven't even spoken of the sin."

"What's there to say? You were a child. He was my husband. He betrayed us both. You, worse, of course—far, far worse." She stops. "How are you, Cassandra?"

It's a strange question, coming from her. Has she ever asked me this before? So directly?

How am I? How am I? "I have no idea," I tell her. "I feel sad—and sorry."

"You have nothing to be sorry about. Not as far as you and I are concerned."

"But to find out in court? Had I known . . . had I thought . . . I'm flailing here, Eleanor. I have no idea what to say except I'm sorry. I should've told you, or said no, or . . . I don't know . . . not done what I did. But the way Lawrence described me, that I was a . . ." I choke on the word *predator*. "That's not true. It wasn't like that; it's not how it happened." I think of Columbia, my apartment, all the hours we spent together. Lawrence and I had a relationship; it happened every day.

"I know, Cassie. It was . . ." She takes another sip. Her hands are trembling. "When you were a teenager, Burt had suspicions, but I didn't listen. I should have, of course. Of course, I should have. But the idea that Lawrence was capable of something so . . . so heinous . . . that he could . . . It was inconceivable. And even if I could believe it, what would I say and to whom?"

Digging into the bag, Eleanor takes out the biscotti, breaks it in half and hands me a piece, then keeps going.

"When I was growing up, parents and children occupied separate orbits. We never spoke of our difficulties. We prided ourselves on our self-sufficiency. I realize this was cowardice. Similarly, I used to consider myself a strong person, but I'm not. I was weak. I turned away . . . I didn't ask . . . I didn't . . ." She shakes her head, bewildered. "When you left for Yale, and I saw Lawrence's grief, I wondered. Then, when Lawrence pushed Billy to take a plea, I think that's when I knew. A plea! To save himself."

"But you still went to trial knowing it might come out."

"It was a risk, but a calculated one. I believe Billy is innocent, and when it came down to saving Lawrence or saving Billy, there was no choice. This meant exposing my family, subjecting you to pain and humiliation, and I'm sorry for that. But it was a price well worth paying to keep my son out of jail."

I gasp. "It was your idea to have DeFiore go after Diana." I remember the way she shouted "no" in the courtroom. The Sphinx, performing for the audience.

Eleanor's face breaks open, and for a second, I think she's going to admit it. Then she pulls herself together. "It's not impossible to repair our name, though it will require money and pandering. But to let my son go to prison? Not in my lifetime." She pauses. "Cassandra, I came here to talk about you. I got it wrong, from the start. As a parent my job was to learn when to step in and when to back off. It's a delicate dance, and I vacillated, every day, between too much and not enough. I smothered Billy and neglected you."

"I wasn't your daughter. I was a burden. You did what you could."

"You were a *child*, Cassie. Not a burden. Though it's true I was skittish with you. You were so small and defiant—and heartbroken. Rachel was your mother. You worshipped her like a religion. I didn't want to come between you and her memory, nor did I want you to feel pressured to love me."

"But she was barely a mother to me. You know that. She was a mess." She was, yes, but she was also mine, my one and only. Sitting here with Eleanor, I ache for Rachel, a real mother, my real mother, someone I don't have to prove myself to or beg affection from.

"Children don't look at their mothers and see a mess. They see perfection. Now you have the luxury of hindsight. But back when you were five, six, seven, you were obsessed with her, and you hated me. Rather, you hated that I wasn't her. So I took a backseat, and I allowed Lawrence to parent you in ways you wouldn't, or couldn't, tolerate from me. I made a choice. But like with any choice, there were consequences. I will never forgive myself, Cassie. I will do whatever I can to make it up to you, which at this point I realize isn't much. My failure as a parent is a shame I will carry the rest of my life." She holds out her hand. "I am so sorry, Cassandra. I am so very sorry."

I take her hand. Can I trust her? I want to believe I can, to allow myself to feel her remorse, but I'm not sure. My relationship with Lawrence has crippled me in so many ways, some irrevocably. I doubt my own instincts. I don't trust myself to know what's right or wrong, true or false. Don't women like Eleanor always forgive themselves? There's always a reason, context, extenuating circumstances. In this manner, she and Lawrence are not dissimilar. In fact, if we're weighing the scales, aren't her crimes worse? After all, Eleanor is the mother. She's the mother. We look to our mothers to protect us from the world, from outsiders, sometimes from our own fathers.

"I'm tired," I tell her. "I need to lie down."

"Cassie, we're not done yet. We need to see this through to the end."

I was right, I realize. She wants something from me. "Which means what?"

"Come to court."

"I won't testify."

"No, of course not. I'm only asking that you show up and sit with your family."

Eleanor's face is gentle. I see softness, a warmth that used to be missing. I don't know if I can trust this. I want to, though.

"You really believe my being there will help Billy?"

"I do, Cassie." She smiles. "A united front," she adds.

Your son is a criminal, Eleanor. Even if I could help him, I don't know if I should.

"Maybe," I tell her. "I'll think about it."

58

THE TRIAL RESUMES MONDAY AT TEN. OVER THE WEEKEND,
the media exploded with the latest twist. Lawrence and I are being compared to Woody and Soon-Yi, with headlines like: "Dirty Dad and Dar-
ling Daughter; Princeton Rapist's Family Secret; Runner Rapist Can't
Flee the Shocking Truth." This morning, we drive from the hotel in separate cars. Having agreed to Eleanor's request, I travel with her, Nate,
Billy, and the Bowtie in his Bentley. Lawrence rides alone in his Mercedes.
Eleanor is concerned about appearances, but even she has her limits.

As we make our way up the courthouse steps, reporters call out to
me and Lawrence: *Are you together? When did your affair start? Is Billy
a rapist?*

It's hell trying to focus. My only salvation is anger—burning-hot,
acid, laced with venom—so I glide demurely into the building, wearing a hand-tailored Calvin Klein suit, silky blouse, and kitten heels,
pretending I can't hear. Lawrence is ahead of me, weaving through the
crowds, the same way he wove through traffic. Watching him I force
myself to remember and remember. Unfortunately, it's the memories I
want to forget that have the most staying power.

Haggerty was right. There are no happy endings for girls like me. Instead, there are agreements, compromises. Eleanor asked me to appear.
In return, she kept her promise to stick by me, going so far as to spend
the weekend in New Haven. I ached for her to lie in my bed and rub my
back while I cried. But I also understood this was a little girl's fantasy.
The Eleanor I want and the Eleanor I have are not the same; to pretend
otherwise is how I created Marcus. Still, I want what I want, which, unfortunately, includes Lawrence. All weekend, I waited for him to show
up and make things right, but Eleanor was there so he couldn't.

How do I explain this? My brain knew Lawrence would not come. I saw that gear turn, the thought *he was bad for you* expressed. But other gears were turning at the same time, different thoughts were also expressed: *I love you. I need you. I'll wait.* Despite everything Lawrence said on the stand, I have to believe our relationship was real, that he felt as deeply for me as I felt for him. How else would I stay sane?

Over the weekend, he continued to call me until Eleanor stepped in. "You. Must. Stop." Her voice was ball-shriveling tight. "Gather your belongings. Leave my home. If you don't, I'll freeze your accounts and secure a restraining order." She hung up. "Whew. What now?"

Ultimately, my time alone with Eleanor was tense, sad, painful, and hopeful. We didn't talk about Lawrence. We got manicures and pedicures. She bought me a cashmere sweater. We ate lunch at the Neighborhood Café. I introduced her to Eddie and her first breakfast burrito. "These are good," I told her. "But McDonald's are sublime."

"Well, I'll definitely have to try one, then."

This made us both laugh; *as if*.

Which is more or less how we acted: *as if*. As if she and I were a real mother and a real daughter. As if her younger son wasn't a rapist. As if I hadn't betrayed her. As if she hadn't betrayed me. As if we could be a family once the trial was over. Eleanor lives her life *as if*, it's why she's so cool, so serene. But I don't want to, not anymore. I need to call everything by its actual name. I need to hang on to known things, to the realness of words, to a world governed by facts, where truth is paramount. I can't do it yet, but I'm trying. This may account for my panic attacks over the weekend—full-throttled assaults that wracked my body like seizures. As if the me that had agreed to bury our secrets was finally saying no.

In our own ways, Eleanor and I are beginning the long, hard process of making sense of the past. For her, this means accepting that her instincts were wrong; for me, it's the opposite. We don't get a happy ending. But it may be a promising start. I recognize that to let Eleanor off the hook is to forsake myself. But to not forgive her means forsaking myself in other ways; it means accepting a life polluted by bitterness and blame.

On Sunday evening, she and I drove from New Haven to the hotel, each in our own car. After a long couple of days filled with unnatural togetherness, I was glad to be alone. In the parking lot, I ran into De-Fiore, who'd stopped by to help Billy prep. "Billy is guilty," I blurted out. To which he replied, unfazed, "I'm optimistic, kiddo. We argued an excellent case." I suspect DeFiore doesn't care about my brother's innocence. Rather, he prefers to win, but he's lost before and will lose again.

"Thank you for appearing today," DeFiore says to Billy now, stepping closer to the witness box. "I recognize this is not easy."

No, it's not, I think, trying to focus on Billy's testimony. I'm torn between believing my brother should pay for what he's done, and my kneejerk need to protect him and satisfy Eleanor. The same way I'm torn between telling the world the truth about Lawrence, and my need to protect him—and myself.

"Lawrence ruined all of you," Haggerty said once. "Why protect him?"

"How do you figure?" I asked.

"Your childhood. Your 'days of wonder.' Three kids, golden beaches, a hidden cove. He destroyed that life. Not just for you. For your brothers too."

"It's complicated," I said, but like in so many other significant ways, I hadn't considered my brothers.

Lawrence did stop calling, though I admit I continued to check my phone and listen to his messages. He moved into a hotel in the West Village, and although he didn't say so, he chose his new location with me in mind: the West Village is my favorite part of the city. Eleanor did shut down his bank accounts and credit cards. But Lawrence has money stashed away, which I know because his rainy-day fund was going to tide us over while we waited for my money to come in. Nate and I spoke several times over the weekend. Our calls weren't long or deep, but they were honest. He was describing how his dad left the Valmont and only packed one bag. "One fucking bag!" Nate couldn't believe it. "He honestly thinks he's coming back."

That's Lawrence, I told him.

At the moment, we're all here together. I'm seated between Nate and Eleanor. Occasionally, they'll each take a hand. Partly for comfort, partly to show the court where their loyalties lie. Lawrence is two people away from me, on the other side of the Bowtie. Billy, the rapist, is on the stand. We're the Quinns. Five strong. A united front.

* * *

An hour later, Billy is deep into his testimony. "Yes," he says to De-Fiore. "I fell hard for Diana. When we met, I felt like the luckiest guy in the world."

My brother doesn't possess the full spectrum of his father's charisma, but he can perform on command. Today, he's peak Billy, everybody's All American. His gray suit is new and almost a perfect fit. Over the weekend, I heard him tell Eleanor he had no time for alterations. "First suit I ever bought by myself, Mom. I mean, without you. Deacon was with me."

Eleanor's voice twinkled like chimes. "Another milestone. I'm proud of you. And Deacon?"

"Two suits, shirts, sweaters—the whole deal. I used your house account."

"Yes," she said. "That's exactly right."

Tailored or not, the suit is a stunner. Billy always looks great, which is a gift or a curse. According to social scientists, handsome men are better liked, more highly valued, and perceived as morally superior to their unattractive peers. Handsome serial killers, for instance, are less likely to be seen as suspects. So, in the right setting, a guy like my brother, like Lawrence, could get away with murder.

Today, handsome as he is, Billy looks waxy. He used too much pomade, so his hair is stiff and shiny. Under the lights, he appears coated in plastic, like a mannequin.

Nate is thinking the same thing. "What's wrong with his face?" he whispers.

"It's not his face. It's his hair."

"He looks demented."

"You're demented," I whisper, out of habit.

For the next two hours, Billy answers questions about Diana, Princeton, running, medical school, and porn. Meanwhile, Nate and I play Hangman. I solve his puzzle quickly: $N A T E T H E G R E A T I S K I N G$. But he takes longer to solve mine: $B I L L Y Q U I N N D I D I T$.

Watching his face, I expect him to cross out the letters. Instead, he lets them stand, and wads up the paper. "Thought you were a true believer," I whisper.

"I was until I wasn't." Nate shrugs. "Still, I don't want him to go to prison."

"He might." I glance at Anderson, who is champing at the bit, eager for DeFiore to wrap up so he can crucify Billy on cross.

"Yes," Billy is saying. "Diana told me about Cassie and my father. But I didn't want to believe it."

"And now?" DeFiore asks.

"Now I have no choice; I have to accept the truth. Nate, Cassie, and I had an idyllic childhood. It was fun and lighthearted. But as we got older, it got darker. My dad was always attentive to Cassie. But when I was ten, he crossed the line from paternal affection to—I don't know—something disturbing. Like a boy with a crush. He treated her like a g-g-g-girlfriend. Touched her c-c-c-constantly. Doted on her in this creepy way. When I think about it now, I'm sickened. But as a kid, I didn't know how to describe what I was seeing. I kept doubting myself. If it was wrong, then why didn't anyone stop it? Eventually, I decided my father must be normal, which made me the abnormal one. A p-p-p-pervert. Disgusting."

"But Diana noticed it?"

"Immediately. She said it was nuts, like the room was on fire but we kept stepping around the flames."

"What was your reaction to her telling you this?"

"Horror, disbelief. But if I'm honest, I also felt validated."

"Were you angry?"

"At Diana?" Billy shakes his head. "No. I got annoyed when she kept bringing it up. But I told her I didn't want to talk about it, and she stopped."

"Did this new knowledge throw a curveball in your relationship?"

"It magnified problems that already existed. When school started in September, my schedule was jam-packed. I pulled away because I had so many demands on my time, but also because I had the issue of my sister in the back of my mind. The more I withdrew, the needier Diana got. Soon, I shut down completely, while she did whatever she could to reach me. It was a vicious cycle, one we kept repeating. In November, we went to my parents' house, which was a mistake. I had d-d-d-decided to end our relationship, so the invitation was a mixed message. While I didn't want to hurt her, it was clear we couldn't continue."

DeFiore nods. "What happened during that dinner?"

"Cassie showed up unexpectedly. It created all kinds of tension. And then, as Diana said . . . she saw . . . she saw C-c-c cassie k-k-k-kissing my . . . um . . . d-d-d-d-dad. That was . . . this mmmmoment was . . . the beginning of the end . . . of our relationship. Me and Diana. We fought all the time. I told myself it was because school was tough. Track too. I had a million reasons. But there was only one, really. Her knowing about Cassie and my dad made me sick and ashamed. But again, the more I pulled away, the more Diana preyed on me. She was relentless. C-c-c-calling, texting, showing up. I felt trapped."

"During his testimony, your father said you were drawn to Diana because her temperament was similar to your sister's. Is this true?"

"In some ways. They're both needy. Cassie is a lot more independent but a lot more self-destructive. Still, I never knew a time without her. Cassie has always been larger than life. The best big sister, hilarious, fearless." Billy's voice cracks. "She looked after me, stood up for me." He starts to cry. "She and Nate were my best friends."

I'm crying too. Beside me, Nate is sniffling.

DeFiore allows my brother to compose himself then repeats his earlier question. "So, when Diana told you she saw Cassie and your father kissing, what was your reaction?"

"I felt sick."

"Angry too?"

"Yes, but not at Diana. At myself. I've always been angry at myself.

I used to think it was because I stuttered. But it's really because I didn't protect my sister. From my dad, I mean."

On the other side of Eleanor, Lawrence starts coughing, then choking. "Excuse me," he says to no one. "Pardon me."

"In his testimony, your father said that he wasn't kissing your sister; that, in fact, it was the other way around. Your sister was the aggressor. Is this true?"

Billy looks at Lawrence. "No," he says with finality. Then he looks at me. For a second, we're alone, but DeFiore's voice breaks in and my brother turns away.

"Are you saying his testimony was untruthful?"

"I don't know," Billy answers. "He must believe it, on some level."

"What else happened after Diana told you what she saw?"

"My worldview cracked. Over Christmas, I saw my dad with C-c-c-c-cassie through different eyes. It was like a hallucination, but I knew it was real. I started replaying all the times I should've spoken up but didn't. Never, not once. She's my sister. I should've helped her." Billy starts to cry again. He takes a minute to compose himself. "So, like I said, when Diana told me, I was angry. But not at her for pointing it out. I was furious with myself."

I've heard enough. I'm sure my brother believes this; it may even be true. But I'm equally sure he was furious with Diana and wanted her to pay. So, as Billy describes all the ways she tried to seduce him and all the ways he tried to fend her off (until, of course, he couldn't), Nate and I resume our game. "Your go," I whisper. I point to the page. *WILL BILLY QUINN GET OFF?*

59

FINAL ARGUMENTS START ON MONDAY AFTERNOON AND run through Tuesday at noon. Clocking in at forty minutes, the State's closing is short, terse, and a body blow for Billy. Anderson restates the most critical evidence and reintroduces each exhibit. He retells Diana's story in chilling detail, reminding us, incident by incident, how Billy's rage sparked, escalated, and culminated in rape. My relationship with Lawrence casts a shadow over the proceedings, which the DA uses to his advantage.

"The defendant was raised in a toxic home. You heard the testimony. You saw the evidence. You know the truth. A predator raised a predator. One married into great wealth, the other was born to it. Brimming with every privilege—race, gender, socioeconomic, you name it—these men are indifferent to the basic tenets of human decency. They ignored their responsibilities to each other, to women, to society. They believed they were above the law. But I'm standing here today to tell you that *no one is above the law*. These men must be held accountable. You, ladies and gentlemen of the jury, have a moral imperative to get justice for Diana Holly. For all women who are mentally, physically, and emotionally diminished, whose lives are destroyed by soulless men."

DeFiore's argument is equally persuasive. "We can never know what really happened inside the Quinn home, but our knowledge of this family's struggles has no bearing on the charges against my client. It has no bearing on how you, members of the jury, should vote. What does bear on your vote, however, is the accuser's integrity. Diana Holly is untruthful. We have seen this over and over. She is untruthful, relentless—and vengeful."

DeFiore finishes by reminding the jury that the burden of proof lies with the State. They must prove without a shadow of doubt what happened between Billy and Diana on March 24. It seems like a tall order for any prosecutor, not just Anderson. I mean, how can any of us say for sure what happens between two people?

By the time both sides rest, it's impossible to tell which way the jury will lean. For me, I know, unequivocally, what Billy is and what he isn't. Billy is a rapist. Billy is my brother. Both statements are true.

*   *   *

The jury deliberates for twenty-four hours. On Wednesday at noon, Eleanor checks her watch. "Peter, you said a not-guilty would come fast." She gives him a murderous look. "What's the holdup?"

"Give it time, Ellie." DeFiore is unfazed. The verdict will come when it comes. Tomorrow is Thanksgiving. He has relatives visiting from Florida. He's looking forward to turkey and all the trimmings, soccer with his girls, and a spate of new clients. He's already told us we should hire a fresh set of eyes if there's an appeal. Once the verdict is read, Peter DeFiore, Esquire, is finished with the Lawrence Quinns.

We're in the conference room. If we do get a decision today, the five of us won't be together again for a long time, if ever. Lawrence is at the other end of this mammoth, sixteen-chair table. The sight of him, alone and cast out, would break my heart if I let it. Except for "hello, how are you," and "fine, how are you?" he and I haven't spoken since last Friday, nearly a week ago.

It's a choice, I remind myself. Loving him may not be but protecting him is. All I know is that it's very hard not to move next to him. Impossible, almost. And this is only day five. How will I survive the rest of my life?

Lunch is delivered, eaten, and cleared away. One o'clock comes and goes. By two, I'm scared. Billy won't survive incarceration. Like I told Haggerty, he's softer than me and Nate, more likely to break. Maybe, given his background, they'll let him work in the library, or better, in the clinic. I acknowledge the privilege he'll bring to that situation, privilege that so few others hold. And yet, I am grateful for it. I hope beyond hope that his looks, money, race, education—any of it, all of it—will serve him as well in prison as it has in life.

At four-thirty, DeFiore's phone dings. "It's in." He stands up. "Let's go."

Together, we head to the courtroom. Inside, everyone—McKay, Anderson, the jury—is already seated. We slip into our seats and hold our breath.

"Will the defendant please rise?"

Billy stands up.

"Has the jury reached a unanimous verdict?"

A woman with curly brown hair and a starburst broach on her lapel stands up. I thought I knew all the jurors, but I feel like I've never seen her before. It's not a good sign. "Yes, we have, Your Honor."

The bailiff hands the verdict to the judge who reads it silently then hands it back.

"He's just a kid," Nate whispers nervously. "Prison will destroy him."

"He's a grown man, Nate. He'll adjust."

"On the two counts of rape, how do you find?"

"We find the defendant . . . not guilty, Your Honor."

"Hell no," someone calls out. "Oh my God," I say aloud.

"Silence!" McKay is pissed. "On the count of attempted rape, how do you find?"

"Not guilty, Your Honor."

"On the two counts of felony sexual assault."

"Not guilty, Your Honor."

"Mr. Quinn," McKay says, "you are free to go."

I turn to Nate; he's shocked too. "He's free?"

60

LAWRENCE IS ARRESTED TWO WEEKS LATER. I WATCH IT ON the news, in the celebration room, on the widescreen TV. A reporter narrates as footage is aired of Lawrence standing on the sidewalk in front of his hotel. His hands are locked behind him. But his chin is up, his eyes are bright.

To the naked eye, he is a supremely confident man. On camera, you see this in the thrust of his chest, his optimistic grin. What you can't see is the rot roiling below the surface. Funny, but watching him on-screen, I can't see it either. I can almost forget it's there.

Lawrence bends his head and Haggerty pushes him forward, into a waiting car. Then he's gone.

A few days later, I text Haggerty:

Thanks for everything. You're not such a shitty cop, I guess.
I'm a detective, Ms. Quinn. Your praise is humbling.
It's Cassie. Maybe one day we can solve crimes together.
Cassie, I look forward to it.

*   *   *

No one is all good or all bad. You can love your father because he clothed and fed you, but you can hate him because he's a man and tragically flawed. I love Lawrence in the childlike way that's rarely questioned. The kind of love that's involuntary, like breathing. The kind of love that's impossible to stop even if stopping is the only way I'll survive.

Lawrence was charged with statutory rape of a minor, along with other crimes related to me. Turns out Billy's testimony, my conversations with Haggerty, and affidavits from Anton, Joey, and Maeve were enough to get a warrant. It's unlikely the case will go to trial. Given the facts, and the havoc Eleanor can wreak, at some point soon he'll make a deal. So, unlike his son, Lawrence is headed to prison. Upon his release, he'll have to register as a sex offender.

I'm not sure that what Lawrence did was a crime, nor am I sure if he committed it alone. We fell in love together and with my full consent. Even if I was too young, as defined by an arbitrary law, I knew what I was doing. Men are men are men. Feral, submissive—it's biology. I appealed to Lawrence's baser instincts and got what I wanted.

And yet.

Recent developments suggest that the concrete pillar at my core has sustained a hairline fracture. After Billy was arrested, I saw cops everywhere. Now I see girls. Twelve-year-olds buying frozen yogurt with their moms. Thirteen-year-olds arm-in-arm on the street, laughing uproariously. The other day I walked past a playground and watched a group of girls huddled in the corner, smoking. They were fourteen, maybe fifteen, max. Their cigarettes were hidden, but smoke plumed in the air. Wearing plaid skirts and school blazers, with their yarn friendship bracelets, Converse high-tops, and swinging ponytails, they looked so childish, so blissfully unaware that I felt my legs give way and had to sit down. Then I started to cry.

The terms of Lawrence's bail agreement prohibit him from contacting me. Even so, two weeks after his arrest, out on bond, he called me and my brothers and begged us to see him. Neither Nate nor Billy agreed, but after a week of yes-no-maybe-I-don't-know, I said yes, okay, I guess.

Lawrence is living in a plush hotel near the Hudson River, far from the Valmont. We agree to meet on Monday afternoon in the lobby restaurant. At four, Nate walks me to the hotel entrance, but that's as far as he'll go.

"I can't." He gestures to the bar next door. "I'll wait here."

"I'll be in and out in twenty minutes."

"It not, I'll come find you." A promise and a threat. Nate knows that without it, I'll waffle. I'll stay too long. I'm not nearly as tough as I think I am.

"I'll be fine," I tell him.

"I'll be here," he assures me.

Lawrence is in the back, in a corner booth. It's almost Christmas, and the walls are decorated with sparkly tinsel and blinking lights. Candles glow on the tabletops. It's lovely and romantic, and yet, the room has an air of tragedy. Or maybe it's just that this feeling is evoked in me when Lawrence lifts his head. "Cassie," he says. His voice cracks.

"Lawrence." Numbness permeates my body even as I start to tremble. *What now? What next?* Panting, I grab the back of a chair to steady myself.

A couple of years ago, Eleanor told me that when her parents reached the end of their lives, she was forced to think of them as strangers. She cared for them with the diligence of a loving daughter, but these cranky senior citizens, who barked orders and called her Eloise, weren't her real mother and father. She said it was the only way she could handle her sorrow and absorb the enormity of what was happening to them, and to her. "They weren't just dying," she explained. "They were also leaving me behind."

I study Lawrence's face. He still has the same arrogant lift to his chin, the same chiseled jaw. But the light is gone. His skin is ashen. His blue eyes are cloudy. He's a shadow of the man I knew.

"You look so beautiful." His cheeks are wet. "My Forever Girl." On the table, there's a gift wrapped in elegant gold paper with a silk bow. He pushes it toward me.

I thank him but don't touch it. This man is a stranger, I tell myself. I've never met him before. I focus on the age spots near his nose. They make him look old.

The next fifteen minutes are awkward, with frequent pauses and small talk that trails off. He doesn't appear nervous, but I can feel his strain. As for me, my body continues to shake.

At one point, he asks if I plan to go back to school.

"I'm not sure. But I'm moving back to New Haven."

"For good?"

"For the foreseeable future, yeah."

Before long, I'm depleted. Standing up, I clutch my bag. "I have to go."

Lawrence watches me. "I keep telling myself that's where I am."

"Where?"

"Home. At the Valmont. Instead of a hotel. That what's happening isn't happening." He offers a sad smile. "You know me, Cass. I've always been good at fantasy."

"Does it work?"

"Not really. Not the way it used to, at any rate. I'm in a hotel downtown. I am going to prison eventually. My life, the life I had, is over." But even as he speaks, his eyes flicker in and out of focus, as if he doesn't quite believe this. "The life we had," he adds.

Lawrence is baiting me, I can see him doing it, and yet I feel the old familiar pull, the flutter and flush, the need to make things right. I begin to waver, weaker still.

He tracks my face. "Do you ever think about us?" His voice is coy. "About me? About what we have?"

I take my time replying. The clock ticks. Nate waits. But I have to be accurate. I shift my bag to my other arm. I want and don't want to go. I could lean over and kiss him. I remember the wetness of his mouth, the weight of his body. His fingers trailing down my thigh.

"Cassandra." Lawrence is urgent; he has to hear yes.

"I don't think about it or not think about it, Lawrence." My voice is grave. "It's what I am."

He doesn't disagree. And in the long silence that follows, we both acknowledge one truth. If, in fact, a crime was committed, then this is by far my worst injury. I do not belong to myself. I belong to Lawrence Quinn.

For him, though, maybe this isn't a crime. Maybe it's his due. Still, he asks, "Can you forgive me?"

For a second time stops. We breathe together. I give us this moment, a gift. He was my whole world, once.

"I'll do whatever it takes," he says. "Whatever you want."

I won't lie. I love hearing this. Deep in my bones, I need it. And in two hours or two months or two years or two decades, when the cravings for Lawrence hit and I'm undone by my feelings, I'll need to hear it again and again and again.

"We'll see," I tell him because I can't yet say no.

There's a glint in his eyes, that same cocky smile. "I'll wait," he promises then pushes his gift across the table. "This is for you, Cassie. Please take it."

What should I do? Time's up. Nate's alone. I have to go. So I grab the package and leave Lawrence behind. I want to turn back, promise yes, of course, I forgive you. I can visit. I'll call. I'll write. Instead, I head out to the street and into the bar next door, where I find my brother. I tap his broad shoulder and say, "I'm done," and he gets up, buttons his coat, and we leave, together.

EPILOGUE

I ONCE READ ABOUT A FANTASTICALLY RICH MAN WHO owned several homes, many cars, and rooms of priceless art. But he felt possessed by his belongings, burdened by their weight. To lighten himself, he distributed his houses, cars, and art among strangers. This, he believed, was the key to contentment. Giving away his personal effects, though, wasn't enough. So he donated all his money, shocking his family. Still, he felt unsatisfied. With no assets left, he decided to offer up his organs, starting with a kidney, which he gave to a woman he met on the internet. And yet he still had more to give. So, he found someone to take his second kidney. I'll go on dialysis, he said. By this point, his siblings stepped in, and the man was institutionalized. They tried to recoup his money, but to no avail. He gave it all away willingly, they were told. It was his choice.

My brothers tease me about carrying the sorrows of the world, but I don't think you can quantify empathy. These days, I'm clear about the facts I know to be true. My brother Billy is a criminal. He raped Diana Holly in a fit of rage while she was unconscious. Then he lied about what he did, and my family covered it up. I am sickened by this; I feel terrible for Diana; and I will live with this knowledge for the rest of my life. At the same time, I'm preoccupied with my own behavior, and making amends to my family, to Nate, Billy, and Eleanor.

But what is my burden and what is theirs? How much is required to balance the scales? What words can convey how deeply sorry I am? You can be both a victim and an offender, but in this case, they don't cancel each other out. You can't shroud yourself in self-pity to avoid accountability. I will apologize to my brothers, whose lives were derailed by my behavior, the younger of whom went on to destroy someone else as a result.

"You guys are really taking off?" Billy is at my bedroom door. Nate and I are packing boxes.

"Yeah," I tell him, closing my suitcase. "The Bowtie is selling the SoHo loft. We'll stay at my place in New Haven."

"And then what?" He looks at Nate.

Nate responds by ripping off a long strip of tape.

Maybe I'm wrong. But I want to believe we are more than the worst things we've ever done. If we are, I may have a shot at a real life. Not normal, just real. I also may have a shot at becoming a better person. Not good, just better. Someone, for example, who uses her money to benefit others.

As for Billy, it's hard to say. Last week he spoke to Princeton about returning. If he takes classes this summer and doubles up in the fall, he'll graduate with his class. Med school is once again a possibility. Turns out some guys can in fact move forward after being accused of assault.

Now, wearing sweatpants and expensive sneakers, my brother looks like himself again. His phone rings constantly; girls are swarming more than ever. His hair is still long, though he keeps threatening to buzz it off, change his name, move west and start over. Doesn't matter. Billy will be fine. Better than fine. If only he wasn't so handsome, if only he wasn't so rich. If only.

I hear Eleanor calling for him. "Coming!" he shouts. "I'll see you guys soon," he says before heading out. "Maybe I'll drive up to New Haven for a weekend."

"Maybe," I say, noncommittally.

Nate still hasn't uttered a word.

Billy pulls us both into a hug. "Take care, Cassidy Cakes. Call me." But he won't meet our eyes, and as I watch him go, I feel a sharp pain in my chest.

This morning, I opened Lawrence's present. It's a knickknack, a hand-carved duck. Around its neck it has a tag with a label written in Sharpie: *I am a drake.* I should've thrown it out. For the moment, it's packed in a box and moving to New Haven. I need to know it's there, just in case.

There are places inside me that will always be broken. I'll always feel unlovable and worthless, dirty and damaged. Maybe, too, I'll never be able to sustain an intimate relationship. I'll sabotage myself or run away or pretend it doesn't matter.

"You ready?" Nate asks. "Cass?"

And yet I have to move forward. Every day I have to make that choice, to live.

I turn to my brother and say his name. "Nate." My throat starts to close.

He's watching me. "Cassandra?" Nate asks. "What's up?"

A ringing in my ears distracts me. My skin is twitching. I feel rising pressure in my head. "I'm terrified," I blurt out. Such a small thing to admit out loud. But here, with my brother, it is everything.

An hour later, Nate and I slip into his car and pull out of the driveway. Neither of us look back. We're headed to our new life. But first we're stopping at Hawkins Cove to walk on the beach, for old times' sake.

My brother is driving. I'm the navigator, so it's my job to entertain. When we reach the highway, he relaxes. "Tell me a story," he says. "Make it epic."

I think for a long time. "I have one. You may not believe it, though."

"Try me," he says.

I do Nate's bidding. After all, he's my big brother, and we have a few hours to kill.

"This is Billy's story. But if I were the one telling it, I'd start with Nate's call. For me, that's the pivot point between before and after. The moment I was, for lack of a better expression, jolted awake."

The dream continues. We pick up speed, and I keep talking. Soon, I grow wings.

I started working on *When We Were Bright and Beautiful* in 2016. A couple of years later, the #MeToo movement exploded. So, it was largely coincidental that I happened to be writing a novel about sexual assault at the same time the world was reckoning with the issue. At first, the overlap was overwhelming; and I considered, if not abandoning the book then at least changing the central crime. In the end, the sight of so many women stepping forward evoked a sense of urgency, and I stayed the course, a decision I've never regretted.

To write this novel properly, that is, to depict the complexity, nuance, and pervasive consequences of sexual assault without demonizing a vulnerable young woman or supporting an ostensible rapist required humanizing the characters. To accomplish this, I read scores of novels and nonfiction books, and watched hours of movies and television. Unfortunately, space precludes me from listing every title. However, I do need to mention *Blackbird* by David Harrower, a play that crystalized for me the insidious ways sexual trauma compels a young girl to sacrifice her autonomy, identity, even her reality, to explain the inexplicable and find a way forward.

In fiction, just like in life, each story is the sum total of all the stories that have preceded it, and my own is no exception. In this way, *When We Were Bright and Beautiful* owes an enormous debt to all the writers who came before me and dared to tackle this subject.

Similarly, I am indebted to the countless women and girls who shared their experiences of sexual violence as a result of the #MeToo movement. Equally important is the debt I owe to the women and girls who shared their experiences long before the #MeToo movement made it feel safer to do so. Finally, I want to recognize the women and girls who continue to suffer alone and in silence.

Jillian Medoff

ACKNOWLEDGMENTS

Fifth novels are killers. This book was uniquely difficult and it exists only because a number of very smart people contributed their time, expertise, and advice. While it's impossible to fully express my love and gratitude for all they've done on my behalf, here is my heartfelt attempt.

I am extremely grateful to the Mercer County Criminal Courthouse staff for their comprehensive description of the detention process, and to Kimberly Worth, Worth Jarrell LLC, for her painstaking review of the legal arguments depicted in these pages. A brilliant but busy litigator (who also happens to be my sister), Kim generously walked me through pre- and post-trial procedures, researched and answered all my questions, and vetted scenes in and out of the courtroom. If errors exist, I claim full responsibility.

I'd also like to extend my deep appreciation and awe to:

Emily Griffin, Jen Gates, and Nicole Dewey for their white-hot brilliance, diligence, encouragement, and kindness. To work with the same publishing team over several novels is a rare gift, one I never take for granted.

Jonathan Burnham for his editorial genius and tolerance for risk.

Erin Files, Alison Warren, and everyone at Aevitas Creative Management.

The Writers Room and the Virginia Center for the Creative Arts.

Tracy Locke, Katie O'Callaghan, Leah Wasielewski, Mary Ann Petyak, Micaela Carr, and everyone at Harper/HarperCollins.

Dr. Nan Jones and Dr. Karen Hopenwasser.

David Blumenstein, the Segal Group, and Jen Benz, Segal Benz, for time, space, and ongoing support. Special shout-out to all my Segal Benz coworkers.

Todd Lane for the insight and laughs but mostly the laughs.

Aimee Molloy for the podcast, for her wit and intelligence, and for sharing the grind, day in and day out.

Laura Zigman, Sue Halpern, Ann Bauer, Karen Bergreen, Liz Kaye, Colleen Magee, Catharine Hamrick, Laura Hanford, Erin Nauman, Jen Schuster, Stacey Simon, Ettore Toppi, Victoria Skurnick, and Diane Swisher for careful readings, wise counsel, foxhole humor, and respite from the absurdity.

Lewis Medoff, Naomi Medoff, Mara Medoff, Joy Dawson, Sam Worth, Alex Crowell, David Crombie, Jack Crombie, and Kennedy Crombie for your presence, warmth, and inspiration.

Finally, my husband, Keith Dawson, and daughters, Sarah, Liv, and Mollie for everything, always.

(Oh, and Goose, too, I guess.)

ABOUT THE AUTHOR

JILLIAN MEDOFF is the author of the national bestseller *I Couldn't Love You More*, as well as the novels *This Could Hurt, Good Girls Gone Bad,* and *Hunger Point*. A former fellow at MacDowell, Blue Mountain Center, VCCA, and Fundación Valparaiso, she has an MFA from NYU. In addition to writing fiction, Jillian has a long career in management consulting and is currently a senior consultant at Segal Benz, a division of the Segal Group.